CLAIMING VALERIA

A FADA NOVEL

REBECCA RIVARD

THE FADA SHAPESHIFTER SERIES

The fada.
   Shapeshifters created during Dionysus's infamous bacchanals from a mix of fae, human and animal genes.
   They're ruthless, untamed—and when they love, it's forever.

Stealing Ula: A Fada Shapeshifter Prequel (Nisio & Ula, set in Ireland)

The Rock Run River Fada
Seducing the Sun Fae (Dion & Cleia)
Claiming Valeria (Rui & Valeria)
Tempting the Dryad (Tiago & Alesia)
Sea Dragon's Hunger (Cassidy & Nic)

The Baltimore Earth Fada (The Darktime Trilogy)
Saving Jace (Jace & Evie)
Charming Marjani (Marjani & Fane)
Adric's Heart (Adric & Rosana)

Fada Shapeshifter Short Reads
Lir's Lady (#3.5—Lir & Isleen)
Shifter's Valentine (#3.6—Jenny & Chico)

Find out more and read exclusive excerpts: https://rebeccarivard.com/shapeshifters/

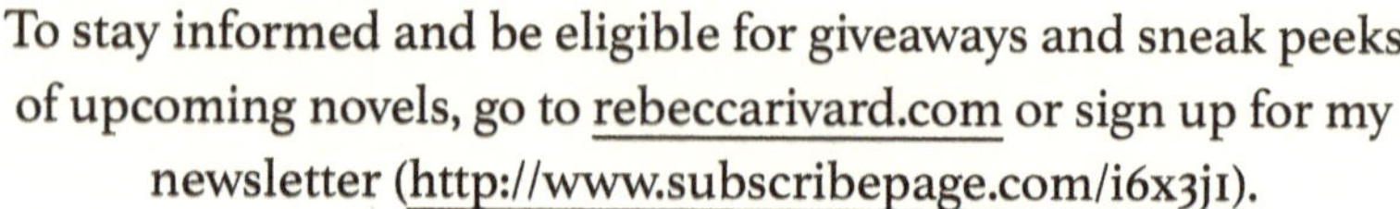

To stay informed and be eligible for giveaways and sneak peeks of upcoming novels, go to rebeccarivard.com or sign up for my newsletter (http://www.subscribepage.com/i6x3j1).

PROLOGUE
TWO YEARS EARLIER

The night fae lord materialized in the darkest corner of the alley.

But Rui was expecting that. The night fae were creatures of the moon. You rarely saw one in the daylight, and even at dusk they sought the shadows.

This man could've been the pattern from which his people were cut: tall and lean, with chalk-white skin, midnight hair and sharp features. And dressed in tight black jeans and a long duster even though Baltimore was in the middle of a heat wave.

Rui's lip curled. He didn't like any fae, but he especially didn't like the night fae. Still, a job was a job.

He inclined his head. "Lord Tyrus."

"Do Mar?"

"That's me. Peace to you and yours."

Tyrus hesitated just long enough to be insulting before returning the ritual greeting. "Peace to you and yours."

Rui's jaw tightened. But he hadn't become Rock Run second by indulging his emotions. "You wanted to hire me?"

Tyrus flicked his fingers and an image of a man appeared in Rui's palm. "His name is Silver. He's in Baltimore somewhere—

my people have tracked him this far, but we can't get a fix on him."

Rui studied the image. The man—Silver—had dark hair and pale skin, although it was clear he wasn't a pureblood. His face was too broad, his eyes a muddy brown rarely found in a fae.

"He's a half-blood," Tyrus said, confirming Rui's guess. "His mother was human." His voice held a sneer.

"Anything I can use to scent him?"

"I have a few strands of his hair. You can use it to do whatever it is you shifters do." The sneer was more pronounced now. The fae looked down on anyone who wasn't a pureblood, but they had a special disdain for the fada with their mix of human, fae and animal genes.

Rui ignored the scorn. Tyrus might sneer at his animal genes, but that was why he was hiring a fada assassin. Rui wouldn't be the hunter he was without his animal. And although hunting a man mainly involved old-fashioned legwork —questioning known associates, tracking him through credit cards and bank accounts—even a few strands of hair would make things easier, allowing him to track the man through his scent as well.

He wasn't sure why he asked the next question. He'd already talked it over with Dion, his alpha and best friend, and together, they'd decided to take the job. But something made him say, "What did he do?"

The image in his hand dissolved.

"The SOB ripped me off," Tyrus snarled. "He knows what that means. Now, do we have an agreement?"

Rui stared back at him without speaking, his face expression-less, but he felt his eyes going night-glow gold, a sign his animal was aroused.

Tyrus took a step back.

Good. He might be the son of a fae prince, but he needed to remember whom he was dealing with. As clan second, Rui was answerable only to Dion. No one—especially some asshole pure-blood from Virginia—spoke to him like that.

The night fae gave an audible swallow. When he spoke again, his tone was more polite. "You don't need to know what he stole. All I want you to do is send a message—no one steals from Lord Tyrus."

So Silver wasn't going to be given a chance to make things right. Rui didn't even blink. If he'd ever been squeamish about acting as a hit man for the fae, he'd long since made his peace with it. Hunger had a way of making a man hard-hearted, especially when his women and children were suffering, too.

"All right."

"Then we're agreed? You'll take the job?"

"Of course." What did he care if the fae picked one another off?

"Good." Tyrus's black eyes flickered with an unholy glee that raised the tiny hairs on Rui's nape. Something was off here. But the night fae tossed him a small black pouch. "That's the deposit. You'll get the spell when I confirm the kill."

Rui opened the pouch. Inside were three small but perfect diamonds. Purebloods loved expensive, shiny things. Frankly, he and Dion would've preferred a direct deposit into the clan account.

He closed the pouch. "I'll let you know when it's done. We expect the rest of the payment within the week."

"Don't contact me directly—go through Hunter." Hunter was a Baltimore earth fada who worked at the Full Moon Saloon, a bar catering to shifters.

Rui jerked his head in acknowledgment. As long as Tyrus kept his part of the bargain, he was just as happy not to have to deal with him again, although it went against the grain to let the Baltimore fada have anything to do with Rock Run business.

"And, do Mar?" Tyrus stepped closer.

Rui's nostrils flared. Night fae stank, an acrid mix of metal and decay. Rumor had it they made their homes in crypts, and smelling Tyrus, Rui could believe it.

"What?"

The reply was low and cold. "Don't fuck this up—or you're next."

Rui's fingers tightened on the pouch. For the amount the diamonds would bring, he could slip a blade in Tyrus's aristocratic chest and walk away with the clan twenty-five thousand dollars richer. Not even a pureblood could survive a knife to the heart.

But Rock Run desperately needed the second half of Tyrus's payment—a promise to renew the concealing spell that hid their base from intruders. The clan was gripped by a mysterious malady that was slowly weakening them. And not just the people themselves, although that was bad enough. Even their crops and river had been affected. The grapes that produced the wine that was the clan's main source of income were rotting in the vineyards, and every year the fishers brought in less fish and crabs.

If Rock Run's troubles became generally known, they'd be easy pickings for the Baltimore shifters, who'd long coveted the clan's large tract of land in northern Maryland.

And to top it off, Rui had recently met his mate, a sexy Portuguese shifter named Valeria. Their mating celebration was in a couple of weeks, which made him even more eager to get that concealing spell. It wasn't just other men's families he was protecting now. It was his own woman and their future children.

Right now, the spell was as valuable to Rock Run—and Rui— as a thousand diamonds.

Still, he couldn't resist peeling back his lips to display two sharp canines. Tyrus went whiter, if that were possible. But he was a pureblood fae, taught from birth that all other life forms were inferior. He held his ground.

Rui gave Tyrus his back—a grave insult, implying the other man was too weak to worry about—and stalked out of the alley.

THE HALF-BLOOD WAS DAMN good at hiding. It took Rui almost a week to find him.

But Rui's primary animal was a shark. He was calm, cold, relentless. As a water fada, he tended to short out computers and other electronics, so he paid a human hacker to track Silver through the digital crumbs he'd dropped. That got him close, and then he kept at it until his questions—and his nose—led him to a shabby little rowhouse on a street less than a mile from the alley where he'd met Tyrus.

Now he studied the narrow house, one of a row of twelve that stretched from one corner to the next. So this was where Silver had gone to ground. The house was as sad and neglected as the surrounding area—a sagging roof, a chipped and faded Form-stone exterior and a yard that was more dirt than grass.

Whatever the half-blood had stolen, he sure hadn't cashed in on it.

Silver roomed with a human who worked nights. Rui slipped into the backyard and waited until the man left. One by one, the lights went out. Rui waited another half an hour before skimming across the lawn to the back door. It was locked, but it was a few second's work to dig out the rotted wood around the bolt and ease the door open. A simple warding spell halted him on the threshold. He withdrew a pinch of precious counterspell dust from its packet, sprinkled it on the doorjamb and stepped into the kitchen.

The air inside was hot and close, not much different than the humid summer night outside. Rui took in his surroundings with his animal-enhanced senses: the red plastic table with three mismatched chairs...the greasy remains of a pizza on the counter...the smear of chocolate ice cream in a bowl in the sink. From upstairs came the sound of a man snoring, the ragged buzz a counterpoint to the distant hum of a window air conditioner.

He glanced down and jolted. A small face was staring up at him. Then he realized it was a doll.

Deus. He scrubbed a hand over his face. He wasn't usually so edgy.

He picked up the doll. It was a clown, its baggy satin suit tattered from much handling. He brought it to his face and inhaled, scenting the child who owned it: sweet, happy innocence.

He cursed under his breath. Tyrus hadn't said anything about a child—a girl, from the scent. Children were rare and special gifts. There was no way in hell he'd harm one.

And how had he missed the fact that a child was here? He was working alone, he and Dion having agreed that since Baltimore was technically earth fada territory, the quieter they kept this the better. Still, Rui had spent the past couple of days observing the house, studying the occupants and learning their routine. The half-blood couldn't have brought her in without him knowing—unless he was working some kind of fae magic to hide her.

Rui placed the clown on the kitchen table and headed for the stairs. With any luck, its owner was somewhere else—with her mother, perhaps.

As he reached the top of the stairs, he slipped a switchblade from his pocket and pressed the button. The blade slid out with a soft snick.

Down the hall, the sleeper mumbled something.

Rui stilled, his back against the wall.

Five minutes ticked by, then ten. The only sound was the bedroom air conditioner and the slow drip of a faucet in the bathroom across the hall. Rui waited, unmoving. His Gift was tracking. With it came a predator's patience, whether his prey was animal—or man.

The sleeper resumed snoring. Rui palmed the knife and continued down the hall. He passed two bedrooms, one empty save for a sagging couch. The other must be the human's room; it was sparsely furnished with an ancient dresser and a mattress and box spring covered by a colorful Indian bedspread.

Rui reached the bedroom where the half-blood slept. The door was closed, presumably to keep the cool air in. The snoring had stopped again, but he could hear the slow, steady breath of someone in a deep sleep. Soundlessly, he turned the knob and pushed the door open a few inches. He drew a breath, checking for the half-blood's unique scent: a mix of iron (from his human half) and silver (from the fae half), along with a touch of salt.

But the girl's sweet scent filled the air as well. The iron and silver notes told him she was related to the half-blood, that he was almost certainly her father.

Rui's hand tightened on the knife handle.

Fucking fae. Tyrus had to have known that the half-blood had a daughter. But he apparently didn't give a shit.

He almost said to hell with it and left. But Tyrus would make a powerful enemy—and Dion had asked Rui to do this job for a reason. He was Rock Run's best assassin—and they needed that concealing spell. They'd never be able to pay the huge amount demanded by the night fae to cast it.

No, they'd been forced to barter: a job for a job.

And in the end, an assassin didn't judge the rightness or wrongness of a kill. He just did what he'd been hired to do.

The door jerked open. Rui released the handle and jumped back into the hall. A shadow barreled out of the darkness, knocking him to the floor. He rolled, barely avoiding the other man's clawed fingers.

Something else Tyrus had neglected to tell him. Silver apparently had the fae Gift of wayfaring, which included the ability to move lightning-fast. At least Rui knew how he'd gotten the girl in without him knowing.

Silently consigning Tyrus to whatever hell would take a night fae, Rui rolled again and with an agile twist was back on his feet, bobbing and weaving as he tried to get a fix on the half-blood.

But the other man was impossibly swift, shifting first to one side, then to the other.

The hairs on Rui's nape stood straight up. He spun around to find the half-blood behind him.

The two of them settled into a deadly dance, searching for a weakness. The half-blood's speed made him damn near invisible as he moved from place to place. A human assassin would've been dead by now, but as a fada, Rui had a touch of fae blood as well, so could track the other man's movements—barely—now that he knew what to expect.

He slashed out with the knife, slicing Silver's arm to the bone. The other man inhaled sharply and hugged the arm to his stomach. Blood dripped to the floor. Rui scented a hint of decay beneath the iron-silver. So Silver had some night fae in him.

The other man fought on for another silent, desperate minute but his breath was rasping in and out of his chest, his movements much slower, his injured arm pressed uselessly to his abdomen.

Now, whispered Rui's animal. He feinted left, and when the half-blood shifted to avoid him, plunged the blade beneath his breastbone and up into his heart.

Silver fell to his knees. His good hand latched onto Rui's wrist. "Please." He dragged in a breath. "Not. Mary." His gaze flicked in the direction of the sleeping girl.

Rui hesitated, but there was no harm in telling the man the truth. "She's safe. The contract didn't include her."

Relief softened the half-blood's sharp features. "Thank the gods." His lips moved but nothing came out but a gurgle. He took a last, harsh breath, and then his chest heaved and he released Rui and crumpled the rest of the way to the floor.

Rui stared down at the dead man, wondering why he didn't feel more: remorse at having killed a man, satisfaction at a job well done, guilt about the girl sleeping in the bedroom. But he felt—nothing, as if his heart were encased in chill gray ice.

He retrieved his knife, rinsed it off in the bathroom and

returned it to his pocket. He should get the hell out of there—but instead he hesitated, listening to the girl's soft, light breaths.

Drawn by something beyond his control, he stepped into the room and stared down at her.

She was younger than he'd expected—maybe five turns of the sun. She was sprawled on her back in the boneless sleep of a child, a nightgown twisted around her legs, her hair braided into five stubby pigtails that stuck out at angles around her head like an off-kilter crown. Like her father, her face hinted at fae blood—sharp chin, pointed ears and wide, tip-tilted eyes—although her skin was golden-brown where the half-blood was pale.

But like him, she was thin. Too thin.

As he gazed down at that small, skinny body, something in Rui clenched. If a child of his were that underfed, he'd do anything to get her food—lie, cheat, steal, even murder.

Which was apparently what the half-blood had done.

Delicate eyelids fluttered. "Daddy?"

Hell. He couldn't leave her here to find her father dead in the hall.

"Shh," he murmured, "it's all right." He lifted her from the bed. She weighed next to nothing, her arms and legs knobby brown sticks.

Her eyes popped open and rounded in terror. Her lips peeled back in a feral hiss. Light shimmered over her skin and suddenly he was juggling an angry, spitting jaguar cub. She hissed again and struck out with her claws. He cursed and tried to hold onto her, but she twisted out of his arms to the floor where she shook off the nightgown and dashed into the hall. She crouched next to her father and raised her upper lip in warning.

He ruefully rubbed his wrist. The little devil had drawn blood. Not that those tiny claws had done much damage, but still...

He followed her into the hall and crouched down on his haunches. "Easy, little one. I'm not going to hurt you."

Her ears flattened and her mouth opened to bare small canines. She growled, a high, baby growl that would have been cute if it weren't aimed at him.

He put out a hand, palm out. "Everything's going to be all right. I just want to help you."

She snapped at his hand, her little tail whipping back and forth in agitation, but he kept it near her face, allowing her to take in his scent. She took a cautious sniff, then growled again, her eyes flashing the green of her jaguar. Keeping her gaze glued on Rui, she inched backward until her head was next to her father's.

He remained still, knowing she needed a few moments to come to terms with what had happened, even as his animal urged him to grab her and leave—now.

The little jaguar licked the dead man's cheek, trying to heal him in the way of a cat.

That's when he realized she'd shifted to jaguar, which meant she was a fada, a shapeshifter—but not a river fada like him, or even some other form of water shifter. No, she was an earth fada.

He briefly closed his eyes. Could this night get any worse? Water and earth fada didn't get along at the best of times, but Rock Run and the Baltimore earth clan were longtime enemies. At the moment, the Baltimore shifters were in disarray, wracked by a brutal internal war. But it was only a matter of time before they regrouped and tried—yet again—to wrest control of Rock Run.

He had to take the cub and get out of here. *Now.* The last thing Rock Run needed right now was war with another clan.

He seized the little shifter by the scruff of her neck, grabbed the nightgown and loped down the stairs.

She yowled the whole way. In desperation, he snatched up the clown and stuck it in her face. To his relief, she snagged it with her front paws and quieted.

He gripped her neck lightly and stared into her eyes, letting her see his dominance. Water or earth shifter, he was her superior in size and strength, and her animal needed to recognize that. Her gaze dropped and she whimpered, all the fight leached out of her.

He reached the back door and then halted. Someone waited on the other side, someone who smelled of metal and decay.

The cub's tawny head jerked up, sensing the danger. She whimpered again, a small, heart-rending sound.

He swore under his breath and dashed back upstairs. Thank the gods, there was an open window in the human's room that let out onto the roof at the front of the house. He stuffed the nightgown in his back pocket, hefted the cub in one arm and climbed out.

Setting her down, he inched up to the peak and risked a look down. Night fae had eyes like a cat, but the two men below had their gazes trained on the back door.

Just two of them. The SOBs were damn sure they could take him. If he hadn't had to get the little earth shifter to safety, he'd have enjoyed allowing them to test that theory.

He jerked his head at the jaguar, knowing she could easily keep up in her cat form. "This way," he said in a subvocal voice only she could hear. The half-blood's rowhouse was a few from the end. The two of them moved soundlessly down the roofs in the other direction.

The second-to-the-last house had a small dormer jutting out of its roof. Rui dropped to a crouch on the far side, the cub hunkered next to him, her small body shivering despite the warm night.

He passed a hand over her fur. *Deus*, she was young. She felt as thin and breakable in this form as she had as a girl.

"Don't worry," he murmured in the same low voice. "They won't find us here. But you have to be very quiet. Don't move. Can you do that?"

Night fae were like vampires, but rather than sucking blood, they sucked energy. The only way to hide from them was to freeze, slowing your breath and heart rate so they couldn't track you—and pray like hell that it worked.

The cub nodded solemnly and pressed against him. To his relief, her shivers slowed and her breathing calmed. It occurred to him that she'd done this before, and the ice around his heart cracked open enough to send pity stabbing through him.

Although it was nearly midnight, the sidewalks were dotted with people enjoying the cooling night air. He heard the murmur of voices, the sound of footsteps. From somewhere nearby a cat in heat screeched, and a man threw open a window and hollered for it to shut the fuck up.

The noises quieted. Then the crack of a door being kicked open shattered the night. The night fae had gotten impatient.

Now was their chance. "Climb on my back," he told the cub. "We're going down."

She took the clown between her teeth and obeyed. He shimmied down a drainpipe, moved the cub to his arms and dashed the few hundred yards to the alley where he'd stashed his motorcycle.

He set the cub on the pavement. "Shift," he ordered.

She shifted. It took her a long time, her small reserves nearly depleted.

When she was a girl again, he dropped the nightgown over her head. It was pink with a cartoon princess on the front, underlining how very young she was.

He felt another unwelcome stab of pity, and it made his voice gruffer than he intended. "Tell me where your mama lives."

She screwed up her face. Fat tears rolled down her cheeks. "I don't have a mommy."

Rui tensed, knowing he wasn't going to like this. But he softened his tone. "What do you mean, *menina?*"

"She died. The bad men hurt her and she died."

Hades. Rui stared down at the girl, flummoxed.

He could leave her near a Baltimore earth fada's den. They had dens scattered all over the city, unlike his clan, who preferred living together in a single underground base. They would know who her mother was.

But with her mother dead, would the earth clan accept a mixed-blood child, especially one with night fae in her? For all he knew, her mother had been caught up in the savage internal war the Baltimore shifters were fighting, one that had left whole families dead. It would explain why Silver hadn't asked the clan for help hiding his daughter.

Handing the little girl over to the Baltimore shifters could be signing her death warrant.

And apparently the night fae were after her too.

That's when it hit him. The half-blood hadn't stolen a *thing* from Tyrus. He'd stolen this child.

Which meant that Rui had killed a man simply for protecting his own daughter.

His whole body went rigid.

The little girl gave a moist sniff.

He scraped a hand through his cropped black hair. "What's your name?"

"Merry Jones," she said, a tremor in her voice. "M-E-R-R-Y. Like Christmas."

He swung her into his arms. "Well, Merry Christmas Jones, I guess you're coming home with me."

Rock Run was about an hour north of Baltimore at the top of the Chesapeake Bay. The clan owned a large, pie-shaped piece of land edged on one side by the bay and on the other by the Susquehanna River, with Rock Run Creek running through the center. The clan base was deep underground in the caverns that ran along Rock Run Creek.

By the time Rui had reached Rock Run, Valeria had already gone to bed. But as he entered his quarters, she emerged from the bedroom, rumpled and adorable in one of his T-shirts, her dark hair tumbling around her shoulders.

"Rui?" She yawned. "What—" She froze, hand still covering her mouth, as she saw the little girl.

"This is Merry. I—" He licked suddenly dry lips. "I found her. In Baltimore."

Valeria's brows lifted but the look she turned on Merry was kind. "*Olá*, sweetheart. Are you lost?"

The little girl shook her head.

"She's part earth fada."

"*Sim?*" Valeria's brow furrowed. "And a bit fae as well, no? But why—"

Merry whimpered and Valeria's face softened. She gathered the child into her arms and sat down in a nearby chair, rocking her gently back and forth. "It's all right, *menina*. It's all right."

Merry had been mute the whole way up from Baltimore, perched before Rui on the motorcycle, one hand clutching his arm around her waist, the other fisted around her clown. She hadn't even complained when he brought her through the narrow tunnel that was the only way for a land dweller to enter the base.

But now she burst into tears. "I...want...my daddy."

"Shh," murmured Valeria. "Of course you do. Don't worry, we'll find him for you."

"Can you?" Merry sniffed. "Please?"

"Of course. Senhor Rui will help me. He's the best tracker in the clan."

Rui swallowed something sharp as glass. "I can't." He switched to Portuguese so the girl wouldn't understand him. "*Ele está morto.*"

Valeria sucked in a breath. She glanced at Merry and replied in the same language. "Does she know?"

"She was there. She didn't see it happen but she saw him after."

"Poor baby." Valeria pressed a kiss to the little girl's head. "But why bring her here?"

"She's mixed—human, night fae, earth fada. I asked about her mother, but she told me she's dead. I was afraid to leave her with the Baltimore clan."

Valeria nodded. She'd only been at Rock Run a couple of months, but she'd heard about the local earth fada and their problems.

Then her full lips pressed together. "Her papa." Her gaze was accusing. "It was you, wasn't it?"

He looked away. "*Sim.*"

"*Madre de Deus.*" The words were a horrified whisper. "How could you?"

The bond between them was still tenuous, not complete until both of them accepted it during the mating ceremony—but he felt her recoil from him.

It sliced at the deepest part of him. Valeria had grown up in a prosperous clan in Portugal—an old, rich clan, where the warriors didn't have to hire themselves out as assassins and mercenaries just to survive. She didn't understand that he'd had no choice.

"*Querida*—" He reached out a hand.

She ignored it to murmur to Merry.

His animal rumbled, puzzled and angry. She was the mate. She should know that if he killed, it was for the good of the clan.

"Valeria," he said, louder this time.

She stiffened but kept her gaze on Merry. He let the hand drop back to his side.

Merry lifted her head from where she was cuddled close to Valeria's heart to scrutinize him with hazel eyes slashed with shards of green, her jaguar very close to the surface.

"Are you a bad man?" The question hung in the air.

Rui opened his mouth, then shut it again. He shook his head and took a step back. At the door, he said, "I have to report to Dion."

Valeria finally lifted her head to look at him. He flinched. His warm-hearted, sensual, *maternal* woman looked as unforgiving as the harshest judge.

"You do that. And then don't come back. Not tonight, anyway. She needs time."

He stared back, despair an icy sludge in his veins. It was then that he realized how much he'd counted on her warmth to balance the coldness in him. He glanced from Valeria to the tearful child and then wrapped the familiar chill around him like a shield and with a curt nod, left the apartment.

He made the walk to the alpha's quarters encased in that same chill gray ice. Despite the late hour, Dion answered on the first knock.

He took in Rui's tension with one sharp look and waved him inside. "What happened, *irmão?*"

"It's done. But—" Rui explained about Merry Jones.

"She's our clan now," Dion said immediately. "I'll go to her, mark her with my scent so the others know she's under my protection."

Rui nodded. He'd expected his friend to see it that way, even though the last thing they needed was another mouth to feed— and an earth fada at that.

They discussed the night fae. They both figured Tyrus had sent the two men after Rui to make sure no one got out of the house alive. Dion was furious, but there wasn't much he could do. Tyrus was a powerful fae, the son and heir of the night fae prince himself. The clan was too weak to go up against him. All they could do was take the bastard's payment and then never work for him again.

And then Rui left Rock Run and went to a bar in nearby Grace Harbor. He started to toss back shots of whiskey, but no amount of alcohol could drown out Valeria's accusing face or Merry's small, clear voice asking, *Are you a bad man?*

But he couldn't blame the whiskey. He was sober enough when the sun fae queen, Cleia, strolled into the bar on the prowl for another fada lover, dressed in a flirty little red nothing.

He couldn't take his eyes off her. He'd seen what she'd done to the men before him—how they returned drained, and fit for little but fishing—but he hadn't cared.

All he wanted was to sink himself into that long, golden body and sex his brains out.

So he went home with Cleia, intending to stay for a night. He told himself it was to give Valeria a chance to cool down. But even then he knew he was lying to himself. What he was really trying to do was forget all the men and women he'd killed—and the children he'd left father- or motherless.

Are you a bad man?

Just one night, he told himself. What harm could that do?

But Cleia was a powerful fae, with a glamour that made her damn near irresistible. He'd lost himself in their dark, hedonistic play. The night turned to a week, and the week to a month.

Each evening he told himself: *Tomorrow. Tomorrow I'll go back to my mate.*

But each morning he found himself staying another day, caught in the fae queen's seductive net.

In the end, he stayed a year.

An entire fucking year.

He returned to find he'd lost his mate—and he had no one to blame but himself.

1

THE PRESENT

*R*ui's glass held only a few dregs of red wine. He raised it. "This is empty," he said in a soft voice that had the half-dressed blonde on his lap—a human named Katie—scurrying to fill it.

They were in a small, shabby house near the Baltimore waterfront, not unlike the one from which he'd taken Merry Jones. He ignored the familiar twinge of guilt at the thought of the little earth fada.

He'd taken Merry back to Rock Run, and Valeria had adopted her as her own. Both females seemed to be thriving. He had nothing to be guilty about...if you discounted the fact that he'd murdered Merry's father and left Valeria for the sun fae queen practically on the eve of their mating ceremony.

Katie poured wine into his glass with hands that trembled. He smoothed the frown from his face. She'd wanted to be with a fada, had come onto him in the Full Moon Saloon with a mixture of boldness and innocence that had pricked his jaded senses. But now that she had him, she was stiff and skittish, fear oozing from her pores in acrid waves.

She wasn't wrong to be afraid. But it irritated him all the same, carving like a knife through his wine-induced haze.

Across the room, Jorge and Benny were occupying themselves with three other women—a sea fada from Jamaica, a slumming night fae who'd conjured a plush rug for them, and Rui's own sometime-lover Beatriz. He eyed the limbs entwined in a sensuous knot of dark and pale. *Was that even possible?*

Like him, Jorge and Benny had been Rock Run warriors. Like him, they'd been taken as lovers by Queen Cleia. And like him, they'd returned different men: colder, more cynical, weaker in mind and body. Rui had turned to wine and women, but Jorge and Benny had given in to their animals and left Rock Run to travel the oceans in their dolphin forms.

Dion thought the two men lost for good. He'd be furious if he found out they'd returned and were attempting to resurrect the bacchas right under his nose. The wild, orgiastic rituals had been banned for a good reason—they brought out the worst in fada, bringing their feral side to the fore so that a fada in the grip of the *Delírio*—the Frenzy—was more beast than human.

Rui should've informed his alpha the first time he'd seen the two men, late one night in a bar just a few miles from Rock Run. But he hadn't, and he wasn't sure why, except that maybe it was his way of thumbing his nose at Dion, who made no secret of his contempt for Rui and the way he lived his life now.

If Dion found out that Rui was here today, he'd be out on his ass. Banished from Rock Run.

He stared into the dark red wine and wondered why that didn't bother him more. Lord knew, Dion had put up with enough from him. No longer fit to be a warrior, Rui had become a fisher instead—the worst frigging one in the clan. Somehow his Gift for tracking failed him when it came to fish.

Or maybe it was that he just didn't give a damn.

Once, he and Dion had been inseparable, raised together from the time they were pups. They'd been born days apart a little over a hundred turns of the sun ago, when the clan still lived in Portugal. When Rui's mother died a few weeks after giving birth to him, it was Dion's mother who'd nursed him along with her son. And ten years later, when Rui's father was killed in the battles over territory that had led to the clan leaving for America, Dion's parents had taken him into their family—and their hearts. The two of them had played together, trained as warriors together, chased their first women together.

When Dion took over as Rock Run alpha after his father's death, it had been a foregone conclusion that Rui be his second-in-command. Rui hadn't challenged Dion for leadership, although he knew his friend had half-expected it. Whenever a new alpha took over, there was a period when everyone in the hierarchy jockeyed for place. They both knew such a battle would be too close to call.

But frankly, Rui didn't want the headaches that went with being alpha. He was content to be second, a powerful position in its own right, and one where his hunting and tracking abilities were best utilized. He and Dion had quickly settled into a comfortable routine, working more as partners than alpha and second.

And then came the night he'd killed the half-blood.

Katie shifted uneasily on her feet, drawing his attention. He ran his gaze over her with an almost clinical interest: blond hair, blue eyes, creamy skin set off by two black scraps of lace that functioned as a bra and panties. He crooked a finger at her.

"Come here."

She flushed, the color tinting her pale breasts in an interesting way, but obeyed. He drew her back onto his lap where she perched tensely, the fear scent overpowering.

He growled lowly, but that made her go even stiffer. *Damn it anyway.*

He hadn't had a woman in over a month. At the bar he'd been more than ready, but now all she was arousing in him was his instinct to protect. Not exactly a turn on, especially since what she apparently required protection from was him.

He tipped her chin up so she was forced to meet his eyes. "Why so afraid, *menina*? I don't bite." Not unless the woman asked nicely.

"I'm not—"

He placed a finger on her soft pink lips. "I can scent a lie."

Katie gulped and nodded. "S-Sorry. I just want to go, please."

A slap sounded across the room. Katie flinched and darted a glance at the tangle of bodies on the rug. The night fae was on the bottom, her pale buttocks marked by someone's hand. Jorge speared his fingers in her black hair and jerked back her head. The night fae moaned, caught between pleasure and pain, and Katie pressed her hands to her mouth.

Deus, what had he been thinking, to bring her here? It was like introducing a baby seal into a pool of killer whales. But she'd begged to go to a baccha and this was the closest thing these days.

Rui opened his arms wide. "You're not a prisoner here."

"Thank you," she whispered and leapt from his lap.

"*De nada*," he muttered dryly but she was already out of the room. He pulled on a T-shirt and shorts and followed.

Out of nowhere an intense uneasiness swept over him. He opened the front door and scanned the dusk, all his senses straining to detect anything out of the ordinary. Nothing, save for the young toughs hanging out on the corner. They knew what he was, were careful not to meet his eyes.

Still uneasy, he shut the door.

Katie emerged from the bathroom, fully dressed. At the sight of him waiting in the hall, her eyes widened and he scented another spike of fear.

He blew out a breath. "Calm down, woman. I'm not letting you walk back to the bar alone in this neighborhood—especially not now that it's getting dark."

She swallowed noisily and ducked her head. "Thank you."

He slid on a pair of sandals and exited first, sending a hard glance in the direction of the young humans on the corner that ensured they wouldn't so much as look at Katie, before standing back and waving a hand toward the sidewalk.

"After you, *querida*."

When he returned fifteen minutes later, the others were still at it. He considered joining them, but he was still on edge. He rubbed his nape, watching as Jorge crawled over Benny and nipped his ear with a rough tenderness.

Rui's brow raised. *So that's how it is.* He'd known the two of them had been Cleia's lovers at the same time, but he hadn't realized that the two of them had become lovers as well.

Beatriz lifted her head. Seeing he was alone, she rose from the tangle and came across the room to him, all smooth, dusky skin and sensuous curves, her full red lips curved in a bold smile.

As she reached him, she shook her head in mock-dismay. "Did that silly little human leave you unsatisfied, *meu amor?*"

He just looked at her. Undeterred, she interlaced her fingers around the back of his neck and rose on her toes to nibble at his lips, her lush body pressed against his from chest to thighs. Beneath his shorts, his cock sprang to life. Beatriz purred and rubbed her pelvis against him. With a growl, he gripped her bare ass and thrust his tongue into her mouth.

Beatriz murmured contentedly and opened to him, sucking his tongue deeper and twining a long leg around his thigh.

Without taking his mouth from hers, he kicked off his shorts and then hitched her higher so that both her legs were wrapped around him and walked with her until her back was against the nearest wall. He kissed her, hard and savage, his erection thrusting against her moist center. She moaned and dug sharp fingernails into his nape.

Taking her hands, he set them against the wall on either side of her head. "Leave them there." He set her down to drag off his T-shirt. She disobeyed him to run her palms over his bare torso.

Busy fingers pinched his nipples, teased the wiry black curls on his chest.

He grabbed her jaw and pressed her head against the wall. "I said, leave your hands on the wall."

She moistened her full lips and placed her hands back on the wall. "I'm sorry."

He kept one hand on her jaw and with the other, fingered a large rose-brown nipple. "This is what you want, *sim?*" He pinched, a bit too hard. "To be punished a little, hm?"

"Goddess, yes." She moaned, her musk saturating the air. "Punish me, Rui. Make me sorry."

Taking in her slit eyes, her dazed expression—from drink or drugs or both—his lip curled in disgust. Not at Beatriz—Lord knew, he had no right to sneer at anyone—but at himself. At the lazy, wine-soaked womanizer he'd become.

"Rui?" She pouted up at him. "Is something wrong?"

He shook his head. "Not a thing." Grasping her ass, he hefted her higher and thrust into her. Hard.

2

Grr...yip...Yeow!

Valeria glanced at the ball of pups rolling around on the rug: Merry, in her jaguar form, and Trina and Marco, her two best friends, as otters.

"No claws and teeth," she reminded them. The three halted long enough to nod, their furry faces the picture of innocence, and then with a mutual growl threw themselves back into the fray.

Valeria shook her head, but she was smiling as she returned to the snack she was preparing in the kitchenette of her apartment. It was good to see the little ones enjoying themselves. The whole base was in an uproar. Their alpha, Lord Dion, had been kidnapped by the sun fae when they'd teleported into his quarters to rescue their queen, Cleia, whom he'd been holding prisoner. The children didn't really understand what was happening, but they knew their alpha was missing and the adults tense, which was making them anxious as well.

Marco and Trina's parents, both warriors, had been called to duty, so Valeria had volunteered to take the children overnight.

As a fisher, she wasn't much use right now, but at least this way their parents wouldn't worry.

They had to get Dion back. She briefly closed her eyes. Maybe he shouldn't have gone up against the sun fae, but she knew he'd believed he had no choice.

She'd never forgotten how kind the alpha had been after word came that Rui had chosen to live with the sun fae queen. Valeria had waited a month, and then asked Dion for an apartment in the wing where her friend Sabela and her family lived.

The alpha had given her a sympathetic look.

She dug her fingernails into her palms. Sympathy she could take, but it was humiliating to see the pity lurking in his eyes.

"You don't have to move out," he told her. "No one expects you to."

"Thanks, but I'd like to be nearer to my friends." And she wanted out of Rui's quarters. He was everywhere: his clothes in the dresser; his spicy male scent; the sturdy wood furniture...even the shaving gear on the bathroom shelf.

Oh, yeah, she needed to move.

"Then the apartment is yours." Dion enfolded Valeria in his arms. Nothing sexual, just an alpha comforting one of his own. His scent enveloped her, calm and reassuring. He smoothed a big hand down her back and something in her loosened. In that moment, she knew she'd been fully accepted into the clan.

She sighed and rested her head on his broad chest. She'd felt so alone ever since Rui had left. Her parents had stayed a couple of weeks—her father had even offered to go to the sun fae and kick Rui's ass for her—but they'd never intended to stay in America permanently. They'd urged Valeria to return to Portugal with them, but she'd seen how uncomfortable they were around Merry. Earth and water shifters were like oil and water, and on top of that, Merry had night fae in her as well. The Rock Run Clan was younger, less steeped in tradition than the clans back home. Merry had a better chance of being accepted here.

And Valeria hadn't been ready to give up on Rui. Not then. So she'd stayed.

Valeria realized she was staring down at the apple in her hand without moving. She resumed slicing, her stomach a knot of worry. Rock Run was hanging on by the skin of its teeth. The loss of the alpha could be a killing blow.

A knock sounded on the front door, and Sabela poked her head inside. "Oh, good, you're here."

She sauntered the rest of the way into the apartment with the languid grace of a pampered koi, tall and striking with black hair and a short dress in an eye-popping chartreuse. But that relaxed, colorful exterior was matched by a sharp wit. It was Sabela who bargained with both the fae and the humans to sell Rock Run's vinho verde, getting the best possible price. More than that, she had a heart as wide as a river.

Valeria didn't know what she would've done without her these past two years.

"Any news?" Valeria set a plate of apples and cheese on the rug for the pups before crossing the room to her friend. They kissed each other's cheeks, European-style.

"Nothing you don't already know." Sabela glanced at the happily munching pups. "I see Merry's okay."

The knot in Valeria's stomach coiled tighter. "Why wouldn't she be?"

Sabela drew her into the kitchenette. "The Baltimore earth alpha was here," she said in a low voice.

"Lord Adric? In the base?" Valeria's heart gave a hard thump. "But how?"

"He came in with the sun fae. He must've been the one who tracked Queen Cleia to Rock Run."

"But no one said—"

"Luis wants to keep it quiet for now. People are upset enough about the sun fae." Luis had become Dion's second after Rui had been ensnared by Queen Cleia. "But he was here, Valeria. Rodolfo told me."

"*Madre de Deus*," she breathed. Adric was alpha of Merry's mother's clan. He had every right to demand her back. Everyone knew he was determined to rebuild his clan. He'd be eager to claim any child, even a mixed-blood like her Merry.

Or worse, execute her for being a mongrel. Adric had a reputation for being ruthless, and some fada were as fastidious about their bloodlines as the fae.

"I know." Her friend's dark eyes were somber.

Sabela had been with Valeria through the worst of it, when not only had she lost Rui to Queen Cleia, she'd suddenly become a mother—of a sad-eyed earth shifter. No one knew better than Sabela how hard it had been, but Valeria had never regretted a moment of it. Merry had become her daughter in every way that counted.

Agitated, she paced the floor. Merry was *hers*. No one was going to take her away.

She threw up her hands. "What was Lord Dion thinking, to capture a fae? He was asking for trouble."

Then she instantly felt disloyal, especially after the welcome the alpha had extended her and Merry. But it was true; Dion had been holding the sun fae queen prisoner for the past two weeks, believing she was somehow sucking energy from Rock Run's men. And not just the men—the women and children too. According to Dion, it was either stop Cleia—or stand by while one by one, the Rock Run fada sickened and even died.

But no one, not even the people who'd disagreed with Dion's decision to kidnap the queen, had expected this. The base was concealed by a powerful spell which hid its location from everyone, fae or not. Adric and the sun fae shouldn't have been able to find it, let alone get in.

"It was the only way," Sabela said. "You've seen Luis—how

weak he is. And now his son, little Xavier, is sick too, with the same wasting disease as the others."

"No." Valeria swallowed sickly. "Not Xavier." The boy was barely more than a toddler.

"*Sim*. And then there's Rui—"

"Don't," Valeria interrupted. "Just...don't." She didn't need anyone to tell her what a drunken SOB her "mate" had become after his year with Cleia. She saw it every day. She swallowed over what felt like a jagged rock lodged in her throat.

Sabela touched her arm in wordless understanding. "You know things have been bad ever since the queen started taking our men as lovers. The alpha didn't have a choice. He had to do something before she wiped us out."

"Adric can't have scented her. She was in the creche with the other children when the sun fae came for Cleia. And Dion's quarters are on the other end of the base." Valeria scraped a hand over her hair. "I can't let him find out about Merry. I should've taken her and gone back to Portugal as soon as I realized Rui wasn't coming back. But no, I had to stay, hoping he'd—"

"Stop it." Sabela grabbed her shoulders. "You stayed for Merry, too, remember? And you were right—look how much everyone loves her. She's safe here at the base. Adric doesn't know she's here, and who's going to tell him? And don't forget, the earth shifters have never come looking for her. If they wanted her, wouldn't we have heard something?"

Valeria glanced at Merry, who was staring at her, eyes big, sensing her distress. She took a deep breath and sent her a smile. Reassured, the little girl went back to her snack.

"That's true," she allowed.

Sabela gave her a squeeze and released her. "Look, I'm sorry I scared you, but I thought you should know. And there's something else—Luis has called a clan meeting for after dinner. You can leave Merry at the creche. They announced a sleepover for the kids so that as many of the adults can come to the meeting as possible. It'll settle them, too."

Valeria nodded. With the alpha gone, the children were upset. The best thing was to distract them with something fun like a sleepover, and they'd be happier in a group with the other young.

"Now," continued Sabela, "why don't you pour us both a glass of wine? There's still a half hour until dinner."

When Valeria returned with the wine—some of Rock Run's own vinho verde—she was reclined on the couch in a very Sabela-like pose, one slim brown leg crossed over the other. Valeria handed her a glass and took a seat at the couch's other end.

"*Obrigada*." Sabela slanted Valeria a glance. "There's something you should know before the meeting."

Somehow she knew it concerned Rui. Her fingers tightened on the wine glass. "*Sim*?"

"You know they called in the fishers when it happened."

Valeria nodded. "I was out on the river myself when they sounded the alarm."

"Well, Rui didn't come in with everyone else. No one knows where he is."

"So? How is that different from any other day?" Everyone knew Rui made only a token effort at fishing. If he and Dion hadn't been old friends, he'd have long since been asked to leave Rock Run.

"It's not." Sabela studied the pale yellow wine, avoiding Valeria's eyes. "But people are saying that someone must have helped the sun fae. They couldn't have teleported into Dion's apartment unless they knew exactly where it was—and that that was where he was holding Cleia."

"No." Her denial was instinctive. "He wouldn't. He doesn't even *like* Cleia. I didn't see him talk to her once the whole two weeks she was here."

And she'd been watching, even though she'd pretended to herself that she hadn't been.

Sabela's teeth worried her lower lip. "I don't believe it myself. But it looks bad. He did spend a year with her, and he's the only person missing."

"No. Not Rui."

But Valeria couldn't help wondering. He'd always had a hard edge, but his time with the sun fae had honed it knife-sharp. He behaved as if their nascent mate bond had been severed—and perhaps it had, for him—but she still felt the connection.

Not all the time, and when she did it was a mere shadow of what it could be. But the emotions emanating from him were so cynical, so full of self-revulsion that it tore at her heart.

She hated his drinking, hated how he took woman after woman, some of them right in front of her as if she were less than dirt to him. Sometimes it made her cry, and sometimes she wanted to slap him—hard—until he snapped out of whatever black pit he was wallowing in. Couldn't he see that he was using alcohol and women as a band-aid? That he could indulge as much as he wanted but it wouldn't erase the darkness?

But somewhere underneath was the man who'd been Dion's second. A strong, proud warrior who'd done everything for the Rock Run Clan. She refused to believe Rui had changed that much.

"It wasn't him," she asserted. "I *know* it. We're not mated, but I still feel him." Sometimes, anyway.

Sabela set her glass on the coffee table to hug Valeria. "I believe you. The alpha's like a brother to him. He'll probably stomp into the meeting and tell everyone they're out of their fucking minds."

Valeria made a sound that was half-laugh, half sob. "That sounds like Rui."

She sagged against Sabela, their cheeks touching, her animal

—sad and lost at losing its mate even after two years—craving a reassuring touch. "Not that I care," she muttered.

"Of course not," her friend agreed.

They sat there for a minute and then Valeria pulled away. "I'd better get these three ready for dinner." She came to her feet and clapped her hands at the pups. "Time to eat. Everybody back to their girl or boy." When they whined without shifting, she added, "Did I mention that if you're good, there's a sleepover at the creche tonight?"

Three enthusiastic yelps split the air. Iridescent sparkles shimmered over their pelts and for a few moments, the pups were nothing but glittering points of light, stars picked out in the air above the rug.

As always, Merry's shift took longer than the others. When she finished, she lay on the rug, panting. Trina and Marco were used to it, but Valeria always held her breath until she completed the change. By age seven, a fada should be able to move easily from one form to the other. Was it because she was an earth shifter—or was there something wrong with her?

Then she was up and joining the other two in chanting, "We get to go to a sleepover. We get to go to a sleepover."

"Thank you, Mama Ria." Merry grabbed Valeria around the waist. "I love you."

Valeria bent down to cup her sharp little face. Goddess, she adored this child. Losing her now would be like losing a piece of her heart. She rubbed her nose against Merry's. "I love you, too, *querida*. So much."

She straightened up and spoke over the din the other two were making. "All right, you three, what did you do with your clothes?"

~

After spending himself in Beatriz, Rui released her legs with a murmured thanks.

She drew her fingers down his chest. "Anytime, *querido*."

Rui glanced over his shoulder at the other four. The uneasiness pressed at the back of his skull. Something was wrong at the base. He knew it with every inch of the warrior he'd once been. He dropped a light kiss on Beatriz's lips and reached for his clothes.

"I'm going back to Rock Run."

She pushed herself off the wall. "Take me, too."

All he wanted was out of there, to cleanse himself of Beatriz's cloying scent. But not even he was such a pig as to fuck a woman and leave her stranded.

"Get dressed, then."

Five minutes later they were on his motorcycle, threading their way through Baltimore. From there, they roared up I-95. By the time they arrived at Rock Run, he was more or less sober. He'd only had a few glasses of wine, and the short swim required to enter the base through one of its underwater entrances did the rest.

As they exited the creek, Rui shook off the excess water. His shirt and shorts were still wet, but as a water fada he barely noticed it. He told Beatriz goodbye and headed inside, but she followed him down the hall.

"Come to my apartment?" She gave his bicep a suggestive squeeze.

He gently but firmly disengaged himself. "Not tonight."

"Tomorrow, then."

He lifted a shoulder. "We'll see."

She reached up to kiss him, and at that moment Valeria came around the corner hand-in-hand with Merry.

Rui froze.

But Valeria just nodded to the two of them, her face expressionless. "*Boa noite.*"

"*Boa noite*," he returned. She was dressed simply, in brown leggings and a pink camisole. His gaze moved over her hungrily, taking in her classic Portuguese features and glossy dark curls, the tanned cleavage exposed by her camisole.

Merry grinned up at him. "Hello, Tio Rui. I'm going to the creche for a sleepover."

He dragged his gaze from Valeria to smile down at the little girl. "That sounds like fun."

Valeria's nostrils flared, scenting the sex on him and Beatriz even after the short swim. For a moment she faltered, her dark eyes wounded.

He swallowed and glanced away, even as he told himself he had nothing to be ashamed of. The two of them weren't lovers, and hadn't been for more than two years.

Valeria's expression went blank again. With a short nod, she continued past him and Beatriz. Against his volition, he turned to gaze after her. Her bottom swished enticingly in the clinging leggings. His whole body went taut with longing.

He swallowed again, then snapped his head around and strode blindly down the hall in the opposite direction.

Beatriz kept pace with him. Somehow her fingers were entwined around his bicep again. When he glanced down, there was a catlike smile on her mouth.

He jerked his arm from her grip and wished her goodnight.

She halted him with a hand on his chest. "Are you sure you won't come tonight, *querido?*" She swiped her tongue over her full red lips. "I can make you forget…"

For an instant he was tempted. At least it would ease his aching cock. But he was coming to see that no one but Valeria could ease his aching heart.

"I'm sorry"— he set her away from him—"but no."

3

———

After leaving Beatriz, Rui turned toward his own apartment, but he hadn't walked ten yards when he heard the hum of voices. Too many for that time of night. Heading toward the sound, he was surprised to find most of the clan's adults gathered in the large cavern that served as the dining hall.

"Please," his cousin Luis was saying from the front of the room. "Calm down and listen to me."

Rui's uneasiness ratcheted up to full-blown alarm. Why was the clan meeting at this time of night—and where was Dion?

Rui's nearest neighbor nudged him. "Where the hell have you been?" A large hulk of a man, Rodolfo had been the first Rock Run warrior to be taken as Cleia's lover. Like Rui and the others, he'd returned home drained, but most of his strength had since returned. And even at less than full strength, the big, square-faced man was one of the clan's top warriors.

"Never mind where I was," Rui told him. "What's going on? Where's Dion?"

"The sun fae have him. The SOBs teleported into his quarters to rescue Cleia and captured him, too."

"Dion?" Rui frowned, not sure he'd understood. Maybe he wasn't as sober as he thought he was. "They have the alpha?"

Rodolfo nodded grimly. "That's not all. The sun fae had an earth fada with them—the new alpha."

"Adric?"

"*Sim*. I saw him myself."

"Hell." Rui dragged a hand over his face. It was bad enough the sun fae had Dion, but for the Baltimore alpha to know the base's location—that was a disaster. And even a fae couldn't teleport somewhere he or she had never been—unless the fae had somehow received coordinates or a clear description of the location. The concealing spell should've prevented that sort of thing. What had gone wrong?

Luis was speaking again. "We've heard nothing from the sun fae yet, but I'm sure Queen Cleia will contact us—or allow Dion to. You all got to know her these last two weeks. She's a good woman. You know that. We would've scented the falseness on her."

Some of the clan nodded. Rui wasn't one of them. As far as he could tell, the sun fae woman didn't let much stand between her and her pleasure. He'd made sure to avoid her while she'd been at Rock Run. It was easy enough; Dion had kept her blindfolded to prevent her from accessing her magic. He'd walked right by Cleia several times without her knowing.

But damn. Even wine-soaked as he was, he'd thought Dion had lost his mind. The queen was the most powerful fae in a clan of rich, powerful fae. His old friend had been playing with fire—and now he'd be lucky if he wasn't consumed by the flames.

Rui glanced across the room. Valeria had slipped into a seat a few tables away and was scowling at him. He didn't need to see her lips move to know what she was thinking: *Do something.*

He looked away. What the hell did she think he could do? He'd spent the past year somewhere between buzzed and full-out drunk. The last time he'd trained as a warrior had been two years ago. He was overweight and out of shape. The lowliest cadet could probably take him now.

But as Luis continued to speak, the clan grew increasingly agitated. The loss of their alpha had sent shock waves through the hierarchy. Worse, no one knew how long he'd be gone. Already, some of the dominants were eying Luis, knowing that not only wasn't he at full strength, his son Xavier was ill with the wasting disease that had taken several other children, causing Luis's attention to be divided.

Those lower in the dominance chain weren't looking to challenge, but their distress was palpable. Someone near Rui muttered that without Dion, the clan was lost. Another worried that they would become trapped in endless dominance challenges and vicious infighting like the Baltimore earth clan.

"Listen to me." Luis raised a hand for quiet. "I know you're upset, but Lord Dion would expect us to stay calm." Nods of agreement. "And as for the queen, this morning she tried to heal my Xavier. She said that it was just a temporary fix, but you all saw him at dinner. He's eating again. He even shifted to otter and tried to slip away from his mama at bedtime."

A chuckle swept through the crowd, relieving some of the tension. They all knew that was a good sign; shifting took energy. If the boy could shift, he had energy to spare.

"For that alone, I would die for the queen. So I'm going to trust she had a good reason for taking Dion with her."

"But what about the earth shifters?" It was Tiago, Dion's youngest brother. "They're probably preparing to attack right now. We have to do something, not remain in the base like sitting ducks, praying everything will be all right. You might trust the queen not to help Adric—but I don't."

Rui lifted a brow. There was something about Tiago's voice, as if he knew something he's wasn't telling. And it was odd, the comment about Cleia.

Tiago had been the queen's last Rock Run lover, although

she'd sent him home as soon as she'd discovered how young he was—barely twenty-one. For the past couple of months the kid had moped around the base like a lovesick fool, his face so long even Rui had noticed. After her capture, Tiago had been one of the queen's staunchest defenders, even clashing with his much older and dominant brother about her treatment. He was the last person Rui would've expected to argue against trusting Cleia.

"Tiago's right," Teresa called. The only female *tenente*, she was a tall, wiry blonde known for her level head. "We should be preparing our defenses, not sitting here arguing. Everyone knows the Baltimore shifters want our land."

More people nodded. But others jumped to their feet, saying they shouldn't just defend, but attack. And then people were shouting and snarling at one another in a way Dion would never have allowed.

Luis shouted for calm, but the dominants ignored him. Ordinarily his cousin wouldn't have stood for that—he hadn't become second by being a pushover—but he was pale, tired, his mouth bracketed by strained lines. Rui had the impression he was holding himself upright by sheer willpower.

Hell. Rui couldn't stand by and watch the clan be pulled into a war. Nor could he let Luis be forced into a dominance challenge —not while he was weak from whatever Cleia had done to him and on top of that, worried sick about his son.

He strode forward. "Enough," he growled, taking his place beside his cousin.

A few people glanced his way, but the shouting continued. He snarled, a vicious rasp that had every head in the hall snapping around. This time the silence was instantaneous.

"That's better," he said, soft and dangerous. "Now sit the fuck down and listen."

"You heard him," Luis added. His tone was harsh, but Rui heard his relief.

One of the *tenentes* called out, "Why should we listen to do

Mar? How do we know he wasn't the one who gave the fae our location? Everyone else has been back for hours."

Several people muttered agreement. Rui growled low in his throat. The man who'd spoken was Davi, the youngest *tenente* and ambitious as hell.

A hush fell as Rui stared at Davi until the younger man dropped his gaze and muttered, "*Desculpe-me.*"

Rui nodded curtly. Hands on his hips, he scanned the crowd, meeting each of the most dominant men and women's gazes in turn until they recalled he'd once been Dion's second—and their superior.

"I may not have been much of a warrior in the past two years," he said, "but I'll be damned if I'll let anyone question my loyalty. I've been a member of Rock Run since Dion's father first led us here from the old country. I've spilled blood for the clan—over and over. God's balls, I'd slit my own throat before I gave away the base's location—or betrayed my alpha. Does anyone here doubt that? Davi?"

People averted their eyes, shook their heads.

Davi swallowed. "No, *senhor.*"

Isa, one of the clan's elders, spoke into the silence. "Rui's right. We wouldn't be here today if it weren't for him and Dion and the other warriors who spilled blood to keep us safe—and ensure there was food in our bellies."

Several others murmured agreement.

"*Obrigado, senhora.*" Rui inclined his head to the round-faced, elderly woman. "But what I did in the past isn't the issue, except that it means I've earned your trust. Right now, we need to stop arguing and start planning. Shouting at each other plays right into the earth fada's hands. They've wanted Rock Run for years, since the old alpha Dionísio's time. The only reason they haven't tried anything recently is that they've been too busy fighting among themselves."

"That's true," another elder stated.

"Now that they have a new alpha," Rui continued, "you can be damn sure they'll be looking at our territory again. They know we're weak without Dion. Hell, if I were them, I'd strike as soon as I could. They could be at our door by morning. The question is: are we going to be ready for them or are we going to be arguing among ourselves?"

Mouths firmed, murmured, "We'll be ready."

"He's right." Rodolfo's deep voice boomed from the back. "Just a month ago, I saw Adric and two other earth fada on our land. They looked as if they were measuring it for size."

"Over my dead body," shouted a *tenente*. The dominants among the clan growled agreement, Davi the loudest.

"And that wasn't the only time," Davi added. "Adric came back another time, left his scent mark right across the creek, not a half mile from the base."

"Good," Rui said. "As for the sun fae, Luis is right. We all know Cleia has a thing for fada males. She probably took Dion back to Rising Sun to use him in her bed." His lip curled. "She won't hurt him—at least, not yet. If we attack first, the sun fae might simply kill him—or teleport him to the other side of the world. But I swear to you on the god Dionysus's staff, we'll get the alpha back."

"I'm with you, Rui," a *tenente* called out.

"Me too," rumbled Rodolfo.

Rui glanced at Luis. It was his cousin's call. He was second, a position he'd won fairly, working hard for Dion and the clan while Rui had been wallowing in his own filth.

Luis nodded. "Rui is Dion's second. We all know my position was only temporary."

Rui's throat constricted. He didn't deserve such trust. "*Obrigado*," he managed to say.

Luis grinned and pulled him into a bear hug. "Welcome back, cousin."

Rui squeezed him back. "*Idiota*," he muttered in a voice that only Luis could hear. "Plant your ass on a chair before you topple over."

His cousin scowled but obeyed.

Rui stared out at the sea of faces waiting for him to direct them. *Deus*, he wished he hadn't drunk that wine tonight. The haze was gone, but his brain felt like warmed-over flan. For a panicky moment his mind went blank, but then his ten years as Dion's second kicked in as the animal rose up to steady him. He hadn't listened much to the animal recently; the alcohol had drowned out its voice.

"Tonight we'll send a couple of men to Rising Sun, see what they can find out. Meanwhile, the rest of you, prepare for a battle —standard procedure. The earth shifters would love this base and the territory we control. It's our job to make sure the cost is too great for them."

Luis came back to his feet. "You heard him. The *tenentes* and the top warrior cohort meet here with me and Rui. The rest of you either go to your assigned duties or your quarters."

Dismissed, the clan rose. The group of *tenentes* and warriors gathered around Rui. He looked around at the men and women awaiting instructions and felt that lump in his throat again.

He swallowed hard. "Luis and I will go over your assignments. But first, we need two volunteers to infiltrate the Rising Sun compound and find if that's where they took Dion—and if so, exactly where they're keeping him."

THE WAY back to Valeria's apartment took her past the creche. She couldn't resist a peek at the children. Merry was sitting in the circle with the rest, her thin face rapt as she listened to a story. Valeria had done her best to put some fat in those cheeks, but although the little girl was no longer painfully gaunt, she had a restless energy that kept her string-bean slim.

The story ended with a ritual "...and they lived happily ever after."

Merry saw Valeria and dashed over for a hug. "Mama! What are you doing here?"

Valeria swung her up into her arms. "I just came to make sure you're being a good girl."

"*Mama*," Merry replied in wounded tones.

"Are you?" Valeria tapped her nose.

Merry sighed, a teenager trapped in a seven-year-old body. "Yes, Mama Ria."

"That's my girl." Valeria gave her a kiss and set her back down. "I'll see you in the morning, then."

"Okay." Merry skipped off, calling to her friend Trina.

Valeria hung around another few minutes to help the creche workers with the kids' bedtime snack before heading back to her apartment, where she found Petros Okeanos outside her door, wearing only a pair of faded jeans and a smile, a bottle of wine in his hand. It was obvious what he was here for.

The two of them had been flirting for weeks. Sabela couldn't understand what was holding Valeria back.

Valeria wasn't sure herself. The man was hot and a little wild, with curly dark hair and a hard, muscled body. Even better, he was just passing through, a Mediterranean sea fada on a visit from Greece. Sex with him would be just for fun. No one's heart would be left cracked and bleeding when he headed back across the Atlantic.

So what was stopping her?

"Hello, *glika*," he said in a thick Greek accent and indicated the bottle in his hand. "I brought you some wine."

"Sim?"

"Come here." He set the wine on the floor and held out his hand. His gaze was hot, predatory.

She faltered, her animal sending up warning signals. She told herself not to be silly and continued forward.

"Hello, Petros." She touched her lips to each of his cheeks.

He turned his head and captured her mouth, pulling her closer so that her whole body was against his. Leaning back against the door, he fingered a lock of hair. "I hear the little ones are sleeping in the creche tonight."

She nodded. "I was just saying good night to Merry."

"You're a good mother."

"Thank you," she murmured even as her animal gave another uneasy twitch.

Water fada often took to the ocean, spending months, even years riding the currents. Fada *tradição* was to welcome such nomads, so when Petros had first swum up the Chesapeake, Lord Dion had readily assigned him a room in the Rock Run caverns. But most travelers stayed only a couple of weeks, whereas Petros had already been here for over two months.

Valeria swallowed. Had she read him wrong? Had he been courting her, thinking of her as a possible mate?

He tugged on the lock of hair. "Invite me in, baby."

And she did *not* like to be called baby.

She pulled back. "I'm sorry, Petros, but it's not a good time. This thing with Dion and the earth fada—"

"So? What can you do? And I offered my help but Luis said there's nothing I can do either—not tonight."

"No, but—" Petros was right; there was nothing Valeria could do right now for either Dion or to defend against the earth shifters, and Merry was in the creche. Sex would calm both her and her animal, which was as upset as the children by the day's events.

So why wasn't she happier to see him?

He closed a hand around her nape. "I brought wine"—he indicated the bottle at his feet—"an Agiorgitiko that's been aged in French oak. I had to go to Baltimore to get it." He stroked the sensitive skin at back of her neck.

Her eyelids drooped. His fingertips were rough, male, knowing. And it had been so long...so very long. She craved touch—intimate touch. And *Deus* knew Petros was sexy. For the first time in two years, she'd thought perhaps—

A fada could mate more than once. But it was almost unheard of if the original mate were still alive. Damn Rui anyway for leaving her in this hellish limbo—mated, but not.

"Don't say no," Petros murmured against her ear. He turned so that his body was pressing hers into the wall and told her exactly what he wanted to do with her—and the wine.

To her dismay, her animal shrank back, arguing he didn't smell right. She'd thought her animal wanted this. They were both going crazy, sleeping alone night after night.

Petros nipped her earlobe. "So? What d'you say, *glika*?"

Valeria moistened her lips. "I—"

A growl filled the corridor. Valeria went stiff. Over Petros's shoulder she saw Rui bearing down on them, his eyes changing from green to the dark, feral gold that signaled his animal was in control.

"She says *no*, damn you."

4

―――――――

Together, Rui and Luis assigned the top warriors where they would do the most good. Two *tenentes*—Justino and Ed—would infiltrate the sun fae compound and bring back any information they could about Dion, as well as a report on the sun fae's current defenses, should the clan need to mount a rescue. A third *tenente* would organize the defense of the base's main entrances, while three squads of their most seasoned warriors would patrol the perimeter of the Rock Run territory on alert for any sign of the earth shifters.

With that decided, Rui sent a clearly exhausted Luis back to his mate and child and gave himself and the two remaining *tenentes*—Rodolfo and Teresa—the task of planning Dion's rescue. He ordered Rodolfo and Teresa to meet him in his *sala* in thirty minutes and headed back for a quick shower before they arrived.

First, though, he stopped at the creche to make sure the children were safe and happy. He nodded to the two guards who'd been assigned to guard the entrance and went inside. The room was relatively quiet due to the fact the children were rapidly downing milk and fresh-baked cookies. His gaze lingered on

Merry, seated at a large round table with the others in her age group. Valeria had done a good job with her. She'd filled out some, although she'd probably always be thin. But it was a healthy, wiry slimness, not the near starvation in which he'd found her.

She caught sight of him and her serious little face lit up. She left her snack to hurtle across the room.

"Hey there, *princesa*." He swung her up into his arms for a kiss.

He was still a little bemused by her obvious partiality for him. From the day he'd returned from the sun fae, she'd been curious about him. At first, she'd kept her distance. But at dinner each night, when the clan gathered for a communal meal, he noticed her studying him as if he were an interesting puzzle. He'd ignored her, too intent on getting quietly drunk. But he'd wondered if her interest was due to curiosity—or hate.

Then one evening she stopped beside him and greeted him gravely in perfect Portuguese, having apparently picked some up in the year she'd been at Rock Run. "*Boa noite*, Senhor Rui."

He'd removed his arm from his current woman and returned her greeting, conscious of Valeria waiting tensely behind her daughter. She placed her hands on the little girl's shoulders, urging her to another table. "Come along. Tia Sabela's waiting for us."

But the next evening, Merry stopped beside him again. He was prepared this time, having taken a seat at a table of all men. "Hello," she said in that serious little voice.

"Hello," he replied. There was a pause which felt awkward to him but didn't seem to faze her. She waited patiently, her big, almond-shaped eyes seeming to take in everything—that he wasn't sitting with the woman of the night before, that his wine glass was still full.

He swallowed and glanced up at Valeria, but her set face made it clear he was on his own.

He looked back at Merry. "Uh...how are you, *bonitinha*?"

She inclined her head in a gesture that would've done a princess proud. "I'm good. What's that mean—*bonitinha*?"

"Pretty girl. If I were speaking of your mama"—his gaze went to Valeria again—"I would say *bonita*—pretty woman."

Merry's face lit. "*Obrigada*, Senhor Rui," she said, and taking her mama's hand, headed off to their table.

Rui felt a curious tightness in the back of his throat. He took a gulp of wine, then with a glance at Merry and Valeria, set the glass back down and didn't touch it until they'd left the dining hall.

Soon Merry was calling him Tio Rui and giving him daily reports on her friends, her school, her mom. He kept waiting for the other shoe to drop. For Merry to ask point-blank why he'd killed her father.

Are you a bad man?

But apparently all she recalled was that he'd saved her from the night fae. He knew he had Valeria to thank for that, and he was more grateful than he could say. But it was a special kind of hell, having the little girl treat him as her hero when he was anything but.

After the first week, Valeria started allowing Merry to talk to him on her own. Occasionally she took her meals with him instead of her mother.

Lately she'd been trying to get him and Valeria back together.

Rui had tried to discourage her—the last thing he needed was a seven-year-old matchmaker—but Merry was a true jaguar: stubborn and independent. And he didn't want to upset her, because the damnedest thing had happened: she'd wormed her way into his heart. They only saw each other at dinnertime—he was afraid to push for more than that—but her chatty reports had become the highlight of his day.

Now she pressed a sticky kiss to his cheek. "Guess what, Tio

Rui? We're sleeping in the creche tonight. I get to sleep next to Trina."

"Sounds like fun."

She put a small hand on his arm and leaned in close. "Wanna hear a secret?"

Setting her on her feet, he crouched down so he was at her level. "Only if it's one you're allowed to tell."

"Oh yes. This is *my* secret."

He nuzzled her cheek, unable to resist her little-girl scent: sweet, a little sweaty. She must've been playing hard before the creche workers corralled the kids for a snack. "Then yes, I'd like to hear it."

She put her mouth next to his ear and whispered, "This is my first sleepover."

"Ah...that's nice." Something made him add, "Are you going to be all right?"

She moved a shoulder.

"Are you sure? If you don't want to stay, I can take you back to your mama."

"I'm a big girl now. I can sleep with the other kids."

"I know. But even big girls miss their mamas sometimes."

She twisted her fingers in the skirt of her nightgown. "The other kids will laugh at me."

His heart lurched. *Deus*, this girl had him, hook, line and sinker. She was the one bright spot in his sorry life. He tucked a wiry black curl behind her ear so he could meet her eyes. "We'll tell them your mama needs you."

The big hazel eyes got larger. "Isn't that a lie?"

"It's not a lie if it's true. And your mama always needs you, right?"

She considered that for a few seconds, then gave him a shy smile. "Yes, please."

He tapped her on the nose. "Let's tell the teachers." He came to his feet and hoisted her onto his hip. She nestled her head trustingly into the side of his neck. He swallowed hard and kissed the top of her head.

It took only a few moments to take Isa aside and explain what was up. Rui was conscious that even six months ago, Isa would've refused to let Merry leave with him. But now she merely nodded and gathered up the little girl's belongings, giving Merry a conspiratorial wink as she handed Rui the backpack.

"See you at the next sleepover, *querida*."

Merry stayed on Rui's hip as he made his way through the labyrinthine halls. The complicated, intertwining paths were typical of a river fada base, part of their defense against an enemy incursion, but he knew the way to Valeria's quarters as well as his own. How many times had he'd made his way there, late at night when everyone else was asleep? To stand outside her door, eagerly gulping in any small trace of her scent—nutmeg and earth—lingering in the hall...hands balled and craving her with every fiber of his being until he feared he'd go mad.

Everyone thought he was cold to Valeria, that he'd decided she wasn't the mate for him after all.

Everyone was wrong. With each day that passed, he wanted her more.

Tonight, with the clan in turmoil, he'd have come anyway if only to reassure her and Merry. Now he had the perfect excuse to spend a few extra minutes with her, something his animal had been pushing for. But as he entered the corridor, he saw her and that damn Greek sea fada who'd been sniffing around her for weeks—and he had Valeria pressed against the wall.

A dark heat filled Rui's head. A growl tore from his throat.

Merry started. "What's wrong, Tio?"

He growled again and she whimpered. He remembered himself enough to set her and the backpack down. "Stay here."

Then he was moving down the hall, his vision edged with red, his animal a roar in his head. He was running by the time he reached the other two.

He clamped a hand on Okeanos's shoulder. "She says no," he said, his voice so close to animal the words were almost unrecognizable.

Okeanos snarled and shook him off. "Like hell."

Rui's lips peeled back. His switchblade practically jumped into his hand. Okeanos reached for his own knife and they circled each another.

Rui wasn't sure what would've happened if Valeria hadn't inserted herself between them.

"Stop it, both of you," she hissed. She looked past them and reached out a hand. "*Querida?* What's wrong? Why aren't you at the sleepover?"

Her distress penetrated Rui's anger. He dragged his gaze from Okeanos to see Merry a few feet away, gazing up at him wide-eyed, her backpack clutched in both hands.

Deus, what was he doing? He expelled a breath and brought his knife back to his side.

"*Desculpe-me*," he muttered to Valeria. "I'm sorry," he added to Okeanos, knowing he spoke only Greek and English.

The other fada stared back with cold black eyes. Then he jerked his chin in a curt nod. "Fine. But stay away from Valeria from now on. She's mine."

Valeria hissed but didn't contradict him.

Rui clenched the knife's handle. When the other man had first turned up at Rock Run, Rui had been in a drunken haze—as usual. It had been weeks before he'd realized Okeanos was courting Valeria. He told himself that was good, that it was time she moved on. Wasn't that what he'd been trying to force by parading his women before her and the clan? But the reality was a blow to the gut.

Still, he was wrong and he knew it. He had no rights where Valeria was concerned; he'd made sure of that.

He jerked his head in acknowledgment before retracting the blade and returning it to his pocket. Okeanos followed suit as

Valeria took the backpack from Merry and lifted her into her arms.

"I didn't expect to see you. You're not sick, are you?"

Merry burrowed her face into Valeria's neck and shook her head.

"She's fine," Rui said, "but she decided she'd rather sleep here tonight."

"I was afraid you'd be lonely," Merry said into Valeria's shoulder.

"*Sim?* How'd you know I was missing you?"

"I just knew."

Despite the tension still thick in the air, Rui's lips twitched. Even a seven-year-old had the need to save face, it seemed.

Merry lifted her head to look at her mama. "Tio Rui brought me back. Don't be mad at him."

"Oh, *querida*. Of course I'm not mad that he brought you back." Valeria gave him a stiff nod. "*Obrigada*, Rui. For bringing Merry home." Her tone made it clear that was *all* she was grateful for.

"*De nada*. It's no problem."

He backed away. But some stubborn, primitive instinct wouldn't let him leave before Okeanos. Instead, he leaned against the wall a few yards away, arms crossed over his chest.

The other man scowled in his direction, then gave Rui his back. Rui's jaw tightened at the deliberate insult, but he remained where he was.

Okeanos stroked a finger down Valeria's cheek. "Would you like me to come back later, *glika?*"

"Not tonight. I'm sorry, but Merry needs me..."

"All right." Okeanos's tone was neutral but the scent of his irritation filled the air. The man wasn't happy at having his plans for tonight thwarted. He wrapped a hand around Valeria's nape, pressed a hard kiss to her lips and stepped back with a triumphant glance at Rui.

Rui's teeth clenched, but he managed to wink at Merry. "Have a good sleep, *princesa*. I'll see you tomorrow."

She gave him a sleepy smile. "'Night, Tio Rui."

Rui straightened up and looked at Valeria. She was clearly pissed off, although he wasn't sure if it was at him or Okeanos—or both of them. She might be low on the dominance chain, but push her hard enough and she pushed back.

"*Boa noite.*" His gaze went to her full lips, reddened from Okeanos's kisses, and he had to fist his hands to keep from dragging her into his arms and erasing the memory of the other man's mouth with his own.

Thick dark lashes lowered, shielding her thoughts. "Good night."

His fingers dug into his palms. Once he'd have known what she was thinking, would've felt her emotions through the mate bond—but no longer. The bond had been well and truly broken, leaving a gaping hole in his heart where Valeria had been.

He'd been numbing himself with alcohol and sex for so long that he'd forgotten how much it hurt when he was stone-cold sober.

Okeanos stood a few yards away, watching them. She glanced at him, then lowered her voice. "I can handle him."

He raised a brow. "That's not how it looked to me."

"Well, I *was* handling it. And if I wasn't, it's none of your damn business."

"Sorry, but you looked like you could use some help."

"You were wrong."

But she didn't meet his eyes, and he knew that wasn't entirely true. Still, if that's how she wanted to play it, there was nothing he could do.

She opened her door. "I have to put Merry to bed."

He placed a hand on her arm. "Valeria. I—"

He didn't know what he intended. An apology, maybe. Or even to beg her for another chance.

But her whole body went rigid, and before he could get anything out, she jerked from his grip and slipped into her apartment. The last thing he saw was Merry gazing forlornly at him over Valeria's shoulder.

For a long moment he stared at the closed door. He lifted his hand to knock on it, to say—what? She didn't have to spell it out. He'd had his chance and blown it.

Okeanos still watched from a few yards away. Rui gave him his back and walked away.

~

DAMN THE MAN.

Valeria blew out a furious breath. The *cabrão* didn't want her for himself, but he wasn't going to let anyone else have her either.

Well, they'd see about that.

Merry tilted her head so that she could see Valeria's face. "Don't you like Tio Rui, Mama?"

Her chest tightened. "Oh, *querida*. I do like him. It's just that I like Senhor Petros better." Which was a lie, she realized as soon as the words left her mouth. Nausea welled in her throat, a warning not to continue in that vein or she'd become truly ill.

"But—" Merry's small brow puckered.

Valeria placed a finger on her lips. "No more questions. It's time you were in bed."

Merry frowned but didn't argue, a sign of how tired she must be. Within a few minutes, she was tucked between the sheets, one arm wrapped around the tattered clown doll that was all she had from her former life. Sitting down on the bed, Valeria placed her hands on either side of her shoulders and rubbed her nose against hers.

"Love you, sweetheart."

"Love you too." She yawned. "Mama?"

"What, baby?"

"I'm *not* a baby," was the automatic reply. "Can I sleep as a cat?"

"*Claro.*"

Unlike water fada, who typically could shift into several different animals, Merry had only ever shifted into jaguar. That she wanted to sleep as her cat tonight didn't surprise Valeria. Young shifters tended to feel safest as an animal; at that age, the human form was by far the weaker. But it hurt Valeria to know her daughter was feeling anxious. She'd spent the last two years doing her best to make her feel safe again.

She smoothed a hand over Merry's head. "Don't worry, we'll get Lord Dion back. Meanwhile, we're safe here at the base."

Merry nodded. "That's what Tio Rui said." She wriggled out of her nightgown and shifted into a petite gold-and-black jaguar.

Valeria rubbed her behind the ears. "'Night, big girl."

Merry butted her head against Valeria's hand before setting it on her paws with a toothy yawn. Valeria continued to pet her until her eyes drifted shut. Giving her one last pat, Valeria closed the door and returned to the *sala*. Only then did she give in to her anger.

She says no.

Her claws sliced out. How dare Rui interfere between her and Petros?

The man was a dog in the manger. She'd smelled the sex on him and Beatriz—and not for the first time, either. And didn't Beatriz like to rub that in her face? Smiling that cat-in-the-cream smile of hers.

Valeria's heart had felt like it was being squeezed by a giant fist. It had been all she could do to hide her hurt and shame.

Well, to hell with him. She paced angrily back and forth. If he didn't want her himself, he'd damn well better get used to seeing her with other men, and she was going to tell him so to his face. So he was a dominant and her superior by several degrees. Sometimes you had to make a stand.

Only the fact that Merry had been present had kept her from having it out with him right there in the hall.

It wasn't like Rui was so special. He drank too much and no longer trained with the warriors. His once hard body had developed a gut. But his face...ah, his face. It was a little too fleshy now but still striking with strong, sculpted planes, hooded green eyes and a full lower lip that she itched to take between her teeth and—

She groaned and threw herself onto the couch, face down. Damn Rui anyway.

Petros was perfect for her. And he wanted her, Valeria. He made her feel sexy, beautiful—and she needed that, after being rejected by the man who was supposed to be her mate.

She curled up in a ball and, retracting her claws, covered her face with her hands. Her lips moved, cursing Rui again, but it came out as a sob. She was so tired of this endless aching, this yearning for a man who'd pushed her away again and again. So very tired.

Because as she'd met Rui's intense golden gaze over Petros's shoulder, she'd felt a jolt clear to her soul.

And she'd known that whatever she might tell herself, whatever she might pretend to Sabela and the rest of the clan, she still wasn't over Rui do Mar.

5

Rui turned the shower handle to ice cold. The adrenaline that had been carrying him for the past few hours had almost worn off. He didn't mind cool water—he was a river fada, after all—but this was straight from an underground well. He sucked in a breath as the water hit his skin. But it would clear his head, give him the boost he needed to keep going.

Soaping up, he lifted his face to the icy stream and thought about Valeria and Okeanos. Something had been off about the whole thing. She might have been allowing the other man to touch her, but she hadn't been enjoying it.

It had been sheer primal instinct that sent Rui striding down the hall to drag the other man off her, but now that he was calmer, he knew why he'd acted like such an ass. It wasn't simply that his animal had been riding him, urging him to claim her. That had been part of it, of course, but damn it, she'd been afraid of Okeanos. Rui had smelled it, an acrid thread woven through her familiar, earthy scent.

She hadn't even seemed aware of it, but on some level the son of a bitch frightened her.

Recalling the other man's hands on her, Rui squeezed the soap bar so hard it shot out of his fingers and hit the stone wall.

He retrieved it and tossed it back into the soap dish. *Deus*, this was fucked.

He didn't have the right to interfere between Valeria and another man, but his animal was snarling that Okeanos was all wrong for her. And there wasn't just her to consider, but Merry.

Rui groaned and scrubbed his hands over his wet face. Once, he'd have gone with his instincts, ordered Okeanos to stay away from Valeria. But he no longer trusted himself. Dion seemed to like the other man. And he'd been accepted by the clan, had made friends here at Rock Run.

And Valeria apparently wanted him in her bed.

Hell. Rui admitted that his distrust could be rooted in jealousy. And what was more, it was selfish. He'd rejected Valeria, but he didn't want her to go to anyone else.

That wasn't fair. Their animals needed touch even more than their human and fae parts did. Valeria was a loving, sensual woman. Celibacy—and he knew she hadn't had a lover since him —must be hell for her. If she wanted Okeanos, he was just going to have to suck it up.

But he didn't have to like it.

With a scowl, he shut off the water and grabbed a pair of shorts.

The two *tenentes* were waiting in his *sala*, Rodolfo on one of his two chairs, Teresa on the couch. The shower hadn't done much to clear his mind. He was exhausted and his mouth was desert-dry. He glanced at the jug of wine on the sideboard.

Just one glass. Surely just one wouldn't hurt.

He licked his lips, wanting that wine so badly he could taste it. Beads of sweat broke out on his forehead and his hands started to shake. He dragged in a breath and reminded himself what the clan was facing. Dion was the only person—man or woman— with the strength to hold them together. And he, Rui, might be the only warrior who could rescue him. No one else had the right combination of experience, tracking abilities and knowledge of the sun fae compound. Even overweight and out of shape, he was Dion's best chance.

He couldn't let Dion down. They might not be the friends they'd once been, but this past year, when Rui had been more interested in drinking than working, the other man had stuck by him, allowing him to keep his place in the caverns.

So no. For Dion, he could go a few days without wine. Fada bodies weren't as weak as a human's. He might feel like hell, but he could function.

He slowly released his breath. Going to a small cooling unit set into the stone wall, he removed a bottle of grape juice and raised it to the other two. "Want a glass? Or there's wine over there." He indicated the jug on the sideboard.

Rodolfo's bushy black brows lifted but all he said was, "Juice is fine."

"Same for me," Teresa said.

It was humiliating, since they were obviously going along to keep him sober, but he'd lost the right to be proud. After handing them each a glass of the tart purple juice, he poured himself one and drained it in a few gulps. It soothed his parched mouth, and he could almost fool himself it was wine.

Almost.

He turned a chair around and straddled it, resting his forearms on the back. "Let's start with you, Rodolfo. You spent even more time with the sun fae than me. What would you say are their weak points?"

The big man rubbed his neck with a beefy hand. "God's balls, Rui. That was almost twenty years ago."

"We need to start somewhere. You may remember something I don't."

Rodolfo nodded and furrowed his brow. "Let's start with Cleia. I'd say that other than her magic—and she can do some serious damage—her greatest strength is those bodyguards of hers. The family's been guarding hers for centuries. Their loyalty is absolute—they'd die for her and consider it an honor."

"Agreed."

"And her greatest weakness is that like most fae, she relies too much on her magic. Take that away and she's just a woman. That's true of the whole clan. They rely too much on magic and not enough on old-fashioned fighting skills. If we could somehow block their magic, they'd be dead in the water, other than the small group of warriors who've worked on their physical skills."

Rui nodded. "Excellent point. On the other hand, that's what Dion thought and look where that got him." Trussed in a net like a goddamn fish, according to the warriors who'd seen it happen, and taken prisoner by the sun fae. "And we might be able to block one or two of them from using their magic, but there's no way we can stop the whole clan. Only the most powerful fae could do that—and not for very long."

"Which is why Dion kidnapped Cleia," Rodolfo pointed out. "He knew he had to stop her, but her clan alone is three times our size, and they can call on the other six sun fae clans as well. On top of that they're fae. A direct attack would've been suicide."

Rui nodded. Knowing Dion, that must have chafed, big time. He much preferred an honest fight to something sneaky like kidnapping a woman, even if the queen were a powerful fae who was behind Rock Run's decline.

Teresa spoke up. She was the clan's expert on the fae, which was why Rui had included her in this discussion. "That's true, but only a small number of fae have Gifts that are useful in combat. Generally it's the ones whose Gifts are some kind of primal magic, like Queen Cleia."

The queen was the sun fae's Conduit. Sun fae needed the sun's energy for life, and they could draw some energy directly from the sun, but they needed the Conduit to keep them at full strength.

"That's why they hire the fada to fight their battles," Rodolfo inserted dryly.

"What about the illusionists?" Rui asked.

"An illusionist can trick a fada's eyes and ears," said Teresa, "but our sense of smell is too good. They can't fool us for long."

"True," Rui said. "But Cleia doesn't just draw energy—she can direct it. They say she can incinerate a man where he stands. And right now, around the summer solstice, she's at her most powerful."

The other two nodded soberly.

"So to recap," he said, "a direct assault would lead to all-out war with the sun fae, and might not free Dion anyway. Our best option is a search-and-retrieve."

Teresa rubbed her chin. "Justino and Ed were in the Rising Sun compound at the time Dion kidnapped Cleia." Dion had been there as the queen's guest, brought there to become her latest lover, but the other two warriors had acted as Dion's backup. It was they who'd helped Dion spirit Cleia out of the compound after he'd rendered her unconscious.

"Good point." Rui hadn't known that until tonight, when Luis had chosen Justino and Ed as the fada's advance scouts. It had brought home to him how far he'd been out of the loop. Save for his interactions with Merry each evening, he'd spent most of the time in his own little world. He hadn't even known that Dion intended to kidnap Cleia until he'd returned to Rock Run with her. "That's why Luis sent them to the compound tonight."

"They're good," Teresa said. "Last time the sun fae never even knew they were there. But this time the fae have probably tripled their guards—both physical and magical. Still, we need to know where they're holding Dion and what barriers we'll have to go through to get him."

"Exactly." Rui smiled grimly. He was the clan's best tracker. Being out of shape didn't affect his Gift. He could find his friend even without the others' information, but it was imperative he got Dion out of there as quickly and safely as possible.

He came to his feet. "All right. Let's give it a day, gather all the information we can. Then we're bringing Dion home—Cleia or no Cleia."

They nodded. He knew he could count on them. Any one of the *tenentes* would gladly give their lives for Dion.

Teresa left, but Rodolfo lingered. "You sure you're all right?"

Rui met his eyes. "Yes. I promise, I won't touch a drop until Dion's back."

The big man broke into a smile. "That's good, then." He clapped Rui on the back and left.

Rui shut the door and looked at the jug of wine. He didn't give himself a chance to think, just crossed the room and upended it into his kitchenette sink. The scent filled his nostrils. Enticing... seductive. Mesmerized, he watched the dark red liquid swirl around the stone basin and disappear down the drain.

He was bending to catch the last of it in his mouth when he realized what he was doing. Horrified, he finished emptying the jug and then dropped onto his mattress to snatch a few hours of sleep.

Tiago went to the quarters he shared with several other unmated males and shut himself in his room. He paced back and forth, a lead weight where his stomach should be.

What had he done?

With each day Cleia had spent in Rock Run's caverns, she'd grown weaker, her energy drained by Dion's insistence that she stay below ground so that her people couldn't rescue her. The only sunlight she'd received were the weak rays that came through slits cut in the rock ceilings. Anyone could see she was slowly wasting away. She was a sun fae; she *needed* sunlight.

Tiago had felt torn between his love for his brother and for Cleia. He'd always looked up to Dion. The oldest of his three brothers, Dion had been more like a father to him, especially after their own parents had left to ride the waves when Tiago was still a boy. Just the thought of challenging the much older, very dominant alpha made his animal cringe.

But meanwhile, Cleia got a little paler and weaker each time he saw her. He loved her, believed she was his future mate. Okay, there was no sign of the mate bond, but that wasn't unusual in someone as young as him. It would come when he was ready—and then she would feel it too. Meanwhile, he refused to stand by and let Dion starve her of the sunlight that was the stuff of life to her.

So he'd given Adric the coordinates that he and the sun fae had used to rescue her, even though he knew that it was a betrayal that could get him banished for life—if his brother didn't kill him outright. But he'd never expected Cleia to take Dion with her. And it hadn't even occurred to him that the earth fada might use the coordinates to attack Rock Run.

Now the clan was in an uproar, trying to get Dion back and at the same time prepare for an attack from either the sun fae or the earth shifters—or both.

Tiago groaned and dropped onto the bed, his head in his hands.

All he knew was that Cleia was his mate. He *felt* her—a constant ache in his heart. If he hadn't helped her, he wouldn't have been able to live with himself.

But what the hell had he done?

One thing he could fix. Opening the top drawer of his nightstand, he removed the chunk of quartz hidden at the back. It was a cleverly engineered smartphone given to him by Adric, its smooth, milky white face a screen that lit up at the touch of a finger. Crouching down, he smashed it against the rock floor. It broke into a handful of shards laced with a metal that appeared to be gold. He swept the pieces into his hand and hurried down the hall and to one of the river exits, only to be stopped by Davi.

Tiago swallowed a groan. No one would leave the base without permission tonight.

"What's up?" the *tenente* asked.

He concealed his fist at his side. "I need to get in the water for a few minutes. My animal—" He shrugged.

Davi waved him in. All their animals were edgy. Sometimes water was the only thing that soothed them. "You can have five minutes. Hugo's in the river, patrolling. Stay where we can see you."

"I will." Tiago saluted and dove in. He swam a few yards before looking around for Hugo. He was a hundred yards away, swimming as a dolphin.

Tiago dove deep and released the quartz pieces into the fast-flowing stream. They spread out and drifted downward, settling on the bottom with the other stones. Then he changed to dolphin because his animal *did* need soothing, and dove back down. Even though it was mid-June, the deep water was cold, bracing.

His panicked heart stopped racing and he was able to think. All he could do now was to support the effort to rescue Dion. And then he'd better start making plans to leave. Because when his brother discovered what he'd done, he was a dead man.

Hugo appeared nearby. He whistled a hello, which Tiago returned. They brushed by each other, a companionable touch. Then Hugo prodded him with his beak, indicating he should return to the base. Tiago obeyed. He was in deep-enough shit already.

Back on land, he shifted to man and returned to his room. As a novice warrior, he wasn't involved in the preparations tonight, but he'd been ordered to get a good night's sleep because tomorrow he'd be taking a turn on guard duty—if the clan wasn't fighting the earth fada.

As he entered the quarters reserved for unmated males, his best friend Chico hailed him. "Tee. Wait up."

Tiago lifted a hand. Despite his name, Chico was as American as they came, his mother a fada who'd grown up in Rhode Island, his father the first child born at Rock Run after its founding some eighty years ago. He had his mother's clean-cut Anglo features and his father's dark hair and olive skin, and like Tiago and the other younger members of the clan, spoke English for the most part.

He reached Tiago and bumped his shoulder in silent sympathy. "Sorry about your brother."

A hot rush of guilt made his reply curt. "We'll get him back. And if the Baltimore shifters try anything, we'll be ready."

"Hell, yeah. There's no fucking way Baltimore can take us. They're nowhere near our size. They were smaller than us to begin with, and they've been killing each other off for years."

The tightness in Tiago's shoulders eased. Chico was right. For the first time since he'd burst into Dion's quarters behind the other warriors and seen Cleia, Adric and a group of sun fae standing over his unconscious brother, he felt better. They'd get Dion back. And if the earth shifters attacked, they'd send them back to Baltimore with their mangy tails tucked between their legs. Hell, everyone knew it was easier to defend territory than take it.

"Damn straight." He reached for his doorknob. "See you in the morning."

"Tee?" Chico's expression was a mixture of excitement and fear. Although they'd been training for years, neither of them had made warrior yet—and they'd never been in a real battle. "You afraid?"

"A little," he admitted. "But I'm ready." His animal bumped against his skin in agreement. He was a young, unmated male. He'd willingly die to protect the clan, especially the children.

Their eyes met, both their animals to the fore. Tiago knew his eyes had changed to a feral silver, while Chico's glowed a spooky green.

"Me too," was the reply.

Their arms came around each other in a tight hug. They half-nuzzled, half-butted each other in the way of male animals before breaking apart and entering their separate rooms.

6

"**M**ama, Mama!" Merry pelted down the hall to Valeria. "Guess what? We're all going to a party."

"*Sim?*" Valeria scooped her up for a kiss. "That's nice, *querida*."

She glanced at Sabela, who was following close behind, having offered to pick up Merry from the creche. "A party?" she mouthed as she set her daughter back down.

The base was on lockdown. Only a few heavily guarded men had gone out fishing. The whole clan was readying itself for war —with the sun fae, the Baltimore fada, or both. Valeria had dropped Merry at the creche and spent the morning helping the healers inventory medical supplies.

Rock Run had been awash with rumors.

Dion's dead.

No, he got away from the sun fae.

No, he had the shit beaten out of him by Cleia's guards.

Finally Justino and Ed had returned with the information that Dion was safe in Cleia's apartment. Justino had scaled the four floors to the queen's balcony and seen with his own eyes that the alpha, although bound tight in a fishing net, was unhurt. Justino had hung around as long as he dared, hoping to speak with him, but Cleia hadn't left his side. In fact, she'd fussed over him—giving him food and water, releasing him from the net. Since it appeared Dion was safe for the time being, Justino and Ed had returned to base to report what they'd learned.

Sabela's grin was almost as big as Merry's. "Dion sent a message to Luis. He's fine. He promised to stay with the sun fae for a couple of days, but he's fine."

"Thank the Goddess." Valeria's shoulders sagged with relief. *And yet...* "Why? Why does he have to stay?"

She could think of only one reason the alpha would've agreed to remain with the sun fae—and it wasn't good. Surely he hadn't fallen prey to Cleia's glamour?

Sabela shrugged. "Who knows? But he swore an oath to stay with the sun fae until midsummer day. Cleia wants him to attend the ritual."

Valeria's brows lifted. The midsummer ritual was normally for sun fae only. "But why?"

"Who knows?" Sabela said again. "But he'll be safe enough. Queen Cleia has promised."

Valeria nodded. Neither the fae nor the fada found it easy to lie, and reneging on a promise was even worse. If Cleia went back on her word, she'd be left weak and ill for days, an easy target for any rival fae clan. And she'd be a target for the Rock Run assassins for the rest of her days.

Merry was chanting, "We're going to a party. We're going to a party."

Valeria shook her head. "Not us. Lord Dion."

"Us, too," the little girl insisted.

"She's right," said Sabela. "The entire clan is invited to the midsummer ritual—and the festival, too. Rui and the *tenentes* are conferring with the elders right now." The sun fae's midsummer festival was a three-day celebration famous throughout the fae and fada worlds.

"Why would she want us there? Unless she wants another chance at our men," she added a little bitterly.

"She says it's to show there are no hard feelings between the sun fae and Rock Run."

Valeria pursed her lips. "And we're going to go."

"It looks that way, *sim*. You can always decline. But if you're worried about Lord Adric, only Rock Run and the sun fae are invited to the ritual."

They both looked at Merry's excited face. It would break her heart to stay home, and there was no way Valeria was letting her leave the base without her.

She blew out a breath. "No," she said. "We'll go."

GODDAMN FUCKING FAE.

Adric lifted the quartz that dangled from a leather cord around his neck and stared at the screen in disbelief. All the data they'd gathered about the Rock Run base was gone, wiped out as if it had never been, his quartz still vibrating as it did after an energy surge.

"Hang on." Adric looked around at his four lieutenants—his sister Marjani and three young but battle-hardened men who'd earned his absolute trust during the Darktime: Lucas, Jace and Zuri. The five of them were seated at a circular table in his den twenty feet below Baltimore.

"Something's happened," he told them. A few quick taps on the screen contacted the clan's head surveyor. "Mason. Do you still have the data on the Rock Run base?"

Mason was one of the few older men who'd accepted Adric as alpha—which was why he was still alive. Now he was silent for a long moment before shaking his head. "The file's empty. Damn it, that's impossible. I encrypted that file myself—three times over. Nobody but you, me or Jace should've been able to access it."

"Nobody but a fae." Adric let out a vicious curse. It had to be the sun fae. They could do things with energy that would make an electric eel green with envy. "Dion got to their queen. Hell, you'd have thought the woman didn't want to be rescued." When he'd arrived with the sun fae, Cleia had been naked and on her knees, about to be fucked by the Rock Run alpha.

"I'll do my best to retrieve the information," Mason said. "But I can't make any promises."

"Don't waste your time. The sun fae are forgetting one thing; I was at Rock Run. I know where the entrances are." Including the single entrance that could be reached from land.

Adric was a Gifted tracker. He only had to be somewhere once for the location to be imprinted in his memory.

Except—his hand clenched on the quartz. "I don't fucking believe this," he breathed. "They messed with my mind as well. I remember being there, but everything else is gone—its location, what it looked like. All I can remember is its scent."

He frantically searched his memory, but all that remained was the odor of Rock Run Creek: lush, moist, organic. Which probably applied to every damn river in the world.

He growled. "How the hell did they do that—get in my mind like that?"

"I'm sorry," Mason said. "I'll keep trying, but it looks like it's been wiped clean."

Adric expelled a breath. "Not your fault."

He cut the connection and looked around at the others. The four lieutenants stared back with varying degrees of shock and anger—except for his sister, whose expression was carefully blank. He knew damn well she was pleased, though. Marjani had been against invading Rock Run from the start.

Lucas spoke first. He was Adric's right-hand man and a shifter with his animal so close to the surface, he was basically a human wolf. "I'll tell the clan to stand down."

Adric's jaw tightened. "Not yet." He refused to accept they'd been cut off at the knees. Not when he'd been dreaming of this day ever since he'd first heard the stories about how the clan had almost taken Rock Run sixty years ago. He'd decided then and there that was what his people needed to become whole again. "Maybe Jace can recover the data."

Jace was the clan's ace hacker and the main architect of the quartz smartphone technology. "Already on it." He frowned down at his own quartz.

He wouldn't touch Adric's quartz except in a dire emergency. No one would. Earth fada had a direct connection to their quartz. Each piece was attuned to its owner's energy, a unique vibration that fed both the owner and the quartz. But as their go-to tech guy, Jace had a backup copy of every important document.

"Sorry." Jace shook his head, scowling. "No can do. Whoever did this didn't even bother breaking the encryption. They just wiped the whole file clean."

Adric's hand went to his own quartz again. The gray-and-orange crystal vibrated in a short, agitated pattern, attuned to his emotions in a way that was eerily sentient.

"I'd say the SOBs broke our agreement, but they never said I could keep the data on Rock Run." In fact, the sun fae had been careful to make no promises beyond the large sum they'd paid for his help in tracking their queen.

Fucking fae.

They were so damn clever with their promises. Well, at least he had their payment safe in a bank account that could only be accessed by him or Marjani. It was money his clan desperately needed. They'd been nearly destroyed by the fighting during the Darktime. They were poor, hungry, demoralized. As alpha, his first priority was to rebuild their crumbling homes, make sure the children had food in their bellies.

"It's for the best, Ric." Marjani leaned forward, hands on the table. "We're not ready. The clan's still recovering. Even if we took

Rock Run, we're not strong enough to hold it. We have the money —more than we ever dreamed of. Be grateful for that."

"You're wrong. We could take their base—and if we did, we'd damn well hold it. Even if we have to kill every male above the age of ten—and the female soldiers too, for that matter."

Female fada were less likely to have the aggressive instincts necessary to make soldier, but every clan had women like Marjani who fought alongside the men. Two years his junior, she was slim, almost delicate-looking with an oval face and large dark eyes. But she'd guarded his back with a pit-bull-like determination as he'd fought his way up the hierarchy on his way to becoming alpha.

She dragged a hand through her short black hair. "This isn't us," she asserted. "We don't go into people's homes and murder them. Not since—" She looked away, throat working.

They all knew what she'd almost said. *Not since the Darktime.* When their parents had been executed by an alpha brutally consolidating power. When a few years later the two of them had almost been murdered in their beds by their own uncle, who had assassinated the previous alpha. When Jace's sister had been raped and murdered, and Lucas had been imprisoned and tortured for over a year—simply for being Adric's friends.

The stories went on and on. The end result was their clan had split into a number of small, weak factions which had nearly ended in them all being exterminated, hunted by one another and the more nasty fae.

Adric crossed his arms. "We need that territory. Our cats and wolves need the space, need the room to run. Even deer need more space than they get here in Baltimore."

Marjani's full lips thinned, but she kept silent. Adric might be her brother, but he was also her alpha.

He glanced at Zuri, who as usual hadn't spoken, preferring to listen to the others as he weighed options. The man was frankly beautiful, with curly black hair and brown skin touched with gold—but he was a lieutenant because of his cool head.

"Well?" Adric asked. "Is it worth a shot?"

Zuri lifted a finger. "One—we know the boundary of their territory. The spell concealing the base's actual location is functional again, but we can work around that. We already knew its approximate location even before the sun fae neutralized the spell. They may have wiped our memories of the exact location, but those are recent memories. An older, more-entrenched memory may still exist."

Adric narrowed his eyes. "You're right. I can still picture the area we'd narrowed it down to. We can start from there, use scent to locate the entrance."

Zuri inclined his head and raised another finger. "Two, their alpha is with the sun fae. They have to be upset, off-balance. They may even be challenging each other for leadership." A third finger. "Three, we're young, hungry. It's their home ground, but our people *want* this. A year ago I wouldn't have thought it was possible, but you've got the whole clan behind you, Ric. If we can just find a way in, this may be our best chance in a long time to take them."

Adric smiled. "My thoughts exactly."

"I don't know why the hell we're wasting our time talking," Luc inserted. "We need to strike now, before they recover from the loss of their alpha."

Jace and Zuri nodded agreement. Only Marjani abstained, her face carefully blank. But he scented her dismay.

Adric came to his feet. He didn't like upsetting his sister, but this time she was wrong. They might never have a chance like this. His animal, coldly ruthless, was in full agreement. It was time. He was opening his mouth to give the order to invade when a white mist formed in the palm of his hand.

He jerked even as he smelled the silver that was the mark of a fae spell. Words in a formal script formed in the mist, one elegant letter at a time.

Queen Cleia requests the pleasure of your company and that of a guest at a Summer Ball to be held at Rising Sun on Midsummer Day at two in the afternoon.

His jaw went slack. "Well, hell." He looked at his lieutenants. "I've been invited to a fucking ball. The sun fae."

There was a stunned silence. No member of the Baltimore clan had been invited to a sun fae celebration. Ever.

Luc recovered first. He snorted. "Probably a trick."

Adric shook his head. "I don't think so."

He read the invitation aloud to the others; a fae message was only for the recipient's eyes. Already the invitation was dissolving, leaving behind only the faint, metallic odor of silver. He stared down at the fading invitation in disbelief. Wasn't that just like the fae?

"They wipe our minds and our crystals of data and then they invite me to an effing ball?"

"You'll go," said Marjani.

He scraped his fingers through his spiky hair. "Will I?"

"You don't refuse a fae invite without a good reason," Zuri pointed out. "Not unless you want to piss them off. And you'll be safe enough. Hospitality is sacred to the fae. They'd be shunned if they treated a guest dishonorably."

Another message appeared.

Lord Dion and the Rock Run Clan will be in attendance as our special guests.

"Fuck," Adric said. "Fuck, fuck, fuck." He could almost hear the crack as his plans collapsed around him like a castle built on a fault line. He stared at the words as the message dissolved.

"What?" asked Marjani.

"They invited Lord Dion and his clan. Damn him anyway. I *knew* that sun fae bitch had the hots for him."

Zuri was the first to catch on. "She's saying he's an ally."

Luc looked from Zuri to Adric, baffled. "Even though he held her hostage?"

"Yes, damn her." Adric turned and slammed the side of his fist against the cavern wall.

It was Zuri who explained. "Word is that Dion took Cleia as retaliation for all those Rock Run men she took as lovers. I'm guessing she decided to cut her losses, declare them even. Everyone knows the sun fae women have a thing for fada men."

Adric blew out a breath and forced himself to think beyond his anger and frustration.

"Order the soldiers to stand down. But this is not over. I'll go the damn ball and see what's what. And then we'll plan our attack—sun fae or no sun fae. If we can't take Rock Run in a straight battle, we'll find another way."

Marjani's full lips tightened.

He stabbed a finger at her. "You want to be a diplomat? Here's your chance. Because you're coming along as my guest."

7

Cleia was beautiful, Valeria would grant her that.

Her mouth turned down as she watched the queen stroll through the crowd of sun fae and Rock Run fada assembled for the midsummer ritual.

A long, incandescent candle of a woman, she drew everyone's gaze without even trying with her bright hair and body like a dancer's. Next to her, Valeria felt like a plump troll with her ordinary brown coloring and a form that was several inches shorter and ten pounds heavier.

She grabbed Merry's hand and edged backward so that Cleia would pass by without seeing her. Most of the people from Rock Run were happily greeting the queen. They had come to like and respect her during the two weeks she'd been imprisoned at Rock Run, but Valeria had kept out of her way, only meeting the queen once, and that briefly. And Cleia wouldn't recognize her; Dion had kept the queen blindfolded the entire time, which apparently bound her powers in some way so that she was as helpless as a human.

As a relative newcomer at Rock Run, Valeria had refrained from weighing in on whether it was right of the alpha to keep a sun fae imprisoned underground. But that didn't mean she had to interact with the woman, because frankly, it was hard to feel warm and fuzzy about someone who'd stolen your mate, then thrown him back like a too-small fish when she tired of him.

And she'd kept her curious daughter far, far away, especially when people began to whisper that Cleia was behind Rock Run's mysterious decline, that she was sucking energy from them like a night fae. She'd been glad of her caution after little Xavier had fallen ill with the same wasting disease as the others.

Now Cleia paused near Valeria. She tensed and placed her hands on Merry's shoulders, instinctively peeling back her upper lip. But Lord Dion caught her eye, his expression warning that she'd better remember she was a guest here. Abashed, she averted her head, and Cleia passed by without noticing her.

The sun was almost at its zenith. The queen entered the center of the small outdoor amphitheater where the midsummer ritual was to take place. The sun fae required energy from the sun for life. Although they could draw directly from the sun, it wasn't enough; everyone in the seven clans depended on the Conduit—currently Queen Cleia—to draw the extra energy they needed. The midsummer ritual was where the Conduit renewed her or his bond with the sun. Without that bond, the flow of energy would gradually cease and the sun fae would wither and die like plants kept too long in the dark.

Cleia raised her arms, and the crowd hushed. "Welcome," she said in a ringing voice, and proceeded to greet each of the sun fae clans by name, finishing with a special welcome to the Rock Run fada. Then she invited Dion to come forward, using his full title, Lord Dionísio, a sign that something serious was about to take place. The crowd held its collective breath when he simply narrowed his eyes and remained where he was.

The queen stretched out a hand in supplication. "Please, my lord?"

A fae queen saying please to a fada. Valeria wouldn't have believed it if she hadn't seen it with her own eyes.

The sun fae murmured in shocked dismay, but Cleia remained where she was until Dion strode forward and drew her back to her feet.

"What the hell are you playing at, woman? If this is a trick, I'll—"

But it wasn't a trick. To everyone's astonishment, Cleia declared Lord Dion was her mate, then admitted to inadvertently draining energy from the Rock Run Clan for years. To make amends, she nearly died trying to heal Xavier when the energy she was channeling nearly overwhelmed her. Lord Dion stepped in to help, adding his strength to hers. With his support, Cleia had used the mate bond connecting her and Dion to replace everything she'd taken from Rock Run—with interest. The lovers she'd weakened, their women and children, others in the clan who'd been affected—all were on the mend.

To cap it off, the two of them officially joined in a mate ceremony.

And then the ball was in full swing. Valeria watched from the edge of the dance floor as Merry danced in a giddy circle of river fada and sun fae children. She was still stunned by what had just occurred. Fae/fada matings were the stuff of fairytales—but it was real. You couldn't fake a mate bond. And like the rest of the clan, she'd felt the energy that had come with their mating.

Everyone was buzzing with it. Valeria felt as if she could dance all afternoon, run the eight miles to the river, swim the couple of miles home and still have energy to spare.

Sabela danced by, her scarlet dress twirling around her legs. Most of the fada were dressed in more subdued blues and greens and purples, but not Sabela. She rivaled the sun fae, who loved bright, sunny hues. Sabela winked at her over her partner's shoulder—a man half her age, Valeria was amused to note—and mouthed, "Why aren't you dancing?"

"In a minute," she mouthed back.

As if on cue, Petros appeared at Valeria's side and slid his arm around her waist. "Let's dance, *glika*."

She glanced at Merry, now holding hands with a golden-haired sun fae, both girls shrieking with laughter. Along with the rest of the children, they were being watched over by a group of fada and sun fae elders.

She turned back to Petros. "Sounds like fun."

Guiding her onto the polished wood floor, he took her into his arms. The ball was taking place outside under a large white canopy. A drummer provided a syncopated beat, a tribal counterpoint to the guitar and bass playing *fado*, the Portuguese blues. A tall, regal woman plucked at a twelve-stringed *guitarra Portuguesa* before beginning a sultry scold of her faithless lover.

Petros steered her easily through the crowd. The man could dance, she'd give him that.

They passed Merry and her new friend. "Hi, Mama!" Merry gave an enthusiastic wave. "Did you see me dancing?"

"I did," Valeria called back. "You look great."

Merry beamed.

As Valeria turned back to Petros, the newly mated couple appeared. Knowing smiles rippled through the crowd. Everyone had seen the alpha leading the queen into a secluded glade as soon as the ritual ended.

Valeria watched as Dion's dark head bent to catch something Cleia was saying, his face so tender that Valeria blinked. Her throat clogged with something black and acrid. *It wasn't fair.* The sun fae queen had stolen her mate; she didn't deserve to find her own.

Ashamed, Valeria dragged her gaze away from them. This wasn't her, this sour, envious woman. Maybe it was too much to expect her to be happy for Cleia, but Dion had been nothing but kind to her. And Cleia had only taken what Rui had freely offered. If he hadn't gone out trolling for a woman that night, she would've never had a chance to sink her hooks into him.

Petros nuzzled her cheek. "Come into the woods with me. Sabela can keep an eye on Merry." When Valeria hesitated, his fingers slid down her back to rest on the curve of her buttocks. "You know you want to."

She edged backward. *No, I don't*, a little voice said. She ignored it to say, "Not now." Too many people would see, and she wasn't ready for Petros to claim her so publicly. "Later. I'll see if Merry can sleep at Marcos and Trina's."

The teeth that closed lightly on her earlobe were both a chastisement and a promise. "Fine. I can wait a few more hours. But no more teasing, *glika*. I'm going to take you. Tonight."

Valeria murmured something in response, but her stomach was a tight ball. *What was wrong with her?* She and Rui were through. At least he couldn't spoil things for her and Petros this time; he'd remained behind with a handful of other warriors to guard the base.

It was time to move on, to stop wishing for something she was never going to have.

With another glance at Dion and Cleia, she made up her mind. "You can try," she murmured—and nipped his lower lip.

He growled and pulled her closer. They both knew that nip had been a dare. *Try to tame me if you can.*

"Oh, I will," he assured her.

RUI PACED BACK and forth in the forest near the only Rock Run entrance accessible from land. He'd posted guards at the water entrances, of course, but this was the most likely place for the Baltimore fada to attack.

With most of the clan at Rising Sun, the base was nearly

empty. For the hundredth time, Rui wondered if he'd done the right thing in allowing the others to attend. But Dion had included a code word in his message, one known only to Rui and Luis, assuring them he was all right and that he wasn't being coerced.

And the rules of hospitality were strict. A fae invitation automatically extended protection to anyone who accepted it. If Cleia tried anything, she'd have every fae and fada in North America gunning for her.

But that wouldn't stop the earth shifters from attacking while most of the clan was elsewhere.

He paused to glance at the sky through the gnarled gray branches of an ancient beech. The sun was at its zenith; the ritual must have begun.

He resumed pacing. His mouth was dry, the skin of his skull pulled tight. The craving was on him again, worse than yesterday.

He raised his wineskin to his lips and took a swig of grape juice. The skin retained the faint trace of the wine it had held up until a couple of days ago. He clenched his teeth. A fada's enhanced senses could be a curse at times. Right now he could smell the wine, a lush dark note above the tart grapes. Taste it in the juice.

His mouth watered. His whole body trembled with the need for alcohol. He took another gulp from the skin.

It would be so easy to slip inside, grab a bottle. Enough to take the edge off but not get him drunk.

Just one.

His head dropped as he fought a fierce inner battle.

What would be the harm?

He clenched his fists and gave himself a hard shake.

No.

He was a fada warrior and Dion's second. He would *not* give in. He knew damn well that one drink would lead to another and then another, until he wasn't fit to guard an anthill, let alone the base's most vulnerable entrance.

He was covered in sweat despite the fact that he was in the shade. He glanced longingly through the trees at the cool pewter ribbon of Rock Run Creek. What he wouldn't give to change to his shark for a long swim.

Later, he promised himself. He drew in a deep breath, taking in the scent of the river, the primal mix of mud and organic matter and fresh water that was life's blood to a river fada. Something about it reminded him of Valeria's earth and nutmeg aroma. He flashed on her mouthing, "*Do something,*" at him the night Dion had been kidnapped, and knew he couldn't disappoint her.

Not again. It would crush something permanent in his soul.

Something settled in him and he knew he could do this...at least for today. At least until Dion returned.

He kept pacing.

Probably a half hour had passed when suddenly, a warm energy suffused his chest. Startled, he brought his hand to his heart even as it spread to his fingers and toes. His skin heated and his brain filled with the same warm golden light. It surged, humming throughout his body like a low-level electric current, healing everything it touched. He instinctively spread his legs and stretched his arms above his head, riding the wave while a part of him looked on in wonder.

The energy increased, and then just as it became painful, began to recede. He bent forward, hands on his thighs, gulping in oxygen.

What the fu—?

He came back upright and glanced around, dazed. The trees were bathed in the same golden light, their leaves an intense, saturated emerald; the sky above a radiant azure. Everything was sharper—his eyesight, his hearing, his sense of smell.

If he didn't know better, he'd think he'd been drugged. But no drug had ever left his brain feeling this keen, his senses this clear. He felt strong and energized, better than he had in years.

He squinted up at the sun streaming through the trees. It was a half hour or so after noon. Could it be something to do with the midsummer ritual?

Eliana, the young warrior helping him guard the entrance, jogged up from where she'd been running surveillance. "Senhor Rui?" She rubbed a hand over her face, her eyes full of the same dazed wonder he felt. "I—what was that?"

She was young, twenty-one or so, but he had a vague, ashamed memory of taking her to bed a few months ago...although he wasn't so sure a bed had been involved. He shook off the guilt—there was no time for that now—and asked, "You felt it too?"

She nodded. "What happened?"

"Hell if I know. But it could be something to do with the ritual. Why don't you check with the others? See if it affected anyone else."

She ducked inside the base. He scanned the horizon, his senses amped from the energy still humming through him. He could detect nothing out of the ordinary.

He rubbed his nape. In a rare sober moment, he'd heard Dion's theory that Cleia was draining energy from him and her other lovers, but had dismissed it as improbable. But now he wondered if some of what he'd attributed to too much drink—and sheer laziness—had been due to that energy drain. Not that it excused what a drunken ass he'd been.

Eliana returned to report that everyone in the base had felt the surge. "You won't believe it. The sick ones are sitting up in bed, asking for food. And Fernando says for the first time in years his knees aren't swollen. He did a little dance to show me." She grinned and shook her head.

A few minutes later a motorcycle roared up. It was Teresa, returning from Rising Sun. "You'll never guess what happened," she began, and then narrowed her eyes. "You felt it, too?"

When they said they had, she confirmed that those at the

ritual had felt the same burst of healing energy, and then dropped a bombshell.

"Lord Dion mated with Queen Cleia."

Rui blinked. "Dion—and Cleia?"

"That's right. The energy surge happened when the mate bond clicked into place. Apparently, we drew energy from the sun through the queen's bond with Dion."

"You're kidding." But it fit, even if he'd never heard of anything like it. "So everyone's okay?"

"They are—better than okay. And little Xavier—" Teresa's throat worked. "He's fine, Rui. He was the first one Cleia cured. He's out there dancing with the other kids right now. You'd never guess how sick he was three days ago."

He briefly shut his eyes. "Thank *Deus*."

"There's something else," the *tenente* continued. "Adric is at the midsummer festival. He knows Dion mated Cleia. Only a complete fool would attack now—and from what I hear, Adric's no fool. Luis said for you to come, that the sun fae are throwing a mate ball for Dion and Cleia. Dion would want you there."

When Rui didn't say anything, she added, "Valeria's there, too, you know."

"I know." Teresa didn't have to spell it out; he'd seen Valeria and Merry leave with Okeanos.

"*Obrigado*," he told her. "You go on back now."

She opened her mouth, but when he just looked at her, she closed it again, and with a nod to them both, headed back the way she'd come.

Eliana slanted him a look. "You should go, Rui."

He was tempted to snarl at her—what was with the women today?—but he reined it in. Still, she must have felt his anger because she dropped her gaze.

"If you want to, that is."

He blew out a breath. "Maybe I will." He saw again Valeria

and Okeanos, the Greek fada pressing her against the wall, and that dark aggression rose up in him, strong and hot.

When he spoke, it was his animal talking. "Hell, why not? Teresa is right—the earth fada would be out of their fucking minds to attack us now. We'll stay on high alert just in case, but take it in turns to go to the party. I'll send a couple of warriors back to spell you."

Eliana's eyes rounded. "You mean it?"

"*Claro.*"

She did a happy little dance, ponytail bouncing. "All *right.*"

"HOLY CRAP." Marjani took in the scene, mouth ajar. "This is—" She waved a hand.

Adric followed her gaze to the huge, canopied dance floor and neighboring dining area. The decorations were understated in a way that screamed of wealth: enormous flower arrangements in blown-glass vases, delicately sculpted fountains, unlit fae lights dancing like soap bubbles above the crowd.

Through it all, the sun fae moved like colorful tropical fish in their shimmering clothes and glittering gems, their bright hair every shade from gold to silver to copper. Threaded among them were the Rock Run fada, no less beautiful with their dark, vivid coloring and simple clothes in rich hues of river and ocean and forest.

"Who would've thought we'd ever be guests at a fae ball?" he remarked.

Their eyes met in shared understanding. Marjani and her fellow lieutenants were the only ones who knew how hard he'd worked to save the clan. And if he'd been brutal at times, well, the end justified the means.

He crossed his arms and watched the dancers. It was mostly sun fae until a young river female took the floor with a tall blond fae. She gracefully followed her partner's lead, her dress an iridescent blue-green, her wavy black hair floating around her shoulders. The music changed to a samba and she grinned up at the sun fae and started to move her slim hips with a provocative innocence that made Adric's lungs seize.

For an endless few seconds he simply stared at her, entranced.

Mine. The knowledge settled in some deep, primitive corner of his soul.

And she damn well wouldn't dance with anyone but him. He was about to stride across the dance floor and take her from the sun fae when Marjani nudged him.

"Ric? That river fada over there is staring at you."

He frowned, not caring.

"Ric? I said—"

"I heard you." He forced his gaze away from the river girl—because she *was* a girl, as much as his body was reacting to her as a woman—and glanced in the direction his sister had indicated.

Ah...

The man could've passed for Lord Dion. He had the same shoulder-length black hair and strong, hard face, although this man was younger, slimmer, not yet fully formed. Adric knew exactly who he was: Tiago do Mar, the man who'd given him Cleia's location in the Rock Run base. Apparently the Rock Run alpha hadn't yet discovered his own brother had betrayed him.

He inclined his head in Tiago's direction. The other man jerked his gaze away and took a gulp of beer.

So he didn't want anyone to know they were acquainted. That suited Adric just fine. Tiago must be desperate to keep his brother from knowing—and a desperate man was ripe for blackmail.

Other fae had started to arrive for the festival—walnut-skinned sun fae from Africa and Australia, ice fae from the far north with their pale skin and cold light eyes, a trio of dryads with long brown hair and shy smiles, and others whom Adric couldn't name, including a group of slim, golden-skinned beings with translucent wings and the air of being not quite of this earth.

A night fae in dark sunglasses strode by Adric. Power brushed over his skin, cold and black. He had to force himself not to shudder. But he'd vowed never again to bow down to anyone—especially a fae.

He looked back at the dancers. The river girl threw back her head and laughed up at her partner. She glanced toward Adric. Her eyes were a rich blue, startlingly beautiful against her light olive skin. Their gazes snagged and she missed a step.

So she felt it too. He smiled at her, slow and dangerous.

She stared back, eyes wide. Then the sun fae spun her around and she returned her attention to him.

"Who is she?" he asked Marjani. He kept files on the Rock Run alpha and his top warriors, but he'd never seen the young river shifter before.

Marjani followed his gaze. "God's balls," she muttered. "You do like to live on the edge, don't you?"

He frowned. "Who?" he insisted.

"Rosana do Mar. The alpha's only sister. His *baby* sister."

"Ah." His file needed to be updated. In the file photo she was young, no more than thirteen turns of the sun, with a stick-straight body and gangly arms and legs. But he'd been struck by the wide grin she'd directed at the camera.

He blew out a breath. She'd certainly grown up in the past few years.

Marjani elbowed him in the side. "Anyone but her, Ric. Dion won't let you within ten miles of her."

"It's a party. We can at least have a dance. And Dion's not even here yet."

"But his brother is."

"So?" Adric flicked him a dismissive glance. The younger do

Mar was going to be powerful one day, but at the moment he wasn't close to a match for Adric.

"You want to start a war, that's the way to do it."

She was right. And while he was willing—no, eager—to engage the Rock Run Clan, this wasn't the time or place.

Adric turned his back on the pretty little river girl. "Let's dance. I think I can still do the damn samba."

His sister's lips quirked. "Since you asked so nicely—"

"Shut it," he muttered.

She chuckled, grabbed his hands and moved into an easy, fluid salsa. But then, their Jamaican mother had had them both dancing from the time they were toddlers.

As the dance ended, Cleia appeared with Dion, both of them wearing shit-eating grins. The two of them were immediately surrounded by people offering congratulations.

Dion caught sight of Adric and their gazes locked. The two of them had disliked each other on sight—and now the other alpha knew that Adric had engineered Cleia's rescue, had been inside Rock Run with the sun fae.

A beat passed, then another, neither of them giving ground. Tension rocketed through Adric. Damn, he wanted to challenge Dion. If he won, he'd have the right to take over the other alpha's clan—and his territory. But this was a celebration and the laws governing a gathering of this sort were rigid. Anyone who broke them with an unprovoked attack would be punished severely.

Adric gritted his teeth and jerked his head. Acknowledging Dion as the dominant—for now.

Cleia noticed him and smiled.

He moved forward to offer his congratulations, enjoying how Dion's teeth clenched as she graciously accepted them and thanked him in turn for the aid he'd rendered the sun fae.

"It was my pleasure." He shot a carefully expressionless look at Dion. "I trust you weren't harmed, my lord?"

Dion's jaw hardened. The man didn't like being reminded of

the humiliation of being captured naked—and in the act of taking an equally naked Cleia. Adric kept his face blank, although inside he was grinning.

Cleia frowned and flicked her fingers as if shooing away an insect. He blinked as a painful jolt of energy hit him. She gave him a butter-wouldn't-melt-in-her-mouth smile and turned to Marjani.

"And is this your sister?"

Adric swallowed. "Yes, my lady." He introduced Marjani to the queen and Dion. They exchanged a few words and then melted back into the crowd.

"Let's go eat," he muttered to his sister. "It stinks of the swamp around here."

Behind him he scented Dion's spike of anger, and a couple of nearby river males sent him heated looks, but they were constrained by the same laws of hospitality that bound him. He flashed them a smug smile and guided Marjani toward the dining area.

8

Rui leaned against a tree, arms crossed. The mating ball was in full swing now. From what he could tell, his entire clan was a little high from Cleia's infusion of life-energy. Those who weren't dancing stood in groups talking animatedly as they sipped drinks or nibbled treats from tables groaning with every food imaginable, including a magnificent white mountain of a wedding cake.

Teens flirted or faked boredom, while the younger kids darted excitedly through the crowd. Nearby, a group of men burst into a raucous off-key song, the Rock Run males trying to outshout the sun fae. Rui shook his head.

But it was good to see the clan enjoying themselves. It had been too long since they'd had something to celebrate.

He strolled along the dance floor. Merry was wearing a new dress that swirled in a blue-and-white bell around her legs as she danced with a sun fae girl. When she caught sight of Rui, her face lit up and she raced toward him, her new friend on her heels.

"Tio Rui! You came!"

"Hello, sweetheart." He swung her into the air.

She entwined wiry arms around his neck. "Did you see me dancing with Gracie?"

"Is that her name?" He winked at the little blonde. "*Boa tarde*, Gracie. I believe I met you when you were this high." He held up his hand at toddler height.

She clasped her hands behind her back and smiled shyly up at him. "Good afternoon, Senhor Rui." She glanced over her shoulder at her mother, a cousin of Cleia's.

He nodded to the woman. "*Boa tarde*, Lady Amelie." For the most part, the sun fae had been friendly enough when he'd lived here, although they'd never let him forget he wasn't a pureblood —and then there were those animal genes. But he'd always liked Amelie.

She returned his greeting with a smile. They exchanged a few words and then she strolled off with Gracie.

He slanted a grin at Merry. "Look at you, *princesa*. Is that a daisy on your dress?" He held her away to admire the large flower appliqued on the front.

"Yes." She beamed and touched a white petal. "Mama's friend made it for me. And did you see my hair?" Her wiry black hair had been woven into a single fat braid and topped with a bright blue bow.

He kissed the top of her head. "*Muito bonita.*"

"*Obrigada*," she returned with a dignity that had him smothering a smile.

They surveyed the dancers. "Where's Mama?" he asked, his tone deliberately casual.

Merry's look was very adult. "She's with Senhor Petros. She said if I need something, I should ask Tia Sabela."

"I see." Something dark and primitive filled Rui's head.

"Don't worry." Merry patted his cheek. "She doesn't like him as much as you."

He grunted something noncommittal. He was *not* going to stoop to discussing Valeria with her daughter.

"You have to be nicer to her." Merry cast him a sly look. "Senhor Petros brings her flowers. She likes flowers. And candy. Chocolate candy. She *loves* chocolate."

His lips twitched in spite of the darkness. "I'll keep that in mind."

Her mouth turned down. "Don't you want to be a family with us?"

He swallowed something sharp and raw. "It's not about what I want. It's about what your mama wants."

"But—"

"That's enough, *menina*. What your mama and I do is between us." He set her back on the grass and gave her a firm pat on the rear. "Now go play with the others."

Merry fisted her hands by her sides and frowned up at him. He lifted a brow. Whatever she saw in his face made her sigh and drop her gaze.

"Oh, all right," she grumbled and stomped off to join the other children. A minute later she was laughing again.

He continued to pace along the edge of the dance floor, stopping to exchange a few words here and there with the sun fae he knew and other members of Rock Run. The Rock Run people were tentative with him, as if he were recovering from a long illness. Which he suppose he was.

But it made him uncomfortable, so he set his back against another tree, this one further from the celebration. From time to time someone glanced at him, but for the most part they let him be. He supposed his set face had something to do with it, but his animal was growing more and more agitated.

Another man was with the mate. His animal couldn't understand why he was allowing it.

Dion and Cleia took the dance floor. His old friend was sporting a midnight blue shirt and black slacks that bore the marks of sun-fae tailoring, but like most of the fada, his feet were bare.

Rui's lips curved. It was clear Dion wasn't going to be dazzled by the sun fae and their wealth.

Cleia murmured something and Dion snagged her for an openly possessive kiss that had the crowd hooting and calling out ribald suggestions. When he released her, she gave a rich laugh and spun out of his arms, bright hair flying around her shoulders. He caught her hand and reeled her back in, the two of them playing to the audience.

Rui grinned along with the rest, but he couldn't help reflecting that fate was a funny son of a bitch. Dion had set out to stop Cleia whatever it took, even if it meant imprisoning her for life—or worse—and had ended by mating with her.

Rui, on the other hand, would slit his wrists before mating with a fae. He'd had his year with Cleia and the woman was good, but he was glad to be out of her clutches. She was strong-willed, used to ruling. Dion was going to have his hands full with that one.

But what did he know? He was the man who'd left his woman just days before their mating ceremony.

Luis halted by the tree along with his mate, Marina, and little Xavier.

"Tio Rui," the boy shouted from his perch in his mama's arms. "I'm all better. Queen Cleia cured me."

"I can see that." Rui ruffled his brown curls and listened to Marina repeat the story of his miraculous cure.

Xavier squirmed to be put down. "I wanna play with the other kids," he whined.

When she hesitated, he gave her a winning smile. "*Por favor?*"

With a roll of her eyes, Marina set him on the grass. He dashed off to join in a game of soccer. Marina's gaze followed him, her face naked with emotion.

Rui took her by the shoulders. "He'll be fine, *querida*. There's not a trace of sickness in his scent."

She nodded. "I know it here"—she pointed to her head—"but not here." She touched her breast.

"Give it time." He kissed both her cheeks and released her to eye Luis. "And you, *primo*. You look like a new man."

It was true. The fatigue that had lined his cousin's face was gone, and he looked as if he'd already regained a couple of pounds.

Marina slanted her mate a smile. "If I didn't know better, I'd think the fae switched him for another man."

Luis growled. "Come here, you. I'll show you which man I am." He wrapped his hand around her nape and kissed her. When he released her, she blinked and then gave him a slow smile.

Rui swallowed a prickly lump of envy. The look the two of them exchanged was so intimate, so loving.

Marina brushed her fingers down Luis's cheek and murmured something Rui didn't catch. He was turning away to allow them their privacy when she said in a louder voice, "And Rui, you don't have to leave. Keep your cousin company while I see what Xavier is up to." She slid out of Luis's arms and headed after her son.

Luis made a rueful face. "She still can't believe he's better. He almost died, you know."

"*Sim.* Even as drunk as I was, I knew. Forgive me for not being there."

"What would you have done? None of the healers could help him." Luis's throat worked. "If Cleia hadn't figured out what was wrong—"

"But I should've been there. Even if all I did was watch over him when you needed to sleep."

Rui slung an arm around his cousin's shoulders, wordlessly offering the comfort he should've offered days ago. Luis leaned into him, unashamed to draw strength from another male. Their animals understood the importance of touch.

"I hear Dion's going to live with the sun fae for part of each month," Rui remarked.

Luis straightened, but they remained where they were, arms around each other's shoulders. "That's right. And Cleia will live part of the time with us. As second, you'll be in charge when Dion's gone."

"He'll only be a few miles away. I'll just be carrying out his orders."

"True. But you'll be acting as alpha in his stead. You up to it?"

"Is that a challenge?"

"Only if you blow it." Luis sent him a sidelong look. "We both know that when you're healthy, you can whip my ass. But I'm damned if I'm going to stand by and let you. Get yourself in shape or expect a challenge."

"Fair enough." As if sent by a malicious pixie, a server stopped to offer them a choice of champagne or mineral water. Rui didn't allow himself a look at the sparkling golden wine. "Water, please."

With a glance at him, Luis took the water as well.

"You want to start working out tomorrow?" Rui asked.

"With you?" Luis returned.

"Of course with me. I've got a lot of time to make up for. And no offense, cousin, but you're out of shape yourself."

A broad grin split Luis's face. "You're on."

The talk turned to the base's defenses. Rui explained that he'd arranged it so everyone could attend the mating celebration, and Luis nodded.

"I'll take my turn tonight. Marina's going to want to get Xavier home anyway."

They covered a few more items. It was an ordinary conversation between Rock Run's second and third, of the sort he'd taken part in many times, but to Rui its very ordinariness was special. It had been a long time since he'd discussed anything at all with his cousin.

But all the time his eyes were searching the crowd for Valeria.

Luis nudged him. "She's over there." He pointed over Rui's shoulder.

Rui turned and there she was, coming across the meadow.

Alone, that dark and primitive part of him noted with satisfaction.

She strolled toward the dance floor in a green dress that flowed like water over her lush curves, the afternoon sun touching her rich brown hair with gold. She'd left it unbound so that it swayed to and fro over her breasts.

He stared at her, mesmerized, chest tight. All around the dance floor, unmated males did the same. Spines straightened and stomachs sucked in. A dozen hungry gazes ran over her voluptuous body.

Rui rumbled a warning. Those fada close enough to hear shot him a look, then dropped their eyes. Even the sun fae men glanced around uneasily.

Valeria appeared not to notice. She wound her way through the crowd, smiling and greeting her friends.

"Mama!" Merry sped across the grass toward her.

"Hello, baby." Valeria swung her up for a kiss. Her eyes met Rui's over Merry's head and her smile faded, but she gave him a nod before setting the little girl back down. Merry launched into a speech about something with great passion and much waving of hands, probably the soccer game.

Rui's fingers tightened on his glass. He hated that he could no longer read Valeria. He hated that she acted as if they were mere acquaintances, as if she'd never lain under him, hot and needy, begging him to take her.

Okeanos appeared, striding across the grass with two other men. Seeing Valeria, he said goodbye to his friends and fell in beside her and Merry. They kissed and then stayed where they were to watch the dancing, Okeanos's hand on her ass.

Rui took a slow breath.

The Greek fada shot him a look and deliberately drew Valeria closer. She glanced over her shoulder at Rui. Their eyes met and for a long moment, she stared at him. Then she raised her chin and turned back to Okeanos.

Rui's whole body went taut. He wanted to tear the other man limb from limb for daring to touch his woman. He wanted to pull Valeria into his arms and give her a deep, claiming kiss like the one Dion had given Cleia. And then he'd take her home and pleasure her long and hard until she admitted she belonged to Rui—and no one else.

But he didn't have the right.

Luis dug his elbow into Rui's ribs. "*Deus*, man, when are you going to wake up and kick that man's ass? Isn't your mate worth fighting for?"

Rui shook his head. "You don't under—" He halted and stared at his cousin, arrested.

He'd told himself it was better this way. He'd left Valeria and she'd gone on with her life. But now he wondered when the hell he'd become so gutless. Sure, he'd returned from the sun fae drained and weak, but he'd had a year to get his shit together.

"You're right," he said. "She is."

Valeria felt Rui's gaze boring between her shoulder blades from where she stood talking to Petros. Because it was him, of course. He might have denied their mate bond, refusing to acknowledge or feed it until it was a fragile, frayed thing, but she still felt *him*—whether she wanted to or not.

She sent him a scowl over her shoulder.

His cousin Luis leaned in to murmur something. Rui stared at him and then looked back at her.

He'd changed. The energy surge had burned away some of his fat. He wasn't back to his old self, but you could see it, there beneath the excess weight: the powerful frame, the long, strong legs. But it wasn't simply his body; his face was more alert too. He'd shaved, exposing a hard jaw and lips that could be either cruel or sensual. His river-green eyes seared into hers: hot, predatory.

A shiver slid up her spine. Not fear.

No, it was because she remembered too well what that look meant.

She resolutely turned her attention back to Petros, who was asking if she wanted champagne.

"Thank you." She took the proffered glass.

All around them, the members of Rock Run were pairing up with each other or unmated sun fae. The clan might not hold bacchas any longer, but they were still fada, descendants of Dionysus and his wild followers, with the blood of the god himself running through their veins. The combination of their alpha's mating and that surge of energy had everyone of mating age reaching for a partner—or two—and apparently the sun fae felt the same.

She couldn't help glancing at Rui again. He was still looking at her.

Their gazes locked. The sounds of the celebration faded and it was just the two of them. His lips curved in a half-smile that made her whole body tingle.

She jerked her gaze away. Drat the man anyway. She just *knew* he was picturing her naked. Fada males liked to master their women, and Rui was very much a fada male. He'd loved to tease her, to make her beg for her pleasure until she was nearly mad with wanting him.

And then he'd pin her wrists to the mattress and take her, slow but firm, and oh, so sweet...

Petros handed his empty glass to a server and placed an arm around her shoulders. "Forget him, *glika*."

"Who?" she returned with a lift of her chin.

He chuckled. "No one." His hand was caressing her bottom now. "How much longer are you going to make me wait, Valeria? I need you."

She felt rather than saw Rui's scowl. She ignored him to slide an arm around Petros's waist. "Not right now. But later..."

There was a tug on her other hand. A plaintive voice said, "Mama Ria, I'm hungry."

9

───────

*A*dric eyed the banquet which had been set out under a second canopy near the dancers: plump oysters on the half shell, crab cakes on frilly little crackers, sirloin tips that looked like they would melt on your tongue like chocolate. Platters of roast chicken, crystal bowls of exotic fruits, and a whole table piled with breads, tarts and other baked goods that he couldn't even name.

Beside him, Marjani gazed at the food in silent reverence. There had been days—not that long ago—when they'd have literally killed to get near even a tenth this much food. And all of it kept at exactly the right temperature by fae technology, colorful rings of light surrounding each bowl or platter to warm or cool it.

"Well, hell," his sister drawled. "They didn't have to go to all this trouble for li'l old us."

Adric chuckled, but it was a forced, envious sound. They picked up plates and began filling them. He got a beer for himself and wine for Marjani and they seated themselves at an empty table. For a few minutes they spoke only in occasional murmurs, all their attention on the food. Adric tried to slow down, to savor what was truly a delicious meal, but he'd been hungry for too much of his early life. His instinct was to bolt it down before it could be stolen by someone bigger or tougher—or denied as a punishment.

At last Marjani set down her fork with a sigh of repletion. "It's too bad the others weren't invited. It seems wrong to be stuffing our faces like this when—" She halted and sent him a guilty look.

Adric forced himself to set down his own fork even though there was still food on his plate. "Everyone has enough to eat these days. It may not be fancy, but no one goes hungry."

"I know, Ric. I didn't mean—"

"I know." He lifted a shoulder. "Hell, I wish the others could've come, too."

He took a sip of beer and looked around him. A family had taken seats at the next table: the hot piece in the green dress who'd caused such a stir when she arrived, a bouncy little girl, and a man he recognized—Petros, the Greek sea fada who'd been spending a lot of time in the Full Moon Saloon lately. Adric had made it his business to keep an eye on Petros. He recognized a man sniffing out new territory when he saw one.

He turned back to Marjani. "Someday our people will be invited to these celebrations, too. The sun fae-Rock Run alliance doesn't mean our hopes are dead."

"Of course not. We don't have to beat Rock Run to—"

He gripped her wrist, silencing her. "Not now." He cut his eyes toward the family behind her.

She winced. "Sorry. Just remember there's more than one way to skin a cat."

"That's what I keep you around for—to remind me."

Marjani snorted but he could tell she was pleased.

He glanced at the family again. But no, it wasn't a family after all. The little girl was calling the sea fada "Senhor Petros."

His eyes narrowed. The girl reminded him of someone. That sharp little face and untamable black hair. It had been worked into a braid but already it was escaping to form wispy corkscrews around her face. Then it hit him. His nostrils flared. What he smelled made him freeze.

He lowered his voice to a level only Marjani could hear. "Find a way to look at that family behind you without their knowing. The little girl."

Marjani nudged her napkin so it fell to the floor. As she bent to retrieve it, she took a long look at the girl. He heard her inhale, knew she'd discovered what he'd scented: the girl was a mixed-blood earth shifter.

When Marjani sat back up, her eyes were wide.

"Oh. My. God," she mouthed. "Do you think—?"

The two of them stared at each other. "We can't be sure," he said in the same subvocal tones, careful not to look at the girl again. "We've been searching for three years." Since the day Jace's sister died and they realized her mate and daughter had disappeared. By the time they'd found them a year later, it had been too late. "Everything we turned up said that Merry died with her father in a house fire. That night fae, Tyrus, swore it was the truth."

The fae had said it with a mealy-mouthed sorrow. But Adric had suspected he'd had something to do with it—Tyrus had practically reeked with satisfaction. Adric had itched to take him somewhere private and work him over until he confessed, but the man had been protected by two thugs and a powerful ward. Adric, on the other hand, had been alone, with his nearest man over a mile away—the only way Tyrus would agree to meet with him.

Adric hadn't forgotten, though. Someday Tyrus would pay for what he'd done.

The night fae's scent had held truth though. He believed Merry had died in that fire. But what if she'd somehow escaped?

"Why was it so important?" his sister wondered. "To kill the whole family?"

"I'd like to know that myself."

"Still, if it's true, Jace is going to be so happy." Marjani's eyes rounded. "Oh, lord. Should we tell him now?"

Jace and Lucas were hiding in the trees at the edge of the meadow—Jace as his cat, Lucas a wolf. They'd refused to let him go unprotected to a celebration packed with Rock Run warriors. Normally the sun fae's wards would've kept them out, but the wards had been dropped in favor of patrolling warriors so that guests could enter the compound. And it would be a cold day in Hades before his best men couldn't slip past a fae warrior.

"I don't know." He dragged his fingers through his hair. "She smells right, but why the hell would she be living with the river fada?"

Then the woman in green called the little girl Merry, and he had his proof.

Rui watched as Valeria and Merry headed with Okeanos toward the dining area. His animal was still urging him to drag the two of them away from the Greek fada, but the man knew that was a bad idea. Valeria had been furious when he'd interrupted her and Okeanos two days ago. If he wasn't careful, he might lose her for good.

He strolled after them as he considered what to do. He'd never courted anyone, not even Valeria. There had been a spark from the instant they first set eyes on each other, a week after she arrived...

He'd returned from a job, another quiet, solitary kill, this one set up by Dion. He'd never liked this part of his work—give him a good, clean fight anytime—but this one had been especially difficult, a fae aristocrat who'd overreached herself and executed anyone who objected. Eventually two of her closest advisors had revolted. It was Rui's job to make sure she disappeared without a trace. He knew she needed to be stopped, but he'd never killed a woman before. It had left him in a dark, dangerous mood.

So instead of returning immediately to Rock Run, he'd spent a few days in the ocean as his bull shark. He was one of the few river fada who could turn to shark, but it was a mixed blessing. It was why he was so good at tracking, but the shark was a tricky animal to control; there were times when it all but took over. The man was always present, making sure that his animal killed only for food, but both had taken a primal satisfaction in fulfilling that need.

Blood lust sated, he'd returned to the base, the animal in him appeased but the man eager for a woman. He'd showered and headed toward the dining hall.

That was when he'd come across her, standing at the intersection of two halls and looking around her uncertainly. He took in a heart-shaped ass framed by tight jeans and increased his stride. As he came up beside her, he angled his head and inhaled deeply.

Earth and spice and warm, sexy woman.

He knew right then he was going to do everything in his power to have her. "*Boa tarde, senhorita.* May I help you?"

She turned her head. "*Sim,* I—" Her eyes widened at finding him so close. Reluctantly, he pulled back but kept his gaze on hers.

Her eyes were the color of rich, dark chocolate. Time seemed to stop. For a few seconds all he could hear was the hard thump of his heart.

Then she blinked and he realized she'd swayed closer to him. She straightened and blushed, a pretty brightening of her smooth olive skin. "I'm lost. I was trying to find the dining hall."

"And you are—"

"Valeria da Costa."

"Rui do Mar." He took the proffered hand, holding it a little longer than necessary. "It's a pleasure to meet you."

"The alpha's second."

"That's me. You've been here a while then?"

"Only since last week. I'm visiting from Portugal."

He gave a slow smile. "Then I'll have to see that you...enjoy yourself."

He scented her desire, knew she was interested in him. But she was a fada female. His animal had already sensed she wasn't a dominant, but that didn't mean she was a pushover.

She blinked again. Then her soft, full mouth curved in an equally slow smile. "And I might let you. But right now all I need are the directions to the dining hall."

"No problem. I was on my way there myself." Placing a hand on the small of her back, he guided her to turn left at the next intersection. "It's right down here."

It had only taken another couple of days before he had her in his bed.

And as he'd entered her that first time, they'd both felt it—a literally magical bond, its first tenuous strands unfurling in their hearts and reaching out for the other. The mate bond expressed itself differently for each couple, but both of them had known that the possibility was there.

Now that connection had been broken—although perhaps not as completely as he'd believed. She hadn't had sex yet with Okeanos; he was sure of that. He'd have seen it on her face, smelled it on her. If the bond were still alive, it explained why not.

He watched as she strolled along between Okeanos and Merry, hips swaying in that pretty sea-colored dress, and bared his teeth in a smile. She was going to smell of sex very soon.

But it was going to be him, not Okeanos, who marked her.

Dion caught sight of him and excused himself from Cleia to approach him. Rui turned his attention to his alpha.

"*Boa tarde*," Dion said. He gave a subtle sniff.

Rui raised his chin. "I haven't had a drink since I heard you'd been kidnapped."

"So I hear—and that you've reclaimed your place as second."

"I had to. Luis was sick, and exhausted from worry about Xavier. Things were getting out of control. But if you have a problem with it, I'll step down."

Dion scrutinized him another moment and then nodded. "Then I owe you my thanks."

"No thanks necessary—you'd have done the same thing."

Rui glanced at Cleia, dancing with a cluster of tiny girls. She was literally glowing, her face radiant with what he knew was her true self, not the glamour she'd used to entice him and her other lovers.

"Congratulations on your mating," he said, and meant it.

Dion followed his gaze. "I'm a lucky man."

"*Sim*. She's a beautiful woman. I'm just sorry I missed your mating ceremony."

"Me too." They shared a sidelong look of understanding, Dion letting Rui know there were no hard feelings. Sure, Rui had had Cleia first, but it had only been sex for him—nothing like the powerful, till-death-do-us-part love that it clearly was for his friend.

"So," Dion asked, "can you do this? Because I can't have a drunken ass as my second. What Cleia did today helped, but it's up to you and me to bring Rock Run back to where it was. She may be my mate, but I'm damned if I'm going to beg her for help."

"Luis already threatened to challenge me if I fuck up." He met Dion's eyes. "But I won't. I'm going to do this. For you. For the clan. For Valeria—because I want her back. And"—he moved a shoulder—"for me."

Because he couldn't live like that any longer—and the only other choice was dying.

Dion searched Rui's face. What he saw there must have satisfied him, because he smiled and clapped Rui on the back. "It's good to have you back, *irmão*."

Brother.

Rui's stomach clenched. He slapped Dion's back in return and then they were hugging. When they released each other, both their eyes were moist.

Dion shook his head. "Damn, I've missed you."

"What can I say? I was an ass."

"No argument here."

"Fuck off."

They elbowed each other—hard—and grinned.

10

———————

The striking couple at the next table were earth fada. Valeria stiffened.

First, she'd caught the man eying them. Nothing unusual there; fada instinctively kept a close eye on their surroundings—and these two were definitely fada. They had a shifter's firm, muscled build, they moved with an animal grace...and when the man caught sight of Merry, his voice dropped to a subvocal level that only another fada could've heard.

But they weren't from Rock Run. After two years, Valeria knew everyone by sight, if not by name. These two were dressed in the funky, Caribbean garb favored by the Baltimore earth fada —the woman in a colorful tunic over brown leggings, the man in a copper-and-black print shirt.

After a searching look at Merry, the man was careful not to look their way again. Too careful. Uneasy now, Valeria angled her body to shield Merry from his view.

Next the woman managed to take a look, even though her back was to their table. As she leaned over to retrieve her napkin, the quartz hanging from a cord around her neck swung free from the bodice of her tunic. Every hair on Valeria's body stood on end as the woman straightened up and tucked the quartz back into her tunic, her gaze on Merry. Expressions flicked across her face —amazement, joy—almost too fast for Valeria to be sure she'd seen them. Then she turned back to her companion.

Valeria shot another glance at the man. Now she was looking for it, she saw he also wore a leather cord around his neck, with the telltale lump beneath his shirt.

She swallowed dryly. Just to be sure, she gave a surreptitious sniff. They were earth shifters, all right, the difference in their scent from a water fada's as obvious as that between a puma and a dolphin. She'd only missed it because it had been masked by Merry's jaguar scent.

She set down her fork and turned to Merry. "Finish up, sweetheart. It's time to go home."

Merry stuck out her lower lip. "But I want ice cream." She pointed to where a server stood behind a table with a dozen different kinds of sorbet and ice cream.

"Merry," she said sternly, then glanced at the earth shifters and gulped. "You can have some at home. If you're good, I'll let you have a chocolate, too."

The pout disappeared. Merry's face took on the shrewd expression of a street vendor. "One of the good ones? From the box?"

Valeria nodded.

"All *right*." Merry hopped off her chair and pumped a small fist.

"I'll come with you," said Petros.

"No, no." Valeria barely glanced at him as she came to her feet. "You don't have to leave yet. We can get a ride with someone else."

He rose to his feet as well. "I'll take you," he said, tight-lipped.

The earth shifter male was watching them openly now. He was frankly gorgeous, with a lean, hard body, spiked-up dark hair bleached blond at the tips, and an arrogant smile that said he knew exactly how good-looking he was. Despite his youth, he carried himself with an air of authority. Everything about him screamed high-ranking dominant.

Their eyes met. His bored into hers, the flat, predatory bronze of a mountain lion sizing up its prey, and suddenly he wasn't so good-looking anymore. Just menacing.

"Ric?" murmured his companion. "Maybe we should—"

Valeria missed the rest as a buzzing filled her head. *Lord Adric.* All the clues pointed to it: earth shifter, dominant, even the fact that he'd been invited to the mating ball when no other earth fada were present.

Panic wrapped tight fingers around her throat. Forgetting Petros, she glanced around blindly for help.

"Look, Mama." Merry tugged on her hand and pointed up. Dusk was approaching. All across the compound, fae lights had started to twinkle on in a variety of hues—gold, silver, pink, amber. They floated several yards above the ground, bubbles of light illuminating the white canopies from inside and creating a fairytale setting as they spread out across the meadow.

Valeria shot them a quick, distracted glance. "They're beautiful, *querida.*" But the interruption broke through her panic. She had to calm down. If Adric saw how agitated she was, it would only confirm his suspicions. "But it's time go now." She took Merry's hand and started for the exit.

Petros grabbed her arm. "What the hell?"

She swung around to face him. Lord, she did *not* need this right now. "I'm going home. It's getting late—Merry—"

"She's fine," he growled. "It's not going to hurt her to stay up late one night."

Valeria's jaw tightened. "Let me go, Petros."

His eyes narrowed. "I'm tired of you teasing me. One minute you want me, the next minute, you're running away. If you leave now, we're finished. There are other women who'd be more than happy to—"

She jerked her arm free. "Then feel free to find one. Because as of right now, we're through."

His face darkened. "By the gods, I just might. You think I haven't seen you making cow eyes at him when you believe no one is looking? The man doesn't want you, baby."

"I. Am. Not. Your. Baby," she said between clenched teeth and strode away, Merry trotting alongside her.

"I don't like Senhor Petros," she stated in a high, clear voice. "Even if he does buy you chocolate."

Valeria squeezed her hand. "You know something, sweetheart? I don't either. I don't like him at all."

They had to skirt the dance floor to reach the parking lot. Valeria risked a glance over her shoulder and got a nasty jolt when she saw that Adric and the woman had risen to their feet.

She picked up her pace. He wouldn't try anything here, would he? The sun fae would be furious if he broke the laws of hospitality—and not even a fada alpha would deliberately anger a fae, especially a powerful one like Queen Cleia.

But she couldn't help recalling Adric's reputation. She had a feeling there wasn't much he wouldn't do if he thought he could get away with it.

And then she saw Rui standing at the exit to the dining area. Relief crashed through her. She didn't stop to think, just headed straight for him.

"Whoa, there." To Rui's shock, Valeria practically threw herself into his arms. He clasped her shoulders. "What's wrong, *querida?*"

He'd bided his time while she and Merry ate, grabbing a plate for himself and eating standing near the entrance. He wasn't alone. Several warriors stopped to speak with him. Everything was very polite, but he knew that like Dion, they were determining his resolve to reclaim his old role in the clan, testing if he were still sober—checking him out in the way fada did when the pecking order shifted.

And all the while he had an eye on Valeria, assessing how best to pry her away from Okeanos. Then she came abruptly to her feet, had what looked like words with Okeanos, and grabbed Merry and headed in Rui's direction.

He would have liked to believe that she was looking for him, but her eyes were on the exit. Still, the relief on her face when she caught sight of him was unmistakable.

"Rui," she said now. "Thank *Deus*." Her eyes were wild, her fear scenting the air. Merry whimpered and wrapped her free arm around Rui's leg.

"What's the matter? Did Okeanos—" He scowled and looked around for the sea fada. He'd taken a seat at a different table and was talking to another woman from Rock Run. His eyes flashed at Rui, cold and dark, then he deliberately gave him his back.

"If that bastard hurt you—"

"No, no. It's nothing to do with him." She took his arm, urging him forward. "Please, Rui. I don't have time to explain, but we need to leave. Now."

"All right." Puzzled but willing, he scooped up Merry and reached for Valeria's hand. "My bike's in the parking lot."

They headed for the cobblestone path that led to the parking lot. As they skirted the dance floor, Valeria shot a glance over her shoulder.

"Oh, no. He's coming after us—Lord Adric."

"The Baltimore alpha?" He glanced back. "Hell. He saw Merry, didn't he?"

"Yes. And Rui—I think he guessed who she was."

He smothered another curse, conscious of the little girl glancing wide-eyed between him and her mother. "This way." He guided Valeria toward a cherry grove that he remembered from his year with the sun fae. "We can cut through here."

They darted off the path and into the trees. The grove was an old, mature one, with thick trees raising large, fruit-laden branches that spread out to form a dense canopy. With the falling dusk, it was like plunging into a dark green tunnel. Rui's pupils widened, adjusting to the sudden loss of light, and he knew his eyes had gone night-glow.

They were deep in the grove when he knew he'd made a mistake. Coming toward him was the unmistakable scent of an earth fada.

"Rui." Valeria pointed to her right.

Make that two earth fada. A large wolf and a big black cat prowled toward them, their eyes glowing in the gloom.

Rui handed Merry to Valeria. "Take her and run," he ordered without taking his gaze off the wolf and cat. "Tell Dion what's happening."

"But—" He heard her swallow.

"*Now.*"

She turned to go but had taken only a few steps when she halted and hurried back to him. "There's more. Behind us."

His jaw tightened as he scented two more earth fada. They were surrounded. Taking Valeria's arm, he drew her and Merry with him until they had their backs against a tree and all four earth fada were in his field of vision.

They were in a small clearing near the center of the cherry grove. Several fae lights had drifted in from the meadow, programmed to seek out party goers wherever they were. The soft illumination allowed Rui to get a good look at the man and woman who'd followed them into the grove. They were clearly relatives: they had the same lean, dark beauty married to a catlike grace. He'd bet good money their animals were cougars or another large cat.

But the man was Adric, all right. He might be pretty, but he reeked of dominance. And he'd heard Adric was young, and this man couldn't be out of his twenties.

Rui released Valeria and straightened to his full height, hands loose at his sides, ready for a battle.

"Take it easy." The earth alpha lifted a hand, palm out. "I don't want a fight. I just want to ask you a few questions."

The big black cat rumbled in agreement. Merry whimpered. When he glanced at her, she was staring, mesmerized, at the quartz hanging from the cat's neck. It was glowing the same eerie green as its eyes.

His blood chilled. "Valeria," he said, "stop Merry from looking at his quartz."

Valeria looked from her to the cat and then clapped her hand over the little girl's eyes. Merry pushed at her wrist. "But it's pretty," she whined. Valeria whispered something Rui couldn't hear, but Merry nodded and Valeria released her.

"You can ask," Rui replied. "That doesn't mean you're going to get answers."

The other man cocked a dark brow. "No? There are four of us, and you have the girl to protect."

Beside him, Valeria went taut, her fear and worry an acrid scent that made his chest tighten. Rui caught her hand and squeezed it.

"Talk," he said.

"Do you know who I am?"

"I'm guessing you're alpha of the Baltimore Earth Fada Clan."

"That's right. I'm Lord Adric and these are three of my lieutenants."

He gave a curt nod. "Rui do Mar. Lord Dion's second."

"Ah."

There was a world of meaning in the single syllable. It was clear Adric knew Rui had spent the past year in an alcoholic haze. His jaw hardened. That didn't mean he couldn't take out a pup less than half his age.

Adric turned to Valeria. "And you are?"

She met his gaze squarely, although Rui felt the effort it cost her. The man was her dominant by several degrees.

"Valeria da Costa. And this is my daughter."

To Adric's credit, he didn't try to stare Valeria down. Instead he simply nodded and turned back to Rui. "We know the girl's one of ours. What we don't know is why you have her."

Merry tugged on Rui's shirt. She was staring at the black cat. Her nostrils flared. "Tio Rui," she said, "I think he's a jaguar like me."

The big cat blinked with what appeared to be approval.

"Very good," said Adric. "He *is* a jaguar. His coat even has some darker spots in it, although you can't see them in this light."

Merry gave the jaguar a tentative smile. "Hello, *senhor.*"

Rui placed a hand on her head. "No, sweetheart. Don't talk to him. Don't say anything. And whatever you do, don't look at his crystal no matter how pretty you think it is."

She nodded but her gaze didn't leave the jaguar's face.

Light cascaded over the cat's black coat in a sparkling rain of gold, silver, copper and that eerie green. A few seconds later a man stood before them, naked save for the quartz crystal hanging from his neck.

Rui glanced from him to Merry. There was an obvious resemblance. The wiry body, the hazel eyes. Even his hard-boned face had something familiar about it, although he lacked the pointed chin and tip-tilted eyes that marked Merry as part fae, and his hair was a straight, shiny black where Merry's was wavy.

Rui drew a slow breath. Beside him, Valeria did the same.

She clutched his arm and he knew she'd scented the same thing he had. The black-haired man was a close relative of Merry's.

The man eyed the little girl with an obvious hunger. "Hello, sweetheart. I've been looking for you for a long time." He swallowed. "And yes, I'm a jaguar. Just like you."

Her face lit up. "I remember you! You're Uncle Jace."

"No," Valeria whispered. Her fingers clenched on Rui's.

"You remember?" The man's eyes crinkled in pleased surprise. He took a step forward, arms out. "I've missed you, Christmas girl."

"Stay away from her." Valeria snatched Merry up.

The little girl looked from Valeria to Jace before burying her head in her mama's neck.

The earth fada's grin faded. "You heard her," he said, bringing his arms back to his sides. "I'm her uncle. She's my sister's daughter."

"If that's true," Valeria replied, "what was your sister's name?"

"Takira. Takira Jones."

Valeria gulped. "No," she said, but her voice held no conviction.

So the man had it right. Rui's heart sank. Merry didn't remember much about her mother, who'd apparently died when she was around four, but she'd been old enough to know her mother's name.

"And I'm Jace Jones," he continued. "Takira mated with a man who was half night fae, half human. His name was Silver. No last name—or at least none that he shared with me. I suppose my sister knew all his names."

The fae guarded their true-names closely, since in the right hands, they could be used to control them.

"You're lying," Valeria returned. "Merry doesn't have any family. Just me."

"The hell I am." Jace's eyes flashed. "Merry is Takira's daughter. M-E-R-R-Y because she was born on Christmas."

Deus, thought Rui. What a fucking mess.

"If that's true," Valeria said, "where were you two years ago when she almost died? She and her father were being chased by night fae. She had nightmares about it for months afterward. If we hadn't hidden her, they would've—" She stopped and pressed her lips together.

"You think I don't have nightmares, too?" Jace's hands clenched. "I was looking for her. We all were. Takira was kidnapped and—" He glanced at Merry and shook his head. "After she died, her mate took their daughter and ran. It took me over a year to find them. By then he was dead, too, and Merry was missing. I—I was told she was dead, too."

"The night fae swore to it," Adric inserted with a scowl. "We would've kept looking but the trail ended at the house she and her father had been staying in. The house burned down, and it appeared Merry had died in the fire."

"It was you, wasn't it?" Jace was looking at Rui. "You're the one who killed Silver. Why else would you have been in the house that night?"

Rui glanced at Merry, praying she wouldn't understand what Jace was saying, and then gave a short nod.

"What about my sister?" Jace was in Rui's face, uncaring of his alpha's restraining hand. "Did you kill Takira, too?"

"No. I swear I had nothing to do with that."

Jace inhaled suspiciously, but it was clear he detected the truth in Rui's statement.

"Jace," Adric said. "Stand down."

He scowled but obeyed.

"I'm sorry about your sister," Valeria told him, "but Merry's mine now. She calls me Mama. I couldn't love her any more if she were my own child."

It was Adric who answered. "She's an earth fada. She belongs with her own kind. You can't officially adopt her without my permission."

"Then give it to me. She's my daughter."

Merry lifted her head to glare at Adric. "Mama already 'dopted me," she said fiercely.

"It's not that simple." It was the earth fada woman. "Tell them, Ric. Tell them why Merry needs to be with us."

He hesitated and then leveled a stare at Rui and Valeria. "As far as we're concerned, the less outsiders know about our crystals, the better. But Marjani's right, you need to know. First, though, I want you two to swear this won't go any further. Not even your alpha can know."

"I swear," Valeria said quickly.

Rui cut her a glance. Damn it, he didn't like being told to hide what they learned from Dion, especially when the two of them had just reached an understanding.

But Valeria bit her lower lip. "Please?" she whispered.

"All right," he growled at Adric. "As long as whatever you tell us won't hurt Rock Run, you have my word that we won't speak of it to anyone else. But you need to know that Merry's one of us now, by Lord Dion's own word. And Valeria's her mother. Nothing you tell us can change that."

"No?" the alpha replied with a cryptic smile. "You're aware that we all wear a crystal, some type of quartz." He lifted his from beneath his shirt. It glowed in the dim light, a milky gray shot with swirls of orange and brown.

"But what you may not know," he continued, "is that we don't have them from the time we're born. At first, we share the energy that emanates from our parents' crystals. Merry, of course, had only one parent's quartz to draw on, but that wasn't a problem as long as her mom was alive. But when Takira died, she lost even that. Tell me something—when you found her, was she too thin, half-starved?"

It was Valeria who replied. "Yes," she said in a small voice. "But they were on the run, barely surviving. Her dad was afraid to leave her with anyone so he could work. He didn't have money for food."

"That was part of it. But without a crystal, she's never going to grow like she should. Look at how thin she is." Adric shrugged. "Even we can't really explain it. We just know that we need a quartz. Does she have trouble shifting?"

Valeria gulped. But she didn't have to say anything; the earth alpha was shaking his head.

"I'm sorry, Miss da Costa—"

"But she's better now," Valeria protested. "She may be skinny, but you should have seen her two years ago. Don't forget, she's only half earth fada. Maybe that makes a difference."

Adric's face softened, and Rui had the surprising thought that he might like the man—or at least respect him—under different circumstances.

"I can see you're a good mother," Adric said. "You may even be giving her some of what she needs. But you can't give her everything. I'm afraid we have to—"

"Then give her a quartz," Valeria cried. "I'll make sure she wears it. Only please don't take her away from me."

Marjani stepped forward. "We're sorry," she said gently, "but it doesn't work like that. Merry will find her own quartz when the time comes, but until then she should be with Jace. As her closest living relative, she can draw the energy she needs from him."

"No," Valeria choked out. Tears were streaming down her face now. "No. Please. There must be something else we can do. Look at her. She's fine. She's not hurting or hungry or sick. *She's not.*"

Merry took one look at her mother and started crying as well. "Mama, please," she sobbed, clinging to Valeria. "Don't make me go with them. I want to stay with you and Tio Rui."

"Enough." Adric jerked his head at Jace. "Take her."

"Like hell." Rui put himself between Valeria and Merry and the earth shifters. "She's managed to survive for three years since her mother died. Don't tell me you have to take her this very minute."

Adric ignored Rui to finger his quartz. There was a flash of orange-gold and Merry's cries stopped mid-sob.

"Merry?" Valeria's voice was high-pitched, panicky. Rui turned to see the little girl hanging limply in her arms, her eyes closed as Valeria frantically patted her face.

She shot Adric a furious look. "What did you do, you bastard?"

Rui's knife practically leapt into his hand. He released the blade, the snick loud in the suddenly quiet clearing.

"I swear on my *avô*'s grave, if you hurt her, I'll cut your fucking heart out and feed it to the sharks."

"She's fine." Adric let go of the quartz. "I just put her to sleep for a few minutes. Give her to Jace."

"The hell we will. Why was she in hiding, anyway? If you Baltimore shifters are so good for her, why didn't her dad come to you after her mom died? Instead he was living in a dump with barely enough food to keep the two of them alive."

Adric's lips tightened. "I'd like to know the answer to that myself. But I promise she'll be safe with Jace. He lost his only sister. He won't let anyone hurt her daughter."

While he was speaking, his lieutenants had formed a semi-circle around the three of them with Jace and Adric at the center.

Jace touched his quartz. "I'd die before I let anyone hurt her."

"No." Valeria crouched behind Rui, her back against the tree, Merry in her arms. "Don't let them take her," she begged, fierce and pleading at the same time.

"I won't," he promised without taking his eyes off the four fada. "They'll have to go through me first."

"I know," was the quiet reply. "Thank you."

He felt a rush of shame, that she would even think to thank him for doing what any mate would do—protect her and her daughter. *Deus*, he had a lot to make up to her—if he just survived the next few minutes.

"God's cat." Adric shoved a hand through his spiked-up hair. "She's an earth shifter mixed with a human and a fae—a night fae, at that. Why the fuck do you want her so bad?"

Valeria just growled. When Rui glanced back, her eyes were a feral aqua-blue.

"Ric, think." Marjani's hands were fisted at her sides. "The laws of hospitality—if the queen finds out, she has the right to bind you."

Uncertainty flickered across the earth alpha's face. To be bound against your will was a fada's nightmare; even a few days of being unable to move freely could drive your animal insane.

He glanced at Jace. Something passed between the two of them and his expression hardened.

Rui braced himself. Time seemed to slow. Cold descended on him, familiar, instinctive. He hadn't trained as a warrior in two years. He was out of shape and still recovering from whatever Cleia had done to him. But some things were bred in the bone.

And he'd fight to the death to keep Merry out of these bastards' hands.

"Fuck their laws." A blade appeared in Adric's hand. "The girl is ours."

11

As the four earth shifters closed in on them, Valeria looked frantically around for help. Even though they were deep in the cherry grove, twenty-five yards from the nearest path, it didn't seem possible to be this close to a large crowd without anyone being aware of what was happening.

But the drumming had become louder. It sounded like several drummers now, pounding out a hard, syncopated rhythm that ricocheted back and forth across the meadow. The noise from the crowd had increased, too, as more and more people arrived for the midsummer festival.

Her heart sank as she realized that even if she called for help, not even a fada was likely to hear. They were on their own.

Rui glanced at her. For an instant, the mate bond flared to life. She *felt* his protectiveness, his determination to defend her and Merry no matter what. His *need*.

She sucked in a breath, shocked at all he'd been hiding from her.

Then he turned back to the earth shifters and the only thing radiating from him was a cold so intense she gave an involuntary shiver. The mate bond clamped shut as if he'd stomped on it. The cold was replaced by an emptiness that was even worse, a void in her chest where she'd been holding Rui for two years. Even when the bond had shriveled, there'd been *something* there.

Now there was nothing.

She shoved that aside to focus on the four earth shifters closing in on them. Rui dropped into a fighting crouch. A chill sweat broke out on her skin as she looked from him to them. Four against one were terrible odds. At full strength, Rui might have a chance, but...

Her animal squirmed beneath her skin, tense and agitated. Desperate to defend her mate.

But both parts of her understood that Merry was more important. Joining the fight would play into the earth shifters' hands. All they'd have to do was snatch Merry and run—and Valeria would never see her again.

The wolf paced nearer, his shaggy body looming over Valeria like something out of a nightmare. Her claws sliced out of her fingertips. He was trying to intimidate her—and doing a good job of it—but she refused to go easy. He pressed too close, his amber eyes intent on Merry.

Valeria swiped out. He snarled and jumped back, four red lines marring his snout. *Good.*

Rui took advantage of the distraction to lunge at the wolf. Metal flashed. The big animal twisted, avoiding the worst of the blow, but the knife slashed his shoulder. The scent of fresh blood filled the clearing as the wolf snarled angrily, his left foreleg raised and dangling uselessly.

But the other three saw their chance. Adric and Marjani came at Rui from either side, while Jace darted forward and tried to grab his niece. Valeria swiped at his arm, but he would've had Merry if Rui hadn't shaken the other two off, striking out viciously with his knife and catching Marjani on the upper arm.

As she backed away, Rui spun around and slammed a foot into Jace, knocking him away from Valeria and Merry.

Adric glanced at Marjani, who had a hand to her arm. Blood welled from beneath her fingers. "You're hurt," he said in a guttural voice.

"It'll heal. Just get Merry. We've got to get out of here—*now*, before someone comes."

Adric's head snapped back around. He glared at Rui, his bronze eyes murderous. "That's my sister you cut."

"I'm only defending what's mine," Rui returned in an equally hard voice.

"The woman's yours, then? I've heard different. And the girl's *ours*—not yours."

"You heard wrong. Valeria's mine. My woman. My *mate*."

Valeria blinked. *Now* Rui was claiming her?

"And Merry's her daughter now," he continued. "Which makes them both mine. You'll have to go through me to get them."

Valeria caught her breath. Rui had claimed her before witnesses—and Merry, too—even though the witnesses were earth fada. Still, she knew—and Rui knew. It didn't mean she was his—the woman had the option of rejecting the claim—but the ball was in her court now.

If the two of them lived through the next ten minutes.

Adric smiled. "If that's the way you want it—"

He lunged forward, knife aimed at Rui's belly.

Rui twisted to evade it, one foot coming up to kick Adric's wrist. The knife spun out of the earth's shifter's grip, landing on the grass near Valeria. Keeping hold of Merry, she scrambled forward, snatching it up just as he dove for it and pitching it deep into the trees.

Adric came back to his feet in one smooth roll. "You shouldn't have done that," he said in a soft voice that made the hairs on Valeria's nape stand on end.

"Adric," said Marjani.

He jerked his head in acknowledgment and touched his crystal. Bronze glowed at the center. Valeria stared at it, mesmerized.

"Give Merry to me," he commanded. "You know it's for the best."

Valeria found herself nodding. Then she caught her breath.

No, damn it. Merry belongs with me.

She tried to wrench her gaze from the crystal's glowing bronze heart. But she couldn't.

She growled lowly but she couldn't look away. She couldn't even shut her eyes. Her animal was entranced by the light like a silly, thrill-seeking deer.

Rui was fighting Jace now. The jaguar shifter didn't have a knife, but he was getting in some good blows, darting in close to punch Rui in the face or the stomach, then dancing away from his blade. She could see the fight out of the corner of her eye, but she felt oddly detached, as if she were watching from behind a glass wall.

The bronze glow was so much more interesting, drawing her closer, closer...

"Valeria," said Adric. "I'm going to take Merry now. Give her to me, love."

Valeria felt her hands releasing Merry even as her mind screamed, *No, no, no...*

Rui roared and slammed into Adric. "Get away from her, you SOB."

Adric lurched to one side, releasing the crystal. With a start, Valeria came back to herself. Letting out a sob, she dragged Merry back against her. "I'm sorry, baby," she whispered, pressing her lips to the unconscious girl's cheek. "So sorry."

Meanwhile, Jace had circled to Rui's left. While Rui's attention was on Adric, he aimed a hard kick at Rui's rib cage. There was the dull sound of bones breaking.

Valeria sucked in a breath.

Rui merely grunted and continued to fight. But he was beginning to tire. His shirt gaped open, and she was horrified to see a bloody gash low on his abdomen. Adric's knife must have found its mark.

Adric caught his balance and growled at Jace. "Let's finish this."

It was just the two of them now. The injured wolf lay nearby, panting raggedly. Marjani had ripped a strip off her tunic and bound it around his bleeding shoulder, then pressed another strip to her own wound. She crouched next to the wolf, watching the fight.

Adric and Jace closed in on Rui, their faces expressionless, hitting him slowly, methodically. He was bleeding from several places now—his forehead, his nose, the slice in his abdomen.

Fear snaked through Valeria's stomach. A knife wound like that could kill. She had to help. She struggled onto her knees, Merry still in her arms, and looked desperately around for a weapon.

Adric's booted foot lashed into Rui's thigh. Then Jace cut in with a hard right to his jaw. Rui grunted again and stumbled backward. As he came upright, Adric slammed his fist into his solar plexus.

The breath left Rui's lungs in a whoosh. His mouth opened soundlessly as he tried to bring the air back in but couldn't. He dropped to his knees.

"*Rui.*" Valeria let out a sob, desperate to go to him but knowing the Baltimore shifters would take Merry.

He shot her a despairing look. "*Desculpe,*" he mouthed. "I—" His chest heaved and he shook his head, unable to speak.

She swallowed sickly. "It's okay, *querido.* You did your best."

Adric reached for Merry. "Give me the girl."

"*No.*" She scuttled backward, Merry clutched to her chest.

Adric eyed them. Considering. He was playing with his quartz again, but this time she knew better than to look at it.

Jace took a step closer. Valeria's claws sliced out and she knew when she looked up her eyes were glowing with her animal's feral green-blue.

No. She wrenched her animal back under her control.

There was no way she could fight off two fada males. Her only chance was to reason with them.

"Wait!" Still holding Merry, she came to her feet and took a deep breath. "Look," she told Jace, "I'm sorry about your sister—truly, I am. But do you think she'd want you to take Merry away from the woman who's raised her the last two years? Merry's mine now. She thinks of me as her mama. I love her—and she loves me. And Rui's the closest thing she has to a father. How—how can you do this to her?" Her voice broke and Merry whimpered.

Jace just stared at her, breathing hard.

On the grass at her feet, Rui inhaled slowly, raggedly. With an obvious effort, he pushed himself back to standing, placing himself between her and the earth shifters.

Adric's lip curled. "Get her," he told Jace.

And then, at last Valeria heard the sound of men's voices nearby. Rock Run men, calling to each other in Portuguese.

"*Socorro!*" she screamed. "Help us! Over here!"

"Get her," Adric snapped again.

Jace tried to shove past Rui, but Rui's hand whipped out, grabbing his arm. "No."

He hung on long enough for Valeria to dart around the tree and run toward the voices. Footsteps pounded after her. She put on a burst of speed.

Two men were running toward her. Luis and Rodolfo.

"Here," she called with her last bit of breath. "This way." She stumbled to a stop, lungs heaving, and fell to her knees, body curved protectively around Merry.

Hot breath touched her neck. "This isn't over," growled Adric. And then he was gone, heading back to the clearing.

Luis and Rodolfo reached her. "What's going on?" Luis demanded.

She looked up at them and dragged in a breath. "Help...Rui." She pointed toward the clearing. "That way. Careful. Four of them."

The men nodded and took off.

She rose to her feet and followed more slowly. Merry's eyes fluttered open. "Mama? What happened?"

At the querulous tone, tears pricked Valeria's eyes. "Nothing, baby." She pressed shaky lips to her daughter's soft cheek. "Don't worry. Everything's all right now."

RUI HAD NEVER TAKEN a direct hit to the solar plexus before, but he'd heard they hurt like a sonuvabitch.

That was a lie. They hurt even worse.

Don't give up, his brain screamed.

But as the pain spread through his abdomen, he couldn't breathe, or even move.

Dark spots danced before his eyes. He dropped to his knees and doubled over. Behind him Valeria moaned. Despair filled him as he realized she'd never be able to fight off the earth fada.

After that everything was a blur. Somehow Valeria managed to get away with Merry. He was able to get back onto his feet long enough to stop Jace from following them, but Adric raced off after them and his heart sank.

When Adric returned a few minutes later. Rui braced himself to die, but the alpha ignored him to sling the hurt wolf over his shoulders in a fireman's lift and lope off, the other two at his heels.

The next thing he knew Luis and Rodolfo were standing before him.

Rui licked his lips. "Valeria? And Merry?"

"They're fine," his cousin replied. "The bastards took off when they heard us coming."

Rui closed his eyes.

"What the hell happened? Damn it, Rui, don't you know better than to get in a fight at a fae celebration?" Luis's voice echoed oddly in his brain, as if he were calling down a long tunnel.

"Wasn't…my choice."

"I hope that's true, because if the sun fae find out—" Luis broke off and cursed as he saw the blood welling around the hand Rui had pressed to his stomach. "Rui? Hell, did one of those SOBs knife you?"

The dark spots multiplied, joined into one giant inky blot. Rui sank to his knees and slid into unconsciousness.

When he came to, Valeria had his head in her lap and was stroking the hair back from his temple. He was content to lie quietly even as the part of him that had been a warrior for more than eight decades took inventory. Besides the soreness in the region of his solar plexus, his lower abdomen was throbbing from the knife wound and his head was pounding. Add in various assorted aches and pains and it meant he hurt like hell—but he'd live.

Then his lungs seized. "Merry?" He tried to push himself up to sitting.

"She's fine, thanks to you." Valeria pressed his shoulders to keep him down. "Just lie still. Rodolfo is getting a healer."

He turned his head, unable to relax until he saw the little girl, sitting a couple of feet away and sleepily rubbing her eyes.

"Mama?"

"It's all right, *querida*," Valeria murmured. "I'm right here."

"You're not going to give me back to Uncle Jace, are you?"

"Oh, no, baby." Valeria held out hand to her. Merry crept forward and catlike, butted her head against Valeria's side, marking her with her scent and taking her scent on herself in return.

Valeria bent forward to rub noses with her. "Nobody's going to take you. You're my daughter now. Okay?"

Merry nodded solemnly. "*Sim*, Mama."

"And *my* princess," Rui added.

Merry rewarded him with a big grin followed by a soft, careful kiss on his cheek.

"Ah...you must have some magic in you. I feel all better now."

Merry giggled and curled up next to him, her head nestled against his neck, a warm, trusting weight. His chest constricted. *Deus,* he loved this little girl.

Luis crouched down and asked Valeria what had happened. "Was that Lord Adric I saw?"

"*Sim*." She explained about Jace being Merry's uncle, and that he and Adric wanted Merry back.

"They have a right to her," Luis said grimly. "Rui never should've been there in the first place. He—" He glanced at Merry. "You know."

"I know," Valeria replied.

Rui waited for Valeria to make her disgust clear. He'd long since decided he should never have killed the half-blood. Even if it meant Tyrus would come after him, too. Even if he knew Tyrus would just hire someone else to do his dirty work.

He'd known there was something funny about the job. And when he'd found Merry there, he should have left immediately.

Some things a man just didn't do. Not and remain with a whole soul. He'd done something unforgivable in depriving Merry of her father. Valeria had been right to reject him.

But she was defending him. He blinked. Had he misunderstood?

But no, she was saying, "If it hadn't been Rui, it would've been someone else. And another man might have left Merry in the house, especially when he found out the night fae were after her.

If Rui hadn't gotten her away from them—" A fine tremor moved over her body.

He turned his head into her hand. She stroked his face, and for the first time in a long while he felt a touch of hope, warming him from the inside out.

"Here comes the healer." Luis rose to his feet. "I'll explain to Dion what happened. There's no reason for Cleia to know."

Rui's lips edged up. "What the fae don't know," he rasped, "won't hurt them." It was practically a mantra for the fada.

Luis grinned down at him. "Exactly."

12

———

Filipa, the healer summoned by Rodolfo, removed her hands from Rui and rose to her feet, her dark eyes sober. "You can take him back to the base now," she told Valeria and Luis. "But have Branco see him as soon as possible." Branco was the base's oldest and most experienced healer.

"We will," Valeria promised.

"And don't let him convince you he doesn't need a healer," Filipa added with a stern look at her patient, who was already struggling to sit up. "What I did was the equivalent of applying a bandage. That knife nicked his intestines. Without further healing, he risks infection or internal bleeding."

"You got it," Luis said. He helped Rui up, ignoring his muttered assertion that he didn't need any help, damn it.

Luis and Rodolfo decided between them that Luis would fill Dion in on what had happened and then remain at the festival with Marina and Xavier.

That left Rodolfo to drive Rui, Valeria and Merry back to Rock Run. As the four of them entered the base, the two men on duty took one look at Rui's battered face and volunteered to get Branco.

"Send him to my place," Valeria told them.

The guards glanced between her and Rui, obviously curious, but just nodded.

Valeria took Merry's hand, sliding her other arm around Rui's waist. Meanwhile, Rodolfo stepped forward and tried to put an arm around his shoulder, but Rui shrugged them both off.

"I'm fine, damn it. Hell, I've felt worse after a day of training."

Rodolfo was a large bull-like man who looked as if he'd as soon grind your bones into dust as speak to you. But Valeria had discovered that his menacing exterior hid a marshmallow-soft core. Now he just said okay and backed off.

The four of them started down the hall. Merry, who seemed none the worse for her brief spell of unconsciousness, skipped happily alongside Valeria. Rui, on the other hand, was fading fast. As they passed the dining hall, he slowed to a shuffle and pressed a hand to his stomach, his mouth white around the edges.

Valeria glanced Rodolfo, but he was already easing an arm around Rui's waist. "Lean on me, you ass. And don't argue—you'd do the same if it were me."

"And have done," Rui muttered.

But he put an arm around Rodolfo's shoulder, allowing him to take some of his weight.

Valeria had never seen the base so empty. The dining hall, normally the heart of the clan's life, held only a few of people. As they headed down the hall to her apartment, their footsteps echoed eerily.

She tightened her grip on Merry's hand and glanced around uneasily. Logic told her it was almost impossible for the earth shifters to enter the base—there were multiple layers of guards as well as the spell that hid their location from any uninvited visitors—but Adric had gotten in once. And as far as she was aware, no one knew exactly how.

As they turned the corner, Merry dashed ahead to open the door to their apartment. "This way, Tio Rui."

He managed a smile. "Thanks, *princesa.*"

As they entered Valeria's *sala,* the fae lights floating near the ceiling were activated. Like the rest of the base, her apartment had been carved out of a system of underground caverns that ran alongside Rock Run Creek, with clever touches like shelves chiseled into the stone walls and countertops of local granite. Now the illumination cast a soft green glow over the rough stone walls, imparting the soothing effect of an underwater grotto.

Rui removed his arm from Rodolfo's shoulder. "Thanks," he said gruffly. "I'll be all right now—go back to the party."

Rodolfo snorted. "I've had a bellyful of the fae, thank you." He glanced at Valeria. "Are you sure you can handle things from here?" She nodded. "Well, send for me if you need help with this fool—or with anything, for that matter."

"I will." She lifted up on her toes to kiss his big, square face. "And thank you."

He colored and with a muttered, *"De nada,"* strode out the door.

Valeria turned around to find Rui eyeing her. "He likes you. All the men do."

"I don't know about all the men, but Rodolfo's a sweetheart. I don't know what I'd have done without him these past couple of—"

Rui expelled a breath. "I'm sorry, Valeria. It should've been me. Your mate. You needed me and I wasn't there for you."

She shook her head. She was so confused. Even a few days ago she would've coldly told him to go to hell. He'd rejected her for Cleia. Humiliated her with women like Beatriz, over and over. But there had been that rush of love she'd felt from him in the clearing—and he'd been willing to die for her and Merry.

What did he want from her?

She drew a serrated breath, conscious of Merry listening to them with great interest. "You're not my mate," she said flatly. "And I am *not* your responsibility."

"Valeria—" He took a step toward her, then halted and brought his hand back to his stomach.

"Here." She helped him to the couch. "Sit down already."

He sank down with a sigh and rested his head on the couch back. His face was sallow beneath the bruises and one of his eyes was swollen shut. She scrutinized him worriedly as he closed the other eye.

"Can I get you something to drink?"

"Yes, please," he said without opening his eyes. "Water."

"I'll get it," Merry volunteered. She scurried into the small kitchen that adjoined the *sala*, returning with a glass held carefully in both hands, then hovered over him while he drained it.

"That was just what I needed," he said, handing it back to her, and her whole face lit up.

Meanwhile, Valeria had gone into the kitchen for a wet cloth and an icepack. Taking a seat on the couch, she bathed the blood from Rui's face and then handed him the icepack.

He hissed as he brought the pack to his swollen eye, but kept it there.

She eyed him doubtfully. "Maybe you should get into bed."

His mouth quirked. "If that's an invitation, *querida*, you picked a helluva time."

She pressed her lips together. "It's not. And you're in no condition even if it was."

He drew in a breath and then pressed a hand to his belly. "I'm afraid...you're right," he said with a rueful expression.

"Just sit still. Branco should be here soon."

Valeria took the bloody cloth to the bathroom to rinse out. She was setting it on a rack to dry when she caught sight of herself in the mirror. She sucked in a breath. Her eyes were wide dark pools, her hair a tangled mass around her shoulders, and at some point she'd torn the skirt of her new dress. For some reason that was the final straw. She poked a finger through the jagged hole and blinked back tears.

In the *sala* Merry was chattering to Rui.

"Mm," he said. "Why don't you sit next to me, sweetheart?"

Valeria drew a shuddering breath and placed her hands on the sink. She couldn't let herself cry. Not now. Merry needed her to be strong. Rui did, too.

For a long minute, she hung over the sink, tears dripping down her cheeks, her fingers digging into the edge of the carved stone basin as she fought to regain control of herself. Then she took another breath and splashed some water on her face before returning to the *sala*.

As she entered the room, she paused in the doorway. Merry was snuggled up on the couch next to Rui. He'd gamely put an arm around her. He was holding the icepack to the back of his head now; he must've taken a blow there, too. If anything, they looked worse than her: Rui with his bruised and swollen face; Merry streaked with dirt and her braid coming undone, her blue bow left behind somewhere in the cherry grove. But all Valeria could think about was how she'd almost lost them both.

Merry turned her head to look into Rui's face. "Tio Rui?"

"Sim?"

"I love you."

"I love you, too." His voice was rough with emotion.

"You won't let Uncle Jace steal me, will you?"

"No way. You're safe, *princesa*. I promise."

"Good." Merry let out a relieved sigh.

Valeria's breath caught. It felt as if her chest was being cracked open, exposing her heart. She pressed a hand to her sternum, trying to massage away the ache.

Rui turned his head. "There you are. Come and sit down." When she hesitated, he set the icepack on the coffee table and held out his hand. "*Por favor?* I...need to hold you right now."

It wasn't that he said please, it was the vulnerable look on his hard face as he said it. The crack in her chest widened and she found herself obeying.

"That's better," he said as she sat down beside him. His big arm settled tentatively around her shoulders. Then it tightened. "Hey, *querida*. Calm down—it's okay. Adrenaline's a bitch, isn't it?"

It was only then that she realized she was trembling. She drew in a shaky breath. "*Sim.*"

He stroked her hair. "It's okay," he murmured. "You're all right. Everything's fine."

Her breath sighed out. When she'd first come to Rock Run, she'd gone straight from her family's close embrace to living with Rui. With him gone, she'd been forced to be the strong one. Oh, she'd been welcomed and supported by everyone at Rock Run from Dion on down, but for the first time she'd been responsible for her own decisions—and not only for herself, but for Merry.

She was proud of how she'd handled things, but even with the friends she'd made, she was still lonely. She yearned for someone to talk to about Merry, someone with whom she could share her worries and triumphs. Someone who loved the little girl as much as she did.

Now sensations poured into her: strength...concern...protectiveness. Even injured, Rui's large frame radiated heat, power. Safety.

She reminded herself this was the man who'd broken her heart, pushing her away again and again. But he'd also been willing to die for her—and Merry.

He pulled her closer and she stopped fighting it.

His thumb moved over her neck in slow, hypnotic strokes. She bowed her head and allowed herself to enjoy it. Even Merry had quieted, her head on Rui's thigh.

He shifted and she tried to pull away. "You're hurt—"

"I'm fine." His fingers closed on her nape, keeping her where she was. "Let me do something for you for a change," he added, seemingly reading her mind. "You're safe now, sweetheart."

She flashed on Adric's flat bronze gaze and shuddered. "I

know we're safe enough here. But—" She shook her head, conscious of Merry hanging on their every word.

He squeezed a little harder. "I know you haven't had much cause to trust me these past two years, but I meant what I said back there in the cherry grove. You're mine, Valeria. Both of you. And I protect what's mine. I promise you, Adric's not going to win this one. He'll have to go through me to get to you—either of you."

She glanced away. She wanted so badly to believe him.

But there was so much hurt, so much darkness still between them. Maybe he really did love her. Maybe he truly wanted her as his mate. But she couldn't forget that he'd promised to meet her in a mating ceremony—and then left her for another woman.

She glanced at Merry. "Why don't you go see if Branco is in the hall?"

"Okay." The little girl hopped up and ran out the door.

Valeria turned to Rui. "Stop it," she gritted. "You've spent the past two years showing me how little I mean to you. Why in Hades should I trust you now?"

The words hung in the air like thick gray smog, sad and bitter at the same time.

Rui met her eyes. "You shouldn't."

She swallowed and looked away. He was agreeing with her. So why did she feel so miserable?

She started to come to her feet, but he caught her arm. "Because you're right, I don't deserve it. But I will. I'm going to earn your trust, Valeria. I'm going to open that bond between us again. And—"

In the hall, Merry sang out, "*Olá*, Senhor Branco."

Rui hung on to Valeria's arm. "This isn't over, Valeria. We need to talk, you and me." He waited until she nodded before releasing her.

Branco entered, Merry on his hip. The healer had seen more than three hundred turns of the sun, but he was still strong, dynamic, his only sign of age his silver ponytail. He pulled Valeria into a one-armed hug before setting Merry down and turning to Rui.

He raised a brow at his patient's battered condition. "Tell me you didn't get into a brawl with a sun fae."

Rui's mouth twisted. "It was the new Baltimore alpha —Adric."

"They attacked us," Valeria added, even as she wondered why she felt compelled to defend him. "Four of them. Rui was protecting me and Merry."

"I see." Branco gave her a quick but thorough once-over. "You and the little one are all right?"

"We're fine. It's Rui who's hurt."

"Even so." Branco took her hands. Energy flowed from him to her, warm, peaceful, soothing away the worry and agitation. She started to protest that he should see to Rui, but he hushed her. "This will only take a minute. And I've got energy to spare today."

"It does feel good," she admitted.

He smiled and released her, then lifted Merry into his arms and did the same for her before setting her back down. He gave her a pat on the rear end. "You look like you need a snack."

She cast Valeria a look. "Mama said I could have ice cream when we came home."

Valeria smothered a smile. She should've known her daughter wouldn't let a little thing like a near-kidnapping to allow her to forget. "You know where it is. Just one bowl, mind."

"And a chocolate, too."

"And a chocolate, too."

With Merry occupied, Branco turned to Rui. "Now," he said, "let me have a look at you. If Valeria will give me a hand—"

Together, they eased Rui out of what looked like his best shirt. His jaw tightened, but he bore it stoically. The purple linen was torn and bloodied. Valeria shook her head and set it on the floor.

"The pants, too," Branco said.

They helped Rui out of his pants, leaving him in black briefs. Even bruised and with an ugly slash across his lower abdomen, the sight of his big body sprawled on her couch made her breath catch.

And he knew it, the bastard. His lips curved and he slanted her a knowing look from beneath inky black lashes.

"Mama," Merry called from the kitchen. "I can't reach the chocolates."

Valeria dragged her gaze from Rui's and crossed the room to get the box. She felt him watching as she let Merry choose one before setting the box back on the shelf. She could tell he wondered if Petros had given them to her, but he wisely didn't ask.

Branco was running expert hands over Rui's body. He sat back with a satisfied nod.

"Other than that cut in your belly, the news isn't bad—a couple of cracked ribs and a slight concussion. Ordinarily, injuries like these would take you a few weeks to recover from, but with the energy you received from Cleia, you should be fully healed in ten days or so. But Filipa is right, that cut has to be closed up before it gets infected. Relax and focus on your breath." The healer hovered his hands over the nasty gash in Rui's lower abdomen. "That's it. Now visualize the energy going here, where you need it."

Rui closed his eyes and inhaled slowly. Branco touched a tender spot, and Rui's jaw clenched, his breath changing to shallow pants.

"Easy now," murmured the healer. "Keep breathing."

Rui nodded and let out an exhale. But he was pale under his tan, his lips taut with pain.

Valeria pulled up a chair and clasped her hands between her legs, wishing she could help. She told herself that her worry was only natural, since Rui had been injured defending her and

Merry, but that was a lie. It was agony, to see him hurting, worse than if she'd been injured herself.

The healing seemed to take a long time, although when she checked only thirty minutes had passed. Merry finished her ice cream and sat on the floor beside the couch, her hand on Rui's wrist.

When Valeria tried to shoo her away, Branco shook his head. "No, leave her. She's helping."

Valeria subsided. Rui turned his palm over to capture Merry's small hand in his and Valeria's heart lurched.

She wanted to hold his hand, too. She wanted Merry to have a father again. She wanted—oh, so many things.

Was it possible? She felt like a weather vane, spinning wildly between hope and distrust.

Unable to sit any longer, she got up to tidy the kitchen. When she returned, Rui was sitting up, his swollen eye open and clear, although surrounded by a dark purple bruise. Most of the rest of his bruises had already faded to a healing yellow-green and the gash on his stomach had closed, leaving behind a ragged red line.

Branco had Merry on his lap, murmuring to her. He smiled up at Valeria. "She'll be fine now. I told her if she goes to sleep now, tomorrow this will seem like a bad dream."

Valeria sent him a grateful look. Maybe Merry hadn't been hurt physically, but she'd had a tough day. Finding her uncle again, who she'd clearly loved. And then having that same uncle attack her mom and Rui, trying to steal her away. The last thing Valeria wanted was for the little girl to go through another bout of nightmares like the ones after her dad died.

"Thank you. If there's anything I can do..."

"It's my pleasure." Branco set Merry down and came to his feet. "All I ask is that you continue raising this fine daughter of yours."

He turned to Rui. "You should be able to make it back to your own apartment now, but don't do anything strenuous for at least a week. Move too soon, and that wound in your belly is going to split open again. And trust me, an abdominal infection is no joke."

Rui nodded. "I'll be careful."

"I stopped the internal bleeding and healed those broken ribs, but concussions can be tricky. Even a slight one can cause problems. Just in case it's worse than I thought, I'll arrange for someone to sit with you tonight."

"That won't be necessary," Valeria heard herself say. "He'll be staying with me."

Branco's brows lifted but all he said was, "Even better. He should continue icing that lump on his head for the next day or so—it'll keep the swelling down. And tonight, you should wake him every couple of hours. Make sure he knows where he is. If you can't wake him or if he seems worse—dizziness, a severe headache, vomiting—send for me immediately."

"I will."

He frowned. "Are you sure you're up to this? You look like you could use a good night's sleep yourself."

"I'll handle it. Don't forget, I have an able assistant."

Merry cocked a thumb at her chest. "That's me."

"I can see he's in good hands." Branco winked. "And Rui," he added sternly, "no alcohol for the next week. Not even a glass of wine."

"I won't," Rui promised.

Valeria almost snorted. Rui without a drink was like a fish without fins. Although that wasn't quite fair. He'd made an effort to be sober around Merry. And his scent was free of alcohol right now—and had been since he'd assumed command of the base in Dion's absence.

"Excellent. Have a good sleep." Branco patted Rui's shoulder. "I'll be back in the morning to check on you."

With Branco gone, Valeria gave Merry a quick bath and put her to bed. The little girl was so tired she didn't even demand her usual book, although she did make a detour into the *sala* to kiss Rui goodnight.

"*Boa noite, princesa*," Valeria heard him rumble.

When Merry returned, Valeria sat on the mattress and pulled her into her arms, nuzzling her neck and breathing in her sweet little-girl scent.

Oh, Deus, she could never let her go.

Especially not to the Baltimore clan. The stories about them were dark, frightening. Lord Adric was rumored to have murdered his own uncle. She recalled again those hard eyes in a deceptively boyish face, the way he'd tried to hypnotize her into handing over Merry. A man like that wouldn't give up easily.

But Marjani. She was obviously tough—she'd had to be, to survive the years of vicious fighting—but she'd seemed like a nice person. And she'd been so happy to see Merry.

And Jace. His expression when he'd looked at Merry had been so hungry...a hunger Valeria understood all too well. He wasn't going to give up either, and if the earth fada were to be believed, then Merry needed to be with him and Valeria was selfish to insist on keeping her.

No, something inside cried. *Maybe you'd love her too, but I don't care. She's mine.*

She hugged the little girl so tightly she squealed. "You're squeezing too hard, Mama."

"Sorry, sweetheart. Good night now."

She gave Merry a last kiss and watched as she turned onto her side, one arm thrown over the clown doll that was never very far from her.

She gently rubbed Merry's back. She'd do anything to keep her.

Anything.

When she returned to the *sala*, Rui was reclined on the couch, eyes closed. He looked so comfortable that she hated to bother him. She turned to tiptoe from the room, but he opened his eyes.

"Don't go."

She came closer. "Do you feel up to taking a shower? Or would you rather go straight to bed?"

He came to his feet. He had to struggle a little, but he was definitely moving easier than he had even an hour ago. "A shower."

But he stayed where he was, looking around. Valeria realized he'd never been in her apartment. He took in the plump blue couch, the large painting of a sunset over the Chesapeake, the colorful cushions scattered on the floor for Merry and her friends. The heated terracotta floor that Rodolfo and Sabela had helped her install for Merry, whose cat craved warmth.

"I like your place." He turned back to Valeria. "It feels like a home."

The naked yearning on his face tugged at her heart. She wanted to wrap her arms around him and promise him...what?

Instead she took a step back. "The bathroom's this way." She pointed down the hall. "There are towels on a shelf near the toilet. You can't miss them."

"Thanks."

She waited until she heard running water and then poked her head inside the bathroom. She couldn't see him because the shower was concealed behind a curved tiled wall.

"Everything okay?" she called.

"I could use some help washing my back."

She *knew* it was a ruse. But there was a weary note that drew her inside anyway. Shucking her dress and undergarments, she came around the wall.

Rui was leaning against the opposite side of the stall, letting the water sluice over his body, but when he saw her he straightened. "Valeria."

By some miracle his mouth had escaped the battering the rest of him had taken. Now it curved in a slow smile as he took in her unclothed state.

She was used to being naked around others; in a clan of shapeshifters, sooner or later you saw everyone unclothed either before or after a shift. But that smile made her flush from the breasts up. Her nipples prickled and hardened.

He swallowed and met her eyes.

She held out a hand. "The washcloth, please."

He looked from her to the cloth in his hand as if he couldn't remember what it was. "What—oh, sure." He handed it to her.

She circled her finger. "Turn around."

He obediently gave her his back.

Ah, Deus. Her tongue felt thick in her mouth. He was darkly tanned all over, and he might have been out of shape but you couldn't tell from this angle. She watched, fascinated, as water slid across his broad shoulders, down his spine and over the firm slope of his buttocks.

Desire pooled in her belly, warm and liquid. She itched to touch him, to run her fingers lightly over all that smooth olive-brown skin and the solid muscles beneath. To press her aching breasts against his back. To rub herself against that taut ass like a cat in heat.

Instead, she soaped the washcloth and began to scrub his back—lightly, so as not to press on his bruises.

He braced himself with a hand on the wall and sighed. "That feels so good, *querida.*"

"Mm," she said. Because it felt good to her, too, and she wasn't sure how she felt about that.

She soaped up the cloth again and then knelt to wash the backs of his legs. When she got to his feet, he turned to face her. She lifted each foot in turn and, setting it on her thigh, scrubbed it thoroughly, including between the toes.

He groaned and she raised her head to see his cock, flushed and hard, just a few inches from her mouth. His lungs were heaving and he had his eyes closed, his free hand fisted at his side.

She finished with his feet and rose back up. Soaping the cloth one more time, she cleaned his chest, rubbing over the wiry black hairs and flat copper nipples. She avoided his ribs and the gash on his abdomen but ran the cloth carefully around his erection and under his balls.

His eyes opened. They were dark with arousal, the black lashes spiky from the water. "You're evil, woman."

"Am I?" She finished by cleaning his penis, pulling back the foreskin and easing the cloth over the sensitive tip.

She'd started this because he needed the help. She'd continued because her animal reveled in the chance to touch him after all these months. And maybe because she *was* enjoying a little revenge.

"Yes. You're torturing me, and right now I can't do anything about it. And you know it."

He was right. She was a bad, bad woman. She turned away to conceal her smile.

"You don't have to wait for me," she said as she started to wash herself. "You must be exhausted."

A strong arm wrapped around her waist. Then his big body pressed against hers, his erection hard against her buttocks. She stilled, aware of him with every single one of her nerves.

"I'll go," he rasped against her neck. "Because I hurt too much to take you right now. And because you deserve a whole man, not one who's still recovering from too much drink and too many women. But we *will* finish this, Valeria. I meant what I said about claiming you. You're my mate, and I *will* win you back."

A shock of arousal raced over her skin, but she held herself stiff, refusing to let her spine unbend even a single inch. Because if she gave him that inch, she might surrender her whole self.

He waited for a few seconds and then when it was clear she wasn't going to reply, pressed his lips to her nape and released her. She waited until he was on the other side of the wall and then released the breath she'd been holding.

When she came out of the bathroom, Rui was already in bed. She considered sleeping with Merry, but if anything went wrong in the middle of the night, she'd never forgive herself. And she was safe enough with Rui—as he'd said, he wasn't in any condition to try anything tonight, and even if he were, he'd never take a woman against her will.

He was turned onto his injured side, which Branco had explained was the best for broken ribs, allowing for deeper breaths. He'd pulled up the sheet but she unfolded the simple blue-and-lavender quilt at the base of the bed and tucked it around him. She'd thought he was asleep, but he opened his eyes to look at her, his gaze soft with fatigue.

She flicked her fingers, turning off the fae lights. "Go to sleep. I'll wake you in a couple of hours." She didn't set an alarm, since like most fada, she had a natural internal clock.

As the lights faded to darkness, he touched her hand. "Thank you for letting me stay here."

She moved a shoulder. "It's the least I could do. After all, you wouldn't be hurt if it weren't for me and Merry."

"Is that all this is? Gratitude?" His voice was harsh.

"*Boa noite*, Rui." She rolled onto her side.

"*Boa noite,*" he replied and then muttered, "But we *will* finish this."

13

———

When Rui woke the next morning, Valeria was curled next to him, her fingertips touching his arm as if to assure herself even in sleep that he was all right.

He knew she'd been exhausted, but she'd dutifully awakened him every two hours throughout the night. Now she was sound asleep, one hand under her cheek, lips parted like a child's.

At some point she'd kicked off the covers. She wore clinging leggings that stopped at mid-calf and a grass-green tank that enhanced her warm-colored skin. His gaze traveled down her body with a hunger that was only partly sexual, taking in the dark curls tumbling over one smooth shoulder, the full breasts beneath the cotton tank, the sweet curve of her hip and her long, strong legs. The familiar heat filled his belly, but for now he was content to lie still and bask in her presence, breathing in her scent, listening to the soft sough of her breath.

Outside the apartment, he could hear footsteps as the several hundred fada who called the base home began to go about their business. But inside, all was quiet.

He let his eyes drift shut again, savoring a rare sense of peace and well-being. *Deus*, he was tired of spending himself in nameless women. He'd rather spend a sexless hour with Valeria than fuck another woman all night, only to rise from the bed wrung-out but restless, unsatisfied. And hungry...always hungry.

Eventually his body started making its needs felt. Reluctantly, he opened his eyes and stretched each arm and leg in turn, taking inventory. He was stiff and sore and feeling every blow, but Branco had been right, he was healing amazingly fast. The worst was the deep ache where he'd taken the knife.

He fingered the wound, disgusted with himself. Compared to him, the earth alpha was practically a kid; Adric should never have gotten close enough to cut him. If Rui hadn't been such a drunken, lazy ass the past couple of years, the other man would be dead now.

He pushed himself carefully to sitting. The pain had definitely eased. Pleased, he limped to the bathroom.

When he returned, Valeria was still asleep. He pulled the sheet up over her shoulders and got under it with her, lying on his side facing her. Long, sooty lashes fanned over her cheekbones. Her face appeared thinner than he remembered.

He frowned. The clan had been through some hard times, but Valeria and Merry should've had enough to eat.

He was ashamed to realize it had been months since he'd really looked at her. He'd been aware of her every moment they were in the same room, of course. But even when he hadn't been drinking, he'd avoided looking at her. Now it appeared she'd lost weight—and he feared it was due more to unhappiness than lack of food.

A fierce protectiveness gripped him. She was his mate. It was his duty to ensure she was safe, happy. And he'd done a god-awful job of it the past couple of years.

Valeria opened her eyes. "*Bom dia.*" Her lips curved.

His throat worked. It had been so long since she'd smiled at him like that—wide and happy. "Good morning."

Then she apparently remembered whom she was smiling at

and the happy curve faded. She propped herself on an elbow and looked him over with a clinical eye. "How're you feeling?"

"Better, thanks."

"That's good." She glanced toward the door. "I should get up. Merry—"

"No, wait." He snagged her hand. "There's no hurry. She's still sleeping."

She hesitated and then nodded. "We should talk, anyway—about Merry." She arranged herself cross-legged on the bed.

"Yes," he said and wondered why he was disappointed. Merry came first with Valeria, and that's how it should be.

He sat up and inched himself backward until his back was against the headboard, keeping his knees bent so as not to overtax his lower abdomen. Pain jolted through him anyway. He closed his eyes and sucked air in through his teeth.

When he opened his eyes, Valeria was frowning at him. "We don't have to do this right now—"

"I'd rather talk to you than lie on my back counting my bruises. Besides, I'm worried about Merry, too. I want to help."

"Okay." She rubbed her palms over her upper arms. "I don't know what to do, Rui. They want her. Not just Jace and Adric, but the woman, too—Marjani. You should've seen her when she first saw Merry. She looked so *happy*. And if Merry needs one of those crystals to be healthy—"

"I'm not sure they were telling the whole truth about that. They didn't lie, but Adric's a slippery SOB. And why should he tell us something that would help us keep Merry?"

"That's true." Hope lit her face.

"It's something to consider anyway. Now, tell me what happened that night after I got Merry away. I gather there was a fire?"

"That's what Dion told me. He figured it was safest for everyone if the Baltimore shifters believed Merry died in the fire. He thinks the night fae believed Merry was still inside the house, hiding. They used some kind of magic to make sure no one got out alive. The house burned to the ground in less than five minutes." Her voice cracked. "She—she wouldn't have stood a chance."

Rui's jaw hardened. "Bastards."

"I still think about it sometimes. If you hadn't been there—"

"Yeah," he muttered. "I was a frigging hero."

"You did save her."

"After killing her father."

"She didn't see you do that, though."

"No. But she did see him after. She tried to protect him—from me." His voice was harsh from the crust of self-loathing lodged in his chest. "But I guess when I saved her from the night fae, she decided I was someone she could trust. Maybe she figured it was them who killed him."

"Was she wrong?" Valeria asked. "About trusting you, that is?"

"No. I'd guard her with my life." He slanted her a look. "I've wondered why you didn't tell her the truth."

She glanced away. "What was the point? She'd only grow up hating you and that's not going to bring her father back."

He swallowed his disappointment. What had he expected? That Valeria would say she couldn't bear for Merry to hate him? She'd done her best to keep the two of them apart.

"I never thought she'd make friends with you," she added. "She looks on you as a sort of father, you know."

"I know." That he'd won Merry's trust was both a heavy weight and an incredible joy.

Her dark eyes lifted to his. "Don't let her down," she warned fiercely. "Because if you do—"

Hurt washed over him. "I'd cut off my own hand before I'd harm a hair on her head. Hell, if you knew how often I wished I could go back in time and change things somehow. Bring back her father—get them both away from the night fae. But I can't. All I can do is spend the rest of my life making it up to her." He lifted a shoulder. "I know I'm a poor second best as a dad, but I've been trying."

She sighed. "I know, Rui. And you're not a poor second best. You—you've made her feel safe again. She's been more at ease these past few months. Those nightmares I told the earth fada about? She hasn't had one since the two of you became friends."

"Yeah?" he asked, surprised and pleased. "I didn't know."

"She wants us to get back together." Valeria gave a short laugh. "Did you know that? I told her there's no way."

He leaned forward, setting a hand on her thigh to support himself while he used the other to cup her too-thin face. He caressed her cheekbone with his thumb. "Is it so impossible?"

"Yes. No. I don't know. I—" She halted, throat working, her expression registering such intense yearning that hope bloomed in him.

He brought his lips to hers, slowly, carefully. Giving her time to pull back if she wished. But she didn't. For a single sweet moment, her mouth pressed back against his. He ran his tongue over the seam of her lips.

"Let me in, sweetheart."

"No," she whispered. But her eyes remained closed, her lips a scant inch from his, so close he could feel the moist warmth of her breath, inhale her familiar earthy fragrance.

"No?" He brought his hand to one soft, full breast. The tank had a built-in bra, so there were only two thin layers of cotton between his fingers and her nipple. It hardened, and he pinched it gently, possessively.

Mine, the animal growled.

"Are you sure?" he murmured. He moved his hand to her other breast, massaging that nipple into a hard point as well.

Her breath shuddered in, and he scented the salty musk of her arousal.

Yes...

Then her eyes opened, and he was shocked to see they were

bright with tears. "No," she said again, and this time he believed her.

That momentary bloom of hope curled back in on itself, but it didn't die. He'd known this wasn't going to be easy. He'd hurt Valeria deeply and it would take time to win her trust again. But he refused to give up. Because she was worth it.

He removed his hands from her body. She pushed off the bed and turned away to knuckle her eyes. When she turned back, her chin was lifted in a way that warned him not to ask about the tears.

"About Merry," she said.

He reluctantly settled back against the headboard. "They're not going to find it so easy to take her back. Dion claimed her as a member of Rock Run, remember?"

"But she's a minor and we didn't have her clan's permission. Lord Adric could say we didn't have the right to claim her."

"So? Who's he going to complain to? A human court? They have no jurisdiction over fada. And the fae could care less if we quarrel among ourselves."

"He's rebuilding his clan, Rui. Sabela says they lost a lot of people during the past twenty years—even more than Rock Run did."

His lip curled. "Because we never turned on our own."

"Yes, but that means a child will be even more precious to them."

"That may be true, but Adric's not going to put his hands on Merry if I can help it. And I'm certain Dion will back me up on that."

She dragged a hand through her hair. "Maybe I should leave. I could take her to Portugal. Adric doesn't know which clan I belong to. He'll never—"

Rui's entire body went cold. "No," he said sharply. "You can't."

She lifted a brow. "Says who?"

"I do. We're mates, Valeria. You can't leave now." As soon as he spoke, he knew it was a mistake. It was too soon. But he refused to take back the words.

She sighed. "Not again, Rui. We covered this last night, remember? I haven't agreed to your claim."

"The discussion is not over."

Her brows snapped together. "It is now. *We're not mates.* Is that clear enough?"

"The hell we're not." It was his animal speaking. To the animal, this was simple. Valeria was the mate. She and Merry belonged with him. End of story.

Forgetting his injuries, Rui came off the bed and crossed the room in two strides. He gripped her arms. "You felt the bond, same as I did."

She looked away. "Did I?" Carefully avoiding a lie, he noticed.

"You did. We both did." He gave her a little shake. "You're my mate, damn it. I won't press the claim for now, but consider this your only warning. I'm going to do whatever it takes to win you back."

She narrowed her eyes. "You can try. You can shout it to the whole damn clan if you want. But it's my right to accept or deny the mate claim. Don't forget that."

He growled. Valeria blinked, but she didn't back down.

He eyed her with unwilling admiration. He was her dominant, and two years ago, she'd have folded in the face of his anger. But she'd changed. Maybe it was being forced to stand on her own for the past two years, maybe it was becoming a mother—or maybe it was both—but she'd matured into someone who wasn't afraid to stand toe-to-toe with him. He approved, although that didn't mean he wouldn't enjoy reminding her who was master in their bed.

But now was not the time.

He released her. "I haven't forgotten. But *you* should know that I'll do whatever it takes. You're mine, Valeria. I know I hurt you, and I'm more sorry than I can say. If I have to spend the rest of my life making it up to you, then I will. But I'm not giving up and I'm not going away."

Her black lashes came down. Shutting him out.

He felt a flicker of panic which he ruthlessly suppressed.

"It's not that easy," she said flatly and turned away.

He stared at her, willing her to look back at him, but she didn't. The rush of adrenaline that had taken him across the room drained away and he was abruptly aware of every still-healing bruise and assorted other aches. He limped his way back across the room and sat down heavily on the mattress.

Valeria bit her lip. "Rui—"

"If you don't tell Branco," he said with a rueful smile, "I won't."

She blew out a breath. "Just get back into bed."

He allowed her to arrange him with his back against the headboard again. He'd always hated fussing, but when it was Valeria, it was kind of nice. She placed a pillow behind his back. He leaned back with a sigh, more sore than he cared to admit.

Valeria set a cool wrist to his forehead. "You don't feel fever-ish, at least. But you should rest."

He caught her hand. "I will as soon as we finish this. Please, sit down and hear me out."

When she hesitated, he swore under his breath. "I only want to discuss Merry. The rest can wait until I'm better." He waited until she was sitting on the mattress again before continuing, "Leaving here with Merry would be playing right into Adric's hands. He has people watching the base. The moment you step off our territory, they'll grab her."

She gave a short nod. "I suppose you're right. We're safer here for now."

He let out a breath he hadn't known he was holding. "I'm sure of it. Dion will be back in a couple of days. We'll talk to him, see what he thinks. He may know of some way we can convince the earth shifters to leave Merry here—something we can trade, for instance."

"All right. I'll wait and see what he thinks. But *I'm* her mother." Valeria shot him a ferocious look. "Whatever Lord Dion decides, she's mine now. If Adric tries to claim her, I *will* take her and run. And no one will stop me. *No one.*"

"Val." He spread his hands. "If it comes to that, I'll take you myself. But give me some time, okay? Let me see what I can do. She's safe here. The Baltimore clan can't get to her, not in the base."

"But he got into the base once. What's to stop him from doing it in again?"

"He only did it with the sun fae's help—and that was to rescue Cleia. Otherwise, the sun fae couldn't care less about the fada. Trust me, Valeria, I lived with them. The fae—even the good ones—only help the fada when there's something in it for them. And besides, Cleia's mated with Dion now. That changes everything."

"Adric had sun fae help? I didn't know." She brightened, then shook her head. "But we can't hide Merry at the base forever. And what if they're right, that she needs one of those damn crystals?" She put a hand on his arm and lifted her eyes to his. "What are we going to do, Rui?"

"She does have problems shifting," he gently pointed out.

Her fingers dug into his skin. "You think I don't know that?"

He set his hand over hers. "We'll work it out, *querida*. I promise."

Running footsteps sounded in the hall. Valeria pulled away as a jaguar cub hurtled through the door, leapt onto the bed, and shifted. As usual, Merry's shift took longer than it should.

Valeria watched with a tiny frown between her eyes, but the little girl was grinning as she came out of it.

"Tio Rui! You're still here." Her smile faded as she took in his bruises. "I thought you'd be all better today."

"I *am* better," he said, reaching for her, "but I could use a hug."

As Merry obliged, he met Valeria's eyes over her head. He ached in places he didn't even know he had, his belly was throbbing again, and he was more worried about Merry than he was letting on.

But he couldn't stop that tendril of hope from setting roots in the soil of his heart. When the chips were down, Valeria had instinctively turned to him: last night at the festival, and again this morning.

What are we *going to do?* she'd asked.

They'd figure out this thing about Merry. And then, please *Deus*, Valeria would be his again.

By EVENING, Valeria could see that Rui was well on the road to healing.

Branco had stopped by after breakfast and confirmed that his patient was coming along nicely. "In fact," he told Rui, "you're doing even better than I expected. Tomorrow, change to your shark and go for an easy swim. The healing will go that much quicker."

They had spent a quiet day in the apartment, with Rui sleeping on and off. When he was awake, he'd played Go Fish with Merry or listened patiently to her endless chatter.

To Valeria's relief, he hadn't tried to have another serious conversation with her. She needed time to get used to this new Rui. One who wasn't drinking. One who seemed to truly regret what he'd put her through. One who wanted to make a family with her and Merry, and prove that he loved them both.

So, after eating dinner in the apartment, they ended up in a cozy tangle on the couch, Rui at one end, Merry cuddled up with Valeria at the other. She and Merry listened, enthralled, as Rui recounted stories of growing up in Portugal a hundred years ago. He'd come of age in the middle of World War II, and although the clan had moved to America in the mid-1930s, he and Dion had returned to work with the Portuguese fada who'd helped the Allies by sneaking food and goods past German blockades.

Valeria was wearing a sundress that left her legs and arms bare. Somehow her feet ended up on Rui's lap. As he described strapping explosives to his body and swimming out to attack a U-boat, he ran a hand up and down her bare calf. Her eyes slit with pleasure even as she cringed at the risks he'd taken.

"Did the boat blow up, Tio Rui?" asked Merry.

"*Sim.*" For a few seconds, his hand ceased stroking her calf as his gaze went inward. When he glanced at Valeria, his eyes were bleak. She suspected his orders had been to leave no survivors. It was one thing to blow up a boat, but to methodically hunt down injured, defenseless men...and Rui hadn't even been out of his twenties.

She instinctively leaned forward and touched his hand. Just touched it, but he let out a jagged breath and the moment passed.

"After the war," he told Merry, "all I wanted to do was forget all about it. I spent the whole summer as a dolphin, touring around the Mediterranean with Dion and a couple other males my age."

Trolling for females, Valeria thought dryly. But hey, he'd been a young, unmated man. That's what they did.

Merry was frowning at Rui. "But if you never went home, what did you eat?"

"Fish, of course."

"But how did you cook the fish?"

"We didn't. We ate it raw."

Merry wrinkled her nose. "Ew."

Rui raised a brow at Valeria. "We're going to have to introduce this child to sushi."

"What's that?" Merry asked suspiciously.

The two of them exchanged a smile over her head, and Valeria realized she was enjoying herself. "Yes," she replied, "we will."

Rui was massaging Valeria's foot now, starting at the top and then working around to the sole and back up. Her breath sighed out. She listened with half an ear as Merry continued asking questions about the war.

"Did the cats and wolves help, too?"

"There aren't any earth fada in Portugal," Rui replied. "But I heard the ones in North Africa and America were very brave fighters."

Merry nodded, satisfied.

Rui moved on to Valeria's toes, gently pulling each one in turn. Then it was time for her other foot, his fingers working her expertly, the pressure just right. She closed her eyes and gave herself up to the pleasure.

If this was how the man intended to win her back, she might just have to let him.

Beside her, Merry gave a huge yawn.

Valeria pulled her feet from Rui's lap. "Time for a snack. And then it's time for a bath, young lady."

As usual, Merry dragged out her snack time as long as possible, but Valeria was onto her tricks, and fifteen minutes later the little girl was in the bathtub. As Valeria added bubble bath, Rui wandered in.

He took a rueful look at his still-bruised face in the bathroom mirror. "Do you have a razor? I was too bruised to shave this morning." He rubbed a hand over the black stubble covering his jaw.

"There's one on the shelf at the left." She indicated one of the shelves chiseled out of the wall on either side of the mirror. "But you don't have to shave on our account."

She meant to sound matter-of-fact. But if he had any idea of how sexy he looked with that stubbled chin and wearing nothing but a white ribbed tank and the loose cotton shorts she'd retrieved from his apartment, then she might as well surrender here and now.

Their gazes met in the mirror. Rui's green eyes went smoky. His nostrils flared, and she knew he scented her arousal. She moistened her lips, unable to drag her eyes from his.

In the tub behind them, Merry squealed. "Mama, the water's running over!"

They both jolted. Valeria hurried the few feet to the tub to shut off the faucet.

Merry giggled. "Look, Mama. The water's up to my neck." She gazed up at them, her wet head emerging from the bubbles, an adorable sprite with sparkling eyes.

Valeria dropped a kiss on her nose as she knelt on the bathmat and reached for the washcloth.

To her surprise, Rui sat on the edge of the tub to help, handing Valeria the washcloth and soap and then carefully rinsing the shampoo from Merry's hair. The little girl played up to him, diving under the bubbles and coming up grinning, showing him how long she could hold her breath underwater, challenging him to a toy-boat race. He allowed her boat to beat his by a good two lengths.

Valeria's chest squeezed. Rui was so good with Merry. He was going to make a great father someday. She'd wondered...

Abruptly, she rose to her feet. "Time to get out, *princesa.*"

And when had she adopted Rui's nickname for Merry?

The little girl stuck out her lower lip. "Not yet, Mama."

"Merry," Valeria warned, but Rui grabbed a bath towel and scooped her out of the water.

"You heard your mama." He wrapped her in the towel. "Time for bed."

The imp gave in without a murmur. "All right. If you read me a book."

Rui glanced at Valeria, seeking her permission, and Merry poked her head out of the towel to say, "*Please*, Mama."

Valeria hesitated. Things were moving a little too fast for her.

Then she caught Merry's pleading gaze and wondered why she was fighting it. The little girl didn't cry for her daddy anymore, but the way she'd latched onto Rui told its own story. From what Valeria had pieced together, Merry had slept through the fight where Rui had killed her father. All she remembered was that he'd saved her from the bad men.

Night fae. Valeria shuddered to think what would've happened to Merry if they'd gotten ahold of her. The night fae fed on any energy, but they especially craved darkness: fear, despair, hopelessness. They'd have tortured her mercilessly.

"All right," she replied. "But just one."

The two of them exchanged a grin which she pretended not to see.

With Merry in bed, Rui took himself off to bed as well. "I'm sorry, *querida*," he said as he smothered a yawn, "but I'm half-asleep."

"Of course. You go ahead."

She took her time joining him, puttering around the apartment for another hour, straightening things up and then relaxing on the couch with a glass of wine. By the time she came to bed, Rui was asleep, but he woke up enough to tug her closer for a kiss.

"'Night, *boneca*."

Boneca had been his pet name for her. It was a little old-fashioned, meaning "baby" or "pretty woman."

Funny. When Petros called her baby, she hated it—but she'd never minded *boneca*.

She let her lips linger on his. She'd learned in the past two years that she was tough. She could work, raise a kid, survive and even do well in a clan far from home. But it was good to have Rui in bed with her, his spicy male scent wrapped around her like a comforting blanket.

She placed a hand on his just-shaved cheek. "*Boa noite.*"

He pressed a kiss to her palm. "Tomorrow," he murmured. "Tomorrow I'm going to start courting you. Like I should have the first time."

Without waiting for an answer, he closed his eyes and was asleep a minute later. But she lay there for a long time, wondering what she'd started.

14

_J_ace slammed his fist into his palm. "I can't believe those SOBs had Merry all this time. And here I thought she was dead—."

He paced across Adric's living room, so agitated his jaguar was a shadow on his skin, his voice more animal than human.

"I know." Dropping onto the couch, Adric spread his arms out along the back and regarded his friend.

This conversation had been two days coming. First, they'd brought Luc and Marjani to their head healer, where they'd passed a tense night waiting to make sure they'd recover. Marjani was home now, healing nicely but weak enough that she'd spent most of the day in bed.

With her out of danger, Adric had invited Jace to the spacious five-room den he'd carved out twenty feet beneath a run-down house leased to a drug dealer. The seedy setting—along with a powerful concealing spell—made for an excellent cover. Not even the most inquisitive fae—or rival fada—had been able to ferret out his home.

"I'm not any happier than you," he told Jace. "But Merry would probably be dead if it weren't for them."

Much as he hated Rock Run, he had to admit that the little girl had appeared healthy, if a bit thin.

Jace's fingers sprouted sharp claws. "Whose side are you on, anyway?"

Adric stiffened. "Yours, asshole. Now sit down and get control of your animal."

Jace hesitated long enough that Adric's own claws sliced out. Then the other man muttered an apology and dropped onto the couch.

"Just tell me one thing. Are you going to leave her there? Because—"

"Are you questioning me?" he asked in a soft voice. Jace might be a lieutenant and one of his oldest friends, but he was seconds from being slammed against the wall and taught a lesson about the respect due his alpha.

Jace averted his gaze. "No. I—it's just she's my only family, Ric."

Adric blew out a breath. "Hell, if it were Marjani's kid, I'd be just as bad. But she seemed happy enough, well-fed." Better than the last time Adric had seen her, actually—and wasn't that a kick in the balls? "And Jace? She called the woman Mama. She—Valeria—wasn't lying. Merry thinks of her as her mom."

"I heard. But damn it, she's an earth fada. She belongs with us. She's all I have left of Takira. And you saw—she didn't have a quartz."

"That's not unusual. I didn't find my own crystal until I was almost nine."

"I could give her a piece of mine. But we'd still have to train her how to use it."

"You could," he allowed. "But that's not the real issue."

Their eyes met. There were only a dozen or so earth fada clans in the entire world, and although for the most part they rarely interacted, they were all pledged to guard the secret of their quartz with their lives.

Because if the fae ever learned an earth fada could be controlled through their quartz, they were doomed. As it was, too many fae treated shapeshifters as their personal servants and errand boys. If they discovered the secret, they could turn the earth clans into slaves.

Adric would sooner slit his wrists than trust someone from Rock Run with their secret. There was too much bad blood between the two clans. And now Rock Run was allied with the sun fae.

No, Adric could never allow the secret to be shared with anyone from the river fada clan. Not even the woman raising Merry.

"We have to get her back." Jace's tone held a craving Adric understood all too well.

The Darktime had been years of terror and backstabbing, culminating in his betrayal by his own uncle, a man he'd once thought of as a second father. He and his small band of friends and family had survived only by digging in and protecting their own by any means possible.

He'd have wanted to claim Merry Jones as one of their own regardless. After all, she was Takira's daughter and Jace's niece. But seeing her had aroused his protective instincts. The too-big eyes in her thin, mobile face; the hair that, like Takira's, seemed to have a mind of its own; the way she'd strutted alongside the Rock Run woman, so clearly proud of her new dress.

His clan had so few young ones. Only a handful of cubs had been born during the Darktime, and of that handful, only a few had survived, dead of either starvation or murder at the hands of a rival faction. Leaving Merry behind had been one of the hardest things he'd ever done.

He squeezed Jace's shoulder. "We *will* get her back."

"How the fuck did they get her anyway?" his friend burst out. "I spent two years thinking she was dead. It was either that or go crazy, picturing Takira's little girl enslaved by a night fae. And now I find out she's been at Rock Run the entire time."

"I'd like to know that myself." Adric rose to his feet and went into the kitchen for some beer. "Merry is ours, Jace," he said as he handed him a can. "We'll get her back. I promise you that as both your alpha and your friend. But we can't just bust in there and drag her out. We need a plan."

"Like what?" Jace's hand tightened on the beer. "The clan's tried to break through their defenses before. You're the only one who ever got inside, and you had help from the fae."

"If I did it once, I can do it again. But it may not come to that. We'll patrol their outer boundaries, keep our eyes peeled. She's a cat. She needs to roam. Sooner or later, we'll have our chance. Meanwhile, promise me you won't do something stupid like try to break in there on your own."

Jace glanced away.

"I mean it," Adric said with all the dominance at his command. "Give me your word or I'll make it so you can't take a step outside this den."

He could do it, too, by keying his quartz to Jace's. He had an unusual amount of power for a man so young, power that had been honed by the hardship he'd endured. He preferred not to use it against his friends, but he would if it meant saving the other man's life.

Jace scowled. "Fine. You have my word. I won't try to break in there on my own."

The talk moved onto other things, but Adric knew he had only a few days to think of something before Jace moved on his own. He stifled a sigh. The man would end up dead or in some dank Rock Run cell, and it would be his, Adric's, fault.

Because if the Rock Run alpha had even half a brain—and he did, unfortunately—he would keep Merry close to home. In fact, that's apparently what the clan had been doing for years. He'd hadn't heard even a whisper of an earth shifter girl at Rock Run.

So to get her back, he and his lieutenants would have to infiltrate river fada territory. They couldn't get into the actual base, not with the concealing spell protecting it. But they could get close, watch where the sentries entered and exited.

And then they'd pounce.

~

Tiago's palms were sweating. He rubbed them on his shorts.

He'd been in hiding for the past ten days after leaving Dion and Cleia's mating ball in a panic. Now he'd returned to the base, but only to gather his things before leaving for good.

Dion *knew*.

He still felt sick when he let himself think about it. Not only had Tiago helped Cleia, he'd given the Baltimore earth alpha the location of Dion's quarters. When the sun fae teleported into Rock Run to rescue Cleia, Dion had been with her. If his brother had died, it would've been Tiago's fault.

Dion couldn't let that go unpunished. Tiago figured his brother had two choices—banish him from Rock Run, or order a quiet execution.

Rather than wait to find out which, Tiago had slipped away from the mating ball and gone to ground in the den of his friend Fausto, an otter whom Tiago had once saved from a trap. The patriarch of a large family, Fausto had been happy to give Tiago sanctuary, but he couldn't hide in his friend's den forever. His animal had been content, but the man needed to walk on two legs again, to speak in something besides grunts, chirps and squeals.

Worse, his mind was becoming hazy, the animal gradually taking control. And Tiago's animal was a dark and frightening beast.

Cleia should be ours, the beast whispered. *If Dion were dead...*

So Tiago had come home. In his otter form, he was large and obvious, his scent recognizable to those fada who knew him well. His dolphin would be equally recognizable, so he shifted to a form he almost never used—a rockfish. It had been years since he'd taken this form. It felt odd, his vision unusually sharp due to the fish's large eyes, his mind confused by the additional information coming in from the lateral line, a sensory organ that detected movement and vibrations in the water.

He was careful to stay deep underwater until he reached the base's marina, located on the Susquehanna River near the mouth of Rock Run Creek. Surfacing beneath the dock, he listened to the workers going about their chores. He soon learned that Dion had taken Cleia on a honeymoon, leaving Rui in command.

That was all he needed to hear. He swam downstream until he reached a hidden tunnel. Built as an emergency escape route, it exited in a pool in the alpha's bedroom, so was rarely used by anyone but the alpha and his family.

As he'd hoped, Dion's apartment was empty. He changed to man, snagged a pair of his brother's shorts, and was settling down to wait for evening when he caught sight of himself in the mirror and winced. His hair was a tangled black mass and stubble shadowed his face.

Well, that he could fix. He washed his hair and worked out the snarls before scraping it back into a ponytail, then used Dion's razor to remove the stubble. When he was done, he felt a little better, more in control.

He still had a half hour to kill until dinner, when the halls would empty as the clan gathered in the dining hall. He sat by the pool, his feet in the cool water, listening to the soothing flow of the waterfall that rippled down one wall.

The last time he'd been here, Cleia had been with him, her face and hair illuminated by a shaft of sunlight like an angel come down to earth. He'd been steeling himself to reach out and touch when Dion had come home and ordered him to leave. Treating him like a boy in front of the woman he loved.

Tiago's face heated. He should've stood his ground. Maybe then Cleia would've chosen him instead of his brother.

Dinnertime arrived, the scent of grilled fish making his mouth water.

Deus, he'd give anything to join the people making their way to the dining hall, to go back to the way things had been just ten days ago. But it was too late.

He waited until the halls grew quiet, then slipped through the base to his room where he filled a waterproof backpack with clothes and a few necessities. As he exited the room he came face to face with Chico.

He froze, but his friend merely grinned and clapped him on the back. "*Tiago*. Where the hell have you been hiding?"

Tiago relaxed a fraction. So his treachery wasn't widely known, although that didn't mean Dion hadn't told his top men.

He thought quickly. "My brother assigned me to scout the Baltimore shifters. There was a rumor at the ball that some of them are going to move against Lord Adric." He swallowed the bile that the lie induced.

"Yeah?" Chico gave him an odd look, and Tiago wondered if he'd scented the lie. "What did you find out?"

He shrugged. "Nothing." That much was the truth.

Chico glanced at the backpack. "Where are you off to now? Aren't you going to eat?"

Tiago hesitated. Sweat trickled down his spine. What reason could he give for leaving the base without having dinner? His stomach clenched at the thought of another lie, so he told a half-truth.

"There's this woman..."

"Human?" Chico's lips curved in a knowing smile.

"Mm. She has a thing for fada." Tiago edged backward, hoping Chico wouldn't scent his nervousness. "I promised to look her up when I wasn't so busy. But, Chico? My leave hasn't been officially approved. Can you forget you saw me?"

"Saw who?" was the reply.

"Thanks, man."

Tiago waited until Chico had turned the corner before heading back to his brother's apartment. A minute later, he was in the pool and strapping the backpack on. This time he shifted to dolphin. When he reached the river, he headed toward the Chesapeake Bay and from there turned south to Baltimore.

It was as good a place as any for a man to go to ground.

FROM BENEATH THE SURFACE, Rui watched Tiago shift to dolphin and then shoot away from the base. As Rui had healed, he'd taken Branco's advice and swum for hours each day, first as his shark and later as a man. Now he watched as Tiago disappeared downriver.

He could give chase, but he had a hunch this was for the best. Before leaving on his honeymoon, Dion had updated Rui on what had happened. An older man would've been banished—or even executed—but Dion hadn't wanted that, and Rui had agreed.

"I can't let him get away with it," Dion had told Rui. "But I can't send him away, or order his death. He's my *brother*. And so damn young. But what the hell am I supposed to do? He gave Adric the coordinates to my quarters—in the very heart of the base. The Baltimore alpha, for *Deus*'s sake. I can't ignore that. If anyone finds out, I'll be fighting off challengers for the next year."

Rui had wrapped his arms around his friend, shocked at how taut he was, a wire stretched close to breaking.

Dion exhaled. "I'd like to whip his ass for putting me in this position."

"Go on your honeymoon," Rui advised, releasing him. "Nobody knows but you and me."

"And Adric and Cleia and her bodyguards."

"And them," Rui acknowledged. "But they're not going to tell anyone at Rock Run. He's a fada male in his first heat. Remember us? Hell, I nearly caused a human-fada war."

"That's true." Dion chuckled. "My father was ready to ring your neck."

"But he didn't. He just made damn sure I never did anything like that again. Go on your honeymoon," Rui said again. "Take the time you need to get to know your mate. You can leave Tiago to me. If he shows up, I'll put him on kitchen duty. He's off-base without permission; that will be enough to explain why he's being punished. It will do him good to peel potatoes for a while. We did our share over the years."

They shared a wry smile, and then Dion nodded. "All right. I can't make a decision about him right now anyway. I'm too pissed off."

And hurt, Rui thought but didn't say.

He understood something of what his friend felt. Tiago was like a younger brother to him, too; he'd tagged along after the two of them from the time he could toddle. Rui felt the same anger and hurt as Dion—along with a healthy dose of regret. Because in the decade since Dion had become alpha and Rui his second, the two of them had focused on the clan and its troubles, leaving the raising of Tiago and little Rosana to elders like Isa, the creche workers or whichever warrior was in the base at the time.

Rui didn't see how they could've done it any differently, but still...

"Get out of here," he said. "And Dion?"

"What?"

"Don't worry about Rock Run. Luis and I can handle things. Enjoy your first few weeks as a mated man."

Dion's smile was very male. "I intend to."

Now Rui watched as, a quarter-mile downriver, Tiago's dolphin skimmed over a wave, a silver flash against the horizon.

Rui could send a couple of men after him, but what was the

point? Tiago was alive and staying close to home. That was enough for now.

The kid had made a serious mistake and deserved to be punished for it. But Dion was wrong. No one would expect him to execute a twenty-one-year-old, brother or not. Everyone knew a fada male in the throes of his first heat had the common sense of a guppy. When Dion got past his hurt and anger, he'd see that for himself.

Rui's stomach growled, reminding him it was time for dinner —and that Valeria and Merry would be waiting for him. He turned and headed back to the base.

15

"Mama?" Merry shot Valeria a winning smile as they entered the dining hall. "Can Tio Rui sit with us again tonight? Please?"

"It's up to him, sweetheart. He might not want—"

"Oh, he will." She skipped off to play.

Valeria gazed after her, a tiny frown between her eyes. Things had been quiet the past couple of weeks, but Valeria didn't fool herself that Lord Adric had given up.

Rui had arranged a meeting with Dion before he left on his honeymoon so that Valeria could explain what had happened. Dion had assured her that Merry was a member of the Rock Run Clan now and that he'd fight any attempt by the Baltimore shifters to take her back.

"This thing with the crystal—" He shook his head. "But Merry's okay for now, right?" When Valeria replied in the affirmative, he said, "So we have some time to figure this out. Let me see what Cleia thinks. She's spent her whole life working with energy —she may know something."

"Good idea," Rui said.

Valeria's jaw tightened. The last thing she wanted was to bring the queen into this, but this wasn't about her, it was about Merry. "I'd be grateful," she forced herself to say.

"Meanwhile," the alpha continued, "don't leave the base without a guard—not even to crab or fish. And keep Merry close to home. They might sense she is here, but they won't be able to find her—not with the concealing spell Cleia had Lady Olivia cast for us. The only way Adric and the sun fae got into the base in the first place was with Olivia's help."

Valeria nodded. It was a relief to know that Adric couldn't come and go at will. But—"How did Adric know where to find the queen? I heard he and the sun fae teleported straight into your quarters."

"They had help," was the grim reply. A shadow passed over Dion's face, and she wondered who it could've been, to make his expression so bleak. "But, Valeria? No one is to know. Understand? I promise you, Merry is safe. The man is no longer at Rock Run—and he won't be returning."

Rui shifted as if in protest but remained silent. Valeria ducked her head. "Of course."

Dion waited another few days until Rui was well on the road to recovery, then left him in charge with Luis as second and departed on his honeymoon. Meanwhile, Rui moved back into his own apartment. He hadn't wanted to leave, but he was too smart to push when he saw he was making her uncomfortable.

But he was courting her as promised. Bringing her flowers and a large box of her favorite chocolates. Inviting her to the regular Saturday night shows put on by the base's musicians and poets. Joining her and Merry at meals.

She couldn't help enjoying it, even as she waited for the other shoe to drop, afraid to trust that he really did want her.

She returned to work. She loved her long, solitary mornings on the river, and now she needed them even more as she tried to decide what to do about Rui. When she'd first decided to remain at Rock Run, she'd asked one of the clan's old watermen to teach her his trade, and it turned out she had a Gift for it.

She crabbed in the old way—baiting a line with a chicken neck and dragging it along the river bottom or a shallow part of the bay, and then, when a crab latched on the bait, scooping it up with a hand net. Her Gift allowed her to nudge water animals like crabs or fish to move in any direction she wished. It had come in handy during the recent dark years as the river's fertility declined. With her Gift, she could usually be counted on to bring in a decent catch.

Although there'd been no sign of the Baltimore shifters since the confrontation in the cherry grove, Rui made sure she obeyed Dion's order to either take a guard or stay within sight of the base's marina. Today she'd chosen to crab alone in a small inlet a few hundred yards downriver from the marina. She hadn't gotten much further in her thinking about Rui, but with the help of her Gift, she'd caught four bushels of crabs, to the cooks' delight.

After lunch, she got Merry from the creche and they'd spent the afternoon playing in the creek along with some other parents and their pups within the protection of the concealing spell.

Back at their quarters, they changed and headed to the dining hall, where Merry darted off to play with Trina. All Valeria wanted to do was relax with her friends and a glass of wine until dinner was served, but the moment she was alone, Petros approached, smiling as if they'd never had that argument at the midsummer festival.

"Hello, *glika*. I've missed you." His black gaze traveled down her body.

"Have you?"

She turned away, but he grabbed her arm and hustled her out a side door into a narrow, little-used hall. She allowed it only because she didn't want the whole clan witnessing them arguing.

He crowded her so that her back was against the wall. "We need to talk."

"I have nothing to say to you," she said through tight lips. She made to pass him, but he slapped his palms on either side of the wall next to her, caging her in.

"No?" He traced a finger down her cheek.

She swatted his hand away. "We're through, remember? There's plenty of other women who'd be happy to—"

"So I got mad." His dark eyes were watchful. "I'd like to make it up to you. Some friends and I are having a party, and I want you to come."

"No. Now let me go." She tried to push past him, but he gripped her chin.

"'No?'" he asked.

She felt a prickle of unease. "No," she repeated more forcefully.

His eyes narrowed. She forced herself to hold his gaze; she was damned if she'd let him see she was afraid. But he knew. She couldn't stop her body from scenting the air with her fear.

He smiled, a slow, cruel stretching of his lips. "I'm going to enjoy taming you, *glika*."

A hand clamped on her nape and his mouth descended on hers in a hard kiss. She tried to turn her head but he pinned her against the wall, his lips grinding painfully against hers. His free hand caught her camisole, shoving it up above her breasts.

She hissed and pushed at his hand, but he gripped her wrist and squeezed. Pain shot up her arm. She jerked her arm but he just squeezed harder. He glared into her eyes, his dominance beating against her, dark and oppressive, willing her to submit. She instinctively averted her eyes, but she didn't stop fighting, her animal scared but determined. He might be stronger than her, but using dominance to force someone to submit sexually was forbidden, against fada *tradição*—besides being just plain wrong.

Somehow she managed to get her other hand between them. Her claws sliced out, digging through his shirt into his skin.

Petros reared back. "You *bitch*." He glanced in disbelief at the blood spotting his shirt.

She took advantage of his distraction to escape.

Her hand was on the door to the dining hall when he said, "This isn't over, Valeria. I just might make a mate claim for you. Who do you think would win—me or do Mar?"

She froze. The last thing Rui needed was to fight a mate-duel right now. He was much better, but he had a way to go before he was back to full strength.

And frankly, she didn't trust Petros to fight fair. He could easily corner Rui somewhere and slip a knife into him with no one the wiser.

"You could. But even if you won, I'd still have to accept you— and that will never happen." She pushed open the door. As she stepped inside, she looked back at him and deliberately drew her hand across her mouth. "And, Petros? No one *tames* me. No one."

His mocking chuckle followed her into the dining hall.

Valeria shut the door with a snap and leaned against it. Her anger was mixed with shock. *Who was this man?*

She'd thought she'd gotten to know him in the weeks he'd been at Rock Run, but apparently not. If this was his true self, she'd had a lucky escape.

Dinner was just being served. Merry was already seated at a table with Sabela and her parents, and Sabela's sister, Carla. Rui, thank *Deus*, was just coming in the main entrance and had missed the whole thing.

Valeria took a deep breath and headed across the cavern. Rui reached the table just before her. He hugged Merry, then set her back on the bench before dropping a kiss on Valeria's lips.

"*Como vai, querida?*"

"Not bad," she returned—which was ambiguous enough to not count as a lie. "And you?"

She sat down next to Merry, with Rui on her other side. Just having his big, solid body next to her helped calm her. The taut-ness eased from her shoulders.

But she should've known she couldn't fool him. He caught her chin, turning her to face him. "Are you sure you're all right?"

"Why wouldn't I be?" With difficulty, she met his gaze.

His thumb came to her lower lip, rubbing gently. It was sore from the kiss Petros had forced on her, but she kept still, not wanting Rui to ask why. He'd go after Petros, and he wasn't ready.

His nostrils flared. "Why do I smell Okeanos on you?"

Valeria shrugged, knowing he'd scent a lie. "He was just saying hello." That was stretching the truth, but it would do.

Rui's face hardened. "Why don't I believe that was all that happened?" He looked around for Petros, but he hadn't returned to the dining hall. He growled. "The man has overstayed his welcome."

She sighed. "Leave it. He means nothing to me. He knows not to do it again. If he does, you'll be the first to know. All right?"

He regarded her, brow furrowed, before reluctantly nodding. "All right. But you'll tell me if he tries anything." It wasn't a request.

"I will."

After that, the talk turned to other things and when Petros re-entered the hall—wearing a different shirt, she noticed with a hint of satisfaction—he had the sense to sit on the other side of the cavern.

"Eat." Rui set a round of crusty bread smeared with olive tape-nade on her plate. "You're too thin, *boneca*." The words were prac-tical, but his green gaze caressed her, warm and protective, and she put Petros Okeanos out of her mind.

When dinner ended, Rui walked her and Merry back to the apartment. When they reached the door, Merry pulled him inside to see the house she was building for her clown from rocks and scraps of wood. Rui listened patiently as the little girl gave him a tour of the rooms she'd finished thus far. But when Merry wound down, he drew Valeria back into the hall.

She eyed him. He'd been working out. His body was nearly back to its hard, toned self, his shoulders broad beneath his moss-colored shirt. Her gaze fixed on the strong column of his throat. She wanted to set her lips *there*, at the sensitive spot just under his jaw.

He inhaled and she knew he'd scented her arousal. He fingered one of her curls. "Ask me to come back later. After Merry's asleep."

She rested her head against the wall. Each night for the past week, he'd asked a variation of the same thing: *Invite me in, Valeria.*

Gods, it was hard to keep telling him no, but she shook her head. "I'd better go. Merry—" But her feet remained planted where they were.

"Valeria." He touched her arm. "I—can't you at least give me a chance?"

Something in her broke. She was already on edge from the confrontation with Petros, and now the hurt and shame and anger she'd carried around ever since he'd left her for Cleia erupted.

"*A chance?* You had twelve months of chances. Even last year, after you came back, I would've—" She flushed and shook her head. "But you didn't even try to get me back, Rui. You didn't even try. So tell me why the hell I should give you another chance now."

He took a deep breath. "You're right," he admitted. "But did you ever ask yourself why?"

"I—of course I did."

"And—?" His gaze was intent.

"I thought what everyone else did. That you didn't really want me."

"No." Sorrow crossed his face. "*Deus*, no. Never that."

"Then why?" She couldn't keep the anguish from her voice.

"Because." His throat worked. "Because I didn't deserve you. Not just because of Cleia, although that was bad enough. Because I'm dark inside...cold. A killer. And you, you're warm and loving and full of life. I felt it, Valeria. I felt you recoil me that night I killed Merry's father—and then you told me to leave. And you were right. I—"

Tears stung her eyes. She swiped them angrily away. "You *ass*."

He blinked. "What?"

"I said, you ass."

"I heard you. I just don't—"

"Then *listen*." She slapped a hand onto his chest. "Killing Merry's father was wrong and we both know it. But I also know you took that job for the clan, and that Dion approved it."

"What are you saying?" He caught her wrist, his gaze searching hers.

"I'm saying that I didn't know the whole story. You were my mate, Rui. All right, so I recoiled, told you to leave. But I hadn't been at Rock Run that long—I didn't know how bad things were, that you only took that job because there was no other choice. You should've talked to me, explained. We would've worked it out."

"It wasn't just that." He seemed determined to lay everything before her. "It was like I said. You're not just beautiful outside, Valeria. You're beautiful inside. You weren't here a month before you had everyone loving you—from Dion on down. But me...I'm a shark, Valeria. My animal is a cold-blooded killer. People respect me, but they don't go out of their way to spend time with me."

She shook her head. "You ass," she repeated, more softly this time.

"You said I didn't even try. Well, I'm trying now. But I need you to meet me halfway. Hell, I'll go more than halfway if it means I win you back. But I have to have something from you. *Something.*"

His eyes burned into hers, asking—no, pleading. But when she didn't say anything, his shoulders slumped. "I'd better let you go inside. Merry—"

She stopped him with her hand on his arm. His gaze snapped to hers, and for a long moment, she looked into his eyes. Recalling the promises he'd broken. Recalling him with his arm around Beatriz just a couple of weeks ago, the two of them rank with sex.

But she also knew he was trying, with his sweet, dogged courtship, when she knew he wasn't a candy-and-flowers man. And then there was that rush of love and longing she'd felt in the clearing.

Her mouth opened before she'd truly made up her mind. But it was only because her animal knew what she wanted before she did.

"Merry and I are going on a picnic tomorrow. Why don't you come with us?"

Rui's eyes widened. Then he smiled. "What time?"

16

———

The next morning, Rui had just reached Valeria's apartment when he saw Okeanos coming from the opposite direction.

He scowled. He knew damn well the other fada didn't have any business in this hall. As an outsider, Okeanos was assigned to a special guest section. Rock Run welcomed travelers from around the world, but they weren't stupid. No stranger would be assigned to a section with families and unmated females.

He deliberately put himself in the other man's path. "What do you want?"

Okeanos returned his scowl. "I'm here to see Valeria."

"She's busy today. But I'm glad you're here. We need to talk, you and me."

The other man hesitated before giving a short nod. It was clear he disliked having to submit to Rui, but he was a guest and whatever his rank in his own clan, in Rock Run he was under Rui.

"I don't want any trouble," Okeanos added grudgingly.

"No trouble. Walk with me, please." Rui strolled away from Valeria's apartment back toward the base's main area, and

Okeanos was forced to follow. "I've been looking for you. I tried to find you last night."

After leaving Valeria, he'd gone looking for Okeanos. It was time the man understood that she was permanently off-limits. But the sea fada had left the base.

Uneasiness flickered across Okeanos's face. "I was out."

Rui couldn't help wondering about the uneasiness, but guests were free to come and go as they pleased. "This way, please."

He led the way into an empty conference room and faced the other man. "Look," he growled, "Valeria's mine. My woman, my mate. The next time I see you within ten feet of her, I'm going to kick your ass. Don't talk to her. Don't bring her gifts. Don't even sit at the same fucking table. Is that clear?"

Okeanos stiffened. "She's not yours until she accepts the mate claim."

Rui growled. "She will," he bit out. "Meanwhile, stay the hell away from her. Better yet, go home. As far as I'm concerned, you've overstayed your welcome."

Okeanos's gaze was a flat, hard obsidian. Rui had heard his primary animal was a Mediterranean moray, and at that moment, he knew he was facing the cold-eyed eel, not the man.

But Rui's animal was an equally cold-eyed shark. It moved restively, urging Rui to kick Okeanos out of Rock Run.

Unfortunately, Rui couldn't do that without a good reason and the other man had been careful not to give him one.

"No," Okeanos said after a pause that was just short of insulting. "I don't think so."

Rui's jaw tightened. "What do you mean?"

"It means no. I'm not going to leave. I like it here."

"Fine." Rui felt the animal in his own gaze. "I can't force you to leave. But stay away from Valeria—she doesn't want you. If you make any further attempts to court her, I'll view it as a challenge."

Okeanos lifted a shoulder, let it drop. "Whatever you say." He stalked out of the room.

Rui stared after him. If only he could toss the SOB out on his ass. But *tradição* forbade it. Once Dion had extended the clan's hospitality, Okeanos had as much right to remain at Rock Run as Rui himself.

And the man was right. Valeria wasn't Rui's until she accepted his claim, and everyone knew it.

He'd been looking forward to the picnic ever since last night, but now he wondered if it was as big a step as he thought. Maybe she'd asked him out of pity—or for Merry's sake.

He slammed the edge of his fist against the wall, then stood there, head down and one arm against the cold stone. He'd spent two weeks courting the woman and she was still as closed to him as ever.

What was holding her back?

The first time it had been so easy. The two of them had connected almost instantly. He hadn't given her pretty words, just told her in raw, blunt language how much he wanted her. Fortunately, she'd felt the same way and by the end of the first week, he had her in his bed.

She hadn't seemed to want or need to be courted. "I can read your heart in your eyes," she'd told him.

He'd been poised above her body, ready to enter her. "*Sim?*" he'd replied, a little uncomfortably. He was still getting used to this mating business. "What does it tell you?"

Her lips had curved. "That you're mine. And I'm yours."

His heart had constricted.

To hide his confusion, he buried his face in her neck and began to move in her. "Read this," he growled against her soft, sweet-smelling skin. "It's saying I want to fuck you." He punctuated his words with a firm thrust.

She chuckled lowly and twined herself around him as if she'd never let him go.

Deus, he'd been an ass to throw that away.

He shook his head and left the conference room. He needed a

drink. Now. Instead of continuing to Valeria's apartment, he turned toward the base's wine cellar.

He was halfway there when he pulled himself up short.

No, damn it. She asked you to a picnic. This is your chance, asshole. Don't blow it.

He wrenched himself around and strode to his room, where he gulped down two glasses of water in quick succession. He'd thought he'd mastered the craving, but it clawed his gut, as bad as it had ever been.

He bent his knees and clenched his fists, sweat beading his forehead, battling for control with every ounce of willpower he could summon. The wave crested, leaving him sucking in breaths. He got another glass of water and washed his face with trembling hands.

Then he sank to his knees and asked whatever gods there were to help him win Valeria, once and for all.

Because without her, all the denial, all the training he'd put himself through until his muscles shrieked for mercy, all those damn glasses of grape juice when he thirsted for just one sip of wine, all those dark hours in the middle of the night when he ached for his woman but forced himself to stay away from her until he'd mastered his demons...without her, all of it was for nothing.

VALERIA WAS PACKING her knapsack for the picnic when Rui knocked. Merry was at the door in a flash.

"*Bom dia*, Tio Rui!"

"Hello, *princesa*." He swung her into his arms with the smile he reserved just for her, and Valeria found her lips curving as well.

He turned to Valeria, taking in her short green-and-white flowered sundress with very male approval. "Ready?" he asked, but before she could reply, he used his free arm to pull her close for a kiss.

As their lips touched, something dark flashed along the mate bond, so quickly she couldn't identify it—danger? Anger? Fear?

She searched his face. "Are you all right?"

His expression was almost too bland. "I am now."

She nodded, not wanting to press him in front of Merry. After slipping on a pair of sandals, she picked up the knapsack and together, the three of them headed for the marina to check out a dinghy. Although it had a small outboard motor, Rui took the oars.

Valeria directed him upriver to one of the small, uninhabited islands on the Susquehanna that were part of Rock Run's territory. "We can picnic on the beach, and Merry can practice her swimming."

"Sounds good." He turned the dinghy toward the island.

Merry was thrilled to be on an outing with her favorite male and chattered the whole way to the island. Rui listened indulgently, but gazed alertly around him as he pulled on the oars. Valeria knew a part of him would always be the hard-eyed assassin, and right now she found that reassuring.

She hadn't forgotten Lord Adric and his flat bronze eyes, even though he seemed to be lying low for now.

Two seagulls screeched nearby, fighting over a fish. Merry whipped her head around and went silent, staring fixedly at the gulls, her nose twitching.

"Cats," Valeria mouthed at Rui, and they both grinned.

They reached the island and climbed out of the dinghy. Merry shifted to her jaguar and got down to the serious business of climbing trees. Valeria felt a twinge of guilt, watching her. Her cat needed to be outside, running, climbing trees, learning all the things a cat needed to know. A river fada would happily spend most of his or her time in caves or the water, but earth shifters needed land and space to play.

Rui shook his head. "Cats and trees, huh?" He and Valeria shared another grin.

Like two proud parents. The idea was both strange—and exciting.

Rui's eyes narrowed and he stalked closer. "But on the other hand, it gives me the chance to do this." Taking her shoulders, he kissed her, long and deep.

"*Deus,*" he muttered against her mouth. "Do you know how much I want you?"

"Mm." She pressed a kiss to his jaw, already shadowed with stubble even though she could tell he'd shaved that morning. He'd shucked his T-shirt in the dinghy, leaving him clad only in a pair of shorts, his upper body tanned and fit from all the swimming he'd been doing.

She slid a hand between them, tracing his scar. It felt cool, the raised line barely detectable. "It's healing well."

"Is it?" He nuzzled her hair, traced the shell of her ear with his tongue.

She forgot about his injuries as she moaned and slid her hands up his abdomen, enjoying the feel of his taut, sun-warmed skin beneath her fingers.

Then she remembered that shadow on the mate bond earlier. She drew back to scrutinize his face. "Something was wrong this morning."

He hesitated, and she tensed. If he held back from her now, she wasn't sure there would ever be a chance for them.

"I had a talk with Okeanos. Told him to stay away from you."

She let out a breath. "Is that all?"

"You don't mind?"

She gave an emphatic shake of her head. "Petros and I are through."

"Good." His tone was forceful, even arrogant, but she could hear the relief beneath it.

"But that wasn't all, was it?"

"No." He glanced away. "Sometimes I'm afraid," he admitted lowly. "That I fucked up too bad for you ever to forgive me."

She swallowed. The part of her that had never stopped loving him wanted to reassure him, tell him not to worry, everything was okay. But even though they'd both come a long way in the past couple of weeks, she wasn't ready to trust him with her heart. And he'd scent a lie.

"I don't know if I can either," she said. "But I'm trying. Don't give up on me, okay?"

"Never." He cupped her cheek with one hand. "As long as you don't give up on me."

"Let's just take it one day at a time, all right?"

"All right." He rested his forehead against hers. "And thank you, Valeria."

His hand came to her nape, the other sliding down to her ass, fitting her body to his as he sealed their agreement with a slow, sweet kiss. Her breasts pressed against his chest through the thin cotton dress, his erection hard against her belly. Arousal spiked through her, a hot, liquid ache that made her undulate against him.

"*Deus*," he breathed against her lips, and it was a prayer.

She had her leg twined around his, her hands caressing his shoulders when he muttered, "Hell. Merry's coming."

He turned so that his arm was around her waist and they were facing the tree by the time the little jaguar came into view leaping joyfully from branch to branch as she made her way back to the ground.

Valeria drew a breath, trying to calm her racing heart. Her gaze went to Rui's. His eyelids were half-shut, the irises a smoky green.

"Don't look at me like that," he said with a playful slap on her bottom.

She rested her hand on his own butt and squeezed. "Like what?" she asked innocently.

"Like you want to eat me up—or maybe be eaten, hm?" He gave her ass another smack before moving away to catch Merry as she leapt the last few feet to the ground. "How about lunch, *princesa?*"

He bent his dark head next to her furry gold-and-black one. She rubbed against his cheek and then curled up in his arms in a relaxed little ball.

Valeria felt a shock of yearning. She *wanted* this—Rui in her life—for her and Merry both.

She swallowed hard and knelt down on the plaid blanket she'd brought to set out the picnic. Merry downed a tuna fish sandwich and a peach, washing it down with a glass of cold milk from the thermos Valeria had packed.

Rui filled a plate for Valeria, then coaxed her to eat every bite. "I like something to hold onto in bed," in a low, wicked voice that had her face heating.

"I am hungry," she admitted as she accepted the peach slice he was urging on her. "It must be the fresh air."

He took a slice for himself. "And the company, no?" He slanted her a grin that reminded her of the old Rui and popped the morsel into his mouth.

With lunch over, Merry stretched out in the sun and fell asleep, while Valeria and Rui dozed on the blanket nearby in the shade.

Valeria was dozing off when Rui said her name. "Yes?" she said without opening her eyes.

He brushed his fingers down her cheek. "I just want to be clear on something. I'll never give up on you, not if I have to wait a hundred years."

She opened her eyes to see him looking down at her, his gaze so tender it made her breath hitch.

His voice deepened. "You're mine, Valeria. My woman. My mate. I'll do my best to be patient, but I won't change my mind."

Her heart skittered. She was too honest to call it fear. Hearing him call her his mate in that low, intense voice sent a thrill through her entire being.

She set a hand on his bare chest and leaned in to kiss him. She didn't often touch him first, and his body stilled. She could feel his heart beating beneath her palm, but he remained still save for parting his lips so that she could slide her tongue into his mouth.

Her bones softened and she melted against him. Goddess, she loved his taste: dark, sexy male.

A few yards away, Merry let out a sleepy sigh. Reluctantly, Valeria moved back to her side of the blanket. He caught her fingers and brought them to his mouth, his gaze on hers the entire time. Her lips parted and she almost gave in right then.

Fortunately—or unfortunately, depending on how you viewed it—he released her hand and rose to his feet.

"How about a swim, *princesa?*" he called to Merry.

Her eyes popped open. She gave a long, very catlike-stretch—arching her spine, extending her small spotted paws—and then the air shimmered and sparked as she changed to girl.

"Last one in's a rotten egg!" she shouted and dashed for the water.

The swim developed into a lesson. Valeria floated alongside, marveling at how easily Rui kept her sometimes-willful daughter on task, so that by the end of an hour Merry was swimming ten yards on her own.

"Look, Mama," she called proudly and launched herself through the water, skinny arms and legs churning.

Valeria caught her in a big hug. "You're doing great."

Merry's smile lit up her face. "Here I go!" She propelled herself back to Rui.

He caught her and dipped her beneath the water. She came up grinning, and the swimming lesson was forgotten as the two of them took turns trying to dunk each other.

Valeria shook her head at them, but inside things were rearranging themselves. For the first time, she could see the three of them as a family.

Rui glanced at her and something in her expression made him halt, an arrested look on his own face, allowing Merry to sneak up on him from behind and wrap her wiry little arms around his neck.

With much giggling on Merry's part, he slid beneath the water's surface, pretending she'd finally dunked him. After that, the two of them ganged up on Valeria and they all played in the water for another hour until they returned to the island, breathless with laughter.

They had just gotten into the dinghy when Valeria's nape prickled. She slowly turned her head. What she saw made her mouth Rui's name.

"Behind us," she said and jerked her head toward the woods, where a black jaguar was staring boldly back. Jace Jones.

Merry was on the bench beside her. Her head whipped around and she made a small, scared noise.

The jaguar remained where he was for a long moment before fading into the trees.

Rui swore under his breath. "How the hell did he get past the sentries?" They were still on Rock Run territory, even though they were outside the protection of the spell.

"I don't know," Valeria said between cold lips as she wrapped her arms around Merry. "But I don't like it."

"Mama?" The little girl hid her face in Valeria's shoulder. "I don't wanna go with Uncle Jace."

Rui had already started the outboard motor. "Don't worry, sweetheart," he told Merry as they moved away from the island at a speed that seemed too slow to Valeria, although rationally she knew it was faster than a jaguar could swim. "He won't follow us into the river. He knows he can't catch us. And even if he tries, a sentry will stop him."

Merry sniffed, and Valeria tightened her grip on her. "He's right."

"Look at me," Rui commanded. When Merry obeyed, he said, "Nobody's going to take you anywhere you don't want to go. You've got my word on that—okay?"

She gave him a wobbly smile. "Okay."

Valeria squeezed her. "We'll be home in a few minutes, sweetheart."

Merry nodded against her chest and burrowed closer. But Valeria could feel Jace's gaze on her neck. How had he found them? She'd only picnicked on that island a few times before, and not at all in the past month.

Or had Jace been out there every day, waiting and watching? She'd never glimpsed even a trace of him before. Had he *wanted* them to see him today?

She suppressed a shiver.

Rui caught her eye and gave her a reassuring smile, but the knot between her shoulders didn't ease until they were safely back inside the base.

17

Rui grunted and heaved himself from the river.

A month had passed since the midsummer ritual. As his body healed, he'd begun to push it, spending hours each day swimming as both shark and man. He'd also started training with the warriors again.

Protecting Valeria and Merry had been all the motivation he needed. His body was lean and hard again, and the exercise kept the craving for drink to a manageable level. He suspected the thirst would always be there, but he was learning to deal with it.

Never again would he let himself be reduced to half a man. If that meant he had to guzzle juice for the rest of his life, so be it.

Meanwhile, Valeria was driving him crazy in slow, tortuous increments. She'd let him back into her life, but treated him more like a friend than her mate. He sat with her and Merry at meals and spent most of his free time. The three of them even went swimming together since he'd discovered that Merry's jaguar loved waters.

I need time, she'd said.

Meanwhile, a month had passed with nothing but a few hot kisses. But if he pushed for more, she withdrew.

Take it slow, he told himself for the umpteenth time. *She has to learn to trust you again.*

Sometimes he wondered if it was a test, with a dose of punishment thrown in for good measure. And the gods knew, he deserved it.

But he found it increasingly hard to resist dragging her into his arms and showing her that both man and animal had only so much patience...

On top of that, the Baltimore shifters were still sniffing around. Rui had lit a fire under the butts of the sentries responsible for the part of the Susquehanna where he and Valeria had seen Jones, but it wasn't entirely their fault. The earth fada were clever bastards. Since that day on the island, the sentries had spotted Jones two more times, but both times, he'd managed to slip away without being caught.

Thank *Deus*, Dion was due back from his honeymoon tomorrow. Rui couldn't wait to turn the business of running the base over to him so that he could focus on Valeria and Merry.

Now, he pulled on a T-shirt and shorts and headed to the dining hall. Dinner was being served, the clan seated at the oak plank tables set with heaping platters of fresh trout and spicy blue crabs.

"Tio Rui!" Merry waved at him from across the room.

He nodded back as Valeria sent him a smile over her shoulder. "*Olá*," she mouthed before turning back to her friend Sabela.

"Rui!" said a cheerful voice about level with his waist. It was little Xavier, completely healed and back to causing trouble.

"*Sim*?" He grinned down at the curly-haired boy.

He tugged on Rui's shorts. "Pick me up."

Rui obediently swung him onto his shoulders. Luis and Marina had just entered the dining hall. His cousin was back to his old self—and from the way he kept disappearing with his mate, Rui suspected Xavier would soon have a little brother or sister. Luis was a lucky dog.

The small boy sent them a disgusted look. "Mama was kissin' Papa again. They're always doin' that." Grasping Rui's ear to keep his balance, he leaned forward to scrutinize his big cousin suspiciously. "Can I eat with you, Tio? You don't do any of that kissin' stuff, do you?"

Rui grimaced. *Not nearly enough.*

Luis and Marina reached them in time to hear their son's question. "Xavier," scolded his mother, but Luis just chuckled.

"Of course he does. And when you're all grown up, you will too."

The little boy screwed up his nose. "No way."

All three adults chuckled, then Luis reached for his son. "Come here. Tio Rui has enough to do without keeping an eye on a rascal like you."

Rui handed the boy over, and Luis and Marina moved on to talk to some friends. A server—one of the teens—appeared with a glass of juice. Rui thanked him and took a drink.

As he took a sip, Beatriz planted herself in front of him. "*Olá,* Rui." She cupped his face and gave him the traditional kiss on each cheek.

"Hello," he returned warily. Beatriz didn't seem to have gotten the message that he was off-limits.

She placed a hand on his chest and slanted him a look from under thick black lashes. "I've missed you, *querido.* Why don't you stop by for a drink after dinner?"

Removing her hand, he glanced at Valeria. Fortunately, her back was to them.

"Thank you, but no. I'm sticking to juice these days." He indicated the glass in his hand.

"I'll make coffee then."

He shook his head. "Look, Beatriz, you should know I'm courting Valeria."

"*Sim?*" Her scarlet lips curved in an irritating little smile. "Does Petros Okeanos know?"

He shrugged. "It's not a secret."

But his jaw tightened. Valeria said it was over between her and Okeanos, and he trusted her. However, the sea fada was still at Rock Run, and Rui suspected that despite his warning, the man still hoped to change her mind.

Beatriz had her hand on his chest again. She scraped a fingernail over his nipple through the T-shirt. His cock twitched; he was a man, after all.

But as he gazed down at her, all he could think was how unmoved he was otherwise.

"I know you haven't had her yet," she murmured. "You're so on edge—we can all scent it. I'd be happy to help you with that."

"But Valeria would know." He gently but firmly removed her hand from his body. "It's over, Beatriz."

As he made to pass her, her fingers clamped on his arm. "Fine," she hissed. "But she's not yours until she accepts the mate claim. And she hasn't, has she?"

VALERIA KNEW the moment Rui entered the cavern. First her spine tingled and then her entire body came alert. Whether she liked it or not, the mate bond was rejuvenating.

Sabela was sitting across the table. She shot a fierce look over Valeria's shoulder. "You need to do something about that woman."

Valeria turned enough to see that Beatriz had her hands on Rui. An unmated native of Rock Run, Beatriz had been jealous of Rui's attentions to Valeria from the start. And this past year, when Rui had sexed practically anything female and of age, she'd been after him like a bitch in heat.

Valeria's teeth clenched but all she said to Sabela was, "It's not up to me."

Her friend made an irritated sound, but Valeria refused to be drawn. Rui wouldn't humiliate her like that. Not in front of everyone. But it was a painful reminder of all those months when he *had.*

Petros paused by their table. He greeted everyone, but his gaze lingered on Valeria.

"Hello, baby."

That smile made her skin crawl. She dipped her chin in a short nod. The man wouldn't take no for an answer. With Sabela's help, she'd made sure she was never alone with him, but she was tired of his advances.

The only thing keeping her from telling Rui was her fear that he'd challenge Petros.

His gaze went past her, and his smile changed to something more shark-like—or in his case, moray eel. The back of her neck prickled; Rui was behind her.

"Do Mar," Petros said, tight-lipped.

"Okeanos."

The two men stared at each other without moving. The tables around them quieted as people sensed the rising tension.

She swallowed. "Rui—"

He lightly squeezed her nape, silencing her. To Petros, he said, "I believe I told you to stay away from her."

Petros held his gaze long enough for Rui to release Valeria and start around the table. Then he nodded curtly and sauntered across the room to another table.

Rui waited until he was seated before turning back. Merry was looking up at him, small brow furrowed.

He smiled and tousled her hair. "How's my *princesa?*"

"Good." She relaxed and smiled back.

He took a seat on Valeria's other side and dropped a kiss on her lips. "Don't look so worried. I can handle him. And I've had enough of him sniffing around you."

"So? Let him sniff. I told you we're through."

"*Sim?* Then you won't mind staying away from him from now on."

A growled order, and although she'd been doing just that, she wasn't going to let him get away with it. Not unless she was accorded the same rights.

"I will when you stop letting Beatriz crawl all over you."

"Sorry." He had the grace to wince. "I told her I'm courting you. I thought everyone knew."

"Oh, she knows," Valeria muttered.

"Well, you're the only one I want," he said, and took her mouth for another kiss, this one deep and unabashedly possessive.

She knew it was partly for Petros's benefit—a dominant staking his claim—but heat curled through her, slow and delicious. When he lifted his head, she blinked at him, dazed.

He brushed the backs of his fingers over her cheek. "You have stars in your eyes," he murmured before releasing her and turning to greet the others at the table.

Meanwhile, Beatriz had paused nearby and was regarding Valeria with narrowed eyes. Then, with a toss of her head, she took the empty seat next to Sabela, which happened to be directly across from Rui.

Valeria's mouth flattened. She wasn't a jealous person, but it wasn't easy knowing that Beatriz—and half the unmated females in the dining hall—had had Rui too.

Rui squeezed her thigh. When she glanced at him, his smile was rueful. The fact that he'd noticed she was upset and was offering reassurance went a long way to soothing her. She brushed her lips over his—staking her own claim—and reached for the platter of crabs.

The talk turned to Dion and Cleia. The two rulers had announced their intention to split their time between the Rock Run base and the sun fae. Now the women speculated as to how that would work, the discussion taking place across several tables.

"Lord Dion said they would spend half their time here and half there," Sabela pointed out. "He won't let her sleep alone, that's for sure."

A passing male overheard her and said, "The queen will follow the alpha's lead. Now that they're mated, he's in charge."

The women hooted him down—Cleia might be crazy in love with Dion but everyone knew she listened to him only when it suited her. Dion might not like it, but he clearly was just as much in love with her. It promised for an interesting life together.

And by the Goddess, Valeria envied them.

Beatriz slanted her a sly look. "When Dion is with the sun fae," she said, "someone has to lead in his place. That would be Rui. He's more than ready. In fact, he looks ready for anything..." She trailed off suggestively.

Every head at the table swiveled in Valeria's direction. She set her jaw and gazed calmly back. But beneath the table, her fingers had sprouted claws.

Rui inclined his head. "I'll do my best to serve the clan and my alpha...as I'm sure we all will."

At his hard stare, Beatriz colored and dropped her gaze. "Yes, of course."

The other fada murmured agreement.

Sabela, bless her, steered the talk to what they could do to welcome the queen into the clan, saying, "It's our turn to throw a party."

The idea spread across the dining hall and soon the whole clan was throwing out suggestions. Valeria forced herself to join in the planning. She was damned if she'd let Beatriz get under her skin.

After dinner, Rui escorted Merry and her back to their apartment. For once, he didn't ask to stay, and she was surprised at her disappointment.

"Luis is expecting me," he explained. "We're meeting to go over things so we're ready when Dion gets back."

Merry tugged at his shirt. "Would you read to me, Tio? I have a new book."

He crouched down so he was at her level. "Not tonight, *princesa*—I have some business to take care of. But I promise I will tomorrow. Okay?"

Her lips pressed into a pout. "Okay. But don't forget."

"I won't. Now kiss me good night and then go inside so I can talk to your mama."

"G'night, Tio Rui." She twined her thin arms around his neck and planted a kiss on his cheek before obediently trotting into the apartment.

Rui rose back to his feet and drew Valeria toward him. Setting his big shoulders against the wall, he pulled her between his legs, tipping her toward him so that she had to set her hands on his chest to keep her balance.

His breath whispered over her lips, and then he was kissing her. Slow, hot kisses. Tasting every part of her mouth until she melted against him.

He sucked in a breath and enclosed her in his arms, deepening the kiss until the only thing she knew was him: the firm wall of his chest against her breasts, his erection hard against her stomach, his spicy scent and the way his heart pounded as fast as hers beneath her palms.

He lifted his head and gazed at her from beneath half-lowered lids. "I can come back later. Merry will be in bed then."

She swallowed—and gave in. "All right."

He blinked and then broke into one of his rare smiles. "Give me two hours. Maybe less." He gave her a last, lingering kiss and strode off.

Valeria let her head fall back against the wall. The old Rui was definitely back.

Sabela poked her head out her apartment. "He's gone?" She inhaled slowly and quirked a brow. "Someone's hot for it."

Valeria scrubbed her hands over her face and pushed off the wall. "It's just me and Merry, if that's what you mean," she said, ignoring the second comment.

"Too bad. But I have reinforcements." Sabela came the rest of the way into the hall and held up a bottle of merlot.

Valeria grinned. "Is that for me?"

"You and your best friend." Sabela followed her into the apartment. When Merry bounced off the couch to greet her, she handed Valeria the wine so she could swing Merry into the air. "Guess what? A certain little girl is at my mother's, asking to see you."

"Katie?" Merry's face lit up.

"You got it."

Sabela's niece Katie was an adorable three-year-old who idolized Merry. Merry, in turn, loved playing mother with her.

"Please can I go, Mama?" Merry hopped from foot to foot.

Valeria nodded. "Be back by eight-thirty." She followed her daughter into the hall, watching until she was safely inside Sabela's parents' apartment.

When she returned, Sabela had the wine open. She handed Valeria a glass and sank onto the couch, long legs folded beneath her.

"That was one hot kiss," she remarked with a grin.

"Which one?" Valeria shot back as she sat on the couch's other end. They both chuckled.

Valeria twisted the wine glass in her fingers. "Go ahead. Tell me I'm a fool. That he's just going to hurt me again. We both saw him with Beatriz tonight."

Her friend sipped her wine. "I might have said that a month ago."

"You did," Valeria pointed out dryly.

"Whatever." Sabela flicked her crimson nails. "But I have to admit, he's making an effort. Rodolfo says he's training as hard as any of the cadets. And if he's drinking, no one's seen it. You weren't facing him and Beatriz, but I was. I couldn't hear them, but it was clear he was telling her to back off."

"That's what he told me." She took a sip of the merlot. "We haven't done anything other than kiss."

"How do you feel about that?"

"I wish I knew." She dragged a hand over her hair. "Sometimes I want him so badly it hurts. He looks at me in that dark, brooding way until my skin feels too tight and I just want to shove him down on the couch and have my way with him. So yeah, I'm frustrated." She expelled a breath. "He's coming back—later, after Merry's in bed."

Sabela regarded her over the top of her glass. "Face it, *amiga*, he's your mate. Maybe it's time to stop fighting it. He wants you. He's not going to give up, and no other man's going to touch you with his scent all over you. But you don't have to make it easy. Take him back, but on your terms."

"Which are—?"

"Well, for one thing, he'd better be faithful this time or you'll break every bone in his body."

"Damn straight," Valeria said and they both chuckled and clinked glasses.

"Now," Sabela said with a disparaging glance at Valeria's tank top and shorts. "Let's take a look in your closet. By the time I'm through with you, the man's going to be on his knees, begging you to take him back."

"But—"

"No buts. You don't have to say yes tonight. You just want him praying to everything he holds holy that you will."

Valeria considered that. Then her lips curved up.

"On his knees begging, huh?"

"There." Sabela gave a satisfied nod. "You look stunning."

Valeria regarded herself in the mirror. Sabela had ferreted out her one black dress, a cotton knit that dipped low in the back with straps that crossed over her shoulders and came around to hold up a heart-shaped bodice. The dress's neckline exposed a tasteful amount of cleavage before nipping in at the waist and smoothing over her hips to end at mid-thigh.

Sabela had then woven Valeria's hair into a thick brown braid that fell over one shoulder and helped her apply a scarlet lipstick. Her cheeks had a slight flush, the bright color set off her full mouth, and she could see those stars in her eyes again.

"Well?" Sabela demanded.

"You're right. I *do* look—"

"Hot," her friend finished with a wicked grin.

"Thank you." Valeria pulled Sabela into a hug. "For everything."

"No problem. I just wish I could be here when Rui sees you. The man won't know what hit him."

After that, all she had to do was wait for Rui to return. Sabela helped her put Merry to bed, then left. Valeria spent the next half hour moving restlessly around the apartment. Washing the wine glasses and the dishes from Merry's bedtime snack. Returning a few scattered toys to the box in the *sala*. Plumping the pillows on the couch.

Rui had been patient, something she knew didn't come easy to him. She loved that he'd spent the past month taking things slowly. Courting her, as he'd promised. He'd convinced her that he was serious about winning her back.

The mate bond was more proof. She wouldn't feel it tugging at her if he wasn't ready for that kind of commitment.

When the knock came on her door, a flutter went up her spine. Placing a hand on her abdomen, she took a steadying breath before grasping the doorknob with firm fingers. She pulled open the door and there he was, big and dark and gorgeous in a forest-green dress shirt and black jeans.

"Hello." He regarded her unsmilingly.

Her heart thumped in her chest, hard and slow. "Hello."

He took in the black dress with hooded eyes. He said nothing as his gaze traveled from her head to her toes.

Then he gave a heartfelt shake of his head. "Sometimes I forget how beautiful you are."

Her lips curved. Rui was never going to give her pretty words, but it was just as good knowing you'd made a man all but swallow his tongue.

He glanced past her. "Merry's in bed?" When she said yes, he placed a hand on the doorjamb, his bicep bulging in the arm beside her head. "Invite me in." He showed her a small white box topped by a gold bow. "I brought you something."

She glanced at the box, then back at his face. He still wasn't smiling. Instead his expression was almost stern, but with an undertone of vulnerability that made her throat stop up.

She reached for his hand and drew him inside. He matched her, step for step, his gaze never leaving hers as he nudged the door shut with his foot. And then her back was against the door with him staring down at her with smoldering green eyes.

His hand went to her braid. He smoothed his fingers down the thick rope of hair to where the tip curled over her breast. Her nipples hardened against the thin cotton of her dress.

He smiled, a knowing uptick of his lips that did funny things to her stomach. "I'm going to kiss you," he said, his mouth a breath away from hers.

"*Sim,*" she whispered, mesmerized.

He placed his hands on either side of her head and slowly, carefully, brought his mouth to hers, tasting her as if she were the most special, delicious treat. Their tongues twined. His body crowded hers against the door. She grasped his shoulders and kissed him back, drowning in his scent and taste, the feel of those hard muscles against her breasts and thighs.

When he lifted his head, they were both breathing hard. Valeria understood that what came next had already been agreed to by them both, but she hadn't forgotten Sabela's advice: *You don't have to make it easy. Take him back, but on your terms.*

His hands were still on the door. She ducked under them and sent him a smile over her shoulder. "How about some coffee?"

He blew out a breath. "That would be nice, thank you."

He placed the box on the coffee table and took a seat on the couch where he could watch as she moved about the kitchen.

Neither of them spoke. A month ago, Valeria might have been unnerved by the charged atmosphere, but tonight, she was completely calm. He might be a male and several notches dominant to her, but in this, she was the one in control. That was the gift of his courtship. Even now, if she said no, he'd leave. He might not be happy about it, but he would leave.

She finished the coffee and then brought in two cups along with a plate filled with small fruit tarts from the clan bakery. Rui helped himself to one, washing it down with coffee before setting the cup on the low table.

"Thank you, *querida*. I needed that." He sat back with a sigh and rested his head on the couch back. "It's been a long day."

She frowned at the exhaustion shadowing his face. "You're pushing yourself too hard."

He lifted a shoulder. "It won't kill me. But it's not the physical stuff—it's some of the other warriors. Not Luis or Rodolfo, thank *Deus*. But a few of the younger men are having a hard time accepting I'm second again."

"It's been two years."

"Nobody knows that better than me. And yeah, I know it's my fault I lost their respect." He rubbed a hand over his face. "I just don't want it to come to a challenge."

She chewed her lower lip. "It won't, will it?" A dominance

challenge wasn't supposed to be to the death, but things could go wrong.

"I don't think so. I took on a couple of the most dominant in hand-to-hand combat today. They're not going to be challenging me in a hurry."

He raised his arms in a long, bone-cracking stretch. The hem of his shirt lifted, exposing his abdomen.

She murmured something, her gaze on all that smooth brown skin. Maybe he was pushing himself too hard, but she couldn't argue with the results. One hand came to his stomach, idly scratching the firm ridge of muscles. A line of black hair disappeared into his jeans.

He stilled, and she jerked her eyes back to his face. He gazed back at her, a smile on his lips. Suddenly he didn't look so tired after all.

He crooked a finger at her. "Come here, *boneca.*"

Her body recognized that husky tone. Her nipples hardened and a lush heat filled her belly. But she heard again Sabela's words: *On his knees begging.*

She concentrated on setting her cup on the table.

"Come here," he repeated.

She moved closer and he traced a finger over her collarbone. "Valeria."

Her thighs clenched at that seductive growl. She swallowed. "Yes?"

This close she could see the flecks of gold in his deep green eyes, feel the heat radiating off his body. She found herself inhaling slowly, taking in his wild male spice, the scent still familiar after all this time.

He moved his hand to her breast, rubbing a knuckle over one hard crest. "No more running, hm?"

"No," she agreed.

His big hand covered her breast, squeezing gently. "Say it, Valeria. Tell me what you want."

And suddenly, she didn't want to make him beg. She just wanted him. That was all she'd ever wanted.

She moistened her lips. His eyes darkened as they followed the movement of her tongue. She thought he might say something but he waited patiently, his fingers massaging her breast.

She slid a fingertip down the outside of his forearm. "I want you."

"Yeah?"

Both his hands cupped her breasts now. He continued the slow, almost-hypnotic massage. Sensation slid up and down her spine, pricks of heat and light and pleasure.

"But," some instinct for self-preservation made her add, "that doesn't mean I'm agreeing to the mate claim."

"No?" His brow lifted. "I can make you want me." He pinched her nipples.

Her reply was half-laugh, half-moan. "You already have."

"So what do you mean, you're not agreeing to the claim?"

"That I'm not making any promises. I have to be sure this time." She glanced away. "You...you broke my heart. Not just with Cleia, but with all the women after you came back. I can't go through that again. I *won't* go through that again."

He stilled. "Ah, *querida*. I wish I had words to tell you how sorry I am. I won't ask you to forgive me. Not yet. But I swear it will never happen again. That from this day forward there will be no one but you. Can you believe that at least?"

She moved her hands in a helpless gesture. "I'm trying."

His eyes met hers. "Thank you. I know I don't deserve it, but thank you." He framed her face and pressed a soft kiss to her lips, then moved his mouth to her eyes, placing a kiss on each lid, before laying his cheek against hers.

"*Amo-te*," he murmured. "I love you. So much."

Something inside her shifted, loosened. She tried to recall her spurt of anger in the dining room at Rui and all his women, but he'd spent the last month focusing on her and Merry. He was polite to his past lovers, but he'd made it clear he belonged to one woman now.

Her. Valeria.

She lifted a hand and stroked his head. And in that moment, she realized she'd already forgiven him, already begun to trust him again.

When he lifted his head, his eyes were wet. He blinked and turned his head, trying to hide it, but she saw.

Her heart squeezed. "Come." Taking his hand, she led him to her bedroom.

18

———

*A*s Valeria turned the lock on her door, it seemed to throw a switch in Rui as well. He grasped her shoulders and pulled her to him for a hard kiss. The apologetic man was gone and in his place was a dominant fada male intent on taking his woman.

"*Madre de Deus*," he muttered against her neck. "If you knew how much I want you—"

Her stomach quivered.

Oh, she knew. If it was anything like how she felt, she knew just how much he wanted her. Desire was a hot, liquid pulse in her core. Need was a red heat in her brain. If he'd asked, she'd have lain down on the floor right there and let him have her.

His nostrils flared, and she knew he scented her arousal. He gave a rumble of satisfaction and turned his head, fitting his mouth to hers. She eagerly twined her arms around his neck and took his tongue into her mouth, sucking hard. He tasted of coffee and the sweet pastry and his own unique male flavor.

He moved his mouth to her neck, nipping and licking the tender skin. Excitement raced up and down her spine.

He brought a hand to her breast. "No promises, then. This is just sex, right?" His thumb traced a circle around her aching nipple.

Her inner thighs clenched. She arched her back and pressed into his caress. "Yes," she managed to say.

"Fine." A fist captured her braid, drawing back her head. "I agree."

"You do? I mean, good."

His teeth closed on the soft underside of her jaw, gentle but firm. Letting her know who was in control.

"But it's going to be all night. And if I want you again tomorrow night—and I will—I'll have you. No going back to just kisses."

She swallowed. "Promises, promises."

Rui chuckled darkly and brought his mouth down on hers again. Pleasure rippled over her skin. She placed a hand on his arm to steady herself. Beneath the shirt, his muscles flexed under her touch.

He muttered something incoherent and gathered her closer with one arm, the other hand holding her steady for his kiss.

"Mm." She fit herself to him.

He growled his approval and deepened the kiss, tasting her in leisurely strokes. She brought her hands to his face, smoothing her thumbs over the black stubble of his night-beard, exploring the strong bones of his jaw beneath. He pulled her closer and she twined a leg around his hip, rubbing herself against his thigh.

Rui bit out something raw and primitive. He raised his head and she saw his animal in his eyes, a rich, wild gold, and then the room spun and she was on the mattress, his big body covering hers, his erection pressing into the notch between her thighs exactly where she needed it.

She shut her eyes and forgot everything but his lips on hers and the hard body pinning hers to the bed.

His mouth moved to her breasts, nipping her through the thin cotton knit. She whimpered and gripped his nape to pull him closer. He lifted his head and, taking her wrists in one of his hands, raised her arms above her head so she couldn't touch him. Then he closed his lips over her nipple and drew hard.

She gasped and arched her back, twining her legs around his body so that her aching center was pressed against his pelvis. He lifted his head, but rather than give her relief, he gazed down at her, one hand keeping her arms against the mattress above her head.

She moistened her lips. "Rui?"

His eyes were dark with some unnamed emotion. "You and Okeanos never...did you? I have no right to ask, but—"

She glanced away. "No."

"Why is that, Valeria?"

She shrugged, and he nuzzled her neck.

"Thank you," he said in a thick voice. "I don't deserve it, but—"

"No, you don't," she agreed, but her words lacked force.

"Ah, sweetheart, you're such a gift. So precious...I swear I won't ever forget that again."

Long, work-roughened fingers pushed up her skirt, exposing the tiny black panties beneath. He cupped her mound. Just cupped her, his fingers firm, possessive. He bent forward to press a reverent kiss just below her navel.

"*Bonita*," he breathed against her skin. "So pretty. So very, very pretty."

Her eyes drifted shut. He rubbed a single finger over her center, a teasing caress through the silky cloth, and her eyes flew open again.

"That's better," he said. "I want you looking at me, remembering who you belong to."

Her head moved back and forth against the sheet. "No," she moaned.

"No?" He drew a slow circle around her clit. "That's not the answer I want to hear, *querida*. Now keep those eyes open or I'll tease you until you're pleading for release."

She stared at him for a moment and then her lips curved in a slow smile. She almost chuckled when he eyed her uncertainly. He'd always been in control of their lovemaking, which was fine with her. He was a hard, aggressive male, and she had no desire to change him. But he wasn't going to have it all his own way.

On his knees begging.

She traced her tongue over her lower lip. "Maybe I want you to tease me."

Rui's whole body went taut. Damn, it made him hard, hearing her husky voice asking him to tease her. He was so attuned to her that he could swear he heard her heart speed up. Her cheeks had a pretty flush and her brown eyes were nearly black with desire.

But she still found the will to resist him.

This doesn't mean I'm agreeing to the mate claim.

And it wasn't because she didn't want him—she couldn't hide how aroused she was—but because she was afraid he'd hurt her again.

Deus, that tore at him. But he'd already resolved to do whatever it took to make it up to her. He'd just have to pray she had a heart big enough to accept him, flaws and all.

Meanwhile, he'd make sure this was a night she'd never forget.

Maybe I want you to tease me.

"Yeah?" His smile was all teeth. It was her turn to look uncertain. "Well, then, let's start by taking this off."

His hands went to her shoulders, helping her to sit back up. The dress's zipper was on the back, so he turned her sideways and eased it down, pressing a kiss to each vertebrae in turn as he gradually exposed her smooth, toned back. When he reached the base of her spine, he rose back up to press a kiss to her nape. She was so soft, so ready, her musk filling his nostrils.

His need ratcheted, fierce and primal. He jerked the wide black straps down over her shoulders, trapping her arms.

"So you want to be teased," he said, this time in a growl against the back of her neck.

"Yes." Her throat worked. "But...not too much."

"Oh, no, *boneca*. You don't get to set the rules. Just be prepared to beg—and maybe I'll take pity on you." He pulled the dress down a little further so that her breasts popped out. He fingered a taut, rose-brown nipple. "I think I'll tease these pretty breasts of yours for a while."

She moaned and dropped her head back against his chest. He brought his other arm around her so that he could play with both of her breasts. She was swollen, sensitive. Even his tiniest touches elicited a whimper.

"Please, Rui—"

He pinched her nipples. "*Sim?*"

"I—I need more."

"I know, sweetheart. But if I give it to you too soon, it wouldn't be any fun."

"Says who?" she muttered, and he gave a bark of laughter.

But he released her breasts to cup her jaw in one hand and give her a leisurely kiss. While he was distracted, she managed to wriggle the dress off her arms so that she could bring them up to clasp him closer. Her head turned, seeking his mouth. He groaned against her lips and then somehow managed to pull himself back.

He reached for the dress bunched around her hips. "Lift your arms."

When she obeyed, he pulled the garment over her head and dropped it onto the trunk at the foot of the bed before standing up to shuck his own clothes. When he turned around Valeria was seated cross-legged on the bed, wearing nothing but those tiny satin panties, her thick braid falling over one shoulder.

He came to stand before her. She flashed him a smile and scooted to the edge of the mattress, where she placed a hand on his abdomen. Her thumb caressed his scar, which had healed into a thin pink line.

"Did I ever thank you for what you did that day? If you hadn't been there—"

He shrugged, his gaze on her hand. "I don't need your thanks."

"What do you need then? This?"

Her thumb moved lower and his cock jerked, eager to be inside her. She stroked her fingers lower, then curled them around his hot, hard length. His breath hissed out. Her fingers were cool and a little rough from crabbing. That hint of roughness on a woman made his balls tighten deliciously.

"That's a start," he managed to say.

But he wanted to draw this out for both of them. Taking her hands, he pressed her down onto the mattress and removed her panties, then brought his hand to the tight black curls that shielded her mound. He moved his fingers in a slow circle, careful not to touch her slick, swollen nub.

She raised herself on her forearms to watch him. He continued to touch her. Light, easy touches that had her tensing and moaning.

"More, Rui. Oh, please."

"But you want to be teased."

Her head dropped back onto the mattress. "I'm an idiot."

"No, you're right. You want this to be slow...perfect—and so do I." Her legs were dangling off the bed. He lifted her hips and shifted her so that she was all the way on the mattress before climbing on top of her and straddling her thighs. "Now let me see —I can tease you here..." He cupped her breasts and played with the rosy furled nipples. "Or here..." He slid his hands lower, stroking down her ribcage to her hips.

She moaned and closed her eyes, the lashes an inky fringe against her cheeks.

"Or maybe here..." He lowered his mouth to her belly, kissing and nipping the soft skin.

She made a low sound and reached for his shoulders, trying to pull him closer.

He nuzzled her palm. "*Eu te adoro, querida.* Accept the mate claim. We belong together."

She stilled and didn't reply. He tightened his jaw but didn't press her, turning his attention instead back to her abdomen, moving lower until his mouth was poised above her warm, moist center. He licked a circle around her clitoris, careful not to touch it.

"Rui—" Her hands clamped on his head, trying to pull him to her.

"Oh, no." He removed her hands and placed them on the mattress. "Remember who's in charge here. Or do I have to tie your wrists?"

She shot him a heated look. "No."

He grinned to himself. He loved Valeria's fiery side. "Good girl," he murmured, just to taunt her, and then licked up her moist, tender slit, savoring the salty musk. He was rewarded by her moan.

He slid a finger inside her, then two, still licking and sucking her, until she broke and her hands gripped his head again. This time he let them remain there, intent on helping her reach the climax he sensed was just seconds away.

"Please, please, please..." She writhed beneath his hands and mouth, her heated core clamping on his fingers.

"That's it," he encouraged. "Beg me."

"Yes, anything." Her head moved from side to side on the sheet. "Just—"

"Taste you? All right." He suckled her swollen pearl of flesh.

She let out a little scream, dug her heels into the mattress and came.

He rode it out with her, bringing her down with soft, easy licks before raising himself up over her. "On your knees." Both man and animal needed it this way, his body covering hers, making her completely his.

Her gaze caught his, the brown overlaid with aqua. He knew his own were golden; both their animals to the fore. He held his breath, waiting to see what she would do, knowing that if she tried to run or fight, his animal would take her down—although gently, because she was the mate.

Then she smiled—a decidedly feral smile—and turned over, presenting her bottom to him.

"*Deus.*" His throat closed. He placed his hands on her hips and sat back on his haunches, taking her in as he tried to catch his breath again.

She was every man's erotic dream. His gaze traced greedily down her body: the strong, elegant shoulders...the graceful dip of her back...the lush curve of her ass. Some of her hair had escaped its braid, wispy curls forming a honey-brown halo around her head.

Something about those delicate wisps made his chest clench; a hot, sweet ache. Gods, he loved her.

Leaning forward, he feathered his lips over the smooth skin between her shoulder blades, grateful just to touch her, to be pressed against her, skin to skin. She shivered and he recalled she was ticklish there. He smiled and did it again.

She moaned his name.

"*Sim?*" He rose back up. "Do you want something, love?"

He slipped his hand between her thighs. She was warm and wet. His balls pulsed with the desire to take her. He inhaled raggedly and caressed her with a single long finger.

Her breath sucked in. "Yes. No. Rui—" Her fingers clenched on the sheets.

"*Acalme-te, querida.* I know what you want."

He played with her a few moments more and then unable to wait any longer, came back onto his knees. Gripping her hips, he nudged his tip against her opening. She made a small sound of pleasure and, reaching beneath her body, took hold of him and slid him back and forth through her hot, moist silk, teasing them both until his teeth gritted with need.

"Enough," he rasped. "Put me inside you."

When she obeyed, he tightened his grip on her hips and stroked the rest of the way inside. Electricity buzzed up and down his spine. He groaned at the sheer wonder of being inside her after all this time. She arched her back and pressed back against him, and his whole lower body tightened.

"*Sim,*" he encouraged. "That's it, love." He pulled partway out and slid slowly back inside. "Is this what you want? Tell me." He flexed his hips and moved back into her again, a little harder this time.

"Yes." Her fingers dug into the mattress. "That's it. Please, Rui."

He settled into a rhythm, stroking in and out of her slowly at first, and then faster. She came down onto her forearms and he groaned again. The angle was so perfect, his entire length buried deep inside her.

But he wanted her with him. He reached under her and, wetting his fingers in her juices, rubbed and teased her swollen nub until she was whimpering.

"Ah, *sim.* That's it...right there..."

And then it happened. Something in her opened and he sensed her need pulsing through the mate bond. A fierce triumph filled him. He went wild, slamming into her, hard and deep.

"That's it, Valeria. Take me. Take all of me."

She arched up to take him as deep as she could, meeting his wildness with her own. He stroked into her again and again, and then she was convulsing around him, milking him with tight little muscles. His balls drew up hard against his body. He thrust another few times and then light sparked behind his eyes and he groaned and emptied himself into her in a climax that seemed to go on forever.

When he came back to himself, she was flat on her stomach and he was resting half on, half off her, breathing hard. He rolled onto his back and pulled her into his arms.

"*Amo-te, querida.* I love you." He pressed a kiss to her hair.

She stroked her fingers through the wiry hair on his chest. But she didn't say she loved him in return and to his dismay, when he reached for her through the bond, she'd closed back in on herself again.

He wanted to say something—plead, argue, demand, whatever it took—but when he raised his head, her eyes held a wariness that made the words dry up in his throat.

But if she wouldn't accept the words, he could love her with his body. And he did, twice more, until they both fell into a heavy, satiated sleep.

19

"Mama Ria?" A small hand shook Valeria's shoulder. "Wake up. I'm hungry."

"Go to breakfast without me," Valeria mumbled without opening her eyes. "You can sit with Tia Sabela."

Merry whined. "But I want you to come, too."

Valeria sighed. "Okay, okay." Then she remembered Rui and her eyes flew open.

But his side of the bed was empty, his clothes gone.

That was good, she told herself. She wasn't ready for Merry's questions. Still, a part of her was disappointed that he'd left without waking her, even though she was the one who'd insisted on no commitment.

Merry waved a small, beribboned box in her face. "What's this, Mama?"

Valeria pushed herself up to sitting. What with one thing and another, she'd never gotten around to opening Rui's gift.

Not that she was complaining. She smothered a grin.

"Tio Rui gave it to me," she told Merry. "Do you want to help open it?"

Merry nodded and scrambled onto the bed. Valeria held the

box while she untied the gold ribbon, the tip of her tongue sticking out as she concentrated on loosening the bow. When she was done, she lifted the lid. Nestled inside was a hand-carved dolphin attached to a brown leather cord to make a necklace.

The little girl clapped her hands. "It's a dolphin—just like you, Mama."

Valeria lifted the necklace out. The dolphin had been whittled from walrus ivory. It was a creamy white with brown striations, the beak, fins and tail flukes lovingly detailed, then the whole thing polished until it shone.

Valeria fingered it, trying to picture a big, hard man like Rui producing such a delicate piece of art. And yet somehow she knew he had, that it had been his hand who'd carved each graceful line.

Hot tears pricked her eyes. She hadn't even known he could carve.

"Can I hold it?" Merry begged.

She blinked back the tears and handed it over. "If you're careful."

Merry ran a small finger down its back. "Can I wear it sometime? Please, Mama? It's so pretty."

"Perhaps. But today I'm going to wear it. Tio Rui gave this to me as a special gift."

Merry handed back the necklace. "He must really like you, Mama."

"*Sim.*" Valeria swallowed over a lump in her throat. When she could trust her voice again, she said, "I hear Tia Sabela and Katie outside the door. Why don't you go to breakfast with them? I'll meet you all in the dining hall after I take a shower."

"All right." Merry darted into the hall, where Valeria could hear Sabela's voice saying that of course it was okay if she came to breakfast with them.

Valeria turned the necklace over in her hands. As Merry had pointed out, the dolphin was her preferred animal. Two years ago, when they'd been courting for the first time, Rui had teased her about it, informing her with a wicked smile that sharks eat dolphins, and then proceeding to demonstrate with his mouth and teeth until she was dazed with pleasure.

She drew in a breath—and then tears were running down her face. She wrapped her fingers around the carving and buried her face in a pillow as she sobbed for Rui and the loss of that first, somehow innocent love.

When she was done, she felt drained, but at peace, the bitterness finally gone.

They could never return to what they'd had two years ago, but maybe they could make something new, something that would be even stronger and more enduring, tested as it had been by what they'd both been through.

She took a shower and then proudly donned the necklace before heading out to breakfast.

SHE FOUND Rui in the dining hall at a table with Merry, Sabela and Katie. As Valeria approached, he rose and gave her a slow, thorough kiss. Claiming her in front of everyone, as if the clan didn't already know from their scents what the two of them had been doing half the night. Then he ushered her onto the bench between him and Merry.

Rui fingered the dolphin, an endearingly diffident look on his hard face. "You like it, then?"

She touched his cheek. "I love it. I didn't even know you could carve."

"I don't, actually—not anymore. It's probably been ten years since I made anything. But I had that piece of ivory sitting around, and I had some free time while I was waiting to heal..."

"Well, thank you." She kissed him. "It's beautiful."

"You're welcome, *meu coração*." *My heart.*

Her own heart contracted.

Across the table, Sabela mouthed, "Guess he liked the dress."

Valeria just grinned and picked up a muffin.

As breakfast ended, there was a stir at the entrance. Dion and Cleia appeared, holding hands and smiling. The clan rose to their feet to applaud the newly mated couple.

As the cheers died down, Dion thanked everyone and officially asked them to welcome his mate to Rock Run. Then he looked around the room.

"Damn if I didn't miss you all," he said, adding with a lopsided grin at his mate, "but not too much."

Everyone chuckled as they retook their seats. Dion got a large espresso and carried it over to Rui and Valeria's table, while Cleia fell into conversation with several of the women who had befriended her while she was Dion's prisoner.

Rui rose back to his feet and stuck out his hand. "Welcome back, *irmão*. I don't need to ask if you enjoyed yourself."

"No." Dion ignored the hand to drag Rui into a hug. They pounded each other on the back.

"You look good," Dion said as he released him. He glanced at Valeria, taking in the fact that she was with Rui. His nostrils flared, and she knew he scented the sex on them. He gave her a wink before turning back to his friend. "It appears everything's all right. No problems?"

"Nothing we couldn't handle. Luis and I can give you a full report whenever you're ready."

"In my *sala* in thirty minutes?"

"Works for me." Rui glanced at Luis, who had just joined them, and he nodded agreement.

Dion hugged Luis next. "How's that boy of yours, anyway?"

He grinned. "With your mate." He nodded at Cleia, who had Xavier propped on her hip as she spoke to Isa and Marina.

"Thank *Deus* I mated her before he was of age," Dion drawled. "I might have had to fight off a challenge." They all chuckled and then Dion turned to Valeria. "Before I do anything," he said with a meaningful look at Merry, "I'd like an update on the situation with you-know-who and the earth fada. You might as well stay and listen, Luis."

Sabela came to her feet. "I'd be happy to take Merry to the creche. I have to take Katie anyway."

"Would you?" Valeria replied gratefully. She tried to keep as much as possible from Merry, knowing it only upset her. Now she hugged the little girl, told her she'd pick her up at lunchtime and then released her to go off with Sabela and her niece.

"*Bom*." Dion took another gulp of espresso and sat down across from Rui and Valeria. "So," he said as Luis took the seat next to him. "What's Adric up to now?"

"His people have been observed nearby," replied Rui. "The first was when I was with Valeria and Merry. It was Merry's uncle, Jace Jones. But since then, the sentries have reported two other possible sightings, although by the time they got close enough, whoever it was had gone. The scent was earth shifter, though. The odd thing was it was faint, as if it had been set down weeks ago."

Valeria lifted a brow. "I didn't know that."

Rui met her frown straight on. "I didn't want to worry you."

"Hm," she said. At some point, they were going to have a talk about him withholding information from her. But right now the important thing was to keep Merry safe.

"What I'd like to know," Rui continued, "is how Jones got so close without our knowing it. He was just a few yards from our boat and none of us scented him. That seems impossible, unless—"

"—they have fae help," Dion completed his thought.

Valeria sucked in a breath. She supposed it should've occurred to her that the fae might be involved, but everyone knew the fae did nothing for free—and the Baltimore clan was dirt poor. Still, it made sense—only the fae could've concealed

Jace Jones's scent so well that none of them had known he was there, watching them.

"Maybe I should contact Adric," Dion said, "see if we can work out something."

"No," Valeria blurted out. The alpha raised a dark brow, and she swallowed uncomfortably but continued, "I'm sorry, my lord, but I don't trust him."

"Hell, neither do I. But we can't keep Merry confined to base until she's an adult. A cub needs to run."

"I know," Valeria said miserably. The little girl was already getting antsy.

"And then there's this thing with the quartz. Cleia says they're telling the truth. Merry needs something that we can't give her."

Valeria's heart sank. "I see."

"Exactly *what* is a closely-guarded secret," continued Dion. "But we know that every earth fada has their own unique quartz crystal keyed to their energy alone. And I can tell you one thing, if you can somehow get their quartz away from them, it hurts—bad. I've seen grown men scream with the pain."

Valeria clenched her fists. "There has to be something we can do. I refuse to believe the only solution is to send Merry back to the Baltimore clan."

Dion expelled a breath. "Look, I may as well tell you, I received a message the other day from Lord Adric. He's making an official claim for her."

Valeria swallowed. "He can do that?"

"And by what authority?" Rui added. Unlike the fae, the fada had no higher court of appeals. They settled things clan to clan—through negotiation, battle or a challenge. The fae derided it as the animal in them, but the fada believed it made more sense than tying things up in court for months or even years, then allowing an outsider to rule on your business.

"He has none," Dion said. "But that doesn't mean we don't

have to take him seriously. If he spreads the word that a Rock Run assassin kidnapped one of his young, we'll be pariahs."

Rui closed his eyes. "Hell. What a mess."

Queen Cleia approached. Valeria's lips drew back in an instinctive curl. She quickly smoothed her face. She didn't blame Cleia for Rui's rejection of the mate claim—he'd done that all on his own—but that didn't mean she had to like the woman.

"Excuse me," the queen said, taking in their serious expressions. "I didn't mean to interrupt."

"No problem, *querida*." Dion caught her hand and drew her closer. "Do you need something?"

"I just wanted to tell you I'm finished here. I'll wait for you in the apartment."

"Actually, we could use your advice. We're talking about little Merry."

The sun fae glanced at Valeria. "If you're sure..."

Valeria wondered if she was recalling how Valeria had snatched Merry away rather than let Cleia touch her when she was Dion's prisoner.

What Valeria said next was difficult, but she'd do anything to keep Merry. "Please stay, my lady. I—we could use your help."

Cleia looked at her, this time full-on.

Valeria blinked. During the time the queen had been at Rock Run, Valeria had never seen her without her blindfold. Now she had the sense those large, unearthly fae eyes, brown shot with gold, could see right into her soul.

Cleia's smile was sympathetic. "If it's about your daughter, I'd be happy to." She took a seat next to Dion. The queen already knew about Adric's claim, and Dion quickly brought her up to date on the rest.

"Well," the queen responded, "I can tell you one thing. If a fae is helping Lord Adric, he or she isn't a member of any of the sun fae clans. We have a strict policy of noninterference with other clans—fae or fada. And frankly, Adric doesn't have the resources to pay for fae help."

"That's what I thought," Rui answered. "And yet none of us sensed him."

Cleia looked at Valeria. "Why don't you take me back to the island? If someone used fae magic in the last couple of weeks or so, I should be able to detect it."

She inclined her head. "Thank you, *senhora*."

"Excellent idea," Dion said as Rui nodded agreement. "I'm supposed to meet with Rui and Luis, but you two can go without us. I'll send Rodolfo to guard you."

"A guard?" Cleia drew herself up, suddenly every inch the powerful fae queen. "Do you honestly think the earth fada would dare try anything with *me*?"

Dion tugged gently on a strand of copper-and-gold hair. "Indulge me, love. *Sim?* No one's invincible—not even the fae. And if another fae is involved—"

She glared at him another moment and then let out an exasperated breath. "Olivia warned me about you."

A corner of Dion's mouth hitched up. "Your cousin's a smart woman."

Rui came to his feet. "I'll tell Rodolfo." Leaning down, he captured Valeria's chin and gave her a hard kiss. "Try not to worry, *boneca*. We'll figure this out."

A few minutes later, Valeria and Cleia were in one of the clan's motorboats with Rodolfo at the wheel. It was a beautiful morning. Despite her worry about Merry and the earth shifters, Valeria felt the familiar lift at being out on the river.

Rodolfo let out the throttle and the wind rushed past, teasing strands of hair from her braid so that they whipped around her face. She donned a pair of sunglasses and glanced at the queen, who had captured her own hair in one hand and had her face raised to the sun, drinking in its rays like the sun fae she was.

Cleia grinned at her. "What a fabulous day."

"Yes."

"You're a fisher, aren't you? You're out here every day."

"It depends. In the summer I work less so I can spend more time with Merry. But yeah, I'm normally out here three or four days a week."

"And you and Rui are back together?" Cleia's smile was knowing. "I'm so happy for you both."

"Are you?" she returned flatly.

Cleia glanced at Rodolfo, then lowered her voice. "Look, I don't blame you for disliking me. But I want you to know that I didn't know Rui had a mate. I'd never have taken him if I'd known. If it helps any, I'm sorry for what it must have done to you both."

Valeria pressed her lips together. "He didn't have to go with you. And we weren't mates—not quite."

"But I didn't play fair. I used a glamour to lure him. Not many men could have resisted me. In fact, no one did—not until Dion. He saw right through the glamour to the real me." Cleia smiled a little self-consciously.

Valeria shook her head. "Rui never said."

"That I used a glamour? He wouldn't, would he?"

"No," Valeria replied slowly, "he wouldn't." Rui would take full responsibility for his actions, whether Cleia had lured him or not.

"There's something else you should know. He eventually broke the glamour. I wasn't ready to let him go—I'd have been happy to keep him for another year or two. But he'd become more and more unhappy, just going through the motions with me. Then one morning he woke up and said he was going home." Cleia moved a shoulder. "So I let him. You may find this hard to believe, but I'm not evil—selfish, maybe, but not evil. Now that I'm mated, I know how strong the bond can be. It was tugging on him all that time."

"I see." Valeria was silent, absorbing that. She tried to imagine how a dominant like Rui would've reacted to being ensnared by a fae. He must have felt so helpless, so ashamed. It explained some of the self-loathing she'd sensed in him since he'd returned.

And all this time she'd thought he found Cleia more beautiful, more sexy, than her.

Deus, she could hate the woman. But that wasn't fair.

Rui hadn't left the base because of Cleia; he'd left because of her, Valeria. Not that it was all her fault, either, but she shared some of the blame for turning from him at a time when he'd needed her most.

She expelled a breath. "Thank you for telling me. It helps."

Cleia moved a slim shoulder. "Rui should've told you himself, but you know what fada men are like."

"*Sim*. They tell us it's in their DNA, but we think they're just stubborn SOBs."

The sun fae's lips twitched. "I once called Dion pigheaded. And that was the nicest thing I could think of."

Their eyes met and then they were both grinning. And suddenly, Valeria understood why so many of the Rock Run women liked Cleia, in spite of the fact that she'd not only taken eight of their men as lovers, she'd mated their alpha. Beneath the golden-girl façade was a genuine warmth and humor.

They were approaching the island where they'd seen Jace Jones. Valeria pointed it out to Rodolfo, and he turned the boat in its direction. A few minutes later, they were securing the boat to a tree.

As they reached the place where Valeria had seen the big black cat, she inhaled slowly. There was nothing out of the ordinary. But for some reason a chilly finger traced down her spine and she shivered despite the warm day.

"This is where we saw him," she told Cleia.

The other woman touched the nearest tree, rubbing her fingers in a slow, considering way over the bark before moving on to the next tree. Her path spiraled inward as if she were following an invisible trail until finally, she crouched to touch the dirt beneath a large maple.

When she straightened back up, her face was grim. "I can't tell if an earth fada was here or not. And that in itself is interesting, because I do detect a concealing spell. What I can tell you is that whoever cast the spell is very good—and that the magic used was dark. There's almost certainly a night fae involved."

"A night fae?" Valeria felt the color drain from her face.

"I'm almost sure of it. Dark magic carries its own costs. Very few fae besides the night fae want to deal with it." She touched Valeria's arm. "What is it? What's the matter?"

"The night fae." Valeria's voice was a rasp. She swallowed, tried again. "The night Rui found Merry—there were night fae after her then, too."

BACK AT THE BASE, Cleia and Valeria found Dion, Rui and Luis sprawled on couches in the alpha's apartment, sipping espresso and listening to Dion tell a very male story about his honeymoon. On seeing Cleia, he broke off and all three men sat up. The guilt on their faces would've been comical if Valeria wasn't so upset.

Dion rose to his feet. "What is it?" He glanced from her to Cleia.

"Night fae," his mate said. "I picked up a trace of dark magic. It appears they're helping the Baltimore shifters."

The other men were on their feet now as well.

Rui growled. "Night fae? Why the fuck do they keep turning up in this?"

"Valeria says they were after Merry the night you found her."

"That's right. And it was a night fae who hired us to take out Merry's dad in the first place."

"And her dad was part night fae," Dion added. "His name was Silver—ever heard of him?"

"No," Cleia said. "But he was a half-blood?"

"Yes. Part night fae, part human."

"And she's half fada as well," Cleia murmured. "Could be the night fae just don't like having their blood mixed with a shifter's."

Valeria set her jaw. "Then why don't they just leave her alone? The shifter genes are the dominant ones. Most people don't even realize she has some fae in her—at least, not any more than all the fada have."

"I agree," said Cleia, "but the night fae aren't known for their tolerance." She glanced at Rui. "Who hired you?"

"Lord Tyrus. Prince Langdon's son."

Cleia nodded. "We've met. He's the heir. He had an older brother but he died a number of years ago, before your clan came to America."

"Assassinated?" asked Dion.

"Not as far as I know. I believe it was some rare disease that no one could treat. It took him very quickly—he was dead within days. But who knows? For the right price, there are fae who can infect you with an undetectable virus."

Valeria swallowed sickly. The terror she'd felt on the island returned. "What are we going to do?"

Rui set a reassuring arm around her shoulders. But when he spoke, it was to Dion. "I think it's time I had a talk with Lord Tyrus."

 $\mathcal{V}$ aleria fingered the carved dolphin and stifled a sigh.

Rui had been gone for two days now, and she missed him: his low, sexy voice, his calm way with Merry, the little surprises he arranged for one or both of them nearly every day. She missed telling him about her day and listening as he talked about his, knowing that only with her did he truly relax. She missed his touches: the soft, teasing kisses and intense, wild lovemaking.

That one night had only left her hungry for more. She had a long dry spell to make up for.

It didn't help that Merry missed him, too. "When's Tio Rui coming home?" she'd asked that evening.

They were cuddled together in her bed, reading. Valeria set aside the book and wrapped an arm around her small shoulders. "Soon, sweetheart."

Merry folded her arms over her narrow chest. "Next time, I'm going with him."

"He's a busy man, sweetie. He can't always be with us."

"But you could mate with him. Then he'd be my daddy and

we could all live together." She slanted Valeria a look from under thick black lashes. "You love him, don't you, Mama?"

Yes. Yes, I do.

And when she saw Rui, she was going to tell him—but it wasn't for Merry to hear first.

"That's between Tio and me." Valeria tapped her on the nose. "Now, enough talk. It's time you went to sleep."

She remained with Merry until she was asleep, taking comfort from holding her warm little body. But with her sleeping and Sabela out on a date, Valeria was at loose ends.

She paced restlessly around the apartment.

Where was Rui, anyway? She hadn't heard from him since he'd left to look for Tyrus. That wasn't unusual—water fada couldn't carry cell phones and could use computers only sparingly —but there were other ways of sending messages. If Rui hadn't contacted the base, it meant he was deep in night fae territory.

She touched the dolphin again and said a little prayer that he was all right. The night fae were dark and unforgiving. If they discovered Rui somewhere he shouldn't be, he was doomed. A fada might be able to assassinate a fae, but only if he took the fae by surprise. In a straight fight, a fae would win nearly every time.

But no, she *knew* he was all right. The mate bond might not be fully active, but the connection was there, alive, vibrant. She would've felt if he were hurt—or dead.

Her mind went to that last night, and the look on his face when he'd told her he loved her. Determined, but vulnerable. Her fingers tightened on the dolphin.

Meu coração.

Why hadn't she told him she loved him back, that he was her heart, as well?

She'd had time to think about what Cleia had said, that she'd used magic to lure him to her. He shouldn't have been in the bar in the first place—because she knew damn well he'd been on the prowl for a woman—but if Cleia hadn't turned up, he'd probably have come to his senses before actually doing anything. It had been Rui's bad luck that Cleia had turned up at exactly the wrong moment. Otherwise he'd probably have come home the next day, hung-over and sheepish, and the two of them would've had a chance to work it out.

She dropped onto the couch and scowled down at the rug. It was time to admit her own part in all of this. She'd all but pushed Rui out the door. She'd seen him flinch, felt his pain through the mate bond.

And a part of her had been pleased, had wanted to punish him. He *should* feel bad for what he'd done. He'd left an innocent little girl an orphan.

She wasn't sure what she would've said if he'd come straight back after reporting to Dion, but she knew she wouldn't have been kind or forgiving. Not then.

But later, as the days turned into weeks and then into long, lonely months, she'd wished she'd at least waited to hear Rui's side of it. To recoil from your mate was to strike at his very core, felt as it was through the mystical, soul-to-soul bond. But she hadn't even given him a chance to explain.

And even if what Rui had done was wrong, who was she to judge? In the two years since then, she'd seen firsthand how bad things were at Rock Run. That didn't make killing Silver right, but it did help her understand why.

And there was the fact that without Rui, Merry probably would've died that night along with her dad.

Valeria scrubbed her hands over her face. She'd probably never sort out all the rights and wrongs of that night. All she knew was that she loved Rui, and it was time to move on—because everybody deserved a second chance.

Meanwhile it was getting late and Merry was an early riser. Rising to her feet, she extinguished the lights and went to bed.

Where in Hades was Tyrus?

After ascertaining the fae lord wasn't in Baltimore, Rui had traveled to the night fae compound, located in an isolated area of Virginia's Tidewater region. There, he'd slipped into one of the streams that ran through the compound and changed into a rockfish.

The night fae had set wards to keep out intruders, but Rui had hidden among a school of menhaden, tricking the wards into believing he was just another fish. Fae wards tended to overlook animals. It was one of the things—along with their innate arrogance—that made the fae vulnerable to fada assassins.

Rui had spent hours lurking in a stream near the night fae's main buildings, which, true to rumor, did resemble crypts, built of granite or marble and set partly underground with only a few feet showing above. The compound reminded him of New Orleans: Gothic stone buildings, towering trees and dank, oppressive shadows.

But Tyrus was nowhere to be seen.

Rui was about to leave when Prince Langdon strolled into view along with a pale, black-haired woman in a short silver dress, both of them wearing dark glasses to protect their eyes from the sunlight.

They stopped just a few yards from his hiding place in the stream and he froze.

Langdon, tall, dark and preternaturally handsome, was cursing out his absent son for missing an important business negotiation without permission. "Damn Tyrus anyway. Sindre was smirking at his empty seat the entire time."

Sindre was the ice fae king. *Interesting.*

The ice fae usually stayed in the far north or south, leaving the middle latitudes to the other fae. Rui would love to know what business Sindre and the night fae were transacting.

"Tyrus ignored a direct order," the prince continued. "And not for the first time. I want him punished, Fleur."

"I'll make sure he's properly remorseful, my lord," the woman assured him. She turned, and Rui saw she wore the black star medallion of a night fae priestess.

"You do that." They exchanged knowing smiles. "I'm counting on you, love."

Rui twitched his fins in distaste. Damn, the night fae made his skin—or in this case, scales—crawl.

He waited to see if the priestess volunteered Tyrus's whereabouts, but if she knew, she wasn't saying. Langdon dismissed her and she strode off, long legs flashing under the short dress.

One of the prince's bodyguards approached the stream. Rui tensed. The sight of a such a large fish in a narrow stream would scream river fada to anyone with half a brain.

He whipped around and shot back downstream.

Back in Baltimore, he cast around for a trail one more time. Still no luck. Even Hunter wasn't to be found at the Full Moon Saloon, and nobody seemed to know the location of his den.

By then it was close to noon, and Rui had been away for almost three days with nothing to show for it. With a muttered curse, he aimed his motorcycle back up I-95. He wasn't looking forward to telling Valeria that he hadn't been able to locate Tyrus.

But as he pulled his bike into the clan garage, Tiago do Rio burst from the shadows, wild-eyed and shaggy and smelling half-feral.

"They have Valeria. You have to come. Now."

～

VALERIA SAT UP IN BED. Was that a knock?

It came again and her heart leapt. It was just a little after six a.m. It had to be Rui.

Merry was already pounding down the hall. "I'll get it," she called.

As Valeria pulled on a T-shirt and shorts, she heard the door open and then Merry said in a flat voice, "Oh, it's you, Senhor Petros."

Valeria hurried to join them. She scowled at Petros. "What do you want?"

"I'm your guard today. I understand you've been having trouble with the local earth fada."

Valeria gripped the edge of the door. His scent reeked of deception—not quite a lie, but close.

"I don't need a guard. The alpha has ordered me not to leave the base." Dion and Rui had decided it wasn't safe for her to go crabbing even with a guard, so she and Merry had spent the last couple of days confined to the base and the small area of the creek protected by the concealing spell. "Now, goodbye—and don't bother me again."

She started to close the door, but Petros stopped it with his foot. The next moment, he was inside and had Merry's face cupped in his hands.

"But Merry wants to come with me, don't you?" Staring into her eyes, he muttered something in ancient Greek.

To Valeria's horror, Merry's small body went taut. She shot Valeria a panicked look, but when she opened her mouth, all that came out was, "Yes, Senhor Petros."

"Good girl." He released her.

Valeria grabbed Merry's shoulders, but something that stank of dark magic had wrapped itself around the girl like an invisible net. She instinctively jerked her hands away as it tried to latch on to her as well.

She took a threatening step toward Petros. "What did you do to her?"

His smile was cold. "I bound her to obey me."

"What do you mean, you *bound* her?"

"I mean I control her. Her mind is her own, but her body will do anything I order. For example, if I tell her to smash her head against the wall, she'll do it. Would you like a demonstration?"

Valeria's hands fisted at her sides. "No," she gritted. "Of course not."

"Good. Now we're going to walk to the marina. Take her hand, Valeria. But lightly, or it will take hold of you, too."

She had no alternative but to obey. She took Merry's hand. Cold tendrils brushed over her hand and wrist. She shuddered and tensed, but they seemed to sense that she wasn't the one they'd been brought into being to control, so didn't latch onto her.

Merry's fingers closed around hers. She gave her a reassuring squeeze.

"Get moving." Petros ushered them into the hall. "And Valeria? If we see anyone, don't try anything. Just nod and keep going. Understand?"

"Yes," she said between tight lips.

They set out, Merry moving like an automaton, her small body stiff, arms against her sides save for the hand clutching Valeria's.

Her only hope was that someone would notice and force them to stop. But at this hour, the halls were nearly empty. The fishers were already out on the water and the rest of the clan was just waking up. The few people they passed were only distant acquaintances, and found nothing odd in Valeria merely greeting them and continuing on.

At the exit, the sentry waved them through with a smile, making Valeria want to scream with frustration. They headed down the path to the marina, where Petros directed them to the *Esperança*, the small skiff Valeria used for crabbing.

"Get in the boat."

Valeria glanced around. *Please, please, someone notice something's wrong.*

But the few people still in the marina were on other piers,

going about their business. Releasing Merry's hand, she edged toward the side of the pier. Maybe she could fall in, pretend to be in trouble—odd behavior for a water fada. That should attract attraction.

"Whatever you're thinking, I wouldn't if I were you." Petros's voice was silky. "Remember, I can order Merry's body to do anything. I wonder how long she could hold her breath if I ordered her to dive to the bottom of the river?"

Valeria gulped, fear a hot mass in her chest. "Look, it's me you want. I swear I'll go with you willingly. But please, leave her here. You don't need her."

"But I do," he replied with a little smile. "Now get in the boat. Unless—" He flicked his fingers suggestively at the river.

"No! I—I'll do whatever you ask." Bending down, she told Merry, "We'd better do what he says, sweetheart. But I promise, it will be all right."

Merry blinked up at Valeria. "Okay," she whispered, lips barely moving.

Valeria swallowed sickly. She had no idea how she was going to keep that promise. "That's my girl."

She helped Merry into the skiff and then sat on a bench near the bow and pulled her onto her lap. The dark net of the spell writhed like a living thing. Tendrils brushed over her arms and face, cold and moist and hungry. She sucked in a breath and went almost as stiff as Merry, but Petros muttered something and they withdrew.

As he took a seat facing them, a shudder went through Valeria. "That's your Gift," she said. "To bind others to do your will."

Very few fada had such a dark Gift. In fact, she'd only heard of one other, and he'd been killed by his alpha when he'd tried to use the Gift against him.

Petros had been careful to hide his ability from the Rock Run Clan.

His mouth curved. "You know what I am, then."

"Yes," she rasped.

He started the motor and cast off, one hand on the tiller. The rest of Rock Run's small flotilla was heading downriver toward the fertile fishing grounds at the mouth of the Susquehanna, but Petros pointed their boat in the opposite direction.

Valeria looked from him to the boats receding in the distance. "Where are you taking us?"

"To a party. Remember?"

And suddenly Valeria knew. Not all the old fada had renounced the bacchanals—and Petros was a very old fada.

"A baccha?"

He smiled without replying, but Valeria knew she was correct. She was too young to have participated in a baccha, but she'd heard the stories. They'd started as rites to celebrate the god Dionysus. Everyone gathered for the ecstatic orgies of wine and sex—fae, humans, animals and Dionysus himself. It was in the baccha that the fada had been born, a magical combination of all four.

But as time passed, the rites grew sadistic: women and the weaker men forced to perform sexual acts with any man who desired it. Wine and drugs forced down a captive's throat. Harsh beatings at the slightest resistance until you begged for the release of death.

And the most depraved had lured children into their games...

Valeria's lungs clenched.

Not Merry. Please, not Merry.

The little girl whimpered, and Valeria realized she was squeezing her too tightly. The dark tendrils touched her arms, seeking, seeking... She loosened her grip on Merry and took a deep breath. She had to stay calm for her daughter.

When she could speak again, she said, "All right," as coolly as she could. "But we don't need Merry, do we? If you let her off, I swear I'll come with you. We don't have to go back to the marina —just let her off anywhere along here."

Petros simply raised a dark brow and let out the throttle. The boat zoomed upriver.

Merry rubbed her head against Valeria's chest. "Please, Mama," she said in a small voice. "I don't want to go with him."

Valeria's heart constricted. "I know." She risked the black tendrils to give her a quick hug and tried again. "Petros, please. I'm begging you—let her go. She's just a little girl."

To her shock, he agreed. "Swear it. Swear that if I let her go, you'll come with me to my den."

"Your den?"

"Me and a few other men have formed a den for those who want to follow the old ways—not like your alpha, with that sun fae bitch leading him around by the balls." Petros spat into the river. "Now swear."

Valeria nodded and repeated his words back to him, all the while conscious of Merry trembling in her arms. They were silent after that, Valeria watching as they headed upriver away from Rock Run.

An odd calm settled over her. She tried not to think about what would happen once she was alone with Petros. At least Merry would be safe.

The old ways didn't just include bacchas. The men had owned the women and children back then, had had the right to keep them in seclusion from other men if they chose. As in much of the human world at that time, a woman's sole purpose was to mate and reproduce.

But all that had changed in the last hundred years, just as it had in the rest of the world. Only a few small dens here and there still followed the old ways, and they were dying out for the simple reason that few females would agree to such complete domination.

They rounded a bend. They were out of sight of the marina now, heading up the Susquehanna River. To their left was Rock Run territory, much of it uninhabited forest, save for a few human farms and the clan's vineyards. The right was more developed, with small towns and the occasional house or farm dotting the land in between.

Petros indicated three wooded islands another half-mile up the river. "We'll let Merry off there—on the furthest island."

Valeria nodded and tried not to see her daughter's pleading expression.

As they approached the island, Valeria rubbed her nose against Merry's. "You'll be all right. Just wave to the first boat. If it's not a fada, tell them you're from Rock Run and they'll take you back to the marina. Or look for a dolphin—it will be a sentry. They patrol here all the time."

"No, Mama. Please don't leav—" Her mouth snapped shut and she whined, animal-like.

Valeria glowered at Petros. "Stop that, damn you. Can't you tell how frightened she is?"

He gazed back without speaking. But something about his expression made her close her own mouth and subside.

Petros guided the boat to a pebbled spit of land at the very edge of Rock Run territory. While Petros tied the boat to a tree, Valeria whispered to Merry, "Remember—look for a sentry. Tell him or her what happened, and that Senhor Petros took me somewhere upriver. Can you do that for me, baby?"

She gave a tearful sniff, but nodded.

"Out," said Petros. "Both of you."

Valeria stepped into the calf-high water and reached for Merry. "I love you, *querida*." She stepped onto the island, the little girl in her arms.

"Set her down," Petros ordered. When Valeria complied, he touched Merry's shoulder and ordered her not to move for five minutes.

"Yes, *senhor*," she replied hollowly.

"Good girl." He jerked his chin at Valeria. "We're swimming from here. Leave your clothes in the boat."

Valeria obeyed and followed him into the water, where he ordered her to shift. She glanced back at Merry. She was standing like a stiff little soldier, tears running down her face.

Valeria felt as if her heart were being ripped out. She swallowed her own tears and told herself it was for the best.

Then two men stepped out of the trees. Jace Jones and another, larger man, also an earth fada.

Valeria snarled. "What did you do?" she snapped at Petros and started running through the water toward Merry.

"What your alpha should've done two years ago. What do you want with an earth-shifter cub anyway? Get back here," he barked at her. "Remember your promise, damn you."

Jace picked the still-stiff Merry up.

"Please," Valeria pleaded as she reached the shore. "Don't take her. I'm begging you."

The jaguar shifter shook his head, his expression regretful. "I'm sorry, but she belongs with us. I'll...let you know how she's doing."

He and the other man faded back into the trees.

Valeria's claws sliced out. She leapt after them, but breaking a vow was even worse than telling a lie. Pain ripped through her. She shrieked even as the change took her. In her fear and anger, something went wrong and her claws turned to flippers.

And then she was a dolphin, wracked by pain and flopping uselessly on the shore, the grit and pebbles digging into her sensitive skin. She watched helplessly as Jace and the other man disappeared into the woods.

The last thing she saw was Merry looking back at her, screaming for help.

Valeria threw herself after them, wriggling frantically along the beach, her animal knowing only that she had to save her daughter.

Until the agony became too much and everything went black.

21

Tiago hadn't lasted long in Baltimore. Too many people —and no clean water. The harbor was a cesspool and even the tap water was chlorinated. After five days he was desperate for fresh, chemical-free water.

A smart man would leave the country. He could lose himself in the Amazon, which had the world's largest concentration of river fada, or maybe travel to Portugal or one of the other southern European countries with river fada populations. But somehow he found himself back at Rock Run.

He couldn't go back to the base, of course, but he made his way to an island in the middle of the Susquehanna River, uninhabited save for a dryad. The clan allowed her and her two sisters to share their territory. Dryads were considered lucky, and besides, they had a special touch with growing things. The three islands that the dryads had claimed were lush green oases, with tall, old-growth trees. The fertility even extended into the river around the islands, which was rich with fish, clams, and other mollusks.

Dryads were notoriously shy. He spent most of his time in the river in his rockfish form, hiding from Rock Run's sentries in dark nooks and crannies. But even when on land, he caught only brief glimpses of her as she darted through the forest, barefoot and dressed in light summer clothing, her tawny hair streaming like a wild flag behind her.

When he first arrived, he left an offering of bread and cheese at the base of her oak, knowing that this would be a treat since she depended mainly on what she could grow on the island. In return, she gifted him with some fresh greens and a sack of early tomatoes. The two of them settled into a wary coexistence—until he realized that someone else was using the island as well.

Five men, who came and went, usually with a female or two: Petros Okeanos, two other Greeks he didn't know, and Benny and Jorge.

Tiago frowned. Jorge had once been his mentor. When Dion and Tiago's parents had been lost at sea, Tiago had still been a kid—just eleven turns of the sun. Dion and Rui had done their best, but they'd been thrust into the role of alpha and second. Jorge had been a *tenente* at the time—far above Tiago—but he'd stepped in, offering comfort in his gruff way and then proceeding to push Tiago. Hard.

"You're the alpha's brother," he'd said. "You have to be twice as good as anyone else."

Tiago had idolized the man. It hurt that Jorge was back and hadn't even bothered to look him up.

He supposed Jorge scented him, but he and the other four men were apparently busy fucking their brains out. They disappeared for long hours with whatever females they brought to the island, returning flushed and smelling of wine and sex.

It was several days before Tiago realized they were using a cavern right beneath the dryad's oak. He was surprised she was allowing it, but then, this was Rock Run territory. She probably thought the illicit little den had Dion's approval.

He felt a twinge of fear for the dryad; she was such a gentle creature. But she seemed safe enough. Dryads had ways of concealing themselves in their trees that made them almost impossible to detect.

Okeanos seemed to be in charge, and although it was obvious what he and the men were doing in that underground cave, it never occurred to Tiago that they were holding bacchanals for the simple reason that there hadn't been one at Rock Run since before he was born.

When he finally realized what was going on, his first thought was that he needed to tell Dion immediately—until he recalled that his brother didn't even know he was still on Rock Run territory.

Mind your own business, he told himself. *They're not hurting anyone.* The few females he'd seen—a couple of night fae, a river fada he didn't recognize, and three humans—seemed willing enough.

Then Okeanos had appeared with an obviously terrified Valeria and her daughter, and Tiago decided it was time to stop lying to himself.

Now he watched as Rui do Mar's brows snapped together. "What do you mean?"

"Your woman—Valeria. Petros Okeanos has her."

Rui had him by the throat before he could react. "Explain. And it had better be good, you bastard."

He gazed back steadily. "You know, then."

"That it was you who helped the sun fae? Yes."

"So am I under a death sentence?"

It would almost be a relief. The weeks on his own had taken their toll. He knew he was on the edge of going feral. A fada his age wasn't meant to live as a solitary; he needed touch, the companionship of the pack. He'd even missed the punishing training his cohort had been undergoing in preparation for their induction as warriors.

"No. Dion wanted to find you first." Rui gave him a hard shake. "Now talk. Where's Valeria?"

"Okeanos has her—and Merry, too. I don't know what happened, but they didn't go with him willingly. I could scent their fear."

Rui inhaled slowly, testing the truth of his words. Tiago saw the exact moment when fear dawned.

"Where?" he asked hoarsely.

"You know those three islands about a mile up the Susquehanna? The dryads' islands?"

"*Sim.*"

"Okeanos and a few other men have a den on the middle one. It's underground, but I know where the entrance is."

Rui released Tiago's throat. "Go on."

"They've been holding bacchas there. Okeanos has brought other women to the island. At first I figured the women were willing, but Valeria was trying to get away from him. And when I thought about it, I realized the other women were too stiff—as if he was controlling them in some way. Dark magic, maybe."

Rui's eyes flickered. "How many men?"

"Okeanos, a couple of other sea fada. And Jorge and Benny."

"And you know where they are?"

"Yes."

"Hell." Rui scrubbed his hands over his face. "Dion needs to know, but there's no time." The garage was a half a mile up creek from the base.

"I'll tell him."

Rui gave him a considering look and then shook his head. "No. I need you to take me to their den. Besides, I could use some back up. You up for it?"

Tiago squared his shoulders. "Yes, sir."

"Then let's go. I'll worry about getting a message to Dion after we're there."

Rui was already on his way out of the garage, tearing off his clothes as he ran.

When he reached the creek, he dove in, changing to his shark in mid-air. Tiago shifted to dolphin a few seconds behind him, and together, they shot downstream toward the Susquehanna.

22

When Valeria came back to herself, Petros was standing on the beach over her scraped and bleeding body. She forced the shift back to human, her animal still in control and gripped by a killing rage.

She growled at him, her claws slicing out. *The man gave the daughter to the enemy. He dies.*

Petros's lip curled. "Fool. I can control you as easily as her."

The words had as much meaning as the barking of a dog or the howling wind. She dropped into a crouch, preparing to pounce.

But Petros muttered a few words in ancient Greek, and the invisible net closed around her. She lunged toward the water, changing to dolphin to try to escape, but the net simply adjusted to her new contours. She thrashed wildly, her animal half-crazed at being trapped.

Petros kept the pressure on, tightening the net until she was gasping for breath.

Still she struggled, maddened with fear and anger, until he waded into the water and punched her in the snout.

"Stop it," he snarled, "or I swear to God I'll knock you out."

Somehow the words made it through the thick terror enveloping her brain. She shuddered to a stop and dragged in air through her blowhole. But she couldn't get enough. The edges of her vision went black and she started to sink as the air was squeezed from her lungs.

Petros swore, but loosened the net enough to allow her to breathe freely. Her chest heaved and she drew in great gulps of oxygen.

Gradually her reason returned, but with it came a cold dread.

The Baltimore shifters had Merry and she couldn't even raise the alarm.

"Swim, baby," Petros crooned in a voice that made her flesh crawl.

He pushed her back into the river and draped one arm around her neck. "I've given you enough slack so you can move that pretty tail of yours. But if you try anything funny, I'll make the net so tight you won't be able to breathe. You'll sink like a stone without me to hold you up. Nod if you understand."

She jerked her head.

"Good girl," he said. "Head downriver. That party I told you about? It's on the next island. Just me and a few friends. And, *glika?* You broke your promise. I'll have to punish you for that. Now swim."

It only took a few minutes to reach their destination. As soon as Petros's feet touched the shore he stood up.

She halted, chest working like a bellows, nearly at the end of her resources. The bastard had kept an arm around her neck the entire way, and rather than helping her swim, he'd let his legs drag so she was forced to pull him through the water.

There was no sign of the sentries and the only boat they'd passed had contained humans, no match for a fada, especially one with a dark Gift like Petros's. She'd hoped he might loosen the net holding her captive, but he'd kept her tightly bound. And even if she did manage to break free of him, she was still bleeding and exhausted.

But Petros had to be tiring as well. He'd bound first Merry, then her. Any prolonged use of magic drained life-energy, and he was using a tremendous amount to keep such a tight control on her.

Now, as she struggled to catch her breath, she told herself that at least Merry was safe. Jace was her uncle. Merry might be scared and upset, but he wouldn't harm her.

"Shift," Petros ordered.

She hesitated, unsure she had the strength. Exhausted as she was, she risked being trapped in a dangerously half-changed state: part dolphin, part woman. She'd die, her body unable to reconcile two such disparate parts.

Petros's hand chopped down on her snout. Pain burst behind her eyes. She squawked angrily.

"Shift," he repeated.

She drew a breath and obeyed.

The change was a slow, painful process that left her very bones aching. She had a terrifying few seconds where she was afraid she wouldn't complete it, but she dug deep and forced the last few parts to form. When she was finished, she crouched in the water, gulping in air, still bound in the invisible net.

The sun had risen. It was going to be a hot, sticky day. Even now, with the sun still low in the sky, it was uncomfortably warm on her bare skin.

Petros waved his hand and the net loosened enough to allow her to move her arms.

Her nose felt wet. She put a hand to it and saw her fingers were stained with blood.

Petros stared down at her, his face an unyielding mask. "When I give an order, you'll obey immediately. Understand?"

She nodded. She'd go along with him for now, wait for a chance to escape.

Because she *would* escape. The alternative didn't bear thinking about.

But the blood had given her an idea. She could use her Gift.

One of the reasons Rui was such a good tracker was that his shark could scent blood in the water in concentrations as low as a few parts per million. She drew several fish toward her and brushed the blood on her hand onto them, and then gave them a powerful push downriver. If Rui was in the river, he'd pick up her scent and follow it to the island.

Of course, that was supposing he'd returned—and that he realized she and Merry were missing. Her stomach sank as she realized how unlikely it was that Rui—or anyone—would come looking for them in time. Eventually, they'd be missed when they didn't show up for meals, but by the time anything realized something was wrong, Merry would be in Baltimore—and Petros would have her, Valeria, hidden in his den.

Petros's hand clamped on her arm. "Get up."

She rinsed the blood from her face and rose to her feet. His gaze moved down her naked body in a way that made the skin between her shoulder blades tighten. His cock began to harden. He raised his gaze back to hers and smiled.

Valeria glanced back and gave the fish another forceful nudge.

Petros waved a hand, freeing her from the net, but he immediately forced her arms behind her back and bound her wrists together with the same invisible webbing while leaving her legs free to walk.

"That way," he said, pointing toward a path into the trees. He slapped her bottom—hard—so that she stumbled forward.

He was trying to humiliate her. Well, fuck him. She raised her chin and calmly picked her way over the pebbled beach toward the woods. He chuckled but fell in behind her.

The path led to a clearing at the center of the island presided over by a tall, slim oak. Petros tapped on the trunk as he spoke some words in ancient Greek, and a magical doorway opened, which by some three-dimensional sleight-of-hand expanded until its width was greater than the actual tree trunk. Stairs led into the shadowy depths below.

Valeria's spine iced. She *knew*, with a deep, inner certainty, that dark souls waited at the bottom of those stairs. Her knees locked and she forgot all about waiting for a chance to escape. She just wanted to stay above ground.

"*Não.*" In her terror, she reverted to Portuguese. With an effort she unstuck her frozen joints and backed away, one step at a time. "*Por favor, Petros.*"

He stalked after her until her back hit a tree. His fingers tangled painfully in her hair. "No?" He forced her head back so that she had to bend her knees to relieve the pressure. "Did I hear you right?"

She licked suddenly dry lips and forced herself to remember her English. "Please don't make me go down there. I'll do anything you want, just please don't make me—"

He slapped her face so hard she tasted blood. "What?" he asked, his eyes glittering darkly.

He was close enough that his erection jabbed her belly. Her resistance aroused him, the bastard.

She brought her hand to her throbbing cheek. "Nothing," she said dully.

"That's better." He gave her hair another painful tug. "Let me explain something, *glika*—the word *no* is no longer part of your vocabulary. Are we clear on that?"

She dropped her gaze. "*Sim,*" she whispered.

Jace sped with Merry to the other side of the island, Hunter close behind him. His heart was full as he cradled the little girl's stiff body. He'd thought Takira's daughter dead. Never in a million years had he thought he'd get to hold her again. Whatever Adric had had to pay Okeanos to get her, it was worth it.

He smiled into the big whiskey-colored eyes so like his sister's. "Welcome back, sweetheart."

She gazed back expressionlessly. That bothered him, but he attributed it to whatever Okeanos had done to her. Then the stiffness wore off and she shifted to jaguar, swiping at his face with her claws so that he almost dropped her.

He caught her by the scruff of her neck and gave her a shake. "Settle down, damn it."

Her upper lip pulled back in a fierce little snarl.

"You're an earth fada," he snapped, exasperated. "You belong with us."

She shook off her clothes, which had twisted themselves around her body, and shifted back to girl. He bobbled her in his arms, almost dropping her a second time.

"I want my mama," she wailed.

"God's balls," Hunter muttered. "Shut her up before she brings a sentry down on us."

"What do you expect?" Jace growled back. "She's just a cub."

Hunter had volunteered for this; he'd known what it entailed. Jace and Adric had agreed that since Hunter had made the first contact with Okeanos, he was a good choice. Besides, the man was a true wolf, his animal close to the surface, worth two or three lesser soldiers. Two men were all Adric had been willing to send. Any more risked detection by the Rock Run sentries.

As it was, he and Hunter were passing themselves off as humans, having rented a local's boat and picked up used clothes at a human thrift store to conceal their scent.

But Hunter was right. Jace tried softening his voice. "Hush, now," he told Merry. "Don't you remember your Uncle Jace?"

She sniffed and nodded, her large eyes shimmering with tears. "Please, Uncle Jace. Don't let Senhor Petros hurt my mama. He's a bad man."

"He's not going to hurt her."

But he couldn't meet her eyes as he said it. It wasn't a lie, but it wasn't the truth, either. He didn't know what Okeanos wanted with Valeria da Costa, but he knew it wasn't good.

Merry's nose crinkled, and he knew she scented his evasion. She relaxed just long enough for him to think she'd resigned herself to coming with him, and then wrenched herself out of his arms and dashed toward the trees.

He leapt forward, catching her up again, but she went crazy, screaming and twisting in his arms, until he was forced to use his crystal to compel calm on her. He didn't have Adric's Gift with the quartz, but Merry was a cub, and also a close relation. He able to quiet her enough that she ceased fighting him, her screams changing to heart-rending sobs.

He gazed down at her helplessly. The last thing he wanted was to get involved in a Rock Run matter. But as he looked at Merry's small, sad face, all he could think of was his sister Takira and how she'd died.

It was obvious that the da Costa woman hadn't gone willingly with Okeanos. And it didn't take a genius to know what the man intended.

How could he, Jace, stand by and let another woman be raped, maybe even worse? It was Takira all over again.

He bit out a curse so sharp that Merry flinched even in her semi-tranquilized state. "I'm going after the Rock Run woman," he told Hunter. "You're welcome to wait here—I know it's not what you agreed to do."

The other man stared at him. "Are you fucking insane?"

"Probably." Jace waded into the water and dropped Merry into the small fishing boat they'd rented. "Don't move," he ordered, "if you want me to help your mama."

She scrambled onto a seat and nodded, face solemn.

As Jace started the motor, Hunter leapt into the boat with a wolf's rangy grace.

"Thanks," Jace told him. "I can use your help. I don't know how many men Okeanos has with him."

Hunter grunted. "I'm not along to help. I'll stay with the cub in the boat. Damned if I'll let you strand me on an island in Rock Run territory."

"Suit yourself." Jace aimed the boat in the direction Okeanos had gone.

THE TOP SPEED of a bull shark was twenty-five miles per hour. Rui hurtled through the water as swiftly as his straining muscles could propel him, but it still wasn't fast enough. He was old enough to have attended a number of bacchas. He'd seen men and women in the grip of the *Delírio*, and worse, seen how it changed a person over time. Sooner or later they lost all sense of right and wrong, caring only about seeking pleasure...and meting out pain.

Okeanos must have crossed that line years ago. The idea of Valeria and little Merry being subjected to his whims had Rui nearly crazed with rage and terror.

Inside, his animal was even worse, growling and gnashing its teeth, threatening to mow down anything in its path to get to the mate.

Blood, it muttered. *Death.*

Rui ruthlessly subdued it. *I promise, he's a dead man. But we have to stay calm.*

His animal rumbled angrily but subsided, recognizing that Rui was correct.

He reached the middle island and waited impatiently for Tiago, whose dolphin couldn't match Rui's speed. The youth had earned his grudging respect. When Tiago had run rather than face the music, Rui had been disappointed, even contemptuous.

But apparently he'd grown some balls in the past month if he'd been willing to face his brother for Valeria's sake.

Tiago arrived and flicked his snout toward a narrow beach. *This way.*

Rui shot forward again, then abruptly halted as he scented Valeria's blood on a school of small fish streaming past him.

She was on the island, as Tiago had said—and bleeding.

Fury and the worst kind of fear roiled in his gut. Hot, black, urgent.

He lurched toward the shore, overshooting his mark and scraping his belly on the grit and pebbles littering the small strip of land. Fortunately, the shark's tough skin protected him. He lost precious seconds changing back to his human form, but Tiago was right behind him.

And then a sentry shot out of the river, shifting from dolphin to woman—Eliana. "What's up?"

"Get Dion," Rui rapped out. "Or Luis, if you can't find Dion. Tell them Petros Okeanos has taken Valeria and Merry prisoner and they're on this island somewhere." Once on the island, they could easily follow his and Tiago's scent.

Eliana didn't waste time with further questions, simply dove back into the river, changing back to her dolphin a few yards out.

"This way." Tiago indicated a narrow path through the trees.

Rui set off at a run. Within a few steps, he'd picked up Valeria's scent, as strong as if she'd drawn a neon trail, overlaid by Okeanos's darker masculine spoor. He didn't scent Merry, which scared him, but his whole body thrummed with the need to get to his mate.

He raced down the path.

A quarter mile in, they reached a clearing dominated by a tall pin oak. Rui halted. "She's here."

"That's the dryad's tree." Tiago jogged up behind him. "There's some kind of door in the trunk that Okeanos and the others use to enter the den, but I don't know the secret."

Rui swore under his breath. He ran his hands over the bark, refusing to believe he could be this close to Valeria and not be able to help her. When he couldn't find even the slightest crack, he slammed his fist against the trunk.

"Open, damn you."

Nothing happened. He changed his tone. For Valeria, he'd plead. Hell, if he thought it would help, he'd crawl on his belly through the cold, dark wastes of Hades.

"Please. I'm begging you. Let us in."

Still nothing.

He caught a fresh whiff of Valeria, acrid with fear. His chest constricted.

"Damn you." He slammed his palms against the oak's ridged trunk. "Open the fucking door."

A bird shrieked and shot into the sky. The oak's leaves rustled and he glanced up hopefully, but saw nothing.

"Tell her," he rasped at Tiago. "Tell the dryad to let us in."

"I can try—but I haven't actually met her."

"I thought you were friends."

"Not exactly." The younger man's expression was sheepish. "She doesn't like fada."

"*Deus*." Rui dragged a hand over his face. "All right. Just—do whatever you can."

"Miss?" Tiago cupped his mouth and directed his voice to the oak's crown. "We know you're up there. We're trying to rescue a friend of ours, a woman from Rock Run. Please ask your tree to open."

Rui held his breath, praying the shy forest dweller would help them. Everything stilled, as if the very trees were holding their breath along with him, but nothing happened.

Tiago tried again. "Please, miss. I swear we mean you no harm. Just let us inside and as soon as we have our friend, we'll leave you in peace."

Still nothing. Rui took a step back, his brain working furiously. He didn't have the power to command the tree to open, but Queen Cleia might; she was a powerful fae. Unfortunately, it could take hours to track her down and bring her back here.

Meanwhile, Okeanos and his fucking den would have Valeria and Merry in their power.

He pressed his fists to his face. *Think, damn it.* There had to be a way to get to them.

Then he heard Valeria scream.

23

———

 aleria froze on the bottom step. Four naked men sprawled on cushions in the dimly lit cave, glasses in hand. The air reeked of wine and lust.

Petros shoved her forward, and she lurched the final step onto the cavern floor.

"Meet Jorge"—Petros indicated a barrel-chested man with hard brown eyes—"and Benny." He pointed to a younger man with a long, soulful face. "They're originally from Rock Run, but we met a few years ago near Crete. The other men are from my clan, Orius and Mys."

She'd heard of Jorge and Benny. Supposedly they were weak, broken from their time as Cleia's lovers.

They didn't seem weak now.

These were large, powerful males in their prime, eyeing her like the unprotected female she was. Both of their primary animals were dolphins—and anyone who truly knew dolphins knew they were far from the cute and cuddly mammals portrayed on human TV. Dolphins could be sexually aggressive to the point of rape.

Jorge gave a curt nod, watching her from beneath lowered lids. Benny raised his glass in a mocking salute.

Orius and Mys didn't even deign to acknowledge her, just stared at her naked body, their eyes crawling with lust.

Ordinarily her nudity wouldn't have bothered her, but these men made her feel like a slab of meat. She shrank into herself, hunching her shoulders and squeezing her thighs together. Behind her back, her hands clenched together so tightly her fingertips went numb.

Petros chuckled. "It won't be so bad, *glika*." He stroked her nape. "You might even like it."

She hunched even more but didn't reply. His fingers slid lower, and she tensed for whatever was coming, but all he did was release her bonds. She shook out her hands, grateful for that much at least.

But then, what did he have to lose? The doorway had closed behind them. She wasn't going anywhere.

Petros crossed to a table by the wall and filled a glass with wine. "Here. Drink this."

She took a cautious sniff of the dark red liquid. The wine had an unpleasant, sickly-sweet odor, and she guessed it had been mixed with some kind of drug.

She glanced at the other men. They watched her avidly, even Jorge and Benny.

Bastards. They must know she was Rui's mate.

She sent Benny a pleading look. "Help me," she whispered in Portuguese.

He merely lifted a brow.

"They're with me," Petros informed her. "All the men here agree that the old ways should never have been abandoned, starting with the baccha. The fada are turning into tame little house pets, doing the fae's bidding. Hell, your own alpha mated with a fae. And the women, well, they need to be taught their proper place."

He raised the glass to the other men. "To Dionysus."

"To Dionysus," they returned as one.

They all took a drink, and then Petros brought the glass to her lips again. "Now drink."

She took a tentative sip. The wine was cloyingly sweet, with an undertone of bitterness. It left an unpleasant coat on her tongue.

Petros kept the glass against her lips. "All of it."

A cold bead of sweat trickled down her spine. She stared into the drugged wine, wishing she dared refuse. But she was outnumbered five to one.

"Drink it," he said evenly. "Or I'll whip you bloody—and pour it down your unconscious throat. The choice is yours."

She drained the glass, then thrust it back at him with a defiant tilt of her chin. "Here."

He took it and placed it on the table. "I can see you require training on the proper way to speak to your lord and master. We'll work on that. But first…"

He trailed off, his gaze on her face, clearly waiting for the drug to take effect. The other men were all sitting upright now, watching and waiting as well—alert, aggressive predators.

Unnerved, she rubbed her palms over her upper arms.

It started as a not-unpleasant heat in the pit of her stomach. Then the drug exploded in her brain.

She gasped and staggered. Someone gave a huff of laughter, but she barely heard as the preparation raced through her veins, bringing an excruciating awareness of every nerve fiber, every tiny cell.

She dropped to her knees, clutching her head. "What," she wheezed, "in *Deus*'s name—did you give me?"

"My own recipe," Petros informed her. "Don't fight it. The pain will soon change, become a sensual agony that only another's touch can relieve. You'll be desperate for a man, any man…

like a bitch in heat. What do you think do Mar will do when he finds you've fucked all five of us?"

"*Não.*" Valeria moaned. "You—*filho da puta.*"

"Enough." Petros grabbed her by the hair and jerked her head back.

She screamed as pain knifed through her, magnified a thousand times. It felt as if her skull was being ripped off.

He eyed her sternly. "I think we need to show you what that mouth of yours is for." He released her hair to take his cock in hand and press it to her lips. "Suck me, woman."

Still reeling, she didn't respond fast enough and he raised a threatening hand. She sucked in a breath, knowing she couldn't take another bout of that agonizing pain.

She opened her mouth and took him inside.

To one side of her, Orius and Mys paired off. From the corner of her eye she saw the larger Orius force the smaller Mys onto all fours, covering him like a dog.

Meanwhile, Jorge and Benny closed in on her, stroking, petting...

Already the pain was transmuting into pleasure. Jorge squeezed her nipples and she moaned with desire, even as tears of humiliation pricked her eyes. Benny knelt beside her and slapped her ass, and she moaned again as the blow vibrated in her cunt.

He leaned close to bite her neck, hard enough to make her jerk with pain, but again the sting was edged with pleasure.

"You like that," he growled, his breath hot against her nape.

She suppressed a sob as Benny slapped her again, then slid his hand between her legs. She clenched her thighs on him, ashamed but desperate for touch—any touch.

Petros gripped the back of her head. "Take it." He rammed his cock against the back of her throat.

She gagged and then caught his rhythm, swallowing in time to his thrusts so that she wouldn't suffocate.

It was too intense. The men stroking and pinching and slap-ping. The man slamming into her mouth, his scent pungent, overpowering. The drug making everything an excruciating plea-sure/pain.

She grasped Petros's thighs to steady herself and blinked up at him woozily.

What would he do if she passed out? The thought seemed to come from far away.

Suddenly he cursed and jerked himself from her mouth with an audible pop. The other men jumped away as well and, caught off balance, she fell to the floor.

She curled into a ball. Someone was whimpering: a sad, desperate sound. It took her a few moments to realize it was herself.

A roar echoed through the cavern. She pressed a fist to her mouth and watched, dazed, as a large, enraged man threw himself at Petros.

She blinked. "Rui?"

24

───────

*H*igh in her oak, the dryad hugged its trunk, scowling.

Somehow the Greek fada had discovered the words that forced her tree to open the passage to the caves below. She hadn't liked it but assumed he had Rock Run's permission. The bargain was that Rock Run left her in peace with her trees and forest creatures, and in return she allowed the river fada to run free on what she thought of as her island.

But the Greek fada hadn't even had the courtesy to thank her.

Alesia had been raised to treat the fada with caution, so the men had only glimpsed her once. Her skin had prickled at how the leader had eyed her body, lingering on her legs, bare beneath a short summer tunic, and then gave her a smile that was all teeth. After that, she stayed well away from them.

And now they'd brought one of their own females to participate in their drunken rites—and she wasn't the first.

Her mother was right; shapeshifters were little better than animals.

But something in her tugged at the sight of the fada female, forced by the cold-eyed male down into his dark, smelly den. At first she'd assumed the woman had come willingly, like the ones before her. If the man slapped her around a little, well, wasn't that what fada women liked?

But Alesia had seen the woman's large, frightened eyes, noted her scratched body and the bruise on her face.

But what could Alesia do? Like most dryads, she was slim and on the small side. Her magic was in keeping the land fertile and coaxing things to grow. She kept nature in balance, assuring the forest and its creatures lived in harmony.

Those big, coarse fada would squash her like a fly if she interfered in their fun.

Two more fada males appeared beneath her tree, their breath sawing in and out of their chests. She recognized the younger one. Underneath that wild black hair he was kind of cute, with silver-blue eyes and a nice smile, and he'd had the good manners to offer her a gift of food in return for sharing her island.

But the older one was a big, intimidating man with bulging muscles and a hard face. At first she assumed he was with the others, but the door didn't open for him even when he begged it to.

She slid a branch aside to study him, curious about this fada who pleaded. He glanced up and she froze, hardening her skin so that its texture resembled bark and she blended into the trunk.

He shook his head and pressed his fists to his face in despair.

And then the woman screamed.

Alesia sucked in a breath and made up her mind. She launched herself from the oak, landing lightly behind the two men. The older one spun around with a snarl, drawing himself up to his full height and baring sharp canines at her.

She held up her hands. "Peace, fada. I'm not here to fight. You want to get inside, yes?"

He scrutinized her for a tense heartbeat. The younger man said, "This is the dryad. She can help us, Rui."

The big man relaxed a fraction. "Yes," he told her. "I'll give you anything—anything you want. Just please help me get to Valeria."

She waved a dismissive hand. "Just promise me that you're here to help the woman, not hurt her." Something occurred to her. "She's yours, isn't she? This Valeria? Your mate?"

"Yes. Yes, she is. And I swear on everything I hold holy that I just want to rescue her from those bastards."

Satisfied, she laid a hand on her oak. "My friend, I beg a favor of you—that you allow these two fada entrance." She thought for a second and then added, "And to please keep the entrance open until this man, Rui, returns with the woman Valeria."

The oak was mature—not ancient, but full grown—with little patience for the foolish doings of the two-legged ones other than its dryad, bound to it at birth. It muttered grumpily at being disturbed twice—no, three times—in the same day.

Alesia stroked its sturdy gray trunk. "Please?"

The leaves above rattled in irritation, but the door slid open. In an instant, Rui was inside and down the steps.

The younger male paused to touch her cheek. Alesia met his silver-blue eyes and blinked. She had the strange, dizzying sensation of falling *up*...into a light-filled sky.

"Thank you, Miss—?"

For a moment she forgot her own name. "Alesia," she blurted.

"Alesia. Well, thanks." He gave her that easy smile. "My name's Tiago. Tiago do Rio." He hurried after the other man.

Alesia put a hand to her cheek and watched as they disappeared into the darkness below. Rui must know he was outnumbered, that he could be rushing to his death, yet he hadn't hesitated to go to his mate's rescue. Goddess, how he must love her. Her heart twisted as she wondered what it would be like to have a man care for her like that.

She loved her trees, her lush little island, but sometimes it was lonely. From time to time her needs grew too great and she left to seek out a lover, but she'd never yet found her mate.

Apparently she expected him to somehow stumble upon her island in the middle of the river. She shook her head at herself, then lifted to her toes and swung back up into the oak.

Ten feet up, she stopped. Somewhere nearby, the woods stirred. She seated herself cross-legged on the branch, waiting. A few minutes later, another shifter ran up. An earth fada with shiny black hair and golden-brown skin.

He glanced up at her. "With your permission, Miss?"

Resigned, she waved a hand. "Be my guest." The tree was going to remain open anyway until the river fada returned with his mate.

The fada darted through the opening.

Alesia settled down to wait. From inside the cavern came the sounds of aggression.

She shook her head. The fada were such a violent race.

Then fine hairs all over her body lifted. Someone was watching her.

She slowly turned her head.

As Rui reached the bottom of the stars, he was dimly aware of other people in the cave, all men: two in a corner, fucking; two others hovering over Valeria.

But all he could see was his mate on her knees before Okeanos, his cock in her mouth.

The bastard had his hands locked on her head, forcing her to take him deep. The two other men had their hands all over her. She shuddered as if in pain and gave a guttural moan that raised the hair on Rui's nape.

He didn't slow as he reached the bottom of the stairs, just leapt for Okeanos, claws out. Let Valeria startle and bite off the *cabrão*'s dick.

But Okeanos saw him coming in time to shove her away. She gasped and curled into a ball.

Rui's heart clenched, but he couldn't stop to comfort her. He barreled into Okeanos, digging his claws into his torso and knocking him to the floor.

For a few seconds Rui was on top. He lunged for Okeanos's jugular vein, canines at the ready, but the other man threw him off and leapt to his feet, chest scoured with bloody marks.

Rui rolled, ignoring the painful jolt to his newly-healed abdomen, and came back to his feet a moment behind him. They circled each other, sizing one another up.

"You think you can take me?" Okeanos flung up a hand, palm out, five fingers extended in a very Greek insult. "Come on then, you *poutanas yie*." Rui knew enough Greek to know that meant son of a whore.

He growled and planted his feet in a fighting stance, preparing to pounce, when suddenly he was enveloped in what felt like a net of cold, black energy.

"What the fu—" He was trussed from chin to toes, arms pinned to his body. He snarled and strained against the net, but the harder he fought, the more it tightened.

Valeria hissed and crawled toward Okeanos. "Fight fair, you— you *coward*." She shoved his legs so that he staggered and stumbled forward.

He caught his balance and turned around, his face so dark that Rui redoubled his efforts to free himself.

"Did you call me a coward?"

She cringed but lifted her chin. "*Sim*. Only a coward would bind a man so he can't fight."

Okeanos slapped her across the face.

She jolted and brought a hand to her cheek, her lips tight with pain. Then her eyes narrowed. "Fuck you."

Rui sucked in his breath. Seeing her being slapped was a

hundred times worse than taking a blow himself. "Valeria, no. Don't—"

Okeanos jerked her to her feet. "Fuck me?" he asked as he slapped her again. "Oh yes, *glika*."

Her head snapped to one side. This time she had the sense to remain silent, the only sound her jagged breathing.

"Stop it, you bastard. You're hurting her."

Rui struggled desperately against the invisible net. It loosened, and hope surged. Then Okeanos flicked his fingers in Rui's direction and the strands tightened again.

Tiago had followed him down into the den. He growled and tried to go to Valeria, but Okeanos snarled, "Take another step and they're both dead."

Tiago looked to Rui. He gave a slight shake of his head in reply. Who knew what a man with Okeanos's Gift could do? If he said he could kill them both, it might be true.

The Greek fada returned his attention to Valeria. "You *will* fuck me, I promise you. Whenever or wherever I wish."

Another hard slap, then another, the harsh sound echoing in the cave and reverberating in Rui until he was nearly blind with fury.

Valeria tried to cover her face, but Okeanos pulled both arms behind her back, gripping her wrists in one hand so she couldn't defend herself.

"You will *beg* to please me," he gritted. "This is only a taste of what I can do. The aphrodisiac increases every sensation. Pleasure *and* pain. If I beat you, the pain alone might kill you."

He raised his hand again and something in Valeria seemed to break. Her face crumpled and she tucked her head into her shoulder.

"No more," she begged. "Please, I can't take any more. Goddess, it hurts."

One of the blows had cut her lip. The scent of her fresh blood, coupled with his inability to help her, scoured Rui's soul like a thousand pieces of broken glass.

"You thrice-damned bastard. Have a little mercy—can't you see she's in agony?"

Okeanos looked at Rui and, holding his gaze, raised his hand and gave Valeria another hard slap.

Rui snapped. A red haze filled his brain. Maddened, he threw himself from side to side, straining his muscles until his heart was slamming against his ribcage.

But the invisible net continued to constrict. Tighter...tighter.

He struggled even harder, but the more he fought, the more it contracted. He fell to his knees, the strands binding his chest so tightly he could barely breathe, but he fought on, sweat pouring down his face, uncaring of anything but the need to help his mate.

Then suddenly, the constriction loosened. Rui's lungs heaved as he dragged in a breath of much-needed air.

Okeanos snarled. He thrust Valeria from him to concentrate on Rui.

Yes.

Some instinct told Rui the other man had reached his limit. He met Okeanos's gaze defiantly and rose back to his feet, not letting up for a heartbeat, no longer a rational being but an animal.

And the animal knew this was a fight to the death.

Okeanos's eyes narrowed. The net tightened again.

Rui gritted his teeth and continued to resist, but he was growing lightheaded from lack of oxygen. Despair washed over him. Because if he died, Valeria was doomed. Tiago was no match for five mature fada.

Spots danced in front of his eyes. He swayed on his feet.

"*No*, Rui." Valeria stumbled toward him, fell to her knees. She crawled the last few feet, wrapping her arms around his legs.

"*Acalme-te.* You can't fight it. You have to stop. He's using dark magic—it feeds on your struggles."

He heard her words with some distant part of his brain, but the animal sensed that wasn't the whole truth—and both parts of him were willing to keep fighting until his mate was free, even if it meant his own death.

Behind him, someone else pounded down the steps, but he was concentrating too hard to worry about whoever it was. Instead, he went deep into himself, drawing on the chill gray center that had made him such a good assassin.

He planted his feet on the cavern floor and shot Okeanos a look so cold the other man took a step back.

"*Sim,*" Rui growled. "You're the one who's going to die." He pushed back—hard.

Okeanos snarled back, but he'd clearly reached his limit. The crushing tightness around Rui's chest loosened. He drew in a breath, then another one. The lightheadedness eased.

He clenched his fists and kept pushing.

Valeria shifted onto her knees, wobbly and yet somehow strong. He felt her touch through the mate bond, a rush of warmth and love and acceptance, the last so sweet it almost dropped him back to his own knees.

"I love you," she said in a low, clear voice, and for one brief second he let himself savor the joy of hearing the words at last.

And then she was helping him turn the dark magic against Okeanos. With a shock, he realized she was using her Gift for directing water-dwelling animals. Of course; at the heart of every river or sea fada was a water animal.

Wonder filled him. At Valeria's strength, at the love he felt pouring into him from her. At the fact that together, the two of them could do what neither could alone. He fed that wonder into the cold determination.

Okeanos's face was harsh with strain. Sweat beaded on his

forehead. His two fellow sea fada started for Rui, but the other two men stepped in front of them.

"Let them fight it out," one of them said. "This is a mate-duel, right, Rui?"

That was when Rui realized the two men who'd had their hands all over Valeria were Jorge and Benny. His breath hissed between his teeth. He'd known Jorge since they were both pups, and he'd helped train the younger Benny as a warrior.

But anger was an indulgence he couldn't afford. If Jorge was willing to force Okeanos into a fair fight, that was good enough for him.

"Yes," he replied. "This is a mate-duel."

"I'll be his second," Tiago stated loudly.

Another voice rang out. The new man. "And me."

He stepped forward, and Rui grunted in surprise. It was Jace Jones.

Rui focused on his opponent. It was hard as hell to speak and maintain the pressure on Okeanos, but he was determined to do this by the book.

"I...Rui do Mar...challenge you...to a mate-duel for Valeria da Costa."

"I accept," Okeanos replied. "With one condition."

First, though, he flicked his fingers. The constriction around Rui's chest disappeared as if it had never been. He put his hands on his thighs and took several deep breaths.

"Thank *Deus*." Valeria dropped her head against his thigh, still holding one of his legs. Her own breath was choppy with pain.

Rui gently disentangled her grip and crouched beside her. He wanted to pull her into her arms, but he recalled what Okeanos had said about the aphrodisiac. He settled instead for stroking her hair, but even that made her wince.

He glowered at Okeanos. "What did you do to her?"

"Just teaching her a lesson." The Greek fada nudged Valeria

with his toe. "Hurts like the devil, doesn't it? Touch me again and it will be worse."

Rui made a harsh sound low in his throat. At that moment he would've sold his soul to rip off the other man's head. But he was bound by the rules of the mate-duel.

He rose back to his feet. "State your condition."

Okeanos crossed his arms. "Valeria has to accept the winner. If I fight you, she forfeits the right of refusal. The winner takes her—whether she wills it or not."

"No." Rui shook his head. "You can't ask that—"

"I accept the terms," Valeria interrupted. She pushed herself to her feet and stood there, wobbling a little.

"No!" Rui put an arm around her waist to steady her. She flinched, and he cursed and loosened his grip. "I'm sorry, sweetheart. Is this better?"

"*Sim*," she whispered.

He brushed a damp curl back from her face, noting her wide, drugged eyes, her cut lip, the bruises marring her soft skin. A rapid pulse beat at the base of her throat, and her breath came in shallow pants.

His gut knotted. It was his fault that it had come to this. If he hadn't rejected her so completely, she'd never have turned to Okeanos. She'd have been Rui's mate already, with no other man having the right to claim her.

He silently vowed that if—no, when—they got out of this, he'd spend the rest of his life making it up to her.

"You're all right? You understand what he's asking?"

Her lower lip trembled. "He made me drink something. Everything feels—strange. It made me—"

"An aphrodisiac," Okeanos said dismissively. "My father's own recipe. He used it often."

Rui's jaw clenched so tight it hurt. Rock Run had never sunk so low as to employ aphrodisiacs, but he'd heard the rumors. No wonder Valeria had been driven nearly mad by the pain.

For that alone, he could kill Okeanos.

He feathered his lips over Valeria's mouth. "It will pass, *querida*."

She didn't seem to hear him. Instead, she frowned at Jace Jones.

"Valeria?" Rui said.

She passed a shaky hand over her face, still looking at Jones. "Wh—where's Merry?"

Rui froze. "She's not here?" He glanced around as he realized for the first time that the little girl wasn't in the cavern.

"No. Petros gave her to him." She indicated Jones.

Everyone looked at the tall, black-haired man. He stared back, seemingly unconcerned that he was the sole earth shifter in a roomful of hostile river and sea fada.

"I left her with Hunter," he told Valeria. "I wasn't sure what I'd find down here."

"Oh. But she's okay?"

"Of course."

Rui narrowed his eyes at Jones. "What's your game?" If all he'd wanted was Merry, the two of them could've been miles away by now. So what was he doing here?

The earth fada moved a shoulder. "Merry asked me to help her mama."

"And you agreed? Just like that?"

"Just like that." The reply was just this side of insolence. Then he expelled a breath. "Look, it was obvious your woman hadn't gone willingly with Okeanos. I couldn't just leave without trying to help. We're not all pricks, you know."

Rui gave an ostentatious sniff. Damn if the man didn't have the clean scent of truth. Still, since when would a Baltimore shifter go out of his way to help a Rock Run woman?

"Thank you," he said, "but you're out of your fucking mind if you think you're going to take Merry. I'll kill you myself if I have to. Still, I agree this is no place for a child. You say she's safe with your man?"

"Yes. Hunter's one of our best. And the only threat I see is down here with you water shifters." He glanced at Okeanos and the other four men.

Rui ignored the dig to turn back to Valeria. Her whole body was trembling now. He guided her to a cushion against the wall and then crouched on his haunches before her.

"You don't have to do this, *querida*. I don't care what Okeanos says. *Tradição* holds the woman has to agree to the mating."

And to the fada, *tradição*—tradition—had the force of law.

She focused on him with an obvious effort. When she spoke, her words were slow but clear. "I know what I'm doing, Rui."

"He can't make you do this," he repeated firmly.

"Unless the woman forfeits the right of refusal," Okeanos inserted. "It's Valeria's choice. If not, I'll bind you again and leave you in the caves to die." He glanced at Tiago and Jace. "All three of you."

"Like hell," Rui muttered in a subvocal voice. "Even if Benny and Jorge go along with him, there's three of us and only five of them. He's drained from using his Gift. Don't let him scare you."

She reached out a shaking hand to him. When he took it, she clasped it in both of hers and brought it to her lips. He could feel her mouth quivering against his skin, but she kissed him and then met his gaze with solemn dark eyes.

He feathered his fingers down her cheek before rising to face Okeanos.

"Well?" the other man demanded.

"She doesn't accept—"

"But I do," Valeria interrupted. "I accept your terms, Petros Okeanos. I, Valeria Lizete da Costa, willingly accept the winner of the mate-duel between you and Rui do Mar."

Rui's gaze snapped to her. She was back on her feet, one hand on the wall to support herself, but her chin was raised and she clearly knew what she was doing. Everyone in the cave felt the jolt as the speaking of her true-name bound her to her word.

He growled. "No, damn it."

Valeria gazed at him, head high and shoulders back, holding herself so straight, so calm, that he suspected only he saw the wild flicker in her eyes.

"This is the only way. It's not just for me anymore—it's for Merry, too." A corner of her mouth lifted. "You'll just have to win, won't you?"

He felt a wave of pride in her, even as he cursed Okeanos for a wily bastard. That was his mate—proud, courageous and stubborn to the core.

Rui had no choice but to accept Okeanos's challenge. He saw now what Valeria had seen: if it came to a fight, Tiago and Jace might die with him, and Hunter would take Merry back to Baltimore. She'd be lost to Valeria forever.

He'd simply have to win, because he'd do anything, say anything, break every rule in the book to save Merry from losing a parent yet again—and prevent Okeanos from taking Valeria for his sick games.

The Greek fada's eyes gleamed with triumph. "So be it."

25

———

"So be it," Rui echoed.

Valeria gave him an I-know-you'll-win smile. "*Boa sorte*," she mouthed. *Good luck.*

"*Eu te amo*," he mouthed back. *I love you.*

Her smile broadened. He felt an echo of warmth in his heart and even though she didn't speak, knew she'd thought it: *Love you too.*

He pressed the heel of his hand to his breastbone, sending her a crooked smile in return before turning to face Okeanos.

The other men stepped back to form a circle with Rui and Okeanos at the center.

Jorge raised a hand, assuming the role of referee. "There is only one rule in a mate-duel. The two of you fight until one of you surrenders—or dies."

Rui inclined his head. He was well aware that a mate-duel was a raw, no-holds-barred fight.

"Surrender," he agreed, "or die."

Okeanos repeated the words. Jorge brought his hand down and Okeanos sprang, his fingers clawing at Rui's eyes.

But Rui was expecting something like that. He raised an arm

to deflect him, at the same time driving his fist into the other man's stomach. Okeanos grunted but retained his balance.

Without allowing him time to regroup, Rui grabbed him and tried to get him in a headlock. But the other man was slippery as the eel that was his other half—and more sly. He slammed his knee toward Rui's balls.

Rui cursed and turned aside so that the blow glanced off his thigh. Lightning fast, Okeanos twisted away. Rui growled and dropped into a fighting crouch. He eyed the other man, looking for an opening.

Okeanos dropped into a crouch as well, mirroring him. They circled each other, their harsh breathing the only sound in the low-ceilinged cavern. Around them the other men shifted to give them space, but Rui barely noticed as he scrutinized his foe, searching for an opening.

Okeanos curled his lip. "I'll enjoy teaching your woman who her master is."

Rui just looked at him. Rather than enraging him, the jibe made it clear what was at stake. He settled in to fight coldly, dispassionately.

Okeanos feinted to the right and then came in with a hard left to Rui's jaw, but Rui had seen the weight-shift and was ready for him. He ducked under the punch and slammed his fist into Okeanos's stomach. The other man grunted and bent double. Rui closed in and rained blows on him—head, neck, kidneys.

His opponent fought hard, getting in a few good blows, but Rui was younger and stronger. In a few short minutes, he had the other man in a headlock.

Desperate, Okeanos tried to use his dark magic again, but Rui resisted long enough to jerk his head to the side. Okeanos's neck broke with a dull snap and the invisible net that had wound itself around Rui dissolved as the man slid to the floor, dead.

Rui's chest heaved. He placed his hands on his thighs, sucking in oxygen, his gaze on the lifeless man sprawled before him.

Gods, he hated killing someone so much older than himself, but the sea fada's soul had become dark, twisted. If Rui hadn't stopped him today, he'd have continued to seek out other women—willing or not—for his perverted rites.

Still, Rui muttered a blessing so that the man wouldn't pass to the next world unsanctified.

Valeria watched him from her place against the wall.

He swiped the sweat from his face and eyed her warily. She'd just accepted the mate bond, and now he'd had to kill a man right in front of her very eyes. Would she understand it had been necessary?

Their gazes locked and everyone else in the cave seemed to fade away.

Her mouth formed a shaky smile. "Rui? Are you all right?"

"I'm sorry." He forced the words through the sandpaper coating his throat. "I had to kill him."

"Oh, Rui—" She shook her head, eyes moist. "Don't apologize for that. You did what you had to do."

Relief flooded Rui. She understood. He hated like hell having had to kill Okeanos in front of her. But this was part of who he was—and if she couldn't accept that, the bond would never take.

He drew a deep breath and took the greatest gamble of his life. "You don't owe me anything. I release you from your promise, Valeria da Costa. We all know it was forced from you. The choice to accept the mate bond is yours."

Her smile trembled. "Rui, I—" Then she looked past him, eyes wide. "*Merry.*"

Several things happened at once: Jace cursed, Merry-the-jaguar bounded across the floor to Valeria, and the air shimmered as Dion and Cleia teleported into the cave.

Rui ignored everything to go to his two females. Valeria was on her knees hugging Merry, laughing and crying at the same time, while the black cub yipped excitedly.

Rui helped Valeria to a cushion. Now that the excitement was over, he could tell she was hurting again.

"Careful," he warned Merry. "Mama doesn't feel good. You have to be gentle with her."

The cub nodded and settled next to Valeria. She gave a shudder and Valeria stroked a hand down her knobby little spine. "I'm better now that you're here."

Merry crept closer and carefully set her furry head on Valeria's knee.

"Oh, sweetheart." Valeria placed a hand on her head. "Mama's so glad to see you." The little jaguar purred and butted her head against her mother's palm.

Cleia knelt next to Rui. "Let me help them."

He glanced at Valeria, who nodded. He touched her cheek and rose to face Dion, who was scowling down at Okeanos.

With a shake of his head, he turned to Rui, taking in his bruises. He quirked a brow. "Eliana told me you were in trouble, but it appears you're handling it."

"Okeanos forced me into a mate-duel. But I would've killed him anyway. The bastard drugged Valeria. He had some kind of dark Gift that allowed him to bind people."

"Then you did all of us a favor," his alpha replied.

Other Rock Run warriors had poured into the cavern with Davi at their head. At a nod from Dion, they ranged themselves around the four surviving members of Okeanos's den.

Dion glowered at Jorge. "What the fuck is going on? Why are you and Benny in Rock Run territory without checking in with me—and setting up your own den from the looks of it?" he added with a glance around the cavern.

The former *tenente*'s lip curled. "Why should we check in with you? As far as we're concerned, you're no longer our alpha. Okeanos was right. Rock Run gets more like the humans every day—weak, easily led. Nothing but pets for the fae. You're a prime example." He cut his eyes at Cleia.

"Maybe so, but I offered Okeanos the hospitality of the clan, and he repaid me by kidnapping one of our own women and her daughter. If that's what the old ways are like, I say the hell with them. Okeanos broke *tradição*. If Rui hadn't killed him, I would've. As for you four, you're dead."

Jorge made a move toward Dion, but Davi had a knife pressed to his throat before he could take one step.

Jorge stilled.

"*Sim*," Dion said, his smile cold. "We could end your lives right now. But I have something even better in mind. My mate is queen over all seven sun fae clans—and the Sudan clan could use some laborers."

One of the sea fada blanched. "But that's in the Sahara."

"That's right. And to make sure you stay, I'll have your vow— or you die right here. Swear it, all four of you. I want your oath that you'll work for the Sudanese sun fae for the rest of your lives."

They stared back, breathing hard. No one spoke.

Rui almost felt sorry for them. If they gave their oaths, they'd be bound to live out their lives in one of the hottest, driest places in the world—hell on Earth for a water fada. Better a quick death than the long, drawn-out decline from dehydration. But frankly, Dion was being merciful. If it were up to him, he'd execute them right here and now.

The silence stretched until Dion jerked his chin at Davi. "Kill them."

"No," Jorge burst out. He looked at the others. "We'll take the vow. But damn you to Hades, Dion."

He went first. The other men reluctantly added their promise to his, saying their true-names at Dion's demand: Jorge Teles, Benny Escobar, Mys Papadakis, Orius Nikolaidis.

Dion looked at Davi. "Get these scum out of here."

"Where?"

"Take them to the boats and wait there. Cleia will send for someone to get them."

Cleia was already talking into a translucent golden bubble, explaining the situation to her cousin, Lady Olivia. "Olivia will be there in ten minutes," she reported.

The warriors sprang into action, binding the four men's hands behind their backs and urging them roughly up the stairs. In a few minutes everyone was gone save for Tiago and Jace—and the dryad, who had apparently entered the cave behind Merry and was pressed against a wall, looking as if she'd like to burrow into it.

Jace edged toward the stairs, but Dion stopped him with a look. "You're not going anywhere. We're going to settle this today."

Dion glanced at Cleia. "You'll take care of this?" He nodded at Okeanos's body.

When she said yes, he turned to Tiago.

Tiago nodded at him, a queer smile on his lips. "Hello."

Dion stared back, his expression unreadable.

"Tiago was the one who told me Valeria was in trouble." Rui spoke quickly, before Dion did something he'd regret. "Okeanos kidnapped Valeria and Merry, him and his so-called den. They gave Merry to the earth shifters and then brought Valeria here. If not for Tiago, I wouldn't have known they had her. *Deus* knows what they'd have done to her."

He dragged a hand over his face and realized it was shaking.

"Is that so?" Dion was still gazing at his brother. "I'll take that into consideration. Meanwhile, Tiago can come with me while Cleia sees what she can do for you and Valeria. I want to make sure those four are off my territory."

Tiago ducked his head submissively and followed him up the stairs, leaving Rui, Valeria, Jace and Merry in the cavern with Cleia and the dryad.

With a resigned shrug, Jace took a seat on a cushion across the room.

Now that the adrenaline was wearing off, Rui's injuries were making themselves felt. The dark net had bruised his ribs, maybe even re-cracked a couple of them, and the battle with Okeanos hadn't helped. His jaw was swollen, his lip split and he was having trouble putting weight on one of his knees.

Trying not to show how much he was hurting, he lowered himself to the stone floor next to Valeria and Merry. He ruffled Merry's fur but refrained from touching Valeria for fear of making things worse. It was enough that he was sitting next to her, close enough to feel the warmth of her body along his side. Both animal and man needed this. To lend her his strength—and take back comfort for himself.

Carefully, he stretched out his legs and leaned against the hard stone. He ached in every bone of his body, but he'd heal. He wasn't so sure about Valeria. The back of her head rested against the wall and her eyes were closed, her chest shuddering with each inhale and exhale as if even breathing were painful.

He sent the sun fae queen a pleading look. "She's hurting, Cleia. Can't you do something? The SOB drugged her."

"Poor thing." Cleia sent Valeria a compassionate look. "Give me a minute and I'll see what I can do."

Kneeling down next to Okeanos, the queen set her hands on his back. There was a white flash and Rui blinked, temporarily blinded. When he could see again, the only thing left of the dead man were ashes drifting down to rest on the stone floor. The queen spoke a blessing and then flicked her fingers and even the ashes were gone.

"Back to the Mediterranean with you," she murmured.

Rui watched with a grudging approval. All water fada, no matter what their clan, desired a return to their own waters when they died. Let Okeanos's mortal remains mingle with the salty blue water of his native sea. It was up to his maker to judge his soul.

Cleia was speaking to Valeria. "Oh, my dear. What did he do to you?"

Valeria shook her head. "Not me—Merry."

"She's fine." Cleia stroked a hand over the cub. "Aren't you, sweetheart?"

Merry rumbled.

"You're safe now," Cleia told her. "No one will hurt you or take you away from your mama ever again. Understand?"

She nodded.

Valeria's gaze was on Cleia. "You...swear?"

"Absolutely." The queen touched three fingers to her heart. "Merry's under my protection now. I'll make certain everyone knows."

"Thank you," Valeria whispered. "I—"

"It's the least I can do." The two women looked at each other for another moment and then Cleia gave a brisk nod. "Now let's have a look at you."

"Okeanos gave her an aphrodisiac," Rui explained. "To increase sensation. Careful—even the slightest touch hurts."

"Stars." Cleia shook her head in disgust. "It's going to have to work its way out of her system, but I can relieve some of the symptoms."

She set her hands lightly on Valeria. Valeria shuddered, then went still, enduring it.

Rui flinched along with her. He suspected the drug was at full strength now. He could only guess how it felt, streaming through her blood, ratcheting up her pulse, stimulating her tiniest nerve endings so that even a touch was painful.

She started to tremble, and he couldn't bear it any longer. He put his hand out, palm up. Valeria set her hand on top of his. He intertwined his fingers with hers, offering what comfort he could. On the other side, Merry nuzzled her mama's leg.

Valeria's breath sighed out. To his immense relief, the trembling gradually lessened. She closed her eyes and withdrew into herself. He sensed the healing energy start to work and he pushed whatever he could through their fragile mate bond, even as a part of him exulted.

The bond was *there*. Connecting the two of them.

He vowed it would never again shut down from his side.

When Cleia removed her hands, Valeria exhaled audibly and opened her eyes. Rui sent up a prayer of thanks. Her pupils were still dilated, but the trembling had ceased and he could sense that she was through the worst of it.

He gently pressed her hand. "How do you feel?"

"Better."

Cleia sat back on her heels. "I wish I could do more, but I suspect you'll feel the effects for several more hours."

"Ah, well. At least I'm free of those *cabrãos*. Thank you, my lady." Valeria released his hand to wrap her arms around her bent legs and rested her head on her knees.

Her breath rasped in, then out. And again. In, out.

Rui made a move toward her, but Cleia shook her head. "Let her be. She's healing in her own way. Besides, you need healing as well."

He drew in a breath to object and winced as his bruised ribs made themselves felt. Still, he was a fada male. "I'm fine."

Valeria chuckled weakly. "Oh, Rui. You look like you've been run over by a truck. Let her help. Please."

"If you insist—" Right now if Valeria had asked him to stand on his head, he'd have cheerfully upended himself—especially if it meant hearing her laugh.

"I do."

Rui nodded at Cleia. "You heard the lady. If it wouldn't be too much trouble—"

"Of course not." The queen set her hands on his chest. "All

you need is another boost of life-energy. Your body will do the rest. You fada are as tough as old boots."

"Thanks," he said dryly and braced himself for a jolt.

It never came. Instead, he let out an involuntary sigh as he was filled with a soothing heat. It was like sunbathing by the river on a perfect day: golden sunlight, a balmy breeze whispering over his skin, his entire body infused with a sense of well-being. Time was suspended as he floated for several minutes in the peaceful, healing warmth, similar to what Branco had done for him after his last fight, but ten times more powerful.

By the time Cleia removed her hands, his swollen eyelids had receded, his cuts had scabbed over, and the ache in his ribs had subsided to a manageable level.

He rubbed a palm over his chest in wonder. "Thank you. I feel—damn good."

"I'm glad." Cleia hesitated, and then blew out a breath. "I'm sorry, Rui. For everything. If I'd known I was stealing energy from you and the clan, I'd never have taken you as my lover—any of you. Please forgive me for what I did to you and Rock Run."

He shrugged, conscious of Valeria just a couple of feet away. It wasn't easy to admit he'd been weak enough to fall under the sun fae queen's spell.

Cleia's large amber eyes met his, a bit regretful. He read the message there: *We enjoyed each other, and it was good—but we've each found our true mates. Can't we be friends?*

He nodded slowly.

Sure, Cleia had worked her glamour on him, but he'd set his feet on the path to self-destruction all on his own. He'd gone to that bar to get fucked. If it hadn't been Cleia, it would've been someone else.

And it certainly wasn't Valeria's fault. Yes, he'd been hurt when she'd recoiled from him—her mate—but she'd merely been a mirror, showing him what he'd become. A cold-blooded assassin, a man who killed even when he knew damn well it was wrong.

Are you a bad man?

He hadn't liked what he'd seen in that mirror, so he'd gone a little feral. No glamour was powerful enough to keep a man enslaved for a whole year. He'd stayed because he'd been too ashamed to return to Valeria.

And by the time he'd returned to Rock Run, he'd been too guilt-ridden to even look at Valeria, much less claim her as his mate. So he'd hurt her, humiliated her in the worst way a man could a woman.

"You didn't know what you were doing," he muttered. "And as for the rest, it was as much my fault as yours."

The queen inclined her head, but her eyes were dancing. He suspected she was laughing at him, but hell, he deserved it. He'd fucked up royally, and he only hoped Valeria would find it in her to forgive him—and finally accept him as her mate.

"I'll leave you three together, then." Cleia dropped a kiss on Merry's head and headed across the room to talk to Jace and the dryad.

Rui turned back to Valeria. "*Are* you all right, *boneca?*"

Her hair was damp. As it dried, her dark curls were springing to life. He captured one of the unruly locks in his hand, rubbing it between his thumb and index finger. It was so soft, so silky, yet full of vitality—like her.

His stomach clenched. Goddess, he'd almost lost her.

If Tiago hadn't come looking for him, it might have been days until he'd found her. And Lord knew what that Greek *cabrão* would've done to her in the meantime.

"*Sim.*" Her voice was scratchy, her pupils huge and dark as a midnight pool. "Just...edgy. You know."

His eyes went to the flush of arousal on her soft, full breasts.

"*Deus*, woman. You're killing me here. But—" He made a gesture that encompassed Merry and the other three.

"Too bad." She gave him a wicked smile, and then sobered and reached for Merry. "I can hold you now, baby."

Merry shifted to girl. "I'm *not* a baby," she asserted as she climbed into Valeria's lap and wrapped skinny brown arms around her neck.

Valeria met Rui's gaze, her smile wobbly. His eyes were stinging. He swiped a hand over them and smiled back, his own lips trembling a little.

"No." Valeria laid her cheek against her daughter's. "You're not a baby, are you? You're my big girl. And I love you so, so much."

Heart full, Rui wrapped his arms around them both. They were safe. A man couldn't ask for anything more.

26

———

*J*ace felt as if his heart were being chipped out, piece by jagged piece.

It was obvious Merry loved the two river fada and thought of them as her mom and dad, just as they'd claimed. He hadn't wanted to believe them. And even if it were true, she belonged with her own kind.

But Rui and Valeria were whom she ran to when she was frightened. Not him, Jace.

He wrapped his hand around his quartz and squeezed so hard the edges bit into his skin.

The dryad crouched down next to him. "You need to know something," she said in a low voice. "That other man who was with you, the one with wolf eyes—"

"Hunter?" His lip curled. The other man was conspicuously absent, having apparently taken off at the first sign of trouble.

"He tried to run away with the little one. She escaped and somehow ended up in my oak. She said he was going to give her to the bad man."

His whole body snapped alert. "What do you mean? What bad man?"

"I don't know. But she was so scared—shaking and crying. She begged me to hide her, so I took her into my tree. She said this Hunter tried to give her to the bad man once before, but her daddy saved her."

"He tried to give her to the bad man once before? When her dad was still alive?"

"That's what she said."

Suddenly it was all too clear. Hunter must have had something to do with Silver's death—and maybe even Takira's, too?

Blood pounded in Jace's ears. He didn't realize he was growling lowly until the dryad edged away.

And who the hell was the bad man?

His heart gave a sickening thump. It had to be a night fae. They'd been in this from the start. What did they want with Merry?

It didn't make sense. To the fae, she was a mongrel, with her mix of shifter, human and night fae genes—and the fae looked down on mixed-bloods. They didn't keep coming after them.

Queen Cleia approached Jace, looming over him like a beautiful, terrible angel. "You see it too, don't you?" she asked, not unkindly.

He jerked a shoulder.

Valeria stood up, his niece wrapped around her like a little monkey.

He jumped to his feet. "Merry?" He stretched out his hands to her, but she burst into tears and buried her face in Valeria's shoulder.

In an instant, do Mar was on his feet, his body between Jace and the two females. Cleia stepped back, signaling that this was between him and the river fada.

Do Mar glared at him, still juiced-up from the mate-duel. Jace knew it wouldn't take much for the man to snap his neck as well.

He raised a hand, palm out. "Peace. I didn't mean to scare her. I just—"

Do Mar stepped closer, his green eyes tinged a feral gold. "I could end this right now. Slit your throat and throw you in the bay for the fish. You're on Rock Run territory. That makes you fair game—as your alpha damn well knows."

"Rui?" Valeria laid a hand on his arm. "He's Merry's uncle."

"Stay out of this," he gritted. When she simply raised a brow, he growled, "Damn it, don't you understand? If we let him go, he'll only try to take her again."

She edged past him to look at Jace. "Will you?"

He squeezed his eyes shut, unable to believe he was doing this. "No. I—she belongs with you. I'll make sure Adric understands how it is."

"But what about the quartz crystal? Doesn't she need one?"

Jace eyed Merry. He could still win her. It wouldn't be a lie.

He just didn't have to tell them the whole truth.

Then she sniffled and buried her head in Valeria's shoulder, her naked body a little too thin, and so vulnerable it chipped another piece from his already hurting heart.

During the Darktime, the alpha—Adric's uncle—had separated families as punishment or simply to keep them weak. Jace's own mother had been sent on a mission to the other side of the world that had kept her away for years. While she was gone, his dad had been killed in the near-constant fighting.

Jace was damned if he'd do that to his own niece.

"Here," he said, somehow pushing the word past the boulder jamming his throat. He removed his quartz from his neck. Before he could do anything, do Mar raised a threatening hand, but Valeria caught his arm.

"Let him," she said.

Jace met the other man's eyes. "I'm going to break off a piece of my quartz for her. It will give her what she needs for the next couple of years, maybe longer. Eventually, she'll have to find her own, though."

He waited until do Mar jerked his head in acknowledgment,

then knelt down and slammed the smoky gray-and-purple crystal against the hard stone floor. A long, icicle-shaped piece broke off. He stifled a groan as pain sliced through him as well. Splitting your quartz was a little like hacking off a chunk of yourself.

But for Takira's daughter, it was worth it.

He offered the chunk to Merry. "Here, Christmas girl. Your mama can make it into a necklace."

Valeria went to take it, but he closed his fingers. "No. She's the only one who should touch her quartz, unless she gives you permission."

Valeria scrutinized him and then she nodded and set Merry on her feet. Merry shook her head and pressed her face against Valeria's stomach.

Valeria touched her shoulder. "Take it, *querida*."

Merry drew a ragged breath and then slowly turned to face him. Her grubby hand opened. He set the piece of crystal in her palm and closed her fingers over it.

"You need to hang it on a cord and wear it around your neck like I do. Understand?"

She nodded, her big eyes solemn.

To Valeria he said, "It's okay to drill a hole in the crystal so you can string a cord through it, but after that, don't touch it any more than you need to. The quartz needs to key itself to Merry's energy patterns. Encourage her to wear it as much as possible. If she's like the rest of us, she'll feel better when it's on, anyway."

He turned back to his niece. "We're going to need to get together for lessons, you and me, but for now, just close your eyes and feel the energy."

She screwed her eyes shut and he couldn't help smiling at the intent look on her small face. Then he swallowed painfully. She wasn't an exact replica of Takira—she had those fae eyes and that sharp chin—but he'd seen that very same expression on his sister's face.

Merry's eyes flew open. "I feel it," she said wonderingly. "Like when Branco touches me."

"Branco is our senior healer," explained Valeria.

"Good," he told Merry. "That's exactly what you should be feeling." He glanced at Valeria. "Someday she'll find her own quartz crystal, but for now my energy is similar enough to give her what she needs. And anyway, she and the crystal have already started the process of attunement. In a few weeks, it will be more hers than mine."

"Listen, Mama." The little girl put the chunk to her ear, then held it out to Valeria. The gray was shot with a line of silver he'd never seen before. "Can you hear it?"

Valeria placed her ear to the crystal, then shook her head. "I'm afraid I can't, sweetheart. But it's good that you can." Straightening up, she held out her hands to Jace. "Thank you, lieutenant. I want you to know you'll always be welcome in my home."

He gripped her hands, hard. "Thank *you*. For taking such good care of Merry. Just—love her. Promise me that."

"I do," Valeria promised. "So much." She embraced him, pressing a kiss to each of his cheeks.

When she stepped back, do Mar surprised him by sticking out his hand as well. "I don't know about a Baltimore shifter in the base, but we'll find a place for you to meet. The hell with just meeting for lessons. Merry should know her mother's brother."

"Thank you." He shook the other man's hand.

Merry was standing in front of him. "Would you like a hug, Uncle Jace?"

His throat worked. "Yes. I'd like that very much, Christmas girl."

She grinned and he scooped her into his arms for a hard hug. When he handed her back to Valeria, his eyes were stinging.

"I'll explain things to my alpha," he told do Mar. "He'll be in touch to set up a meeting place."

"That should work."

Dion had loped back down the stairs in time to hear the last of this. "She wouldn't be safe with your clan anyway. Someone was trying to sell her to the night fae."

Jace looked around for the dryad, but she was nowhere to be seen. "The dryad said something like that. I'm afraid it was the man who came with me—Hunter."

"Hunter?" do Mar asked. He and his alpha exchanged a look. "He was the go-between for Tyrus, the night fae who hired us to take out Merry's father."

Fuck. Another bastard selling them out to the fae. Would the Darktime never end?

"We didn't know," Jace said between tight lips. "I'll inform Adric. I promise you, Merry will never have to worry about Hunter again. That much we can do for her."

The queen spoke up. "And I'll handle the night fae. Tyrus has gone too far if he thinks he can kidnap a child from my mate's clan."

Jace glanced at her. She looked calm enough, but he was damn glad he wasn't Tyrus.

"Thanks, love." Dion touched her cheek. "But first, can you take Valeria and Merry home? The rest of us can take boats or swim it."

"Of course."

Cleia had Valeria pick up Merry again, and then, wrapping an arm around Valeria's shoulders, muttered a few words in ancient Greek. The air shimmered and they were gone.

With them gone, Jace headed back upstairs with the river shifters. The dryad was already back in her the tree.

As the last person left, the oak slid shut behind them with an audible click that seemed to say, "Good riddance."

More Rock Run warriors were waiting at the river's edge. Three of them escorted Jace to a boat, depositing him just outside

Grace Harbor, which was fine with him. Adric and several soldiers were waiting nearby.

One of the Rock Run men gave Jace a rough shove as he exited the boat, snarling, "Stay the fuck out of our territory if you know what's good for you."

Jace simply walked away. The man would learn soon enough that he *would* be back—an invited guest. He'd let the Rock Run alpha explain.

Meanwhile, he had his own alpha to pacify. Adric wouldn't be happy Jace had left Merry with the Rock Run fada. It was partly because Adric loved all the young ones, was genuinely sad that so many had been lost during the Darktime.

But Adric was also concerned Merry might spill earth fada secrets. Jace would just have to make sure she didn't learn the quartz's real secret until she was old enough to understand why she couldn't share it with anyone, even Valeria.

Meanwhile, Adric would come around. Hell, before a week passed, he'd probably be calculating the potential of an earth fada at Rock Run.

Adric was one of his oldest friends, but sometimes Jace almost hated him.

He blew out a breath and looked down at his quartz. Already the crystals were reconfiguring themselves, making up for the piece he'd shared with Merry.

He tapped the alpha's icon.

Adric responded immediately. "Jace. Where the hell are you? I expected you to check in two hours ago."

"We've got another goddamned rat," was his grim reply.

"Who?" A chilly growl.

"Hunter."

With Jace gone, Dion directed the three other warriors still on the island to conduct a sweep. "Make sure there's no one left—above or below ground—but the dryad."

With that handled, he headed back to Alesia's tree. She met him halfway—dryads always seemed to know what was happening in their forests.

He offered her a formal apology, assuring her that Okeanos and the others had been acting without his knowledge. "I promise you, this will never happen again. I'll make sure the sentries keep a closer eye on your island—and your sisters' as well."

She accepted his apology gravely. "I understand, Lord Dion. And we thank you for allowing us to live on Rock Run territory."

"It's our pleasure," he returned. "We're honored to have you and your sisters."

She inclined her head and then with a quick, unreadable look at Tiago, disappeared back into the trees, although he suspected she'd keep them under close observation until they left the island.

That left his brother. He turned to face Tiago.

Deus, he looked terrible: at least ten pounds thinner, his hair in long, matted coils and the lower half of his face covered in black stubble. But the worst thing was the hopeless look in his eyes.

Dion felt a stab of pity which he firmly suppressed.

"Maybe I should go, too," Rui murmured.

"No," Dion replied without taking his gaze off his brother. "I want you to stay." He lifted a brow at Tiago. "Well? Give me one reason why I shouldn't banish your sorry ass."

He hung his head. "I can't. In fact"—his throat worked—"I deserve to be executed."

"Forget the fact that you betrayed your own brother—and your alpha. You also risked the life of everyone in the base. Once Adric and the fae were inside Rock Run, what would've prevented them from leaving my quarters and killing everyone they could? Half of the clan would've been dead before we even knew the base had been invaded."

"I didn't think—"

"Damn right," he bit out.

"Dion," Rui interjected. "Remember our talk. A male in his first heat is not in full control of his animal."

Tiago's head snapped up at that. "I wasn't *in heat*—and she wasn't just some woman. I loved her. I thought she was my mate. And you were *hurting* her. A sun fae needs the sun. She was getting weaker every day."

"Do you think I didn't know that?" Dion returned. "But I had no choice. She was draining our energy. If I hadn't stopped her, Rock Run would've fallen. We were getting too weak. Sooner or later we would've all died from disease—or been easy pickings for the Baltimore shifters. And what you don't know is that Cleia had finally convinced me that she wasn't doing it deliberately, and had no way to stop it. I was going to let her go, but I would've released her somewhere far from Rock Run, not invited an enemy alpha into the base. Your actions endangered not just me, but every single member of the clan—including the pups."

All the fight went out of Tiago. "I know," he admitted lowly. "I didn't think. It never occurred to me that Adric would bring fae with him."

Dion squeezed the back of his neck. He'd been alpha for a decade, and had long since made his peace with dispensing justice. It was for the good of the clan; he had to be strong or Rock Run would be torn apart by the same infighting that had devastated the Baltimore shifters.

By all rights he should execute Tiago, or barring that, banish him for life. But this was his brother, the kid he'd loved from the day he'd lifted his head from their mother's breast and given Dion a bright-eyed, milky-mouthed smile.

And he *had* come for Rui, ignoring the danger to himself. Without Tiago, who knew what would've happened to Valeria and Merry?

Dion expelled a breath. "First," he told Tiago, "I want your oath that it will never happen again."

"You've got it." Without prompting, his brother put his hand on his heart. "I, Tiago Gallagan do Mar, swear an oath of loyalty to you and the clan. I promise that never again will I act in a way that could harm either you or the clan."

"All right." Dion crossed his arms over his chest. "This is how it's going to be. You can return to the base as part of your cohort, but you're the lowest man for the next six months. We won't tell people why, just that you're being disciplined. Some of them may guess it was you who gave our location away, but I'd like to keep this as quiet as possible."

Tiago's throat worked. For a natural dominant, it was a harsh punishment: to be forced to take orders from those lower than him in the hierarchy. But he jerked his chin in assent.

"Yes, sir."

"Any night you're free, you'll report to the kitchen to help the cooks. Anything they need—peeling potatoes, shelling oysters—you're to do it."

"Yes, sir."

"And finally, you'll work in the creche for one day each week for the next two months. That isn't a punishment, by the way. It's to remind you what you risked by giving our location to the Baltimore alpha."

Tiago swallowed noisily. "Thank you. I promise you won't regret this."

Dion gave a curt nod, and then opened his arms. "Welcome back, *irmão*."

Tiago practically jumped the few steps between them. Dion gave him in a hard hug.

"*You asshole*. I could wring your neck."

Tiago let out a single sob and hugged him back. "I'm sorry," he choked out. "So sorry. I never even thought about the kids."

"Well, you're not the first man to make a fool of yourself over a beautiful woman. And if it hadn't happened, you probably wouldn't have been here when Okeanos brought Valeria to the island. *Deus* knows what he would've done to her—and we'd have lost Merry to boot. We're all in your debt."

Tiago nodded. For a few seconds they stood there, arms wrapped around each other. Dion didn't know about his brother, but he was too full to speak.

When they stepped apart, Rui slapped Tiago on the back. "Dion's right. We owe you, all three of us—Valeria, Merry and me. If you hadn't come for me right away—" A muscle in his jaw jumped. "Anyway, I'm in your debt. Anything, anytime—I'll be there. And I mean that."

"Thank you."

Dion glanced at Rui, who even with the benefit of Cleia's healing Gift, still sported some colorful bruises. "Take a long swim. Go out to the bay, give yourself some time to heal. I'll make sure Valeria knows."

Rui hesitated, and then agreed. "Tell her I'll be back in a couple of hours." With a nod to them both, he strode into the Susquehanna and changed to his shark.

Dion turned to his brother. "Let's join the sweep. I want to be sure it's safe before I leave."

It was a subdued young shifter who fell into step beside him.

Dion only hoped Tiago had truly learned his lesson. Because if not, someday his youngest brother was either going to leave or challenge him for alpha—and that could set off the same sort of civil war that had nearly brought down the Baltimore clan.

aleria had lied.

Well, not exactly. She *was* feeling better.

But Cleia's healing energy had only dented the edge of the aphrodisiac. She was so hot, she was surprised her skin wasn't steaming, and the sight of Rui, naked and sweaty after the mate-duel, had her entire body clenching.

Hades take Petros anyway. Just as he'd predicted, she was like a bitch in heat. But at least with Rui she didn't feel shame, didn't need to fight it.

But Merry came first. With a huge effort, Valeria managed to calm herself enough to function normally. By the time they got back to Rock Run, it was afternoon and Merry was whining that she was hungry, which Valeria took as a good sign. The two of them ate lunch in the dining hall along with a few stragglers who shook their heads over Petros, Jorge and the others.

As they ate, Merry kept examining her quartz, fingering it, staring into it, showing it off to everyone at the table. She seemed to have bounced back from her ordeal, but Valeria took her to Branco anyway.

He swung the little girl into his arms. "You're a ball of energy today, aren't you?"

"Did you see my new crystal?" Merry held it up for him to see. "Uncle Jace gave it to me. Earth shifters have to wear one."

The healer duly admired it before setting her down. "I'm no expert on earth shifter metabolism," he told Valeria as Merry danced away, "but it looks to me like she's a little high on the energy from the crystal."

Merry was belting out a song now using her quartz as a mic.

Yeah, she was definitely feeling no pain.

"But is that okay?" Valeria asked Branco.

"If it came from her uncle, I'm sure it's fine. He knows what she needs."

"Look, Branco," Merry said. "I can shift really fast now." She changed to jaguar and then a heartbeat later, was back to her girl.

Valeria's jaw dropped. That was fast even for an adult fada.

The healer chuckled. "Don't worry, she won't stay this hyped-up for long. She's just excited, probably because she was craving the energy all along. She'll calm down, but feel free to bring her back in a day or two if you're still worried."

Reassured, Valeria took Merry outside so she could run off some of that excess energy as her jaguar. Rui still hadn't returned, but Eliana stopped by to let her know that on Dion's advice, he'd changed to shark and swum out to the Chesapeake.

Valeria nodded. The needy, edgy part of her wanted Rui *now*, but he'd heal faster in his animal form.

The younger woman slanted her a knowing smile. "You're mated, aren't you?"

Valeria knew, of course, that Rui had had sex with Eliana, but she also knew it hadn't meant anything. If she were jealous of every woman he'd had, it would poison their mating. Besides, how could you dislike someone who was so clearly thrilled for them both?

So she smiled back. "Yeah. But it's not official yet."

"I knew it!" Eliana threw her arms around Valeria. "Congratu-lations. I'm so happy for you both. I can't wait for the mating ceremony."

"Remember, it's not official—"

But Eliana had jogged off. Valeria shook her head ruefully. By sundown, the entire base would know.

Merry-the-jaguar trotted up with a fish in her mouth and dropped it at Valeria's feet, and Valeria knelt to admire it. They found a bucket in the marina, filled it with water and spent the next hour catching fish and playing in the river with a group of other pups including Trina and Marco who'd come outside with their teachers from the creche.

Trina and Marco took one look at Merry's quartz and immedi-ately announced they wanted their own. Merry offered to help them search, one of the teachers went inside for some leather cords, and soon the entire group was sporting various stones—including a few pieces of quartz—as jewelry.

Thank the Goddess. Valeria had been afraid that Merry's need for a quartz would only emphasize her difference from the other kids.

She was sitting on the river bank watching Merry play in the shallows when a large gray bull shark swam up. She knew it was Rui even before she saw the intelligent green eyes. He glided toward her, intense, powerful.

Valeria stared at him, unable to look away. It was times like this that brought home that he was at heart a hunter. Two years ago, she might have been a little frightened, but now she was just grateful that his massive strength would always be there, protecting her and Merry.

He shifted and strode onto the bank, his big body glistening in the sunlight. Valeria's mouth literally started to water. Her gaze traveled from his feet to his face, lingering on all the hard, lovely places in between. His cuts and bruises had faded until they were barely visible.

She swallowed. "You look better."

"So do you." Rui's lips curved in that knowing way that always sent heat curling through her.

She stared back, forgetting everything but the fact that this strong, gorgeous man was her mate and she needed him.

It was Merry who broke the spell, bounding through the shallow water toward Rui, her tail high and happy.

"Well, hello, *princesa*." He swung her into the air. "How's my girl?" She gave a joyful yowl and he said, "*Excelente*," and planted a kiss on her furry head.

As soon as he set her down, she streaked across the grass to her friends, where she scurried up a tree, lording it over the more earth-bound otter pups until one of the teachers quietly rebuked her.

He glanced at Valeria. "She's okay?"

"Yes. I took her to Branco and he says she's fine, that the extra energy is her adjusting to the quartz."

"Good. And what about you, *querida?*" His gaze traveled over her body.

She'd donned a light cotton sundress, all she could stand against her skin. She knew he was looking her over out of concern, but that intent scrutiny made her whole body catch fire. Her nipples tightened, pressing against the damp material, and his nostrils flared.

"Are *you* all right?" he asked, voice rough.

Valeria tugged the dress away from her skin. Even the light material felt too constricting. "I'm fine."

But her gaze settled hungrily on his naked body.

"*Deus*"—Rui glanced at the children—"don't look at me like that. Not when I can't do a damn thing about it."

A drop of sweat trickled down the side of her face. He frowned and touched a finger to her damp temple.

"You're still feeling it, aren't you? The drug?"

"Yeah," she admitted. "But I'm better than I was—just edgy."

"Why don't you go for a swim? I'll keep an eye on Merry. If she gets bored, I'll take her for a ride."

Merry gave an excited yelp, proving that young shifters—whatever their animal—had an owl's acute ears. She scrambled down the tree, shifting to girl as she reached the ground.

"Can you take me across the river, Tio? On your shark?"

"*Sim, sim.*" Rui placed a calming hand on her head. "Now settle down while I talk to your mama."

She nodded vigorously, then took a step away and clamped her mouth shut.

Valeria pressed her own lips together so that she wouldn't chuckle.

"So?" Rui said. "You know it will do you good."

She glanced at the river. It beckoned: cool and silver-green, a siren's call to her overstimulated system. "If you're sure it's all right..."

"Of course. We'll be fine." He moved closer. A hand slipped around her nape and he deliberately rubbed his cheek against hers, marking her with his scent. "Tonight, though," he husked, "you're all mine."

And just like that, her animal turned belly-up, accepting him as the mate. The bond that had flowered into life in the cavern settled deep, weaving into her heart like the roots of a sturdy plant.

She turned her face toward his. "Mm," she said against his lips.

He gazed at her in wonder. "Valeria—"

She pressed a finger to his lips. "Tonight."

She sensed his impatience through the bond. His animal wanted to claim her right here and now. Then he glanced at Merry, hopping from foot to foot, and blew out a breath.

"Tonight," he agreed.

Valeria bent down to hug Merry. "I'll be back in an hour. You listen to Tio Rui, all right?"

"Yes, Mama Ria." She tugged on Rui's hand. "Come *on*, Tio."

Valeria left them to it, confident that Rui could handle her little ball of fire. Walking to a large rock overhanging the river, she dragged off the too-confining dress and moved to the edge. With a deep inhale, she sprang up and out in a long dive that took her to where the current was fast and so cold against her overheated skin that it stole her breath.

It felt wonderful.

She broke the surface long enough to fill her lungs again and then shifted to dolphin and headed downstream.

BY THE TIME SHE RETURNED, most of the drug had worked its way out of her system, but the few hours before she was alone with Rui seemed to crawl by. The three of them shared a quiet dinner in her apartment. She wasn't in the mood to face a crowd, especially when everyone was expecting them to announce their mating.

Her closest friends stopped by anyway—Sabela and her parents, Marina and Luis, Trina and Marco along with their parents, and the old man who had taught her to crab. They alternately hugged her and exclaimed over how Petros had fooled everyone.

Meanwhile, Merry continued to do an excellent imitation of a wind-up toy, bouncing from person to person and giggling with her friends. Rui came in for a few congratulatory backslaps from the men for winning the mate-duel. He accepted with an easy grin, more relaxed than she'd ever seen him.

Dion stopped by with Luis and his mate, Marina, to check on all three of them. Marina took one look at Valeria and gently but firmly ushered everyone from the apartment.

With the three of them alone again, Merry flopped onto the couch, gave a big yawn and was asleep within minutes. Rui carried her into her room and laid her on the bed while Valeria drew up the sheet.

Together, they stood looking down at her. She'd rolled onto her side, her quartz clutched in one hand, her hair sticking up in wild punctuation marks around her head.

Rui put an arm around Valeria. "*Deus*, it must have been hard for Jones to give her up."

She nodded. "I don't know if I could have done it."

"You would have," he said with certainty. "If it was the only way to keep her happy and healthy, you'd have let the earth fada have her. You love her too much to do anything else."

"I guess. But I'm glad it didn't come to that."

"Me too. But she's safe now. Cleia will keep the night fae away, and I can handle anyone else."

"I know you can." She turned into him. "I'm a lucky woman, to have you."

"I'm the lucky one." His face was grave.

"Mm." She nuzzled his cheek. He still smelled of his swim, a mix of fresh river and salty bay. Her heart started to pound, slow and hard. She slid her lips over the strong cord of his neck, flicking her tongue out to taste him.

He shuddered and she smiled against his skin.

With a last look at Merry, he drew Valeria into the hall and backed her up against a wall, his hands on either side of her head. "Now where were we?"

She cupped his face. "Here." She set her lips to his.

He caught her hands, entwining his fingers through hers, and kissed her back, slow and sweet. When he lifted his head, they were both breathing hard.

"Come." He drew her down the hall to her bedroom.

At some point during the evening, he must have slipped into the room. Lit candles glowed on every possible surface, infusing the whole room with a golden haze. On the nightstand three candles floated in a bowl of water, and a single red rose rested the pillows.

Valeria bit her lower lip. "Oh, Rui...it's beautiful."

"*Sim*," he agreed, his gaze on her. "*Muito, muito linda*." He took her into his arms for another deep, sweet kiss.

She responded with her whole body. Breathing him in. Wanting him so badly it hurt. She supposed some of it was the drug, but mostly it was Rui. His scent, his presence, *him*.

His lips moved to her neck, kissing and nipping the delicate skin.

She ran her hands over his shoulders, reveling in the hard swell of his muscles. "Rui." Her voice was a low, taut vibration. "I need. Goddess, I need."

"I know, *querida*. I know." He gave her a last kiss and then released her to remove her dress and panties. He dropped them on the floor without removing his gaze from her. "So beautiful."

His hands smoothed over her naked skin in feather-soft touches. Something twisted low in her abdomen. Hunger for Rui, yes, but hunger touched by yearning.

A soul-deep need that had been simmering in her for not just hours, but years.

She swallowed and cut her eyes away from his.

He stroked a finger over her jaw. "Is this too much, sweetheart? Tell me what you need. I'll do whatever you want..."

Love welled up in her. She knew how hard it was for him to say that. He wasn't a man who easily relinquished control.

But she didn't want control, she wanted Rui. Her man. Her mate. Her very skin craved his touch, the need for his hands on her chafing like too-tight clothing.

"Touch me." She brought his hand to her chest. "I just want you to touch me."

Rui's eyes darkened to the color of a forest at dusk. He obediently cupped her breasts, caressing her as carefully as if he were handling fine silk. Sensation rippled through her in honeyed waves. Her eyes drifted shut in sheer pleasure.

Her already sharp senses heightened to an almost unbearable pitch, boosted by the small amount of the drug still in her blood. She could hear Rui's breath, harsh with desire; scent his rich male musk with that overtone of salt. A heavily-muscled thigh pressed between her legs.

He gathered her closer to press kisses to her neck, her shoulder while he continued to caress her breasts and belly, his fingertips rough against her skin.

Rough—and perfect.

"*Meu amor*," he said in ragged tones. "When I heard that bastard had you, I thought I'd lost you both."

He backed her up until she was seated on the mattress's edge and then came down on his knees before her. Carefully, he lifted each of her breasts in turn, pressing kisses to the outside of each curve before moving on to her areola, tracing each sensitive circle with his tongue until her nipples were wet and tightly furled and she was dizzy with need.

"Rui," she rasped. She took his hand and set it between her thighs. "There. Touch me. Please?"

A corner of his mouth kicked up. But his fingers slid into her wet folds, gently rubbing.

The craving ratcheted up. Her pulse quickened and a flush heated her cheekbones.

His mouth touched hers. "This is good? What you need?"

"Wha—" She gazed at him from under half-closed lids, her whole body pulsating. "*Sim*. Oh, yes."

His fingers halted their lovely motion. "You're sure you're all right? The drug isn't controlling you anymore?"

"*Sim*. I mean no, I just need you—"

"Then put your hands behind your head."

The soft command sent a jolt of heat to her womb. He liked games, her Rui. But then, so did she.

She obeyed, her gaze latched on his.

"That's it. Interlace your fingers behind your neck and keep them there."

The position thrust out her breasts. He regarded them with hooded eyes.

"*Deus*, your breasts are beautiful. Like lush, perfect fruit. I want to eat you up."

Still stroking her between the legs, he brought his mouth to one nipple and nipped. The small pain made her moan.

"I know that *cabrão* hurt you," he told her. "And I'm sorry. It never would've happened if I hadn't rejected you and our mating. But I think you need to be teased a little, hm? Just to remind you who your mate is."

She moved her head from side to side. "Rui, no. Have mercy. I've been waiting for hours—"

He nipped her other breast. "You'll get what you need...when I decide it's time."

"Damn you," she muttered, even as another wave of heat flooded her belly. The man knew her too well.

He chuckled darkly but said nothing. His hands moved over her body, sure and knowing: plumping her breasts, pinching her nipples, cupping her hips...sliding a finger between the crease of her buttocks until her mind was hazy with desire.

She moaned and tried to reach for him, but he stilled and told her to place her hands behind her head again.

"You know the rules."

She groaned but obeyed. "Please, *querido*," she said in a jagged voice. "I need you."

"All right," he said, taking pity on her. "Lie down."

He guided her the rest of the way onto the mattress and then crawled on top of her, his face stern with desire. Her hard, beautiful predator.

"Come here." She reached for him and this time he let her,

coming down on his forearms to give her a deep, sensual kiss, his tongue sliding in and out of her mouth, tasting, teasing.

Pleasure rippled through her, wave after wave of it. Her fingers dug into his shoulders and she moaned softly.

He pushed himself upright, his knees on either side of her hips, and gazed down at her, his eyes so dark they were nearly black. Her hands fell to either side of her head and he grunted his approval.

"Keep them there." He fisted his hand around his cock and began to stroke himself.

Her breath snagged in her chest. It was the most erotic sight imaginable, watching him pleasuring himself, inky eyelashes shading high cheekbones while his large, blunt fingers slid over his heavily veined erection.

Desire pulsed in her, a hot, heavy beat. "Rui," she pleaded, reaching for him.

He chuckled, the bastard, and brushed her hands away.

But to her relief, he came down to her, his mouth sliding down her stomach, over her mound. His fingers spread her, stroked her open. His face moved between her legs, his stubble rubbing over the soft skin of her inner thighs, and then his mouth touched her most sensitive place.

Her body tautened. "*Rui*," she said in a strangled voice.

"Hm?" he said without stopping the magical things he was doing with his lips and tongue.

She could only moan.

Fire raced over her skin, lashed at her core. Her hips rose, wordlessly begging for more. She lost the ability to think, just melded with her animal as thrill after thrill whipped through her.

She was close...so close...

He slowed and she let out a sob. "*Por favor*, no more teasing. I ne—"

"Hush. I know what I'm doing. I know *you*, Valeria. Don't ever forget that."

He slid two fingers into her, stroking in and out. Her passage clenched around him. Still sucking her clit, he twisted the fingers, touching a single perfect spot behind her pubic bone. White heat exploded behind her eyes and she screamed with pleasure as a climax took her.

He rode it out with her, licking and stroking her as he murmured dark, erotic words of love. When she went limp beneath him, he crawled up her body with a panther's grace and settled between her thighs, forearms on either side of her head.

She gazed up at him, her breath coming in soft huffs.

His face softened. "*Deus*, I love you." And then to her shock, he drew in a serrated breath and his eyes filled with tears. "I'm sorry. So sorry. About everything." His head dropped to her breasts. "Forgive me, *querida*."

Her heart squeezed. "Oh, Rui," she said as she enfolded him in her arms. "Don't cry. Please don't cry. I forgive you. And I'm sorry too. I—"

"Please." He lifted his head to meet her eyes. "I need to say this."

"Okay." She nodded.

"I should never have left you that night. But I was so ashamed. I'd killed a little girl's father. I felt so...cold. Like there was nothing worthwhile about me at all.

"And then you looked at me like I was lower than a worm. I *felt* it, Valeria—and...it hurt. All I wanted to do was get the hell out of here. Because you were right. I didn't have to make that kill. I could've left, explained things to Dion. He left the final decision up to me. He always does."

"Oh, Rui." She was crying now, too. She stroked her hands over his close-cropped hair. "I'm so sorry. I had no right to judge you."

"No—you were right. It's my fault that Merry is an orphan.

You don't know how many times I wished I could go back in time, fix it somehow. Keep her father alive."

"But that might not have helped. That night fae—Tyrus—wouldn't have given up. They'd probably both be dead now. And who knows what he would've done to her first?" She stifled a shudder.

Rui swiped a hand over his wet cheeks. "That's what I tell myself. But who knows? Maybe Silver could've kept them both alive somehow. He was doing okay up to then."

"Let it go." She cupped his face. "What's done is done. You can only be the best father you can be to Merry...and to the rest of our children."

"I will be." He gave her a hard kiss. "I love her so damn much. I swear I'll treat her as if she were my own."

"I know you will." She pulled back so she could look into his eyes. "But you're wrong about one thing. I do owe you an apology—for turning away from you that night you brought Merry home. I knew even then how much I'd hurt you, but I was too angry to care. But that only lasted for the night."

She shook her head. "And damn you, Rui, for running. That's the only thing you need to be sorry for—for running from this thing we have. Mates don't always agree with each other. But they don't run and they don't close themselves off from each other. They talk it out—or they fight it out. But they don't go to someone else. When you were hurting, you should've come to me, *not* Cleia."

"You're right." He took her hands and folded them in his, before pressing a contrite kiss to her fingers. "When I left, all I wanted was to drink myself into a stupor so I didn't have to think about you—or Merry. I can still hear her asking if I was a bad man. And then somehow—"

He briefly closed his eyes. "But I thought of you every day. Every single day. But with each day I stayed away, it got harder to come home, and by the time I did, I was so sure you were better off without me that I blocked the mate bond with everything I had. That was wrong. I was an ass."

"Yes, you were." She grasped his shoulders and gave him a little shake. "But you're my ass, got it?"

His mouth curved. "*Sim.*" He set his lips on her breast bone, right where the mate bond originated.

Warmth filled her, spread to every part of her body. She stroked his head, his shoulders, her eyes drifting shut the better to savor the wonder of it.

When she opened her eyes again, he was sliding into her. Around them, the candles seemed to flare, painting his cheekbones a warm gold.

His gazed bored into hers. "You feel it too, don't you? The bond."

"*Sim.*" It was a heated pulse in her heart, one she knew would bind them for the rest of their lives.

"Say you love me."

It was a demand, but she sensed the vulnerability behind it.

"I love you." Her arms came around him in a tight embrace. "I love you, Rui do Mar. More than I can say. I never really stopped."

"*Deus*, I was a fool to ever leave you. But I love you, too." He moved slowly in and out of her. "Now I'm going to fuck you, *querida*. Slow and deep...hard and fast. And you're going to let me, aren't you? You're mine. Tell me."

He thrust a second time, a little harder.

"Yes. Oh, lord, yes." Her hips lifted without her volition and they started moving together, one body, one heart, one soul.

The fire in her blood heated again, a slow burn this time, the kind that promised to build and build until it exploded into wonder. She bent her knees so she could take him deeper. That first climax had been amazing, but its own kind of tease; she wanted him deep inside her when she came this time.

Her arms wrapped around him at the same time that he cupped her face with big, blunt fingers. At first his strokes were slow and deep as he'd promised, each one touching her most intimate places and increasing the pleasure. His body pressed hers into the mattress, big and hard and perfect.

She dug her heels into his thighs and urged him on with breathy sounds that she barely recognized as her own. In response, he slowed even further, dragging the flared head of his penis over her sensitive inner tissue, then thrusting back in at an excruciatingly deliberate pace.

She threw back her head. "Take me. Please..."

"Yes," he gritted, spearing his fingers in her hair and tugging her head back. "Mine."

He brought his lips to hers in a hard kiss. She opened her mouth to him and his tongue thrust inside.

There was no more teasing, just a man taking his woman, pleasuring them both.

She sucked his tongue deeper and his hips sped up, deeper, harder. She clung to him, each stroke shuddering through her. For long moments they moved like that, their mouths and bodies tight together, dancing to the same intimate rhythm.

Rui tore his mouth from hers to kiss her neck, her breasts, his breath hot and ragged against her skin.

"Mine," he said again.

He slid out of her and she whimpered, thinking he meant to play with her some more. Then he reared back and thrust into her, hard and firm. A shock wave vibrated through her womb.

It was perfect, exactly what she craved. Liquid heat gathered in her core, seared lava-hot up and down her spine. His fingers tightened on her hips, holding her in place as he drove into her. She arched her pelvis, taking him deep.

"It's so good," she sobbed. "So good."

Rui's breath grew harsh. "Mine," he said with each firm thrust. "Mine."

"Yours." She ground herself against him. "Rui, I—"

He slid a hand between their bodies and rubbed his fingers

over her tight, aching nub. She bucked and made a sound that was half-moan, half-scream as her climax took her and she convulsed around him in a seemingly endless series of exquisite shocks.

"That's it." He pumped into her forcefully. "Take me." Then he groaned and muttered, "*Madre de Deus*," in reverent tones and emptied himself into her.

He collapsed half-on, half-off her, his legs entangled with hers.

Valeria smoothed a hand down his back, moist with exertion. She'd missed this most of all: the weight of his body on hers, his rich scent in her nostrils.

He lifted himself off her and rolled onto his back, pulling her into his arms, her head on his chest. She combed her fingers through the mat of wiry hair under her cheek, listening to the rapid beating of his heart.

"Tell me," she murmured, "did you mean what you said after the duel? That you release me from my promise?"

"Of course." She sensed his affront. "I wouldn't take you like that. The gods know I want you, but not because of a vow you were forced to swear. I want you to come to me freely."

"Good." She'd hoped that was the case, but it was nice to have it confirmed.

"But the bond, Valeria. It's there, connecting us. I know you feel it too. Are you still refusing me?"

She propped herself up on her elbow to look at him. He stilled, eyes wary. He had a warrior's body, the fresh cuts mingling with old scars. She traced a finger over the red line on his lower abdomen.

He'd stopped drinking.

He'd gone six weeks without a woman—and there'd been no shortage of those willing to take him into their beds, especially now, when he was nearly back to his old self.

And he'd fought for her, only to set her free.

A smile welled from deep inside, spilling onto her face with a joy too immense to contain.

"Oh, no. You're not claiming me. *I'm* claiming *you*."

THE NEXT MORNING, they walked into the dining room hand-in-hand, Merry skipping alongside them. When they reached the center of the cavern, Valeria stopped and raised her free hand. The room went silent.

Rui quirked a brow at Valeria. *What was up?*

She ignored him. "Some of you may have heard that Rui won a mate-duel for me yesterday."

Everyone nodded. Gossip traveled fast in the close-knit clan.

"But the promise was forced from me."

Rui went as still as the rest of the room. *Didn't we settle this last night?* His heart told him they were already mates, but he'd lost her before.

Still, when she looked at him, he nodded. "It was. So I set you free."

"So he set me free," Valeria repeated. "Which was the sweetest, most romantic thing he could've done." Her voice was softer now. Everyone strained to hear her, and being fada, they got the gist.

Rui started to grin. Somehow he knew what was coming next, and it just wasn't done in the tradition-bound fada world. They'd banned the bacchas, women fought as warriors or went out with the fishers, but the mate claim remained the prerogative of the men.

But then this was Valeria, the woman who'd adopted an earth fada cub into a water fada clan—and made sure she wasn't just tolerated, but loved.

"So *I'm* claiming *him*," she stated in a ringing voice. Her gaze swept the room, lingering for an extra few seconds on Beatriz. "Before all of you, I—"

Wrapping a hand around her braid, Rui reeled her in. He was still a fada male, after all. He had to retain some self-respect.

"I accept," he said against her lips, still rosy from his loving last night and again this morning.

Valeria halted, mouth still open.

He gently tugged her braid. "I accept the claim. Isn't that what I'm supposed to say?"

Her smile lit her face. "That," she informed him, "is exactly what you're supposed to say."

Around them, pandemonium broke out. Merry squealed, Sabela jumped up and rushed toward them, and Dion grinned and started to his feet as well.

But all Rui saw was Valeria and that wide smile. "*Eu te adoro,*" he told her. "You know that, don't you?"

Her response was to wrap her hand around his nape and give him a kiss that left him blinking and the clan hooting.

And then they were surrounded by well-wishers.

With a rueful grin at his mate, Rui turned to accept their congratulations.

EPILOGUE

Rui leaned against the wall, watching as the Rock Run clan poured into the dining hall along with a sprinkling of sun fae. They were boisterous and excited, the unattached adults already pairing off, the children running wild.

He smoothed down his sleek green shirt. Valeria had chosen it for him, saying it matched his eyes. On his wrist he wore a brown leather bracelet with three flat gold rings on which had been inscribed different words for beloved: *querido, amor, amado.* It had been his father's, a gift from his mother on their mating day.

He toyed with one of the flat gold rings, wishing that his *papai* could be with him today. He'd never known his mother, of course, but his father had been a strong, loving presence in his life. Rui had a feeling he'd have liked Valeria. The older do Mar had had an eye for beautiful women.

But he'd have appreciated her warmth and loving care of Merry, too—his *papai* had been a gruff, old-world Portuguese male but he'd adored children—and they'd adored him right back.

Until his death, Rui and Dion had spent as much time with

him as with Dion's family. He'd never been too busy for the two boys, making time to play with them or take them swimming whenever he was free from his duties as a *tenente*.

Rui let go of the bracelet and glanced around impatiently. Where was Valeria, anyway? Wasn't it time to start yet?

It had been a month since the mate-duel. He, Valeria and Merry had met twice with Jace. The young earth fada had honored his word, teaching Merry the basics of her quartz crystal and then simply spending time with her while Rui and Valeria watched from a discreet distance.

Merry already had more energy, and could shift as easily as anyone her age, if not better. She hadn't fattened up any, but that was probably because she'd shot up another inch. But she was happy and healthy and that was all that mattered.

The night fae were another problem that hopefully had been eliminated. Rui had insisted on heading the squad that had tracked Tyrus to his lair. The night fae lord had been hunkered down in a decrepit stone villa in the Vosges, a mountain range in eastern France.

Rui and his men had waited until noon, when night fae were at their weakest, and then closed in, knocking out Tyru's body-guards and dragging him into the sunshine. Dion had made it clear he didn't want a fae-fada war, so Tyrus was still alive when they dumped him in the villa's foyer—barely.

Meanwhile, Cleia had sent an official warning to Prince Langdon. He'd been shocked that his son had been so stupid as to attempt to steal a child from a fada clan under the sun fae queen's direct protection. He'd also cleared up the mystery of why Tyrus was so interested in Merry. Silver was Langdon's illegitimate son by a human woman, which made Merry some sort of night fae princess.

Langdon requested that they keep his secret, as the night fae frowned on procreating with outsiders. Fucking them was fine—you just weren't supposed to make a child with them.

Cleia agreed, in return for the prince's promise that Merry was under his protection for as long as she lived.

Someday Merry would have to decide if she wanted anything further from Langdon—like a portion of his vast fortune—but for now the prince had protected Merry with a special ward that would shock any night fae who got within ten feet of her. And if they were stupid enough to try to touch her, they'd die—even Tyrus.

Dion strolled up to clap Rui on his shoulder. "She'll be here."

"Of course she will." He dragged his gaze from the door. Not even to Dion would he admit his fear that Valeria wouldn't show for their mating ceremony. But no, he felt the bond, warm and steady.

His friend gave him an understanding grin. "Stop worrying already. It's her big day, you know. She's just doing whatever women do to get ready for these things."

"I know." Rui grinned back. *Deus*, it was good to have his best friend back.

He blew out a breath and forced his shoulders away from his ears.

"I know this is your mate day," Dion said, "but I wanted to say I'm sorry."

"For what?"

"Sending you out on that last job for Tyrus. You were our best assassin, but I saw how it was affecting you. I should've pulled the plug before—"

"Like hell," Rui returned. "Whatever happened was due to my own poor judgment. And the clan needed that concealing spell. Don't try to tell me we had an alternative. I was your second, remember?"

"Well, we're done. Rock Run is officially out of the assassination business."

"Cleia—"

"I'm not taking a penny from her." Dion's eyes flashed silver. "I don't care if her clan practically shits money. You know me better than that."

Rui jerked his shoulder in apology. "Sorry."

"We'll still work as mercenaries if the money's good enough, but to hell with being the fae's pet assassins. Let them get someone else to do their dirty work—or better yet, do it themselves. Cleia is happy to have Olivia renew our concealing spell as needed—she insists on it, in fact—and the rest we can handle ourselves. The vineyards are going to have the best harvest in two decades and the fishers are bringing in more than we can eat. And I just heard that another mated pair is having a baby." Dion's grin couldn't have been more smug if he were the father. "That makes five now."

"The midsummer ritual?"

"Guess so. That energy Cleia draws is potent stuff. Hell, you felt it all the way here at Rock Run." Dion pulled Rui into a hug. "I'm sorry, *irmão*. I don't care what you say, I should've said no to that last job. We both knew Tyrus was up to no good."

"You have nothing to be sorry for. What I did, I did for the clan."

But for a few seconds, Rui let himself bask in his alpha's—and friend's—forgiveness. It wasn't until then that he realized that on some level, he'd needed that forgiveness to fully heal.

"You may change your mind." Dion released him and stepped back, his hard mouth taking on a sly curve.

"Oh, yeah?" Rui raised a brow.

"Since you're going to have some free time, I'm putting you in charge of Cohort D. I need someone who will bust their asses— and decide who's ready to be promoted to warrior."

It took him a moment to understand. Then he said, "That's Tiago's cohort."

"That's right. And I want you to work his tail off. He knows what to expect."

"*Obrigado*," Rui replied dryly, but his animal perked up,

pleased. Even five years ago, he'd have balked at having to instruct a bunch of wet-between-the-ears pups, but now he welcomed the challenge.

"You did the right thing," he added.

Dion shrugged. "I hope so. Hell, his main mistake was falling under Cleia's spell—and Lord knows, he wasn't alone in that." They exchanged rueful glances. "Being the low man in his cohort will be punishment enough for a young dominant like him."

Rui nodded.

Dion's gaze went to his young sister, Rosana, who was flirting with one of Cleia's bodyguards. A big, blond bodyguard.

"Excuse me," he muttered and strode off in her direction.

Rui stifled a grin. There were times he was thankful he was an only child.

And then there was a murmur near the doorway and Valeria and Merry appeared.

Rui's heart lurched.

Her dress was a soft rose that made her bronze skin seem to glow. Her dark mane of hair had been left free to tumble over her shoulders and she had a matching pink rose tucked behind one ear. Around her neck was the dolphin pendant along with the lavender quartz that, to Merry's delight, he'd given Valeria as a mating gift.

Rui pushed off the wall.

Valeria walked toward him, spine straight, her expression proud, if a bit shy. Beside her, Merry marched along self-importantly, wearing her favorite blue dress and carrying a small bouquet of matching daisies, and Valeria's parents followed close behind.

Rui met the little group halfway. He winked at Merry, then his gaze went to Valeria. The other fada glanced at him and grinned, and he realized he was beaming from ear to ear.

He ignored them to reach out his hand to Valeria.

His love, his mate.

This last month had been the best of his life. With Dion home, he'd been free to concentrate on Valeria. He'd put his whole heart into wooing her: bringing her flowers and wild raspberries, hunting blue crab and fish and then working together to prepare the best-tasting paella he'd ever had, going for long swims together in both their human and dolphin forms.

Making love every night and any other time they could steal. Knowing he'd almost lost her, his lovemaking had been sometimes urgent, sometimes simply grateful. He'd drenched himself in Valeria: her taste, her sweet scent, the feel of her beautiful body wrapped around his.

And when they hadn't been making love, they'd talked. Sharing secrets and dreams. He'd exposed his inner self as he never had to another woman.

They'd included Merry in much of what they'd done, but he'd also had days when he'd stolen Valeria away, leaving Merry safe in the creche or with Sabela.

It was Valeria who'd coaxed Rui to speak of his biggest fear: that someday Merry was going to ask for the truth about the death of her father.

"Ah, love," she'd said. "We'll face that when we have to. But she knows that if it weren't for you, she'd have been taken by the night fae. And she knows you love her. She asked if after the mating ceremony, she can call you *Papai*. Not Daddy, because that's her other father's name. But *Papai*. Like the other kids."

A lump had filled his throat. "Of course," he managed to say.

"That's what I told her. That you love her like a father."

"I do. You know I do.'

He just hoped that when the day came that Merry found out the truth she would weigh that love against the terrible thing he had done.

Valeria had caught his hand. Her eyes met his. "I love you, Rui do Mar. And we're going to make a family, the three of us—and hopefully a few more just like her." She brought his hand to her mouth and pressed a kiss to his palm.

Something had moved in his chest. He'd swallowed and, fisting his hands in her wet hair, brought his mouth to hers in a fervent, almost desperate kiss.

"I want that too," he'd said and bore her down to the forest floor, where she'd taken him into her body with a willingness that warmed the last cold gray corners of his soul.

Now Valeria took the hand he offered and gave him a wobbly smile. Rui gave her fingers a reassuring squeeze, and her parents leaned in from either side to kiss her. Then with a look at Rui that promised retribution should he ever hurt Valeria again, Mic da Costa put an arm around his wife and stepped back.

Rui nodded, accepting the warning. He understood completely; it was how he'd feel if it were Merry.

The little girl tugged on his other hand, urging him to keep walking. "C'mon, Tio. Lord Dion is waiting for us."

He exchanged an amused look with Valeria. "*Sim, princesa,*" he replied, and together the three of them walked to the center of the hall, where Dion and Cleia were waiting to bless their mating, along with Luis and Sabela, acting as their official witnesses.

Rui inclined his head to the alpha couple. "My lord. My lady."

"Welcome." Dion looked from him to Valeria with a positively paternal smile.

It was the right thing to do. Valeria smiled back, and Rui felt the last tension ease from her.

Dion raised his arms to the assembled crowd. "Welcome, the clans of Rock Run and Rising Sun. We are here today to celebrate the mating of two of our own, Rui do Mar and Valeria da Costa. What say you?"

Merry's hand shot up. "Does this mean Tio Rui belongs to us now?"

"That's right," Dion replied. "And you belong to him."

"So no one can ever take me away?"

Valeria went to say something, but the alpha waved her to silence.

"Never, *menina*." He crouched so he was eye-level with the little girl. "You're a member of Rock Run as long as you live. I swear that before *Deus* and the mother goddess and everyone present."

"Good," she replied with satisfaction. She made a shooing motion with her hands. "Keep talking, then."

Laughter rippled through the crowd. Dion gave her a hug and then rose to his feet as Valeria turned back to Rui.

He grasped her hands and gazed her eyes, lovely and mysterious as the night sea. His heart thumped in his ears.

All he could think was: *At last. At last.*

"*Amo-te*," he said in a voice for her ears alone.

"*Amo-te*," she whispered back.

He raised his voice, keeping his gaze on his mate. "You heard the child, Dion. Keep talking."

ALSO BY REBECCA RIVARD

THE FADA SHAPESHIFTERS

Stealing Ula: A Fada Shapeshifter Prequel (Nisio & Ula, set in Ireland)

The Rock Run River Fada
Seducing the Sun Fae (Dion & Cleia)
Claiming Valeria (Rui & Valeria)
Tempting the Dryad (Tiago & Alesia)
Sea Dragon's Hunger (Cassidy & Nic)

The Baltimore Earth Fada (The Darktime Trilogy)
Saving Jace (Jace & Evie)
Charming Marjani (Marjani & Fane)
Adric's Heart (Adric & Rosana)

Fada Shapeshifter Short Reads

Lir's Lady (#3.5—Lir & Isleen)
Shifter's Valentine (#3.6—Jenny & Chico)

Find out more and read exclusive excerpts: https://
rebeccarivard.com/shapeshifters/

The Vampire Syndicate Romances

Pursued (Gabriel)

Craved (Rafael)

Taken (Zaquiel)

The Vampire Blood Courtesans

Ensnared: Star (Star and Remy)

Compelled: Cerise (Cerise & Bard)

Find out more: https://rebeccarivard.com/vampires/

Join **Rebecca Rivard's newsletter** to stay informed and be eligible for giveaways and sneak peeks. As a thank you, Rebecca will gift you with "Lir's Lady," a steamy short story!

Sign up at rebeccarivard.com or go to this link: Rebecca's newsletter

ABOUT THE AUTHOR

Rebecca Rivard read way too many romances as a teenager, little realizing she was actually preparing for a career. She now spends her days with dark shifters, sexy fae and alpha vampires—which has to be the best job ever. When she's not writing, she walks, bikes and kayaks in the Chesapeake Bay area with her guitar-playing, storytelling husband.

Her debut novel, *Seducing the Sun Fae (#1, Fada Shapeshifters)*, was a 2016 EPIC Awards finalist for Best Fantasy/Paranormal Romance, and her novella *Ensnared: Star* was a *Night Owl Reviews* Top Pick (5 stars).

Five of her novels have been awarded the coveted Crowned Heart Review from *InD'Tale Magazine* and the FADA SHAPESHIFTER SERIES was voted Best Shifter Series in the Paranormal Romance Guild Reviewer's Choice Awards.

Her books have also won the prestigious PRISM Award (*Charming Marjani*) and the PRG Reviewer's Choice Award (*Saving Jace*), and have finaled in both the RONE and the HOLT Medallion.

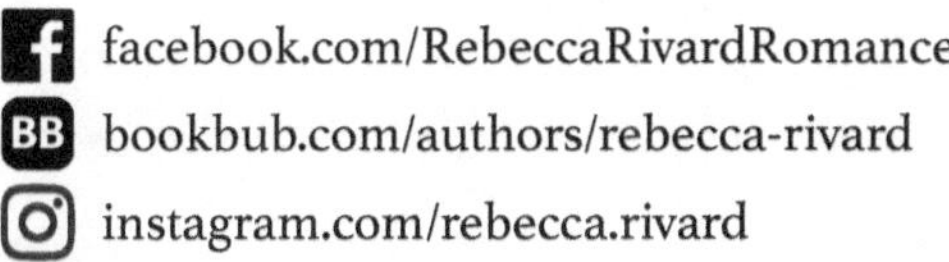

facebook.com/RebeccaRivardRomance

bookbub.com/authors/rebecca-rivard

instagram.com/rebecca.rivard

twitter.com/RivardRomance